Endo

Th

"An impossible marvel . . . *The Alchemy of Flowers* by Laura Resau is a spellbinding journey of one woman's journey toward hope and healing, set amidst a garden of both promise and peril. Full of lush sensory detail, this tale is a vivid reminder that while the path to healing may be fraught with challenges, it is often through confronting the shadows that we find our true strength. A beautifully written, atmospheric novel that will leave readers both mesmerized and moved."

—Sarah Penner, *New York Times* bestselling
author of *The Amalfi Curse*

"Set in a secret garden, *The Alchemy of Flowers* offers a lush blend of myth, magic, and mystery. Beautifully written and brimming with heartache, danger, and enchantment, this is a moving, memorable story about hope, healing, and starting over."

—Heather Webber, *USA TODAY* bestselling
author of *Midnight at the Blackbird Café*

"Utterly captivating. This beautiful novel casts a whispery spell of dark enchantments, secrets, and myth."

—Evie Woods, bestselling author of *The
Mysterious Bakery on Rue de Paris*

"For everyone who has dreamed of teleporting to the paradise of Provence, do I have the book for you. *The Alchemy of Flowers* is a treat of transporting, incandescent storytelling, with a riveting undercurrent of suspense and mystery, too. With tender, heartfelt prose and characters who will break your heart and then stitch it back together, Resau's adult debut feels like the modern French

Provençal take on *Under the Tuscan Sun* we've all been jonesing for. Capturing the magic of beloved childhood reading experiences, while dealing with hard adult topics lovingly and achingly explored, the book is at once an enchanting journey and an unforgettable, page-turning read."

—Jaclyn Goldis, author of *The Chateau* and *The Safari*

"Laura Resau's *The Alchemy of Flowers* is an immersive, sensory experience. Resau treats bone-crushing-hard topics, like pregnancy loss, with love and sensitivity, all the while taking the reader on a mystical journey. Deftly crafted and imaginative; a rare treat of a book."

—Aimie K. Runyan, bestselling author of *The Memory of Lavender and Sage* and *The Wandering Season*

"*The Alchemy of Flowers* is a pure magical and sensory delight. Like roots in soil, though, the gift of this book goes deeper. Resau's novel offers an honest and compassionate portrait of the physical pain and health-related sorrows that go along with being human. So many of us can relate, and we can also relate to the wondrous alchemy and healing found in nature. This gorgeous novel captures both the heartbreak and the true healing at our disposal, if only we seek to turn difficulty into blooms."

—Laura Pritchett, author of *Three Keys*

"*The Alchemy of Flowers* captivates the senses as well as the imagination in a magical tale of healing and forgiveness. Yet this Paradise harbors its own dark mystery that threatens the tranquility of the gardens and the well-being of its inhabitants. Resau has written with great heart an eerie yet deeply touching story that keeps the pages turning until the very end."

—Melissa Payne, bestselling author of *In the Beautiful Dark* and *The Wild Road Home*

"A haunting, immersive tale set in prose as lush and magical as the garden itself."

—Kate Khavari, author of the Saffron Everleigh mystery series

"Gorgeously written and threaded with herbal wisdom, floral intuition, and mythology of the feminine, *The Alchemy of Flowers* is a journey into how nature and friendship can deeply heal. Resau tangles sweetness and bitterness, tenderness and fierceness to offer a thrilling tale rich with emotion. A delight in every sense of the word."

—Bailey Cattrell, author of the Enchanted Garden Mysteries

"This book made me want to sleep in a hammock in a treetop bungalow surrounded by the novel's lush, magic-steeped gardens. Eloise's journey to healing is poignant and tender—a testament to the strength of love, the power of tending to earth and growing things, and found family."

—Suzanne Nelson, *The Librarians of Lisbon*

"I devoured this in one sitting! Immersive, enchanting, and packed with mystery, *The Alchemy of Flowers* drew me in from page one. I was rooting for the curious and brave heroine, Eloise, and her cryptic compatriots in the Jardins du Paradis, as each finds friendship and healing after their own separate heartbreaks. The dreamy Provençal walled garden is the perfect escapist setting. Fans of Sarah Addison Allen will love this charming, feel-good novel."

—Andrea Jo DeWerd, author of *What We Sacrifice for Magic*

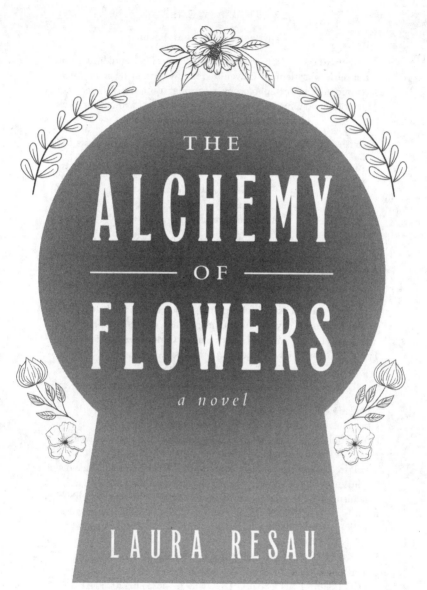

THE
ALCHEMY
— OF —
FLOWERS

a novel

LAURA RESAU

HARPER MUSE

Published by Harper Muse, an imprint of HarperCollins Focus LLC.

Author represented by Kim Lionetti, literary agent at BookEnds.

Designed by Jackie Alvarado
Map illustration by Matthew Covington
Author photograph by Tina Wood

Library of Congress Cataloging-in-Publication Data

Names: Resau, Laura author
Title: The alchemy of flowers : a novel / Laura Resau.
Description: Nashville : Harper Muse, [2025] | Summary: "A woman takes a job at a secretive French garden to avoid reminders of children; there she meets a mysterious girl needing help. This debut adult novel blends the charm of The Secret Garden and magic realism of Where the Forest Meets the Stars"—Provided by publisher.
Identifiers: LCCN 2025002245 (print) | LCCN 2025002246 (ebook) | ISBN 9781400349098 paperback | ISBN 9781400349104 epub | ISBN 9781400349111
Subjects: LCGFT: Magic realist fiction | Novels
Classification: LCC PS3618.E794 A43 2025 (print) | LCC PS3618.E794 (ebook) | DDC 813/.6—dc23/eng/20250411
LC record available at https://lccn.loc.gov/2025002245
LC ebook record available at https://lccn.loc.gov/2025002246

Printed in the United States of America

25 26 27 28 29 LBC 5 4 3 2 1

To my mom . . . and all the nurturers cultivating
your own kind of motherhood

Les JARDINS du PARADIS

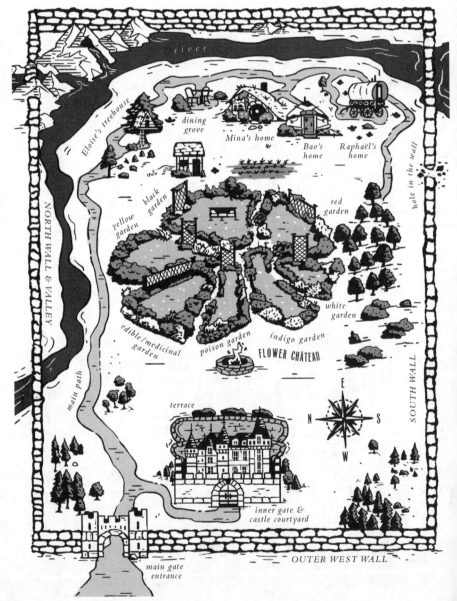

EAST WALL & VALLEY

river

Eloise's treehouse

dining grove

Mina's home

Bao's home

Raphaël's home

hole in the wall

NORTH WALL & VALLEY

black garden

yellow garden

red garden

white garden

edible/medicinal garden

poison garden

indigo garden

FLOWER CHÂTEAU

SOUTH WALL

main path

terrace

N E S W

inner gate & castle courtyard

OUTER WEST WALL

main gate entrance

HERE LIE THE BONES
OF THOSE WHO BROKE THE RULES

Dear Reader,

This book is about healing and hope (and maybe a little bit of magic), but it does deal with issues related to infertility, loss, and heartbreak. We hope you find inspiration in Eloise's journey and your own healing behind the walls of the Jardins du Paradis.

The Gardens of Paradise

Dizzy with jet lag, I stood on the wooden platform in Sainte-Marie-des-Fleurs as the train vanished into the distance. Cicadas hummed in a mesmerizing rhythm. The scent of lavender curled around me and a surreal blue stretched above the hills. The air itself somehow shimmered.

As I made my way to the front of the station, people whirled past, going about their lives, rolling suitcases, holding hands, kissing cheeks, strolling to tiny cars.

Watching them drive away, I waited alone with my single bag—I'd packed light for my job in the walled Gardens of Paradise. No one to impress but the flowers. Back in Denver, packing had felt therapeutic, choosing what to bring into my new life. Mostly practical khaki-colored things.

Colorado seemed a lifetime away. Tying up the threads of my past had required a tangle of online and phone logistics. As I'd moved through automated voice options, I'd marveled at how *archaic* the process of getting the job had been—a magazine ad, a snail-mailed résumé, a handwritten offer of employment, and paper plane tickets. An impossible task from a fairy tale . . . yet here I was.

In my dazed state, I took in the absurd beauty of Provence on the brink of summer. Perched on a ridge stood a cluster of creamy stone buildings topped with red tile roofs. Walled terraces and haphazard stairs wove through the village, which was dotted with cypress and olive trees. Green velvet unfurled over slopes and valleys, rows of lavender ribboned into the horizon, rock outcroppings pierced the sky—all of it begging to be Postimpressionistically painted.

The afternoon sun shone on my fuzzy-brained head as I scanned for someone resembling a personal assistant. At least she'd know what I looked like, thanks to my passport photo.

Oleander blooms whispered in the breeze, and French conversations drifted by, snippets of pleasantries and greetings. Then I registered soft crying, the whimpers of a child.

I locked eyes with a towheaded toddler, slumped against the stone wall, his face pink and tearstained. Lost in the bustle. I hurried to him and knelt down to eye level. Somehow the French word for *lost* came to my hazy brain. *"Perdu?"*

He gave a miserable nod, his face damp with snot and tears. Resisting the urge to comfort him, I stood up and glanced around, noting a woman just looking up from her phone, scouring the crowd, expression frazzled.

When I pointed her out, the child rushed toward her, calling out, *"Maman!"* in his hoarse little voice.

I looked away and swallowed the lump in my throat. This would be the last child I'd see for a while. A fact that made me want to cry, even as I welcomed it.

As the parking lot emptied, I clutched my job offer in my sweaty hand like a talisman, something to reassure me this was real. It had arrived last week, a month after I'd mailed in my application—an assortment of documents, a copy of my passport, two photos, a cassette tape, and a plastic baggy of ashes . . . per the instructions of the job ad. I'd knelt in my garden, opened the airmail envelope with a whispered prayer, then read the hand-scripted letter to my rosebuds:

One is delighted to inform you that one is offering you employment as a gardener in Paradise. Enclosed, please find an airplane ticket from Denver to Paris and train tickets to Sainte-Marie-des-Fleurs. One will meet you at the station.

Respectfully,
Antoinette Beaulieu
Personal Assistant
Le Château du Paradis

I stuffed the letter back into my pocket, my stomach tightening. Now I was the sole person left at the train station. I had no phone or even a number to call. What if this Antoinette Beaulieu didn't show?

There was no going back to Colorado. No job, no home, no friends or family there. I'd switched all my bills to autopay and hadn't left a forwarding address. I'd donated my cheap belongings and sold my decade-old Subaru, which put a slight dent in my debt. I'd called my parents in Vermont to tell them I'd be off grid.

Then—*poof*—I'd flown out of my life.

And now there was no life to return to.

Just when cold fingers of panic were setting in, a rumble broke through the cicada hum. I squinted up the road. The engine noise grew louder, and a burgundy Peugeot convertible rounded the bend.

It glided into the lot, parking smack in the center. A woman stepped out, somewhere in her sixties, dressed in tasteful, summery shades of silk—a skirt, blouse, scarf, and stockings over slim legs. Her hair, too, was pale and smooth, coiffed in a twist, somehow intact despite the breeze. Sunglasses covered half her face à la Brigitte Bardot or some other mid-century French film star.

I felt like a country bumpkin, my hair scraggly and mousy. I'd worn the same gray leggings and tan tunic for twenty hours, slept and sweated in them. I'd assumed someone in soil-stained cargo pants with dirt under her nails would be picking me up—wasn't this place off grid? *Mon Dieu*, had I even packed a hairbrush?

The woman extended a manicured hand. "Mademoiselle Bourne?"

I shook her hand. How odd that she considered me a mademoiselle—I was well into my thirties—but of course, she knew I was partnerless and childless.

My brain felt so slowed down that I couldn't conjure up the words I'd rehearsed in French. I met her hand and squeaked out, *"Oui. Je suis Eloise."*

"Bonjour. I am Antoinette Beaulieu. Welcome to Sainte-Marie-des-Fleurs." She spoke in the most refined French.

I urged my brain to launch into my thank-you speech. *"Merci"* was as far as I got. To make up for my rusty French, I forced a big smile.

"One must be exhausted after so much travel." She opened the tiny trunk of her car.

"Oui." I heaved my bag inside, hoping it wouldn't dirty the interior.

Antoinette slid into the driver's seat as I climbed in beside her, pressing my arms close to my torso to prevent BO from saturating the Peugeot. Thankfully, the top was open.

As we sped past vineyards and olive groves, I tried to ask about the length of the drive, but all that came out was: *"C'est très joli."* It's very pretty.

Antoinette gave a curt nod. *"Alors,* any questions?"

I shook my head. Thank God I could at least *comprehend* French in this brain-addled state. It helped that she spoke formally, not unlike *Mon Jardin*, the magazine with the ad that had brought me here. I'd splurged on a subscription so that I could hang on to the French from my junior year abroad fifteen years earlier.

I braced myself for French from here on out.

"*Alors*, you are aware there is no cell service or internet?"

"*Oui.*" At home this idea had seemed delicious. No social media, no baby posts I'd have to "like." Still, an online French dictionary might have come in handy.

"And no electricity or plumbing?" Antoinette continued, maybe giving me one last chance to change my mind.

"*Oui.*"

"*Alors*, La Patronne has a few simple rules."

La Patronne could mean the lady boss or the owner—in this case, I assumed she was both. "Okay."

"The first is never to break a rule."

"*Oui.*" Curious, I waited for the rest.

"*Bien sûr*, one is aware that children are not allowed."

"*Oui!*" My reason for coming.

And she was on to the next rule. "One must not *raconter des potins*. For example, if one chooses to go to town, one must not *raconter des potins* about what goes on in Paradise."

I struggled to remember what this meant. To gossip? Was this a verbal NDA? I nodded along—I'd never been the gossipy type.

"*Bien sûr*," she continued, "one will have everything one needs. There is no reason to leave." She adjusted her sunglasses over her delicate nose. "The final rule is that you stay in your quarters during the hour of *la crépuscule*."

"*Crépuscule?*" My brain cells scrambled to remember the meaning. Wasn't it a cognate? Alas, the neural pathways were dead ends.

"Doosk," she said in English with a thick accent. "Ze blue hour." So she did know some English, just avoided it at all costs.

I considered this bizarre rule. Well, it wouldn't hurt to stay inside—I was usually at home by dusk anyway, eating alone with the TV. Still, I couldn't help asking, "Why, Mademoiselle?"

She paused, stroking her chin.

Merde. She was probably a *madame* despite the lack of a wedding ring.

Finally, she said, "Because that is the rule of La Patronne."

"Oh, okay, *d'accord.*" I tried conjuring up a vision of La Patronne. Nothing. Why hadn't I searched for her when I'd had internet access?

I moved my gaze back to the landscape. We were zipping through the valley, passing flowered meadows and shadowy groves, no signs of houses. In the sideview mirror, the hilltop town of Sainte-Marie-des-Fleurs had vanished behind us. "How much longer?" I asked, wishing I'd peed back at the station—and then, realizing that sounded rude, added, *"s'il vous plaît?"*

"The Gardens of Paradise are quite remote, Mademoiselle. We are already on the property. There are many hectares that serve as a buffer zone to keep out society. In a few kilometers we will arrive at the heart of it. *Et voilà.*"

She pointed her chin ahead, and sure enough, a rooftop came into view. Well, *turrets*, to be precise.

My jaw actually *dropped.* A limestone castle rose from the hill. Beyond its inner walls, an outer ring of fortified walls enclosed the grounds farther down the valley. Only treetops were visible within.

I blinked at the view—something from a Maxfield Parrish painting, complete with golden haze crowning the palace. "Wow."

"Oui. C'est magnifique, Mademoiselle." Magnificent indeed.

The corner of her lip turned up. "The château was built in late medieval times, added to and renovated over the past millennium. Before that were Roman structures, a couple thousand years ago.

Before that, a Celtic village. And before that, Ligurian tribes. That was around, oh, three thousand years ago."

Would I be living in a *castle*? On top of ancient ruins? Is that what the job ad meant by *unique et rustique* lodging? My boggled mind could only muster up another "wow."

As we grew closer, I could distinguish the château's patchwork of history, even with only its top half visible over the walls. The heavier elements from the Middle Ages—slit windows in thick walls, crouching gargoyles, crenulated turrets—contrasted with the large, elegant windows and red-tiled roofing of the Renaissance sections.

Antoinette continued in her museum guide voice. "Of course the castle suffered from looting and damage during the Revolution. For added protection, stones from the ruins were used to build the outside wall two centuries ago. Truly, it is all a masterpiece."

Why on earth would anyone leave this place? How could there be a job opening here, ever? I scrounged together the question: "What happened with the last gardener, Madame?"

Antoinette pursed her lips together in distaste.

Oh, *merde*, so *madame* wasn't right, either? Maybe I should have stuck with Antoinette.

After a stretched-out moment, she said, "The former gardener did not follow the rules of La Patronne."

Looking straight ahead, Antoinette added, "She is no longer here."

When I'd come across the job ad in my French gardening magazine last month, it was as if the universe, in all its mystery, had dropped a ball of yarn into my lap. And over the course of that day and the days to follow, metaphysical knitting needles had prodded me to follow my particular strand across the ocean to the South of France. Maybe that was why I could overlook the strange rules that came with Les Jardins du Paradis . . . and the disturbing tone in Antoinette's voice when she spoke of the previous gardener.

The road turned to dirt, patterned with dappled light from ancient plane trees, and soon the Peugeot pulled up to the gates of Paradise. Limestone walls towered over us, twenty feet high. The tree canopy poked above, and to our right, the château's turrets rose toward a few pearly clouds. Outside the walls, swaths of green held the afternoon light—the buffer zone.

I climbed out of the car and lifted my gaze up the walls, which joined to form an archway over spiked iron gates, hand-forged and well-worn. Just inside the entrance was a fountain encircled by three stone women in robes, holding spools of thread and scissors. Water bubbled up at the center.

I tried to recall my world mythology class from college. Some kind of triple goddess? The Fates?

Beside me, Antoinette pulled a key ring from her purse. She picked out a handcrafted skeleton key, six inches long, the silver smooth and dark, swirled into an intricate flower design. It looked more like an ancient artifact than something functional in the twenty-first century. Yet it worked. She swung open the heavy gates, then opened the car trunk. "Epona goes no farther."

"Epona?"

She nodded at her mint-condition car—1960s was my guess.

"Of course," I said, confused. I'd thought the make was a Peugeot. Maybe Epona was the model? Wasn't Epona the horse's name in my ex's favorite video game? That horse had been paused mid-gallop the night I realized our marriage couldn't be salvaged.

I had the urge to lighten things up with a joke, but Antoinette didn't seem the gamer type. Maybe I could comment about the key instead, like, "Guess we can't just pop by the hardware store for a copy!" But there was no way I could pull it off in French, not with my current state of mind.

Instead, I heaved out my bag and asked, "Will I get a copy?"

She slammed the trunk shut. "There is but one key. And I carry it."

After breezing through the gate, she turned and beckoned to me.

I paused, holding my bag, scanning the landscape around us, empty of people or even any *sign* of people.

I asked my jet-lagged mind if this lack-of-key situation was acceptable. No clear answer. "Then how will I leave?"

"As I said, one will not want to leave Paradise."

Glancing at the Fates, I rubbed my forehead. *Think, think, think.* "But if I do? I mean, to go to town. To go to a library, a store, a bank. Not to gossip."

She regarded me with disapproval. "If you wish to leave, simply ring," she said, gesturing to an enormous brass bell hanging just inside the gates.

I furrowed my brow at the strangeness of it all.

"But there is no need to go to town, Mademoiselle. Hundreds of books are available here. Food and necessities are provided." Businesslike, she pulled a pen and folder from her bag. "Fill out this form, please. The accountant of La Patronne will deposit one's payments electronically."

I gave a nervous laugh. "High-tech."

Lips pressed together, she waited. I noticed the amount of my paycheck in euros and mentally converted it to dollars. I redid the math. Twice. This salary was more than I'd made as a play specialist in Denver. Since my living expenses would be covered, my paycheck would automatically go toward reducing my debts.

With sweaty hands, I dug through my purse and found the number of the French bank account I'd opened online, then balanced the paper on my knee to fill it out.

She handed me more forms—work permit documents, tax info, and a job contract—which I signed by the X's without reading. It would have taken hours to go through legalese in French.

Once I handed back the forms, crumpled and smeared, she said, "Come inside."

Still, I wavered by the gate, my duffel bag beside me.

Antoinette removed her sunglasses and locked her eyes onto mine. Hers were the color of mist. "Mademoiselle, this is a place of power. Power to heal or harm. Two sides of the same *médaille*. If one does not lock the gates, Paradise will be overrun. For the protection of all, the gates remain closed."

My feet stayed rooted. I tilted back my head at the turrets. The tallest one—thick and toothed—had crumbled, as if gargoyles had come to life and flown through. I shook myself, reining in my imagination. Still, the château morphed between a fairy-tale castle and Gothic lair, like that famous optical illusion of maiden and crone in one.

How to interpret my sweating and trembling and dizziness? Excitement or terror? I picked up my duffel, unsure which direction to take: forge ahead into the unknown or return to my burned-down old life.

As if pushed to the edge of her patience, Antoinette demanded, "Mademoiselle, do you want this or not?"

I took a few tentative steps closer to the entrance, catching the scent of rosemary and thyme on the breeze. I ventured farther, until I could peer inside, to secret pathways winding through rose-covered trellises and wisteria arches.

The blossoms murmured, beckoning me inside. *A place of power. Healing.*

Fountains gurgled, a brook babbled, a lark sang, cicadas chirped. Above it all, the château towered and the soft light shone, and somewhere inside the gardens, composting *toilettes* called to me.

"Oui," I said, "I want this." And I walked toward the Fates, through the gates of Paradise.

The Impossible Marvel

lank.

Antoinette locked the gates behind us and stuck the key ring into her handbag.

A rush of something swept over me: delight, awe, fear, elation. I was inside the Gardens of Paradise, and *mon Dieu*, they lived up to their name! Green blanketed the landscape, layered and textured, so many leaves playing with the light—oak and maple and ash. The air smelled like nectar from a thousand honeysuckle blooms. And the background of birdsong and running water was a massage for the soul.

A cobbled path to the right led uphill toward an arched iron gate in the interior wall around the château. To my left, a dirt path sloped down toward rushing water sounds and disappeared into fragrant jasmine.

Antoinette swept her arm gracefully to the left. "*Alors*, Mademoiselle, you need only follow the stream to your *unique et rustique* lodging. Make yourself at home. Mina will come by with further instructions."

"Mina?" I echoed, hoping for more details.

Antoinette offered a formal smile, then walked toward the inner gate.

"Um, Madame?" I called after her. "Mademoiselle? Antoinette?"

She tossed an impatient look over her shoulder. "*Oui?*"

"How will I know which is my *unique et rustique* lodging?"

She waved away my question, unlocking the inner gate. "It will be obvious. Mina and the others are quite competent."

The others? Did this mean I'd have help with the flowers? I hoped so. There were *lots* of them.

She clanked the gate shut behind her, locked it, and vanished into the inner courtyard.

With a deep breath, I started down the dirt path. The earth softened beneath my footsteps, and all around, bees darted among purple asters and flax and harebells. I walked along the river, brushing petals with my fingertips. *Hello, beauties!*

"I can't wait to get to know you!" I whispered. I'd spoken with flowers my whole life, but never so many all at once. Here, I was in the motherlode. "How will I handle you all?"

The flowers reassured me that of course, they'd help out.

Flower voices were subtle—they spoke in songs, sighs, breezes, hums. Thankfully, there didn't seem to be much difference between the flower language here and in my Colorado garden, other than the sheer quantity of greetings and species.

Ten minutes later I reached the bend in the river at the northeast corner and followed the water's flow to the right. Here the river tumbled off a cliff twice my height, churning into a natural pool of white foam. The cascade was just a few yards off the path, close enough that I felt its mist.

Perched on a nearby boulder was a winged mermaid, carved from stone, gazing at the waterfall as butterflies flitted around her. The beauty made my head spin—or maybe it was the jet lag and thirst and hunger.

I walked past the mermaid and heard a splash. And a squeal. As I turned, I caught a movement in my peripheral vision. My first unfiltered thought: *That mermaid jumped into the river!*

But no, the statue remained gazing at the waterfall. I squeezed my eyes shut, then opened them. Had the mermaid's mischievous smile been there before?

I tromped onward, now with some caution. After rounding a curve, I came face-to-face with a wooden sign reading "*Bienvenue*, Eloise!"

And behind it, the most *unique et rustique* lodging I'd ever seen.

A smattering of houses hovered in the trees.

Swinging bridges made of wood and rope connected them. Stained glass windows and French doors opened onto decks, each with potted geraniums and tables and chairs.

A voice came from above, through the leaves—a rich, deep woman's voice: "You must be Eloise! And I bet you need the *toilettes*!"

I stretched back my head and saw, on the highest balcony, a woman wearing clothes as brilliant as tropical birds—bold prints of orange and yellow and red on a cotton dress and head scarf. Her face was rosy brown and exuding warmth.

"*Oui!*" I called back.

"Well, let me show you the way, my friend." She spoke French with an almost singsong accent, easy to understand. She took confident strides along the rope bridges. As she approached, I saw she was a decade or so older than me and large in a comfortable way.

"I'm Mina." She was now halfway down. Her smile was huge, her teeth bright. "I was just getting things ready for you, Eloise."

"*Merci, Mina. Enchantée.*" And I meant *enchantée* not as shorthand for "enchanted to meet you," but rather, in all ways . . . *enchanted*. "So, which house is mine?"

She laughed, deep from the belly. "All of them!"

Something in my chest flew. "But where's yours?"

She continued down the bridges, slow but sure-footed. "Oh, the boys and I, we have our places over there." She gestured through the leaves.

"*Uniques et rustiques?*" I ventured.

"*Mais bien sûr!*" Nodding, she hooted with more laughter.

She reached the bottom, her face gleaming with sweat. She planted a kiss on each of my cheeks. "Oh, Eloise, how good to have another woman here!"

I allowed her to embrace me, unaccustomed to human touch. I wondered if I should warn her I'd forgotten how to talk to friends—I couldn't move from sunny small talk to broken insides.

As if we were already besties, Mina took my arm and led me through the trees to a wooden shack with a crescent moon burned into the door. Wisteria draped over the structure in a sweet, musky cloud.

"*Voilà, Eloise!* Your *toilettes!*"

I entered and closed the door, breathing cedar and nectar. Light poured through propped-open stained glass windows. Before me was an olive wood toilet seat affixed to a bench, polished to a sheen.

I lifted the lid, peered at the pine sawdust and wood shavings in the tin bucket. A composting toilet, as I'd assumed—but far more pleasant than anything I'd imagined. With a content sigh, I peed, then washed my hands outside with lavender soap and water from a copper jug.

"The most magnificent *toilettes* ever," I announced.

Mina threw her head back and laughed, then gave me another hug. "Oh, I can tell we'll have fun together, my friend."

I felt myself give a real smile back.

"Now, Eloise, why don't you unpack and make yourself comfortable. I'll get dinner ready. Hope you like Senegalese food—that's what you get on my nights to cook! Raphaël will be up soon with an *apéro*." Her eyes crinkled. "He's the one who built the most magnificent *toilettes* ever!"

"*Merci*, Mina."

She gazed at me with undeserved affection, then headed down the river path.

I grabbed my bag, not caring what the hell an *apéro* was, or who Raphaël was—just feeling lighter in all ways. The swinging bridge threw me off-balance, but a jungle-gym kind of off-balance that made me giggle.

My unique, rustic lodging was a *playground!*

With a deep breath, I stepped across the threshold of the first tiny treehouse—a sumptuous room of cushions and candle lanterns and vases of lavender and rose and peony. Floor-to-ceiling shelves of French books, leather-bound and trimmed in gold leaf. A velvet fainting sofa, an antique cast-iron stove, a tiny kitchenette. A cabinet with a glass jug of water, liqueurs of every color—*crème de violette, crème de cassis, chartreuse*—jars of loose tea, honey, and cookies.

I helped myself to a handful of cookies—buttery shortbread with pansies in the center—so delicious I pretended to faint onto the fainting sofa.

I breathed it all in, and then, like a child with a second wind, I ran, limbs flailing, along the swinging bridges to the next structure—an atelier. A wooden drafting table held old-fashioned lab equipment—copper distillation vats, clear tubes, glass flasks and funnels, a vintage Bunsen burner. Shelves displayed mason jars of dried petals and leaves—and strung above were flowers and herbs drying. My gaze landed on a shelf of books: *Les Plantes Médicinales, Savoir des Herbes, Les Essences de Fleur, Les Fleurs Hallucinogènes.* It felt as if someone had left everything just waiting for me.

I raced onward to a small bedroom, airy and bright, all windows and French doors, smelling of sunshine-dried linen. Lacy curtains, soft light, a woodstove, lanterns galore, and vases of peonies.

Resisting the urge to sink into the bed, I let curiosity pull me one more level up, to a dressing room with robes and towels and an armoire. The centerpiece was an old-fashioned makeup table, inlaid with mother-of-pearl, holding bottles hand-labeled with EAU DE ROSE, EAU DE LAVANDE, EAU DE LILAS.

I sat down at the vanity, breathless, and splashed *eau de rose* on my neck. Something caught my eye beside the mirror—a black leather book, pocket-size and bound by hand. I flipped through it, skimming ink sketches of goddesses and typewritten descriptions. My gaze landed on a drawing of the Fates statue at the garden entrance. I read its caption in a whisper:

> The Fates weave destiny. The Triple
> Goddess also takes other forms, some
> more dangerous than others: The Furies,
> the Morrigan, *Les Dames Blanches*, *Les
> Matres*, *Les Trois Maries*, and more.

Curious, I flipped back to the first page.

> Welcome to Paradise.
> Not everyone may enter My realm. Only those
> who master an impossible marvel. You—if you
> stay in My graces—are a fortunate one.

Impossible marvel. *Merveille impossible.* A twist on the mythical *impossible task*? According to the job ad, my principal duty would be turning *merde* into *fleurs*. Shit into flowers. A strange alchemy, a task within the realm of spinning straw into gold. Only ickier.

> I trust you will care for My gardens well.
>
> Respectfully,
> The Goddess of the Gardens

> PS: You should know that strictly speaking,
> this is not Paradise.
> More like a nook of *l'Autre Monde.*

L'Autre Monde. The Celtic Otherworld. A magical land existing in a parallel plane of existence. A place of beauty, joy, abundance, and health, where time moved differently.

I stared at my face in the round mirror with its wavy, silver-backed glass. I thought I'd find the usual exhausted face staring back, but instead, it was a fresh, enraptured face. The face of my hopeful fifteen-year-old self. Or maybe my curious five-year-old self. Or my wild toddler self. Cheeks pink, eyes wide.

I entertained the thought that the mirror was magical and moved my face closer. The crow's-feet were still there, but softened, along with the furrows over my nose. And my eyes looked practically aquamarine, the usual circles below almost vanished. Green surrounded my head like a halo—reflections of the foliage outside.

And as the leaves rustled and flowers whispered, I heard the giggle of a girl.

Or was it me, giggling inside my head? I felt my mouth part, my throat open, and a ripple of laughter pour out.

I was still laughing when a man's voice called up. "Eloise! The *apéro* has arrived!"

Raphaël.

Refuge for the Broken

I descended the swinging bridges, attempting Mina's grace, without much luck.

From above, I registered this man's hair, thick and nut brown and pulled into a wavy ponytail that ended below his shoulder blades. His white T-shirt glowed against tanned, muscled arms. There was something solid and compact about him, nothing wasted.

He raised his face to me. Strong jaw, light stubble, smiling eyes, earthy vibe. Objectively, he was good-looking.

I sighed, unsure what to make of this new development.

"Eloise! *Bonsoir!* I am Raphaël."

"*Enchantée,*" I called down.

He was carrying a tray of drinks and snacks. Right. *Apéro,* shorthand for *apéritif.*

Once I reached the second level, I noticed his hands. Ages ago, they might have made my insides flutter. In a previous life, something about certain men's hands would get to me—usually ones who built and fixed things outdoors.

As if from a distance, I wondered if he might be considered sexy. It had been a very, very long time since I'd thought of anyone as sexy. I hadn't thought of sex for the sake of sex for a very, very long time. Over a decade, I'd transformed from maiden to crone.

Anyway, he was too young—late twenties or early thirties? Sure, I was thirty-seven, but an *ancient* thirty-seven. I wondered if he noticed that I'd given up on my body, let the outside deteriorate to match the inside.

In a split second, I took inventory of my state of disrepair. My feet were calloused and my toenails ragged, legs unshaven beneath stretched-out leggings, basically glorified pj's. My long shirt was drab and shapeless—the kind of thing a non-spunky grandmother would wear. And my hair, oh, my hair—ragged and frizzed, long and formless, the dirty blond of dead leaves, devoid of products beyond shampoo-and-conditioner-in-one. My face wore basic sunscreen—no makeup, no antiaging serums, no wrinkle creams. Why bother? I was in debt with no one to impress.

Well, this took the pressure off. If I was in cronehood and Raphaël was in strapping-young-manhood, he'd see me as tacitly off-limits beyond friendship.

I paused on the lower deck and called down, "Monsieur, would you like to come up and have the *apéro*?" My French sounded funny and formal.

His face lit up. *"Oui, avec plaisir!"*

As he walked up the swinging bridge—quite nimbly considering he had no free hands—I smiled to myself. I was inviting a French man *up to my place* for drinks. And he was coming *with pleasure*. Who would've guessed?

Up close, his eyes looked hazel green, foresty and warm in a dappled-light way. He was an inch or two taller than me, which meant we were more or less at eye level. He leaned forward to do the cheek kisses.

I struggled to remember which cheek came first and picked the wrong one, and we promptly bumped noses. Eventually, laughing, we managed to touch our cheeks together, then—with relief on my part—sat at the little table.

The clouds were shifting from gold to orange to pink, the castle towers shining through a gap in the tree canopy. The whole situation was ridiculously gorgeous. The *apéro* turned out to be Kir—white wine with a splash of berry liqueur. Beside the drinks sat a small olive wood bowl of a nut mix and another of homemade rosemary crackers. Thankfully, I'd stuffed those shortbread cookies into my mouth earlier, or I would've been ravenous now.

"Eloise, welcome to Paradise." He raised his glass in a toast.

I clinked mine against his. "To the Otherworld!"

"Pardon?" He tilted his head.

"Oh, that's what the little goddess booklet said." With amusement, I added, "I love that the Goddess of the Gardens wrote it herself."

I expected a smiling admission of who really wrote it, but he only sipped his Kir, so I joined him, savoring this piece of berry heaven.

In stops and starts, we chatted about my journey. Raphaël spoke French quickly, but when he realized it was over my head, he slowed down and simplified the slang.

"Oh, Eloise, I am just so excited to meet a new friend." Whenever his eyes met mine, they'd flicker away, making me think he was as self-conscious as I was.

Of course I would let him down, just like I would let Mina down. They thought I was an intact human. Still, I resolved to act like a normal colleague. "So," I asked, "what did you do before you came here?"

A cloud passed over his face. *"Eh bien, alors, euh . . ."*

I waited as he *umm*ed and *uhh*ed in French and looked everywhere but at me.

He finished on an anticlimactic note. "Nothing much."

I felt a desperate need to compensate for his lack of eye contact and fill the empty conversational space. "Well, before this, I was doing nothing too. I mean, as far as a job. But there were other things going on, you know, divorce, sadness, anger over my ex's new girlfriend, more sadness, friendships dying, talking only to flowers, setting my old life on fire. Literally."

For a moment, I was back in Denver, engulfed in smoke, dumping flammable liquids into the fire, watching the old Eloise burn as flames rose.

After a beat, he said, "You talk to flowers?"

I gave a tiny shrug, then, desperate to redirect the focus, asked, "What about you? Married? Divorced? Single?"

I pressed a firm hand over my mouth. The Kir had gone straight to my head, removed every inhibition.

He offered a slight nod. It was unclear which marital status he was confirming.

More silence. Just crickets chirping their sunset songs.

Raphaël sipped his Kir and gazed at the trees. "Eloise, all of us here, we have been hurt—and that is why we are in the Gardens of Paradise." His voice was a mix of rough and tender, straightforward and philosophical. "This is a refuge for the broken."

My eyes filled at this unexpected gift. He *understood*. I blinked and sniffled and resisted grabbing an ancient tissue from my pocket. Then I sipped my Kir and waited for details about how, exactly, this beautiful man before me was broken.

He offered none. His foresty-sunshiny eyes met mine for a moment, then looked back at the treetops. He seemed skittish at making friends. I could relate.

"*Merci*," I said. "*Merci*, Raphaël."

A squirrel scampered along a branch, pausing to chirp at us with gusto. Despite myself, I sputtered a laugh, and Raphaël laughed too. Somehow, even rodents seemed more *amusant* in the Gardens of Paradise.

I sipped more Kir. "So, Raphaël, what do you do here?"

"If something needs to be fixed, I fix it. Or built, I build it. Structures, fountains, irrigation, solar panels." He leaned back, tossed a cashew into his mouth, appearing more comfortable talking about his work. "And I love working with leather, metal, wood—or really, any materials I can find."

That explained my objective appreciation of his hands. And the exquisite *toilettes* he'd made. I remembered my delight learning the French word for "tinkerer" or "handyman" in high school French class. "A *bricoleur?*"

"Exactly." The corner of his lip turned up, revealing a tiny dimple.

I sighed. "I guess I'm in charge of the *fleurs* and *merde*."

"*Pardon?*"

I flushed. Twenty minutes into a sunset *apéro* in Paradise with a handsome, kind French man and I was bringing up shit. I willed the blood vessels in my cheeks to constrict.

At first, when I'd read the job ad back in Denver, I'd had no idea how to interpret the *merde* to *fleurs* line. *Shit to flowers?* It hadn't been until the middle of that night when the answer had come to me. I'd been dreaming of overflowing toilets and feeling distressed . . . until I flew away, to the Gardens of Paradise, and landed beside composting *toilettes*. In my dream, when I'd dumped out the contents, flowers had sprung up—lavender and roses and jasmine, sage and rosemary and thyme. I'd awoken, still smelling nectar, then scrawled out my résumé.

"Compost," I clarified for Raphaël, hoping my solution to the riddle was correct. "That's what I'm in charge of. I think."

"*Oui*, that is true."

I smiled, satisfied, even as my nose wrinkled. This kind of task seemed more palatable in a dream or fairy tale.

"Don't worry." His eyes sparked. "There is a system. It is not stinky."

"I'm up for it. That's my *merveille impossible*."

I tried not to look too long at that dimple when he smiled, which was often. From the corner of my eye, I glimpsed something in the trees, larger than a squirrel and shaking the lower branches. A yellow blur swung and dropped behind the trunk with a light thud and a giggle. It vanished.

My first thought: a child in this wild playground.

My second: a woodsprite in a magical garden.

My third: an apparition from my jet-lagged mind.

Raphaël said nothing about it, so I shook myself, refocusing on the conversation. "So, who's this big boss?" I asked, squinting at the far-off turrets of La Patronne's castle.

He puffed out his cheeks in the endearing way French people do. "I have been working here for years, and I still do not know. We have never met. She stays sequestered."

Surprising. And mystifying. "But if she doesn't use the gardens, what's the point?"

He took another sip. "At the weekly market, customers pay triple for products grown and made here. Our plants have . . . *talents*."

Talents? A strange word to describe plants. Maybe it was a language thing. Or maybe because this was a *place of power*.

Before I could question him, he continued, "La Patronne desires the bounty from the gardens yet never enters."

I remembered the rule about staying inside at dusk. "Except for the hour of *crépuscule*?"

"Perhaps. That is one theory."

"You've never been tempted to break the rule, Raphaël?" I raised an eyebrow—a skill I'd forgotten I had. "Spy a little?"

He chuckled. "Life is good here. Why risk ruining it . . . without a reason?"

Standing up, he set down his empty glass, stretched, and looked at the sky. "Speaking of *crépuscule*, the sun is setting. Soon it will be time to stay in our quarters. I will give you time to relax."

"*Merci*, Raphaël."

He picked up the tray. "It is good to have a new friend here, Eloise."

Friend. I gave a breezy smile like a normal person—and I felt, if not exactly normal, then more *intact* than usual.

He walked down the swinging bridges, slowing his pace to accommodate mine. I clutched the ropes—this would take some practice.

"We meet at the dining grove for dinner," he explained when we reached solid ground. "Just follow that path along the river. Nights are chilly, so bring a sweater. We dine at twenty-two hours. *Ça va?*"

I did a quick calculation and came up with ten o'clock. Could that be right? *Ten?* Then again, summer dusk would probably last till about nine thirty, and we were in France, after all. Back in college, when I'd studied abroad, dinners with my host family sometimes lasted past midnight. Anyway, my bio rhythms were screwed up with the time difference. I'd just have more cookies to tide me over. "*Oui, ça va.*"

He leaned in for the kisses, and once again, we bumped noses.

I hoped the tree shadows would hide my flushing cheeks. "One of these days I'll get it right," I assured him. *Or else you'll need a nose splint.* But with no idea how to say "nose splint" in French, I left it there.

Still, he gave a warm laugh. "I am so glad that you are here," he said, like he truly meant it. Then he turned to leave, disappearing around the bend.

I let out a sigh of disbelief at my good fortune, then climbed to the top floor of my treehouse, feeling the echo of laughter. I explored the jars of beauty supplies on the vanity, smoothing almond oil infused with calendula over my face, then spreading mica-flecked hibiscus balm over my lips and the apples of my cheeks.

On impulse, I rummaged through my bag and pulled out my one nice article of clothing—a wrinkled little black dress, simple cotton jersey, short enough to show my knees, with a neckline that revealed some cleavage. Of course Raphaël and the others would discover the frumpiness of my wardrobe soon enough, but at least for this night, what might happen if I played at being the maiden and not the crone?

The Deepest Sleep

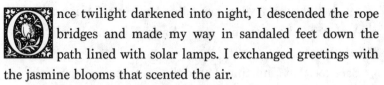nce twilight darkened into night, I descended the rope bridges and made my way in sandaled feet down the path lined with solar lamps. I exchanged greetings with the jasmine blooms that scented the air.

Shivering, I buttoned the khaki shirt over my dress and patted the pocket containing the little leather book—a guide to this strange land. In the spaces between treetops, the Milky Way shone.

I rounded the bend and came face-to-face with a white statue at the side of the path—a stone woman in flowing robes, holding a harp. I pressed my hand to my heart, willing it to calm, then flipped through the handy goddess guide, pausing at a drawing of this one halfway through. I whispered the caption aloud, translating the French.

```
In My Aoibhell form, I play My gorgeous
and deadly harp music, which kills those
who have disobeyed My commands.
```

I studied the statue's eerie smile as if I were visiting a nighttime museum, then continued along the path, wondering what other goddess statues might be waiting to illuminate me. Moments later, I rounded another bend and the magic hit me, full force.

Fairy lights glowed through the trees, pulling me to the edge of a clearing. In the center sat a round table, lit by candles and set with pottery plates and wooden utensils and vases of feathery ferns, steaming pots and pitchers of water and bottles of wine. Lanterns hung from cedar and pine branches.

A one-room stone kitchen, its windows yellow against the darkness, was tucked into the trees. I peered through the doorway at an old-fashioned stove, breathed in the scent of spiced stew. Mina and Raphaël and another man were seated at the table in the grove. Seeing me, Raphaël gestured to the empty chair.

"*À table!*" declared Mina, spreading her arms. *Time to eat!*

As I headed toward my chair, Raphaël said, "*Bonsoir*, Eloise. This is Bao."

Bao stood up. This time I aced the kiss greeting, remembering that one offers the left cheek first in the South of France.

"*Bienvenue,* Eloise." His voice was quiet and kind.

"*Enchantée,* Bao."

He was a thin, ropy man with straight black hair clipped short. He wore a neat khaki outfit, not unlike my practical clothes back in the dressing room. Drab-green binoculars hung around his neck. His canvas shirt had many pockets with all manner of small things poking out—a notebook, pen, handkerchief, pocketknife, twine, tiny bottles, dried mushrooms and flowers and seedpods.

"We are happy to have you, Eloise." His heritage could be Southeast Asian—but his French was clearly native, so I guessed he was born here or came as a small child. "How do you like Paradise?"

"It's magnificent . . . and bizarre." I quoted the Goddess: "More like a nook of the Otherworld."

"Well said." He held up a bottle of rosé. "May I offer you some?"

"*Merci.*" I held out my glass.

As Bao poured me wine on one side, Raphaël poured me a glass of lemon water on the other. A few violets fell into my glass like magic.

"Help yourselves!" said Mina.

And we did. Peanut stew with an exquisite combination of spices, carrots, and potatoes, alongside herbed rice and crusty baguettes.

I tasted a spoonful and moaned in pleasure. "Mina! This is *incroyable!*"

She beamed. *"Bon appétit!"*

I couldn't tell if the meal tasted this divine because it was ten at night and I was starving . . . or if it was the candlelight and flowers and stars . . . or if Mina was truly an out-of-this-world culinary genius.

As we ate, she and Bao chatted about their own jobs in Paradise. Along with personal assistant duties, Mina was in charge of fruits and vegetables, making jams and preserves and pickles. Bao had a background in forest ecology—he managed the bees, fish, rabbits, birds, mushrooms, trees, and nature miscellanea.

Mina held up the bottle of rosé. "More wine? It's from a vineyard nearby."

I noticed my now-empty glass. I wasn't much of a drinker. Not for the past decade at least. Every aspect of my diet had been tightly controlled. Caffeine, alcohol, gluten, meat, dairy, sugar, you name it. I'd been a frantic rat in a maze, trapped in trial after trial. Most of my adult life had been about withholding every indulgence, tempering every pleasure—daily sacrifices for something monumental that never came to pass.

Now, the wine made my head float. "Sure, *merci.*" What if I could escape the maze altogether, fly right out, up and away? This was my first night here, these people seemed to like me, I was wearing an LBD, and my face glowed with flower potions.

I sipped the rosé, floral and mineral, light and deep at once. *Live a little, Eloise.*

As we feasted, the moon rose, full and luminous.

We opened a bottle of Chardonnay and toasted the stars. For the next course (there was a *next course!*), Mina served delicate grilled fish in a lemon-garlic-mustard sauce. Then came garden-fresh greens drizzled with vinaigrette and sprinkled with nasturtium petals that matched the brilliant orange of her headscarf. Then Bao opened a bottle of Burgundy as Raphaël brought out pungent cheeses and another baguette.

Soon a guitar materialized and Raphaël plucked soft jazz melodies. In a starry haze, we lit more candles and lingered over dessert—a mouth-tingling *tarte au citron*. We sipped sweet Sauternes as Bao told us of his youth, working with his Vietnamese immigrant parents in their little café in Marseille.

"What brought you from there to here?" I asked.

He stared at the stars. "Oh, not much." Tilting his head, he murmured, "Hear that?"

An unearthly *hoo*-ing came from the trees.

"Eagle owl." And just like that, he changed the subject, launching into the wonders of eagle owls. Clearly, he wasn't one to talk about himself. Which was okay. I was reluctant to talk about my past too.

He was still fun to chat with, offering generous laughter at my jokes that translated awkwardly at best, incoherently at worst. He and the others radiated warmth, and I soaked it up.

Mina and Bao touched often—she'd slap his knee, he'd pat her hand, she'd rub his shoulder. And they looked at each other the way a couple does, an iceberg of shared history under the surface.

Of course she would know what Bao was hiding from his glossed-over decades. I yearned for what they had, what I'd lost, or maybe never had to begin with.

Deep into the night, Mina said, "Why did you come here, Eloise?"

An image flashed in my mind of my ex's new girlfriend, her naive smile, the pain and the blood—my darkest nightmare made real. Tamping it all down, I offered a vague, "The flowers."

Mina raised her eyebrows, as if expecting more.

"I just—it seemed peaceful, I mean, without sirens and kids bothering me."

She studied me as if she knew full well there was brokenness under my excuses.

But I refused to lead the conversation down a dark path. "I only want peace and quiet."

Raphaël rested his hand on the guitar, regarding me with curiosity, as if he, too, sensed my lie.

I opened my mouth to tell the truth, or at least some of it. But no, I wouldn't ruin the mood with the ashes of my old life.

Soon the conversational momentum wound down and my companions started gathering dishes. Carrying as many as I could hold—a fair amount from my days as a bus girl in college—I followed the others to a counter by the exterior kitchen wall, where two basins sat beneath a spouted water jug. *Right, no plumbing.*

"Go home and sleep, Eloise," Bao said as he and Raphaël started washing.

I gave in without a fight, bidding them *bonne nuit*, and then, wobbly from wine and exhaustion, headed home.

Even though I'd braced for it, the harp lady on the path startled me. I let my eyes linger on her surreal stone smile. And I wondered how her gorgeous and deadly harp music might sound.

❀

Back at my treehouse, I headed up the swinging bridges, illuminated by fairy lights that saved energy from the sun and flicked
on in the dark. On a whim, I stopped by my library to fix some
herbal tea—it made sense to stay hydrated after my wine drinking.

I lit a candle lantern, breathed in the smoke and beeswax.
Scanning jars of tea, I found one labeled CALME. I filled the kettle
with water from the glass jug and heated it on a small burner
fueled by a hidden butane canister. Then I made myself a strong
pot of tea. Well, technically, this would be a tisane, an herbal
infusion—my French host family had been particular about the
distinction.

Once the tisane had brewed, I added honey and sipped. Lavender,
rose, and chamomile I recognized. I noticed some leaves—maybe
passionflower and skullcap—that gave it a grassy smell. And valerian
root and mugwort? Maybe that accounted for the pungency. And
there were mysterious blue petals I couldn't put my finger on.

I settled into the fainting couch. Oh, how *relaxing*. I thanked
the plants in this tea, along with whoever had made it.

After the second cup, my troubles drifted away. After my third,
drowsiness overtook me.

I walked down the bridges in a trance. Starlight, lantern light,
moonlight. Cricket chirps, frog songs, flower whispers.

Somehow, I made it to the *toilettes*, then found my way to bed.
With sleepy delight, I put on a silk eye mask, settled into pillows,
and replayed the magical dinner. It appeared I had three real,
live, human friends.

Soon I slipped into sleep. My dreams were vivid, as if I'd stumbled across another realm, the colors brighter, the sounds more
vibrant, the tastes more intense. A realm where I transformed into
flowers, one after another, from warm calendula to cool violets.

My petals flew in skies full of stars and my nectar trailed like the Milky Way.

And somehow, my flower-self became a goddess, shifting forms, morphing into a mountain, then an ocean, then mist, then lightning, then a torrent. Goddesses flowed through me and I flowed through them, darkness and light intermingling like rivulets.

And as an undercurrent, always, from sea to sky: the laughter of a little girl.

Laughter that felt familiar, as if it had been with me all my life.

First, I became aware of birdsong. One song in particular, clear and sweet—a warbler maybe. Next, I smelled roses, an ancient variety with notes of musk and clove. My mind lifted, bit by bit, from the realm of sleep. Dreams floated away like feathers, and I remembered where I was and why it was pitch black.

I removed the sleep mask.

Light shone through the wavy glass. Green surrounded me— the canopy of oak and maple leaves, finches and wrens hopping around the branches.

I took in my lack of hangover. In fact, it was the opposite of a hangover. A crystal-clear mind. An open heart. *A good night's sleep.* When was the last time I'd had that?

I glanced at the analog clock. Only seven? I wouldn't even be late to my first workday. When had I even gone to bed? It couldn't have been before four a.m., which meant I'd gotten a grand total of three hours of sleep and felt . . . *glorious.* I'd heard of people who needed only a few hours per night. Maybe Paradise was to thank. Maybe that herbal tea.

Humming, I made a fresh pot of tea—a mix of leaves and

twigs labeled RÈVEILLE-TOI. Wake up, *indeed*. It didn't skimp on the caffeine. In a silk robe from my dressing room, I ventured across a small meadow to my shower, a spiral structure hidden inside a veil of wisteria and honeysuckle. I peeked behind it, spotting a solar panel and battery that must have stored energy to heat and pump water from the tank. Most of the gear was cleverly concealed by trellised vines.

In the heart of the spiral, I savored the warm spray until my belly started demanding food. Back in the treehouse, I threw on my khaki outfit, splashed rose water on my face, then smoothed on chamomile-infused almond oil.

Strolling along the river path, I gave a friendly nod to the harp lady statue, greeted morning glories, and inhaled scents of rosemary and sage. *This is my life!*

In the clearing, breakfast was laid out on a linen tablecloth—golden granola, creamy yogurt, stone fruit, toasted nuts, an array of croissants. Coffee steam rose in the honeyed light.

Raphaël emerged from the kitchen, sleepy-eyed. There was an odd intimacy to having breakfast with a man who wasn't my partner yet who'd made me this gorgeous spread, right down to a vase of pink rosebuds.

"*Bonjour*, Eloise." When he leaned in for the cheek kiss, this time I offered my left cheek, then my right. Success!

"*Bonjour, mon ami!* Where are the others?"

"When it's not their turn to cook, they sleep in."

We sat down across from each other, and he poured me coffee. Apparently, he was too groggy to be self-conscious—his drowsy gaze met mine. "Help yourself, Eloise."

"*Bon appétit.*" I stirred cream and sugar into my coffee. "I slept so well!"

He grinned, showed the dimple. "*Oui*, that is evident. We were worried when it was noon and still no sign of you. But Mina checked on you. Sleeping like an angel."

I blinked as my brain put it together. "How long was I asleep?"

"Oh, thirty hours."

I set down my coffee with a splash. "I slept *all day?*"

"You were jet-lagged. It is fine. But you must be starving. Eat."

Baffled, I took a bite of granola, tasted caramelized berries and roasted seeds. I made a moan of pleasure—this was becoming a pattern now. "Delicious, Raphaël. *Merci.*"

"You are feeling good here?"

"Never better," I admitted. "Before bed, I had a pot of tisane. Labeled CALME."

"Ah, one of Iva's concoctions."

"Iva?"

Before he could answer, the leaves rustled and footsteps sounded. Down the path shuffled Mina, wrapped in swaths of lemon-yellow cotton, yawning and stretching. Here was a woman unafraid to take up space and color.

"Oh!" She beamed at me. "Our little bear is out of hibernation." Tossing Raphaël a mischievous glance, she asked him, "You told her how she slept for a week?"

I gaped. "A *week?*"

5

Curiosities

Mina is kidding," Raphaël assured me. "You just slept for thirty hours."

I realized that if I *had* slept for a week here, I'd have no way of knowing it. There were no cell phones or computers updated with the time and day. I'd have to be more careful with those teas. I recalled myths of Celtic heroes taking journeys to the Otherworld and, upon returning home, finding that centuries had passed.

Mina laughed and leaned toward me for cheek kisses. "Oh, Eloise! Just like Rip Van Winkle!"

Once I gave in to laughter, Raphaël joined in, eyes crinkling with delight. Still, something about his gaze wasn't entirely here—he kept glancing at the edges of the grove.

Soon Bao rounded the bend, greeting us with a quiet smile and cheek kisses and *bonjours*. With slow, deliberate movements, he helped himself to breakfast.

Raphaël fixed himself more granola, then stood up, holding the full bowl. "I've got some things to do before work. *A tout à l'heure.*"

A wave of disappointment hit me. Meals with my new friends brought me back to college days, made me feel part of something. Raphaël struck me as the creative introvert type—one who liked his friends but his alone time too. I could respect that.

"So, Eloise, do you often sleep for a day and a half?" Bao asked.

I gave a bewildered smile. "Only when I drink a strong pot of *calme.*"

"*Alors,* that explains it," said Bao. "Iva created that blend. The gardener before your predecessor. An older Czech lady, very wise."

"A witch," added Mina, eyes shining. "The good kind, *bien sûr.* She called herself 'a woman wise in flowers.'"

Bao patted her shoulder. "Iva put together that atelier herself, filled all those notebooks. If any of us had a problem, we'd go to her."

"Did she retire?" I asked.

"One day she said she'd learned what she needed from the garden." Mina wiped her eyes, put a hand over Bao's. "She hugged us all goodbye and left."

I was about to ask about the gardener who'd replaced her—and hadn't followed the rules—but Bao said, "We're happy we have you now, Eloise. You remind us of Iva."

"You have a sense of wonder." Mina deepened her voice. "'Wisdom begins in wonder.' Socrates."

Bao added, "You're like a child, finding joy in everything."

This was all very strange. "Wouldn't anyone feel that way here?"

"Not everyone is open to wonder," said Bao.

"And you make us laugh," Mina added. "Like Iva!"

"She always moaned over our food too," said Bao.

"Oh!" said Mina. "And Raphaël said you talk to flowers. You belong here."

I didn't mind being compared to a wonder-filled old witch. It seemed, oddly enough, like the ultimate compliment. I wanted to be part of this strange little group. I resolved to let my happy moans loose, channel the woman wise in flowers, and embrace whatever this nook of the Otherworld offered me.

"*Alors,*" I said, determined. "I'll do my best to fill Iva's shoes."

Which resulted in confusion all around, as the expression didn't translate literally, and no one understood what the hell I intended to do with the good witch's shoes. Which resulted in a round of teary-eyed belly laughter. Which resulted in even more fondness for these strangers who were, beyond all comprehension, now my friends.

Mina stood and clapped her hands together. "Ready for the tour of Paradise?"

❀

As we set off, the crispness of morning was already melting into another warm day. The Mediterranean light felt lemony and creamy, a whipped dessert you could spoon onto your tongue.

Pointing past the dining grove to a stone cottage with a chimney, Bao said, "That's where we eat in winter. Raphaël's been renovating it."

I admired it, wondering what *bricoleur* stuff he was up to.

"Let's start at my house," Mina said, as eager as a child.

As we headed along the river path in the opposite direction from my treehouse, I asked about the wildlife. Pleased, Bao pointed out tracks and scat, lizards and snakes, and even loaned me his binoculars. He had the endearing habit of picking up little treasures—pine cones, seedpods, pebbles—and placing them into my palm. After he illuminated me about them, I wasn't sure if I was supposed to drop them onto the ground or keep them as treehouse décor. Not wanting to offend him, I tucked them into my pockets.

"You know," Mina said, laughing, "you and Bao could be twins!"

True, we were both clad in unisex khaki gear from head to toe. With plenty of pockets.

We joked and walked until Mina cried, *"Ouille!"* and plopped down onto a log.

"You okay?" I asked.

"Just arthritis," she said, kneading her leg.

Bao pulled a tiny bottle from one of his multitude of pockets and poured a reddish-gold liquid onto his palm. Gently, he rubbed it onto Mina's knee.

"Ah, *merci*," she said, closing her eyes in relief.

"Crushed chili and olive oil," Bao said. "Grown in these gardens. Eases the pain."

After a few minutes, Mina clapped her hands and declared, "All better!"

Satisfied, Bao tucked the bottle back into his pocket. He pulled a lemon from another pocket, sliced it open with his pocketknife, then rubbed its juice on his hands.

"Removes the chili," Mina said, patting his shoulder with affection.

It touched me, their tender ritual.

We continued walking a few dozen meters, until Mina announced, *"Et voilà,"* motioning ahead with her chin. "My house."

Through the leaves, my gaze landed on a hobbit hole. It was earthen, tucked into the side of a grass-covered hill, with a round, wooden door that swung on its axis. Potted geraniums, bright pink and red, lined the cobbled path to the entrance. On either side, stained glass windows ushered in sunshine.

"I'm a fan of *The Lord of the Rings*," she said. "Not so much the war parts. Mostly the hobbit holes and elves."

Around back, I glimpsed a fig tree, heavy with purple fruit. Honeysuckle vines draped her outdoor *toilettes*, not far from an outdoor tub—bronze-footed and cast iron and ancient. A slab of olive wood rested across it, holding a candle and a book of African women's poetry. Even as someone who had terrible associations with baths, I almost longed to take one here. *Almost.*

Mina and Bao led me through the revolving door into a round

living room. Piles of books dotted the central area, and in a side nook was a desk heaped with papers and notebooks.

"Pardon the mess." She laughed. "I'm writing my memoir."

"How's it going?"

"*Comme ci, comme ça.*" She wobbled her hand in a so-so gesture. "At least I'm doing it. Like Samwise says, 'It's the job that's never started as takes longest to finish.'"

Ah yes. *The Lord of the Rings.* I took in the room's patterns—an abstract lilac print on a tangerine backdrop, lime stars dotting raspberry swirls, turquoise dancing with pink and yellow. Rainbow sunshine beamed through windows and skylights. Her home felt warm and cool and dark and light at once.

"I love this, Mina!"

"*Merci.* The cloth is from Senegal. Where I was born and raised. I asked Antoinette to order it from Marseille."

She paused, as if debating something, then said in a matter-of-fact tone, "When I left my country, I had no time to bring pretty things. I was a child. Thirteen. I was married to an old man. And I had just nearly died. It was a matter of time before I would nearly die again. Or actually die. So when I was well enough to run, I ran. I ran far away. My journey took years, but it brought me here."

I had a million questions . . . the first being, what was the etiquette for this situation? Finally, I said, "*Je suis desolée.*" I'm sorry.

"Me too," she said emphatically.

"Is that what your memoir is about?"

"*Oui.*"

"I'd like to read it. I mean, if you're okay with that. When it's ready."

She crinkled her eyes. "Who knows when that will be!" She put an arm around my shoulder. "Oh, Eloise, where would we be if we hadn't made it through hell?"

"Not in Paradise."

She laughed.

This was an invitation for me to share my hell, but where to start? How do you say these things? The time never seemed right. Mina had shared the tip of her hell-iceberg so succinctly—there was no way I could do that.

She'd said she was a former child bride. Who'd been on the brink of death? A brave refugee fleeing for her life?

There was no way I could tell her my woes. She'd been a young girl forced to marry an old man, while I couldn't even make a marriage work with a sweet guy my own age whom I'd chosen myself.

The familiar shame started to fill me, that *drowning* feeling.

Mina squeezed me again. "Now you come over anytime at all, Eloise. Anytime you feel like a chat or a laugh or a cry!"

And all at once, I felt myself open. I let myself feel the pain of a terrified thirteen-year-old girl facing death. I let it flood through me. I looked at this woman in front of me, emanating warmth, and I understood that somewhere inside her was a scared child.

"*Merci*, Mina."

She hugged me. Something about her hug felt like a revelation— the idea that maybe laughter and hurt and darkness and light could coexist the way it did in this hobbit hole home. Her hug was a feeling that maybe pain wasn't a number on a scale, but something that could connect us instead of separate us.

After a moment, she drew away and ushered me outside, arm linked with mine. "Come on! We'll show you Bao's place."

Our arms stayed interlocked as we passed by a cheery vegetable garden—complete with tomatoes, cucumbers, chilis, squash, courgettes, aubergines, lettuce—then rounded the bend to Bao's home.

It was a yurt, handmade in true Mongolian style. The round wooden frame—about twenty feet in diameter—was covered with gray felt.

"Sheep's wool," Bao said with pride when I touched the material. He opened the door. "Come on in."

The interior was one large space with lattice walls, sectioned into three areas—bedroom, living room, and office. Or more accurately, a mini natural history museum. On display were feathers, bones, shells, pebbles, mica, and shelves of books on wildlife. Binoculars hung by the desk, arranged from small to large.

Mina looked at home, picking up a bone here, a stone there, blowing off dust and polishing them against her shirt. I was surprised she and Bao didn't live together, but then again, each home was meant for one person.

I peered at his cabinets of curiosities and wondered what hell he'd been through. One thing didn't fit in with the rest: a photo. The only one in the entire home. It was tucked into a shelf between a framed butterfly wing and a cicada shell.

I looked closer. The picture had been taken in a garden, gladiolas and hollyhocks in the periphery. The girl at the center was maybe six years old, with long dark hair. She was smiling—a joyful smile with endearingly crooked teeth. The lower half of her face was smooth, with golden skin and cupid-bow lips.

The top half of her face was marred with scar tissue—her cheeks, nose, eye sockets, forehead. Her irises were amber brown, but there was something strange about one of her eyes—it was glass, I realized, the pupil staring ahead while her real eye glanced at something to the right.

My chest tightened at the damage to her young face . . . but then there was that impossibly open, genuine *smile*, caught mid-laugh.

I glanced at Bao, standing by the open door. For an instant, our eyes locked, and his filled with such sudden vulnerability, I had the urge to look away. But he averted his gaze first. Clearing his throat, he said, "Ready to move on?"

I paused. Who was this girl to him? Did he have secret pain around children too?

Giving myself a little shake, I took one last look at the photo. "*Oui*. Let's move on."

Mina linked her arm in mine again as we headed toward Raphaël's place, past a fragrant herb garden. She plucked a sprig of rosemary and held it beneath my nose, smiling as I breathed in its fresh, clear scent. It took a little getting used to, this casual physical contact, this closeness.

My sense of the garden's layout was becoming clearer—at least the parts I'd seen so far. The castle was perched on a hill at the western edge of the grounds, mostly hidden behind treetops and inner walls. The estate seemed to be a rough rectangle, maybe a half mile long and a quarter mile wide, bordered by the curving river valley along the north and east walls. Across the river, rock outcroppings merged with the stone wall to form the far boundary.

Nestled near the northeast corner, my treehouse had a partial view of the boulders and cliffs and water. Along the eastern wall—farthest from the castle—the river path branched into smaller trails to the dining grove, and farther along, Mina's hobbit hole, and farther still, Bao's yurt, and finally, Raphaël's home—where we were heading now.

Bao jogged ahead to let him know we were coming. This seemed odd, but who knew the privacy rules here? I was a stranger in a strange land.

Soon Mina and I reached the edge of a small clearing surrounded by cedars. Illuminated by a beam of sunshine, as if spotlit
on a grassy stage and flanked by an audience of flowers . . . was a
caravan.

My heartbeat quickened—this was pure magic. The wooden
exterior was painted forest green with gold and burgundy swirls,
topped by a curved, sky-blue roof. A white rabbit nibbled grass by
the closest wheel.

The Dutch door opened, and Raphaël appeared with a wave,
then closed the door and sat on the steps, blocking my entry. "It's
a mess. Another time I'll give you the full tour." He looked into
the trees and I followed his gaze.

I realized Bao wasn't here. "Where's Bao?"

After a pause, Raphaël said, "Following a bird."

"Oh." I let it go and moved my focus back to the vardo. As I ran
my hand over the horses and fruits painted on the smooth wood,
Mina said, "Raphaël made this himself, right here in the gardens."

"For my ex-girlfriend," he said. "She was Romani."

Awe swept over me. My ex had struggled to assemble IKEA
cabinets. "You built this for her?"

"After she left." His face fell.

He'd used the French verb *quitter*—to leave *or* to pass away. Was
she dead or just . . . *gone*? I couldn't think of how to tactfully clarify,
so I just said, "I'm sorry."

My mind went to the last time I'd seen my ex. That morning
had been my personal hell, materialized by the Platte River. My
foot had been gashed and my soul shredded, and it had all made
me muster up my last bits of courage to head to Paradise.

Raphaël led us to his workshop—a nearby shed, filled with
wood and metal scraps, old tools and equipment. In the center of
a long table sat an elaborate palace made of twigs and twine. It
looked about two feet cubed, every inch crafted with artistry.

"My impossible marvel," he said.

"Which was . . . ?"

"Build a château from *brindille et ficelle*, fit for a royal family."

I deduced that *brindille et ficelle* meant twigs and twine. "Tell me more."

He brushed his hand over the château's roof. "I was living in Paris. I saw the job ad in a magazine at the doctor's office. This was about five years ago and my life had just . . . changed. I made this in one night, then traveled here." He laughed at the memory. "I presented this château for a royal *fairy* family."

I recalled the job ad—not only the impossible task riddle, but the strange request for a résumé of ashes. "Did you give a résumé of ashes too?"

"We all did. We each had different tasks, but the ashes were for everyone. Ashes of our old lives." He gave me a meaningful look.

Right. I'd mentioned setting my old life on fire, literally.

Mina gave him an affectionate pat on the shoulder. "And since he came, he made Bao a yurt and me a hobbit hole. Before, we were living in ruins from the Middle Ages."

I raised my brow at the *bricoleur*, impressed. "Did you make my treehouse?"

"I wish. I just do maintenance on it."

I was trying to figure out how to politely insist he show me his vardo's interior when Mina declared, *"Allons-y!"* tossing one arm around Raphaël's shoulder and one around mine.

We hooked back up with the main river path and headed south, joking about the downsides of living in ruins from the Middle Ages, until we rounded a bend and I gasped.

6

The Poison Garden

hree statues loomed over us with wild grins. Bat wings sprouted from shoulders and snakes intertwined wild hair. Poised for attack, the stone women wielded whips and daggers.

"Sorry, should have given you a heads-up," Raphaël said with a sheepish smile.

Mina tossed her arm around my shoulder as I pulled out the little book.

"What's that?" she asked.

"My goddess guide. You didn't get one?"

She shook her head, looking puzzled.

"Written by the Goddess of the Gardens. I'm thinking it must be La Patronne, or maybe Iva." I flipped through the pages. "Oh, here it is." In museum docent manner, I read the description.

We are the Furies, born of Our mother Gaia
and Our father, Uranus. We sprang from
drops of his blood that fell to earth
upon his castration. We dwell in the
Underworld. Vengeance is Our essence.

I glanced up. "What is it with these goddesses?"

Mina tittered. "An eccentricity of Paradise."

With a grin, Raphaël added, *"Une bizarrerie."*

"Une bizarrerie," I repeated, bumbling through the throaty r's.

Amused, my companions tried to help me pronounce the impossible word, to no avail. Soon the river disappeared into a culvert beneath the wall near the southeast corner. We followed a graveled path uphill. The southern exposure made this area less forested, just neatly spaced rows of orchards—the classic Mediterranean olive, fig, and almonds, along with the more prosaic lemon, orange, and lime.

Raphaël and Mina plucked ripe fruits and dropped them into my palms faster than I could eat: sun-warmed apricots and sweet-tart cherries and soft, zingy plums. I was something new and different and exciting in their lives, I realized—what a strange thing to be.

As we progressed, the slope grew steeper, and the orchards were replaced by berry brambles. Here I had a clear view of the top of the castle—the gargoyles and towers, one of which evoked a crumbling rook chess piece.

I pressed my hand to the outside wall, craned back my head. "Any more gates from outside?"

"Just the one in the front," said Mina.

"What if Antoinette loses the key?"

Mina smirked. "Impossible. She's the most . . . *particular* person I've met." She paused. "Next to La Patronne, perhaps, but we've never met her."

Raphaël gave a lighthearted smile. "That's why only outsiders like us work here. Supposedly, locals might steal plants and gossip."

I considered this. "Ever leave?"

"We have weekends free," Raphaël said. "But we usually stay here."

We headed uphill and to the right, where terraces of wild-flowers and grasses met the inner wall, split by a tall wooden gate. I gestured with my chin. "Locked?"

Mina nodded.

I assumed these inside walls surrounded a courtyard, accessed through the castle. "What's it like in there?"

"Never seen it." Mina sighed.

"Antoinette lives there too," said Raphaël.

"She never talks about La Patronne?" I asked, mystified.

He shook his head.

"Maybe La Patronne is a hypersensitive person?" I joked. "Agoraphobic? Retired dictator? Drug lord in hiding?"

Raphaël laughed. "I used to wonder too. But now? I just let it be. We all do."

We reached the gate, pausing to catch our breath. "What's the history of this place?" I asked. "I mean, the not-so-ancient history."

Raphaël answered in a hushed tone. "Until half a century ago, a secretive family owned the estate." With a touch of melodrama, he added, "There were a series of disappearances and deaths, and then La Patronne took over."

Without warning, the gate swung open. There stood Antoinette, hands on hips.

Merde. How long had she been on the other side? Raphaël had been discreet, but I'd played the loud American. What exactly had I said, except some bad jokes at La Patronne's expense? Would that count as gossip?

"Bonjour," said Antoinette in a cool voice. She wore a silver silk dress, belted at her narrow waist. Her nails were pale lavender opals, her hair in a side twist, fastened with a jeweled hairpin. "Mina," she said, "one has need of more *calme* tisane."

"Of course." Mina's voice sounded oddly formal. "I'll leave a jar of it at the gate today."

Antoinette gave a terse nod and rested her gaze on me. "Mademoiselle, one must replenish the supply. *Tout de suite.*"

A *calme* emergency! I gave a nervous smile. "That *calme* tea is *super cool*, right?"

Antoinette turned to Mina. "La Patronne's nightmares are worsening."

Mina offered a sympathetic cluck, keeping her arms folded. As much as she touched everyone else, she kept a respectful distance from Antoinette. "I'll pass along some other tisanes that might help too."

"When did her nightmares start?" I asked Antoinette, eager for information.

Again, she ignored me. My question probably fell into the category of gossip.

Turning on her heel, she said *au revoir* over her shoulder and vanished through the gate. The lock clicked behind her and the atmosphere lightened.

"Allons-y!" said Mina. "On to your flower gardens, Eloise."

"They're *super cool*," Raphaël murmured, showing the dimple.

"Hyper cool," added Mina.

"Vachement cool," I said, remembering the slang term "cowlike" from my study abroad.

Mina laughed. *"Oh, la vache!"*

Oh, the cow, indeed.

Poppies and harebells joined in with soft laughter.

And as an undercurrent came the mysterious giggle of a child, bright and twinkling.

We headed downhill to the interior of the gardens, to what Mina called the beating heart of Paradise and Raphaël called a flower château.

"Et voilà!" he announced as we passed through a tall cypress barrier.

This was an open-air palace of blooms, thrumming with the voices of so many flowers. Each garden room was a secret nook, with stone seating and color-themed flowers, surrounded by living plant walls.

Special talents. The oddly long blooming season allowed for these petals to intermingle like old friends. Was it the soil—something about the terroir? Or had these unique varieties been cultivated here over the years? Or was it something else—something *otherworldly*?

Raphaël gestured to a large garden across the path. "Welcome to your flower pharmacy and supermarket in one."

I surveyed the colorful crowd of medicinal and edible flowers, their faces sweet and open—nasturtiums and violets and calendula, murmuring their welcomes, and beyond them, lavender and chamomile and sage, perfuming the air, offering greetings, the voices sunny and curious. I thanked them under my breath, whispered how eager I was to get to know them.

Mina whispered something to a violet, plucked a petal, and placed it on her tongue.

At this I relaxed even more—apparently, talking to flowers was normal behavior in Paradise. I *belonged* here.

As my companions lingered, I wandered toward a nearby room we'd skipped. Pausing beneath a trellis of morning glories, I surveyed angel's and devil's trumpets, blooms like bells. The devil's trumpets, pointing upward, were datura, and the angel's trumpets, pointing downward, were brugmansia—both hallucinogenic and poisonous. Some gardeners even recommended wearing gloves when handling the flowers.

Their whispers floated toward me in a dissonant chorus. *We are not for you. Leave.*

A shiver passed through me. I'd never encountered flowers who spoke like this, in such dark tones, in veritable *hisses*. In a whisper, I explained that I was just exploring.

No use. Their harsh voices felt suffocating. *Leave. Leave. Leave.*

I stumbled backward toward the exit, nearly running into a flower-crowned woman atop a rock. Her face was frozen in silent fury, and she was flanked by clusters of pink foxglove and deadly nightshade blossoms. Another goddess statue.

I glanced at Raphaël and Mina at the entrance.

"You're not responsible for this garden," she said.

I kept my hands in my pockets, aware of wispy clumps of poison hemlock as tall as me. I had the urge to run from this room but felt a pull of curiosity too. "Who takes care of it?"

"No one," she said.

I swept my gaze over the plants, which were unkempt, but only to a point. Someone had been pruning and shaping them, snipping off spent blooms and dead leaves. I opened my book and found the flower-crowned goddess. Any terms I hadn't encountered in French Lit were straightforward cognates.

```
In My  ine form, I have healed with herbs . . .
   and driven humans insane. Those who break My
     rules sit on My magic rock and lose their
    minds. Sometimes My wrath is more visceral.
      There was that king who tried violating
 Me . . . and suffered the bloody consequences.
```

Mon Dieu. At the sound of footsteps behind me, I startled.

When I turned and saw Raphaël, I breathed out.

He rocked on his feet, eyeing the exit. "Ready?"

I gave a nervous laugh. "Don't want to hang out in the death room?"

"Some other time," he said with a grin, slinging an arm around my shoulder and guiding me to the exit.

The poison flowers seemed relieved at my departure, urging me out. *And don't come back*, they spat.

I focused on Raphaël's arm around me—it felt so gentle and *right*. "Perfect place for a picnic," I said, trying to lighten the mood. "I'll bring the poisoned apples."

"I'll bring the toadstools." He winked. "*Hyper* delicious."

His arm stayed comfortably on my shoulders as we exited the cypress walls of the flower palace, passing cheery poppies and sunflowers that murmured welcomes. I felt a pang of disappointment when he removed his arm, but we kept up our banter about poison picnics. "I'll bring the chocolate," I said. "It disguises the bitter edge of poison."

Finding excuses to elbow each other, we walked along the interior wall until we reached the front spiked gate and the three goddesses guarding it. I stretched my head back, soaked in the fairy-tale castle towering above, its turret in sweet decay, covered in orange trumpet vine. What a strange and wondrous realm I'd found myself in. A nook of magic and myth.

Which reminded me of impossible marvels. Gold came from straw, flowers from *merde*. The flower part of the tour done, it was time for the compost. The stinkiest part of my duties. Raising an eyebrow, I said, "On to the *merde, mes amis?*"

Raphaël grinned, revealing *two* dimples this time. "*Oui*, Eloise."

Mina hooked one arm with his and the other with mine, and in true *Wizard of Oz* fashion, we headed down the path, the gaze of the Fates following us.

7

Merde to Fleurs

It felt like I'd stepped right into *Mon Jardin*—the magazine with the job ad that had brought me here. I stood at the entrance of a centuries-old stone shed, drooling over the gardening tools—shovels, hoes, spades, watering cans—each one charming. My companions were smart to show me this before the *merde*.

"A gardener's dream," I murmured, breathing in the scent of must and soil.

Raphaël and Mina led me to the kitchen compost area. This concept, I was familiar with—a straightforward place to toss food scraps, used for edible and medicinal gardens.

After nodding along to their simple instructions, I braced myself. "*Eh bien*, show me the *merde*."

Eyeing each other, they led me to the wooden compost bin where the *toilettes* buckets were dumped. The slightest stink was overpowered by the scent of grasses and pine needles. "This compost is just for the decorative gardens, *bien sûr*," Raphaël said in a matter-of-fact tone. "But for the edible gardens, we use only kitchen compost."

I nodded. "Understood."

He went on to explain that every day I'd collect the compost from the *toilettes* outside each home and bring the buckets—containing feces (his word) and sawdust—to the composting bin.

My stomach turned. This part was not a glossy spread in *Mon Jardin*. Not by a long shot. I tried not to grimace when he demonstrated how to aerate it. Periodically, I'd empty the first bin into a transition bin, where the microbes would continue making nutrients beneath a layer of grasses and leaves. Finally, there was a third area—one-year-old compost that had become rich soil. That was what I would use to fertilize the decorative flower gardens.

"*Et voilà!*" he concluded, eyeing me cautiously.

Mina crumpled into laughter. "Oh, you should see the look on your face, Eloise!"

"You do look *vachement* grossed out," Raphaël observed, tilting his head in sympathy.

My nose was scrunched up, and I couldn't quite relax it—or get rid of the nausea. I asked myself, really and truly, could I turn the *merde* into *fleurs*?

Last month, sitting on my patio in Denver on a chilly spring morning, I'd noticed the word *merde* leap out from the last page of *Mon Jardin*. *Très intéressant.* What kind of classified ad involved *shit*? I'd read it aloud to the lilacs and still recalled it word for word now.

> In search of a gardener for the ancient walled Jardins du Paradis in the South of France. Unique and rustic lodging provided. Off the grid in all ways. One must grow flowers from one's merde. One must send copies of the following documents along with a résumé of ashes to: Le Château du Paradis, Sainte-Marie-des-Fleurs, Provence, France.

A laugh had sputtered out. Shit, ashes, flowers . . . perfect. The last line had been the coup de grâce:

> Absolutely no children allowed on the premises.

Mon Dieu! My dream job. I remembered the lilacs murmuring encouragement, those sweet purple blooms, grown from—if not exactly *merde*—the blood of my blood and flesh of my flesh.

Now, I stared at the pile of compost. *Eloise, can you do this?*

The others were eyeing me with caution. Raphaël shifted his feet while Mina pulled out a notebook and scribbled something down.

Stalling, I glanced at the page. "Will this be in your memoir?"

She winked. "Maybe in the sequel."

This cut the tension enough for Raphaël to ask, "*Alors,* Eloise, are you all right with the compost duty?"

Mina gave me an encouraging nod.

I covered my nose with my hand. My job was shoveling shit— but it was also making beauty. It was transforming this devastated mess of a body and spirit called Eloise . . . into flowers. This, of course, was why I'd answered the job ad, left my old life, followed my strand of fate here. What I hadn't expected was to find friends who cared. *Interesting* friends. *Fun* friends. Oddly enough, here with them, after just a couple of days, I felt more valued than I had in ages.

I stared at the compost before me, overwhelmed. *What the hell will I do with you?*

The answer came on flower whispers. *Alchemy.*

I lowered my hand. "I've got this."

"*Bon courage,*" Raphaël said.

And they left me to my task.

As I shoveled, I let myself unravel the events that had led me here—memories I'd tamped down since my arrival. They came with a certain sharpness that pierced, a darkness that ached. But facing them head-on seemed necessary to transforming them.

The morning I'd brushed off the job ad in Denver, I'd hurt my bare foot on a shard of a broken plate that I'd hurled across the patio months earlier. Feeling shattered myself, I bandaged my bloody foot, put on sandals, and limped along the Platte River in an effort to keep up the Sunday stroll ritual I'd had with Josh before he'd left. It shouldn't have surprised me that I'd run into him, nose pink from springtime sunburn that made his eyes extra blue. What surprised me most was the young woman at his side, looking so fresh and fertile. So *whole*.

Panting beside the compost pile now, I wiped sweat from my forehead, expecting the usual tears and anger over the memory. But to my astonishment, I wasn't crying. I wasn't aching. I wasn't smashing anything. I was just here with the *merde*, and it was okay.

Maybe I could do this impossible marvel after all.

I shoveled the year-old compost—now fertile soil—into a wheelbarrow and pushed it toward the color-themed garden rooms. I started with yellow, the cheeriest, and sprinkled handfuls of rich earth among marigolds, murmuring wishes for growing and blooming.

And the flowers responded, their whispers loud and clear. Since childhood, we'd had a special bond, but it wasn't until I'd spent hours alone in my garden as an adult, broken open from loss, that I started to deeply listen.

It felt easy to sense when they needed more or less water, more or less fertilizer, sun or shade or dappled light—but on the day I buried Iris beneath them, their whispers slipped into the realm of love. We cried together, my flowers and me, and on the morning I said goodbye, the voices of columbines and yarrow urged me onward, across the ocean.

Listening to these new flowers in Paradise, I relocated some calendula, then trained golden bougainvillea up a trellis. I snipped dead leaves and spent blooms, pulled weeds here and there. Hearing that some pea flowers were thirsty, I made a mental note to ask Raphaël how to work his irrigation system, involving solar panels and pumps and buried tubes from the river.

These blooms understood my sense of loss—they whispered comfort, made my mind feel safe enough to drift back to that last encounter with Josh by the river. The piercing pain, the deep ache.

His girlfriend had eyed the bloody bandage poking out from my sandal and asked if I was okay. That was when I'd noticed her rubbing her belly. I'd flinched. Her breasts were large, pressing against the too-small T-shirt—early second trimester was my guess. I recalled the sensation of sore, swollen breasts, how satisfying it had felt to rub my belly—not just to encourage the life within, but to show the world that I was *creating a new human*.

Even now, as I crouched beside yellow broom flowers, that pain echoed through my core. I took deep breaths in and out, the blooms encouraging me to replace the hurt with nectar.

Bidding farewell to the golden blooms, I moved on to the white garden as peonies beckoned me. These flower conversations were far more intricate than anything I'd experienced in Denver. Each plant had her own personality, quirks, and curiosities. Their questions floated on the breeze. *What brings you here?*

I rocked back on my heels, wiping sweat from my forehead, remembering the moment I'd decided to come. When faced with the girlfriend's fertile belly, I'd heard myself rambling about my new job in France—which I hadn't even applied for yet—claiming that it would be *paradise*.

As I whispered to the honeysuckle and jasmine around me now, they giggled sympathetically at my memory. I laughed at myself too, at the sad absurdity of circumstances that had led me here.

Then I heard another giggle. A child's. The same bright laughter I'd heard earlier today.

I squinted through the trellis, saw nothing but vines and blooms, heard only petal voices. I must have imagined it. I'd envisioned my future children so vividly over the years, sometimes it felt as if they'd taken form as spirits or ghosts, fabricated from the depths of my unconscious mind, the part that couldn't quite let go. This must be a ghost girl of sorts. A fantastical child. A magical woodsprite.

I moved on to the indigo room next—the gladiolus and hydrangea blooms seemed eager to meet me, made Paradise live up to its name. A place of healing. My mind conveniently omitted the second part of Antoinette's statement. *Or harming.*

I worked for hours, stopping only for a fresh baguette with creamy brie and sliced ripe tomato. My body embraced digging and weeding and clipping—it was exhausting yet exhilarating, even the scratches and bug bites and stiff knees.

When valerian in the red room asked me to sing, I obliged, without self-consciousness. Oddly enough, the songs that came out were the ages-old folk songs my mom had sung to me as a child. The lullabies conjured that intimate space, the timeless love between mother and child. It felt strange hearing the songs in my own voice, with only flowers listening.

> *I gave my love a cherry that had no stone*
> *I gave my love a chicken without a bone*
> *I gave my love a story that had no end*
> *I gave my love a baby with no cryin'*

The lyrics were seeds planted inside me ages ago, and here they were now, somehow, fragile shoots in the garden. The poppies whispered to me: *Sing sing sing.*

And at times, a little girl's voice seemed to join in the chorus. *Chante chante chante.* The imaginary girl. The ghost girl. The woodsprite.

So I sang. "Scarborough Fair" came out next in its eerie-sweet melody.

> *Tell her to find me an acre of land*
> *Parsley, sage, rosemary, and thyme*
> *Between the salt water and the sea strands*
> *Then she'll be a true love of mine*

LAURA RESAU ◆ 59

Riddles. Impossible tasks. The story of my life for the past decade. How to grow a baby in a broken womb. No clever answer to that one.

Once upon a time, another riddle had been given to me, in the form of a divination. The healer had pronounced it when I'd been freshly beaten with white carnations and pungent rue in her mobile home bathroom. It was her answer to whether I'd ever have a child—a riddle at once hurtful and hopeful, something that seemed unsolvable. So I'd left it buried, this seed of fate.

I worked and sang and kissed the flowers, letting their strange talents sweep through me. In Denver, too, I'd pretend to smell flowers while secretly letting my lips brush their petals. It always made me think: *When I die, this is something I will miss on earth.* Kissing petals—number one on my list of reasons to live.

Here in Paradise, more reasons flooded in. My new friends. My treehouse. The sumptuous food. The magic that infused it all.

I plunged my hands into the dark, damp soil, rich with compost, whispering encouragement to buds daring to open their petals. In return came their honeyed laughter, punctuated with the giggle of a child, always just out of sight.

The days softened into each other like lemon and sugar and butter on a warm crêpe, rich and sweet and oh so alive. Bliss, beauty, *bonheur* around every bend. Gardening, sharing meals, bonding in sunlight, starlight, moonlight. Golden soaks in the stream after work.

This was my life now, and there was no reason it couldn't last forever. This was, after all, the Otherworld, Wonderland, Eden, Elysian Fields, Avalon. A place of abundance and joy without end.

A few weeks later—I was already losing track in Paradise—I found myself in the edible and medicinal garden beside Mina, before clumps of chamomile. We planned to replenish the jars in the atelier to keep the tisanes flowing, both for our little work family and for La Patronne. Apparently, she was an avid tisane sipper.

Under my breath, I asked the chamomile permission to pluck some blooms.

"Admit it." Mina eyed me playfully. "You were born a flower witch, right?"

"Maybe more like a flower whisperer." *Chuchoteuse*—I guessed at the word and apparently got it right, since she bobbed her head in approval.

I held up a chamomile blossom, cute and innocent in my palm. I'd been sipping *calme* tea before bed every night—just a single cup—and it lulled me into a deep six-hour sleep that left me refreshed. My dreams were vivid, of flowers and stars and goddesses. "Really, Mina, how could these little cuties knock me out for an entire night and day?"

"Well," she said, tilting her head, "there are other ingredients too."

I skimmed my gaze over the blooms around us. "Lavender and rose and passionflower. Skullcap and mugwort and valerian. But at home, that blend would just make me a little sleepy."

Mina stroked her hand over the white and yellow blossoms as if they were tiny, beloved pets. "Flowers here have talents. They heighten the healing effects. Some might call it magic. But it takes a flower witch"—she winked—"or *whisperer* to bring out these talents."

I let this sink in. "I've always felt a bond with flowers. Then, about ten years ago, they became my friends." I steadied my voice. "My only friends."

"Why?" Her eyes brimmed with empathy. Somehow, she was able to move from light joking to genuine compassion in seconds. It felt safe to be honest.

"I was lonely. I was on one side of a river and everyone else was on the other."

Mina nodded, patted my shoulder. "*Alors*, now you have new friends, human and flower. The best of both worlds, *mon amie*."

I gave her a grateful smile, savoring her words: *mon amie*. My friend.

After we filled our baskets with chamomile, lavender, rose, and passionflower, I stood up and heard a splash. My gaze landed on a little pond, just a few feet in diameter, half hidden among nasturtiums. Two shiny frog eyes peeked out from murky water. Curious, I walked closer, careful not to step on the orange blooms.

Prints marred the mud, about six inches long, and looked nothing like the rabbit or fox tracks Bao had pointed out earlier. Smudged imprints of toes and heels made these look human, but far too small for an adult. I had a vision of a woodsprite frolicking at the water's edge, bare feet squelching in mud.

I was about to ask Mina about it when I noticed, floating on the pond's surface, blue lotus flowers with starry yellow centers. Of course! The mystery flower from the *calme* tea. Just yesterday in my library, I'd read that blue lotus brought on euphoria and lucid dreaming, opened the third eye. A doorway to the divine. The essence of Isis herself.

I hadn't made the connection until now, staring into the lotus's golden center. Surprising that these would grow here, but then again, flowers from unexpected zones thrived in these gardens. Just in case, maybe I'd move them to my atelier for the winter or cover them with a blanket on cold nights.

"I bet this is what gives me strange dreams," I murmured.

I was vaguely aware of Mina nodding and craning her neck to see the flowers. She said nothing about the footprints.

Now that I had the lotus's attention, their ethereal melodies greeted me, rising from muck and mud. I whispered a request to pick three blooms, then thanked them.

My head snapped up at a rustle from the next room over, the yellow garden. I caught a peal of laughter and a flash of pink moving behind the rose trellis, as if petals had transformed into a child playing hide-and-seek.

I glanced at Mina, who was now arranging passionflowers in her basket, grazing her fingertips over purple and white coronas. She didn't seem to notice anything amiss.

Maybe this child was conjured by my imagination, with help from these talented flowers. Maybe she was a garden fairy or woodsprite, part of the magic of this place. Either way, it was clear that no one but me could see her.

Another rustle, now from the honeysuckled arch of the garden entrance. I spun around to see Bao peeking his head inside and waving.

"Come, join us!" Mina called out.

I calmed my breath, then waved back.

"Want some help?" he asked, eyeing our bounty.

"*Bien sûr!*" said Mina with gusto, grabbing his hand. "We don't even need baskets with all those pockets you two have!"

Bao offered me a smile of camaraderie, looking proud to have a khaki-chic style twin.

As Mina tucked sprigs of scarlet bougainvillea in Bao's and my pockets, I considered asking about the woodsprite. But there was no point bringing her up. Not when I was finally reclaiming normal, happy, human friendships. Why make my friends question the sanity of their new *amie*, the flower whisperer?

8

Une Bizarrerie

In the afternoon, we lunched on a gratiné of tomatoes and courgettes sprinkled with *herbes de Provence*, dripping with local olive oil that we soaked up with thick slices of crusty baguettes. We sipped Beaujolais, chatting about our mornings.

Bao showed us jars of dried mushrooms and seeds and nuts he'd gathered months earlier, and encouraged us to use them before foraging time came around again.

"Oh, you're like a diligent squirrel," Mina said, ruffling his hair, then setting tiny cups of espresso before us.

Raphaël reported on progress tweaking the solar panels, then offered to help me in the atelier. "I loved helping Iva with this stuff."

"Merci." I sipped my espresso and tried not to let happiness shoot out of my eyes. "I can be your new old-lady friend."

"Our flower witch," Bao said wistfully. *Sorcière des fleurs.*

"Flower *whisperer*," Mina said. "Right, Eloise?"

I couldn't help smiling through lunch, and even through dishwashing, and then afterward, as I floated beside Raphaël on the path, heady with midday wine, uplifted by espresso.

At my treehouse, we made our way up the swinging bridges with our baskets of blossoms. When I lost my balance, Raphaël's hand swiftly came to the small of my back, quite a feat considering the baskets looped over his forearms. For a moment, his palm stayed there, warm and comforting, until I steadied myself and he removed it.

"*Merci*." I laughed. "You'd think I'd be better at this after years as a play specialist."

"True, this place is like a playground." He looked around at my forest queendom. "I could add a slide."

"Ooh, maybe a swing right there?" I nodded my head. "And a zipline right there?"

"*Bien sûr*. I am your personal *bricoleur*." He gave a little bow.

I raised an eyebrow. "They didn't tell me Paradise came with my own tinkerer."

"At your service, Mademoiselle."

Inside the atelier, sunlight filtered through leaves as we spread flowers over screens on the huge, worn oak table. Our hands and arms grazed each other, and the blossoms urged us closer. The rose petals sounded especially enthusiastic, almost pushy. The flowers didn't seem sad to be snipped and dried—*au contraire*, they sounded eager for this next stage of existence.

I murmured thanks, a little self-consciously, then remembered that Raphaël did, in fact, *enjoy* hanging around crones who talked to flowers. Okay, so maybe I wasn't a crone quite yet. And maybe I wasn't at a drying-up stage of life either.

When we ran out of space on the screens, I tied twine around lavender to form bouquets, and then Raphaël stood on his tiptoes to hang them from rafters.

"*Magnifique*," I declared, because I loved that word and because this was indeed *magnifique*—all of it, every moment in Paradise, filled with swirling scents of rose, chamomile, lavender, passion-flower, and the cerulean essence of blue lotus.

"Things feel different with you here," he said, studying my face.

"Hopefully, *good* different?" I bit my lip, oddly nervous.

"*Oui!*" Then he flushed, letting his gaze dart away. "Iva added her own touch to the flowers. And now you're adding yours."

I tilted my head. "How so?"

He stumbled over his words. "It's just—your smell, how it mixes with the flowers."

"My smell?" I sniffed, doubting my lemongrass deodorant. It was supposedly antimicrobial, but I wasn't used to wearing it this close to anyone.

He backpedaled, looking desperate. "*Eh bien*, it's just that your hair, and your skin, *euh*, they absorb the smells of sunshine and plants and, *euh*, they blend with your sweat."

"My sweat? Like BO?" I asked, mortified. Though I had to admit, *l'odeur corporelle* sounded elegant—almost romantic—in French.

He pressed his lips together, as if determined to dig himself no further into this hole.

He looked so adorable, I had to let him off the hook. "Maybe I should make you a love apple."

"A love apple?"

Une pomme d'amour was the translation I'd used. Pretty straightforward, but maybe the French term was different. Or maybe I'd lost my ability to distinguish between basic cultural knowledge and my own quirky facts.

"Sixteenth-century maidens stuck apples in their armpits to soak up sweat," I explained, "then gave them to their suitors." I had no idea how to say armpits in French, so I said "holes of the arms," pointing to my own armpit, which was indeed damp, but now more from nervous perspiration . . . because why was I talking about something so *dégoutant*?

"Ah, *les phéromones*."

Now it was my turn to blush. "Apples must absorb them well." I paused, then added, "Don't worry, I won't add any love apples to your tea." And then kicked myself for putting this image into our heads. *What the hell, Eloise?* On my first day, I'd gone on and on about *merde*, and now I couldn't shut up about sweat. Thankfully, seduction wasn't on the table with the *bricoleur*. I would've thoroughly screwed it up.

A laugh escaped from me, then from him, and after we calmed down, he wiped his eyes and said, "I'd accept a love apple from you, Eloise."

There was something about Raphaël's hands.

Was it my imagination, or did they tend to linger against mine?

His fingers brushing mine as he offered me coffee. His hand pausing to touch mine as he passed dishes or tools. And sometimes, casually, his palm grazing my back, helping me balance as I carried buckets of earth or water. His hand flicking away a mosquito from my shoulder, making the lightest contact with my arm.

I savored these moments when skin touched skin, willing them to last.

One sunset during our *apéro*, I noticed his left hand holding his wineglass. Tanned and calloused, muscled and tendoned. It wasn't even touching me, but something deep inside me fluttered, a feeling long forgotten. Later, when we said goodbye, his fingers brushed mine, ignited something in my core. As I watched him walk down the swinging bridges, my entire body was bursting with sparks.

On a whim, I changed into my robe and grabbed a towel. I'd gotten in the habit of showering before breakfast, but something about the way the pink and violet sunset smeared the sky made me want to be outside, naked, roofless. I figured I'd have enough time before twilight came.

Heading to the shower, I waded through mallow and poppies, still reeling from modest skin contact with Raphaël. And from the fun intrigue of our conversations. Along with the warmth, he evoked mystery undercut with moments of raw honesty that I didn't quite understand.

Nor did I understand the visceral effect he had on me. It had been so, so long since I'd felt this way. I clasped my fingers together, recalling how his felt brushing against mine, imagining his hands on other parts of my body. A heat blasted through me.

In a kind of domino effect, another heat filled me—*embarrassment*—along with all the *merde* that sex had brought in the past. My last honest chat about sex was the nail in my friendless coffin—the humiliating café outing when a friend had asked how fertility treatments were going. And I'd told her the truth. "Shitty," I'd replied, my voice raw, and proceeded to tell her how much it sucked to have to copulate on certain days . . . every single month . . . for *years*.

And when, with a gleam in her eyes, she suggested sex toys, a pang of tenderness hit me—this woman was so unscathed, her reality so far from mine. So I explained how we couldn't use lubrication because it interfered with sperm motility and vaginal mucus function. No alcohol or weed to get horny because those affect sperm count. Temperature monitoring and ovulation testing indicated the ideal time to conceive, usually when we were tired and busy, but I'd pretend to be turned on and stick it in there, which made me writhe in pain from endometriosis, but I'd try to act orgasmic. Afterward, I'd hide my tears and think, *Crap, we have to do this for the next five days.*

On the other side of the meadow, I stepped into the shower draped in honeysuckle and wisteria. As always, I appreciated how—although it had no door—the design made it private, a curving wall of wooden poles, forming a spiral pathway.

I hung my robe and towel on a hook, then walked into the structure, following it to the center. Here was a nook of a nook of the Otherworld—smooth stones beneath my feet and a copper nozzle above, connected by hidden pipes to the water tank.

As cicada songs swirled outside, this space held a sacred silence. And oh, how it contrasted with the heavy, humiliating silence that had followed my infertility tirade in the café. I remembered realizing the coffee grinder had quieted, conversations had stopped, people were staring. That friendship had drooped and dried up. As had my other friendships—even the truest, deepest, realest one— and eventually, my marriage. And sex of any kind meant only failure and loss.

Now, all around, blossoms were sneaking into the shower, murmuring in soothing tones, urging me to let go of desiccated memories, make room for something fresh and alive. I leaned my head back, thanking the vines that formed a latticed ceiling. I breathed in lavender and rose from the soap and shampoo and conditioner.

As I washed myself in the warm shower, a strange thing happened.

A *bizarre* thing. *Une bizarrerie.*

A breeze swept across me . . . and my skin became . . . *alert.* I wasn't one to use the word *caress* in any situation, but that was the best way to describe what the evening air was doing to my wet body. My skin felt *alive.* And it felt connected to nerve endings in deep places I'd forgotten existed. I rinsed off the soap lather, not in my usual rushed way . . . but *luxuriously.*

Ever.

So.

Slowly.

And then, there was this one angle, where the shower spray hit me right there—yes, *there.* I adjusted the nozzle and realized with a thrill that it was removable. My eyes closed and my heart pounded and heat gathered and radiated, and I felt myself swelling and opening in a way that hadn't happened for, oh *mon Dieu*, something like a decade. And then it was growing, this quivering pleasure for the sake of pleasure, and I was holding my breath, then gasping, and then came the delicious pinnacle.

I dropped the nozzle.

There I stood, moaning, trembling, pulsing, smiling. I soaked it all in, the wonder of it, the bizarreness.

Maybe my body was not forever broken.

Maybe sex—or some form of it—could, indeed, bring me pleasure.

Maybe this garden didn't just make plants with special talents . . . maybe it could awaken what I'd thought was dead.

And what if this was just the beginning?

For the first time in ages, I felt a true fondness for my body, a gratitude, as though we'd been old friends who'd gotten into a massive fight, in a standoff for years, and now we were remembering the good things about each other.

Merci beaucoup, body.

But I also had the gardens to thank. A place of power. A place of healing. Full stop.

My eyes were still closed when, all at once, I perceived a change in atmosphere.

Flower whispers were escalating, trying to tell me something.

Jasmine sang with a strange sense of urgency.

Open your eyes.

9

Soul-Case

I opened my eyes.

Immediately, I noticed the color of the sky. Golden pink morphing into violet-indigo. Dusk was coming. *Crépuscule.*

I thought of the ominous goddess statues, their warnings about breaking rules. Their dire consequences, their vengefulness. In minutes, twilight would descend in full.

Merde.

I made my way out of the spiral and dried myself off, still with that quivery aftermath feeling. In my robe, I jogged across the meadow toward the treehouse. The solar lights had sparked on, turning it into a fairy kingdom of fireflies. Beyond their glow, the sky was the deepest blue, a few stars emerging.

I tried to pick up my pace as I ascended the bridges, but my body insisted on savoring the pleasure. Still, I reached the top room just in time—at least, that was what I told myself. After all, dusk was a liminal space, without fixed boundaries. Right?

I sat at the vanity, lit some candles, and surveyed my flushed face and chest. *Une petite mort,* a little death. And now my body was coming back to life, blood rushing like a springtime river.

Running a brush through my damp hair, I thought of Raphaël's hands and his stubbled chin and my miraculous orgasm. What if one day my body let me feel this kind of deliciousness *with a man?* What if one day I could have sex again, without pain or sorrow or rage, only joy?

At dinner I was very aware of Raphaël sipping his Bordeaux. His gaze flickered to the trees, the sky, the kitchen, and landed briefly on me. "So, Eloise, how's my shower?"

I stopped mid-forkful. "Your shower?"

He laughed. "Well, *your* shower. I made it for you."

"Really?" I forced myself to swallow. How had he known? Oh, my hair. I touched my damp hair, the waves smoothed with almond oil.

"The old shower was falling apart, and since I'm the . . . *bricoleur*"—he gave me a secret smile—"I made a new one before you came." There was that dimple.

Heat gathered in my center as I thought about the shower—the shower that he'd *built for me.* More heat rushed to my face. *Mon Dieu*, could everyone see me blushing? "Your shower . . . ," I said, "is *magnifique.*"

"As magnificent as the *toilettes?*" Mina crinkled her eyes.

"Even more."

"Have you noticed one can remove the nozzle?" Raphaël spoke without innuendo. Just a *bricoleur* making sure his creation met its potential.

His question seemed innocent—he probably knew that American showers generally didn't have removable nozzles. And French people used these nozzles every day, just to take regular, nonorgasmic showers. *Right?*

Still, I lost any last shreds of control over my blushing. "I have, in fact, noticed the removable nozzle."

Mina gave me a sideways glance.

I changed the subject to flowers.

❁

The next day after work—a particularly *sultry* afternoon—Raphaël strolled by as I was soaking in the stream with the ducks. From a distance, he waved and then looked away, as if he feared invading my privacy.

"Don't worry," I called out. "I'm wearing practical underwear and a sports bra." It hadn't occurred to me to pack a swimsuit. "Want to swim?"

My *bricoleur* was gentlemanly, almost to a fault. "You sure?"

"Come on in."

He unbuckled his tool belt and set it on a rock near the mermaid statue. Then he pulled off his shirt.

I'd seen him working bare-chested in the afternoon heat, tweaking the irrigation system or repairing a fence or adjusting solar panels. It was different seeing him up close.

I took it all in. The golden skin flecked here and there with freckles. The triangle of his torso, the broad shoulders, the ponytail curved between the blades. The dark pattern of hair on his pecs and the little trail down the center of his abs, disappearing below the waistband of his shorts. The movement of muscles beneath his skin—traps and biceps and lats working in harmony.

The way the sunlight shone on all of it.

This body was the result of growing things, building things, fixing things. A side effect of making beauty. Muscles grew from thousands of micro-tears in the fibers, tiny wounds leading to sculpted flesh.

Oops. I was staring.

He walked into the river, scrambling over rocks, and gave a shiver of pleasure as he slid underwater. The stream wasn't much deeper than our waists, and only about ten feet wide, so we just glided around water bugs and chatted about mushrooms and flowers and frogs. As always, he was patient with my language skills, listening with lips pursed in that French way, asking questions when he didn't understand.

After a while, we climbed onto the sun-warmed stones. He sat just a foot away.

"So," I said, "what have you been tinkering with lately?"

He squeezed out his ponytail. "Patching some spots where the wall is crumbling."

I gave him an elbow jab. "Keeping us in the gardens?"

"Not such a bad thing, is it?"

I looked upstream at water cascading off the small cliff into the idyllic pool. A sparkling piece of paradise. "Maybe not."

He listed other projects: securing cobbles on the hobbit hole path and repairing rope on my treehouse bridge.

"Glad you quit your desk job to do treehouse upkeep?" I asked playfully, hoping he'd tell me more about his past.

His eyes danced and met mine. "You know the best part?"

"Enlighten me."

"Being the on-call *bricoleur* for a flower witch."

"Flower *whisperer*," I corrected with a grin. "Well, I'm lucky to have you. Clearly, you can fix anything."

A mist passed over his face. "Sometimes it is out of one's hands."

"True." I rested my palm over my Little-Engine-That-*Couldn't* reproductive organs.

He sighed, waxing philosophical. From time to time, he did this—dropped from light joking to something far deeper. "Sometimes one must focus on other things. Things that don't break. This sunlight. This river. This air."

What was it about his life that had broken? Did it have to do with the girlfriend? And the fact that he never invited me into his caravan?

I waited for him to expand, but he only leaned his head back and closed his eyes, as though savoring it all—the warm stone, the scent of lavender, the sound of the waterfall.

Mon Dieu, I couldn't stop staring at his soul-case—a term I'd heard somewhere before, maybe in an old poem. I liked that word for *body*.

"I'd like to open your soul-case," I said, improvising a translation: *suitcase of the soul.* "I'd rummage through your secrets."

"And I would rummage through yours."

I laughed. "Mine is a scary, chaotic mess. You'd run the other way."

He propped his head on his elbow. "Well, I think your soul-case is *vachement belle.* And what's inside too."

Truly beautiful. Or, literally, cowlike beautiful. But the way he was looking at me made me think he meant the former.

Our gazes locked, and I looked away.

The most important thing was this: My soul-case *felt* good. The muscles were happy-tired from hard work. The skin was freckled and tanned, despite a good faith effort with sunscreen. My hair was drying in natural curls. The brazenly nonpregnant curve of my belly was nourished with gourmet food. My eyes felt bright and well rested.

When I looked back at him, Raphaël's face was brimming with emotion, his gaze still fixed on me. *Longing?* Or was I just projecting?

Either way, sex was out of the question. Now that I was liking my body again, I couldn't give it the chance to betray me. And I couldn't ruin my friendship with the *bricoleur* with an awkward sexual encounter. Just thinking about it gave me a stomachache.

Instead, I let myself fall into the pleasures of river and stones and flowers and sunshine and conversation and the soul in the case beside me.

❦

The next morning, Raphaël showed up when I'd finished dumping waste buckets into the compost. I was jabbing it with a pitchfork when he asked, tentatively, "How's it going, my friend?"

"Shitty," I joked in English.

He grinned. He understood English better than he admitted. "I can help you. I helped the previous gardeners."

"*Non, merci.*" I held up a palm. "I'm familiar with piles of symbolic *merde*. It's what I signed up for."

Was it my imagination, or did he look *disappointed*? Then again, last night over dinner and this morning over breakfast, we'd bonded, bantered, and laughed more than ever. I wanted more of it, and maybe he did too.

I took a gamble. "But with all your free time, you could prepare an *apéro* for us after work."

He brightened. "Meet you on your porch?"

I tried wrapping my head around the fact that this man wanted to spend time with me. Lots of time. I went along with it. "*Oui.* You can keep up with your playground skills."

Late that afternoon, he installed a wooden swing on a low oak branch as I watched him from above. Then he walked up my bridges, balancing a tray of Kir and almonds.

I planted long kisses on each cheek and patted his tool belt. "*Merci, mon bricoleur.*"

"It's only the beginning," he said. "Monkey bars, seesaws, you name it."

I poured our drinks, and we sat side by side, sipping and chatting and laughing until the sun fell to the treetops.

Our delicious new ritual borne of *merde*.

Over the days that followed, as I did my compost duties, I sang with the flowers. Our refrains: *Shit becomes beauty, death becomes beauty, hurt becomes beauty.*

When I thought of what I'd lost, I had a stirring inside, a feeling that maybe I could bear it after all.

We become flowers.

Every day before the *apéro*, I soaked in the river with Raphaël, letting cool, fresh water flow over me, brushing my fingertips over my skin and channeling love.

Hello, body. Maybe, for so long, you've been the Little Engine That Could, chugging along with all your steam. Maybe it's not your fault you never got us to Toyland. Maybe you just need to stop on the tracks and enjoy yourself.

And as I felt my skin, wet and alive beneath my hands, I glanced at the soul-case of my *bricoleur*. What would it be like to have his hands on my waist? Would my body shrink and harden? Or would I come to life like a perennial that wasn't dead after all?

One evening after our sunset *apéro*, I bade farewell to Raphaël, watching his broad shoulders and easy stride as he walked away down the wooded path. Instead of going inside, I found myself heading to my wisteria-clad shower. My body was vibrating after our time sipping Kir together, keeping our cordial distance except for hands grazing and arms brushing.

Inside the spiral, I savored the warm water and scents of lavender and whispers of honeysuckle. I let myself sink into the pleasures of this place. The healing.

This time, when jasmine blooms whispered, *Open your eyes,* their voices seemed so far away that I ignored them. Until an entire chorus of flowers, from mallow to moonflower, joined in the warning: *Open your eyes!*

Finally, I did. And found myself immersed in a sea of indigo.

Twilight had fallen, utterly and completely.

Merde.

I threw on my clothes and stumbled across the meadow and up the swinging bridges. Heart pounding, I sequestered myself in the uppermost treehouse room. As my pulse calmed, I peered out the open window at the deep violet sky, wondering if anyone could possibly know I'd broken the rule.

Of course not. There were no hidden cameras or spying drones. My friends were already closed up in their own yurt and hobbit hole and vardo—they would have no idea of my transgression. I gazed at the dark silhouette of turrets in the distance, rising from the tree canopy. There was no way anyone from the château could have seen me.

In my peripheral vision, something moved. Below, several hundred feet away by the river, a moon-white glow drifted along. Cautiously, I craned my head out the window, peered through the branches.

Three forms floated, ghostlike, along the riverbank. A trick of the diminishing light?

They paused, motionless. Their long white cloaks looked gossamer, woven from starlight. One of them raised an arm and gestured toward me.

I ducked back into the shadows of my room, pressing a hand over my heart. Had they seen me? And worse, had they seen me run across the meadow during the forbidden hour?

When I dared to sneak another look out the window, the trio was vanishing around the bend. I blinked, willing them to reappear. Nothing.

With a shudder, I lit a candle and flipped through the goddess booklet, landing on a drawing of *Les Dames Blanches*, a trio of white-cloaked figures walking along a riverbank, faces hidden. The caption read: "A French version of the Triple Goddess, often appearing by rivers and caves as three ghost-women in white."

I hadn't heard of this in my world mythology class. Not that I believed they were goddesses. Or anything beyond products of my imagination.

I picked up the welcome letter from the Goddess of the Gardens, reread it by candlelight. I focused on the conditional part of the sentence: *You—if you stay in My graces—are a fortunate one.* I stuck the letter in the drawer, but its warning echoed in my head.

An hour later, I still heard it as I walked along the path to dinner, hugging my arms close, wondering if there were faces in the shadows. When I turned the bend and encountered the harp lady, I jumped. *Mon Dieu.* Her smile looked so sinister now.

For a brief, irrational moment, I wondered if she came to life every dusk and roamed the riverbanks with other statues. *Don't be ridiculous, Eloise.* Still, a wave of fear weakened my legs. What if the figures in white were in some way *real*? What if they'd seen me break the twilight rule? What would be the consequence?

Why break the rules already, Eloise?

If I were being honest, I knew exactly why: Rules did not apply to me. For most of my life, I'd followed them—been a good student, graduated from college with honors in early childhood development, gotten a job in my field with insurance and benefits, dated my kind and responsible boyfriend for three years, married him in my midtwenties, gone off the pill and tried to get pregnant in my late twenties.

But no baby. Only pain.

Still, I'd kept following the rules: healthy diet, vitamins, ideal BMI, exercise, ovulation tracking, natural treatments, specialists, medical workups, HSG, laparoscopy, IUI, adoption applications. I was a good wife, a good patient, a good human. The universe did not live up to its end of the bargain.

After I'd lost Iris, I stopped believing in rules. I crossed streets when there was no walk signal. And maybe, just a little, I wished a car would hit me, hard enough that I'd lose consciousness . . . I wouldn't necessarily die, just be in a coma for a while, feel nothing, have a breather, put distance between me and the pain. Then I broke the rule about not taking a hefty dose of opioids and slipping into a hot bath, but I'd kept the razors in the cabinet.

I remembered sinking down, down into oblivion, then choking and coughing, then standing up, naked and dripping, and in a fit of despair, grabbing the ceramic toothbrush holder and hurling it against the tile wall. The crash and subsequent cleanup brought me back to my senses.

Now, in the dark garden, I stared at the stone woman, wincing at her eerie smile. No, I wasn't *entirely* fearless of the consequences of breaking rules, especially one made by a goddess.

Ladies in White

In the fairy-lit dining grove, my friends were already seated, sipping rosé. Scents of roasted aubergine and courgette and tomatoes drifted from the kitchen. I sat down as Raphaël poured me a glass and offered cheek kisses.

Faire la bise. Make the kiss. My *bricoleur* and I found any excuse for it—greetings, farewells, thanks, congratulations for completing a minor task—a dozen times each day. We were naturals at it now—it went smoothly, and always lingered.

"Your soul-case is looking lovely tonight," he murmured playfully.

"Merci," I whispered back. Taking a moment to center myself, I let the rosé slide down my throat, cool and bright, fresh and floral. I wasn't about to admit that I'd broken the twilight rule, but I did need more information.

With some hesitation, I asked, "Can you all tell me about this whole Triple Goddess thing?"

Mina tilted her head in confusion. "What do you mean, *mon amie?*"

I took a long breath. "I thought I saw three figures in white at dusk."

"Did you approach them?" Bao asked evenly.

"Of course not." Hands shaking, I set down my glass. "I just saw them through the window." I blinked. "Wait, are you saying . . . they're *real?*"

Bao raised his shoulder in a noncommittal gesture.

After a beat, Raphaël said, "What is it that Einstein said about mysteries?"

Mina answered with gleaming eyes. "'The most beautiful thing we can experience is the mysterious.'"

"She reads a *lot*," said Bao, patting her shoulder. Clearly, they were changing the subject.

"Who are *Les Dames Blanches?*" I asked.

Bao responded matter-of-factly, "A French take on the Triple Goddess."

I bit my lip, wondering if I should just admit I'd been out after twilight. But no, I couldn't risk our friendship. The former gardener was kicked out for breaking rules. My friends wanted me to stay. And I wanted to stay.

"Eloise," Raphaël began, his expression sincere. "We recommend that you ignore the bizarre things. *Les bizarreries.* Follow the rules and you have nothing to worry about. Enjoy Paradise."

❧

The next morning, on the way to the dining grove, everything felt clear and sunny—the gardens, my mind, my conscience. A clean slate. A new day.

A white rabbit hopped across my path and scurried down the riverbank, leaving a cute trail of prints in the wet sand. I did a double take, noticing a trail of larger prints nearby. Human prints?

But not child-sized this time, probably from women's flats or sandals—daintier than my hiking boots. Maybe Mina's?

I knelt down, assessing the prints, badly smudged and spanning just a few yards of riverbank. I couldn't tell if they came from a single woman . . . or three.

Curious if there were tracks on the other side, I hopped

across the river, balancing from stone to stone. And yes, the wet sand held depressions, possibly shoe prints, though I couldn't be certain.

I surveyed the shore—a narrow swath of sand and rock, rising into ten-foot-tall craggy cliffs, and just beyond, the garden wall. I craned my head back and spotted a sign on a ledge above.

Squinting, I made out the word *interdit* burned into the wood. That word . . . it had something to do with parking lots, right? *Stationnement Interdit.* Parking Forbidden, or something like that. *Forbidden.*

Despite the morning sunshine, a shiver passed through me. I wasn't about to break any more rules. And the others were waiting for me with café au lait and *jus d'orange* and tartines and croissants and *pain au chocolat* and apricots and strawberries. So much cozier and safer than anything on this side of the river.

Oleander blooms beckoned me back toward the far shore, and I hopped stones across. The river had now lapped the prints away. Or maybe they'd never been there to begin with.

Mind spinning, I headed down the path toward the warm scents of breakfast and friendship.

The day unfurled in its usual sunshiny, blue-skied, rose-tinged way, and no one brought up *Les Dames Blanches.* Including me. I had no proof of their footprints, after all, and Raphaël had recommended ignoring *les bizarreries.* Which I planned to do, damn it.

After dinner, in my bedroom, I closed the French glass doors, then hesitated, wondering if I should lock them. I felt the skeleton key resting in the keyhole. But now, through the glass, I saw only the magic of Paradise, moonlight spilling over the gardens. No, locking the doors would be paranoid.

I pulled off my dress, put on a long T-shirt, and plopped onto the flax linen bed.

With reverence, I picked up my foil card of birth control pills and pressed a blue one from its plastic bubble. I'd started taking them in December to lessen pain from my endometriosis, fibroids, and cysts—to limit the growth of the crap on my reproductive organs. And having my period just once every three months had made me teary with relief.

As much as I loved herbal medicine, no plant had made a dent in the pain. There was a time and place for modern Western medicine, and for me, these little pills were it.

Before the pills, every month I used to brace myself to enter the medieval dungeon. My torturer, black-hooded endometriosis, had me shaking with fear. At times I couldn't walk or talk, only writhe. Sometimes I crawled to the bathtub. Scalding baths helped. At some point, I'd reach a place beyond, where I'd focus on making it from one breath to the next. The worst of my pain would hover at a nine or ten on the scale, bring me to the verge of passing out. Over and over and over.

But with these pills, I had only mild cramping during my period—they were the only reason I'd been able to fly across the ocean, live without a bathtub for burning-hot soaks. Sitting on my bed, I laid my palms on my belly and imagined it as a vessel, ready and waiting, anticipating only joy. Not a baby, just *joy*.

I was reaching for the water glass when the pill slipped between my fingers and vanished.

Zut! I dropped to my knees and moved the lantern beneath my bed. After searching, I found the pill caught on the mattress piping.

Then I saw something poking beneath the mattress, wedged between the slats of the bed frame. I tugged on it, freeing an envelope.

How strange. I downed the pill with water and positioned the lantern near the envelope, which was addressed to a woman in Iowa, with a return address of Amber Featheringham-Offenburger, Le Château du Paradis, Sainte-Marie-des-Fleurs, Provence, France.

Well, it wasn't unethical to read a letter I found in my own bedroom, was it? How could I *not* take a peek?

I unfolded the letter, loopy purple print on pink, flowered stationery. It was dated a couple of months ago.

> *Bestie! Miss you, babe!*
>
> *Oh. My. God. Can I just say how sick I am of compost and dirt and bugs and sun and the total lack of movies or shopping or scrolling? And how sick I am of the people here?*
>
> *Last night I finally made the first move with Raphaël. After brandy, I pulled my shirt over my head. So he just stares at my face all confused, then looks away. He doesn't even look at my boob's—I wore the scratchy black lace bra all through dinner just counting the minute's till I could take the thing off. He just says, well good night. And he turns to go.*
>
> *So there I am shivering and thinking, is my fat bulging under my bra straps? God, I thought I left all that behind me in Iowa. No offense to you or Iowa, babe.*
>
> *I was trying so hard not to cry. I was like, wait, dude, what the hell's wrong with you? But all he says is: I'm so sorry Amber but your not the woman I need in my life.*
>
> *WTF? He knows I have body image issues! I'm getting literally sick of being here. Most of all, I'm sick of the rule's and tomorrow I'm gonna start breaking them. Wish me luck, babe!*
>
> ### XOXO,
> *Amber*

My heart went out to my predecessor and her insecurities. But kudos to Raphaël for resisting young flesh and cheap lace. Maybe he was a stretched-out-beige-sports-bra-over-a-monoboob kind of guy.

I shuffled to the next paper, another letter, this one dated two days later. Rusty smudges stained the edges. Blood?

Ridiculous, Eloise. Shaking myself, I read onward, ignoring the probably-not-blood and trying not to be judgy about her apostrophe usage.

> *OMG Bestie! Things are way too messed up here. Like, super creepy. Antoinette says if I leave I'll be cursed. She's all, when you reject Paradise you go straight to hell. Ummm . . . okaaaay? I say she's full of crap. Tomorrow, babe, I'm packing up. Getting outta here. I'll deliver these letters to you IRL, can you believe it?*
>
> *So here's what happened. I snuck out during twilight and followed those freaky ghost ladies. I lifted up one of those solar light's (why is there no flashlight anywhere in this garden btw?) I was like, hey! Who the hell are you?*
>
> *And then, get this: One of the ghost's threw a rock at me. It hit me on the hip. Hard! And then she walked closer and totally pelted me. I was literally frozen in fear. Terrified!!!*
>
> *I'm back in the treehouse now and I just looked at the damage: a gash and red spots on my hip, my back, my shoulder and my forehead. I better not get a concussion or I'm suing someone. Literally!*
>
> *R and M and B will just freak out and say it's my fault, like I'm being punished for the weirdness that goes on here. And I think they literally mean like a *supernatural* punishment.*
>
> *Luv ya, babe! See you soon!*
> *Amber*

My pulse quickened. Why had Amber hidden these letters? And why hadn't she taken them when she'd left? *Had* she left . . . or had something happened to her? The unsettling tone of Antoinette's voice haunted me: *"She did not follow the rules. She is no longer here."*

11

Spirit Child

Walking along the river path to breakfast, I considered Amber's fate as I stared up at the distant turrets, stark against the morning light. I had mixed feelings about her, which was unfair—I shouldn't have read her letters. And I'd put Josh's girlfriend's face on her, also unfair. And the truth was, we all had mortifying insecurities and imperfect grammar, right?

My selfish response was fear that Amber had gotten punished—and that I'd be next. *Mais c'est ridicule*, of course.

In the grove, Bao was rubbing chili oil onto Mina's arthritic knee. Upon seeing me, they lit up and called out cheery *bonjours*. Bao tucked the bottle into his pocket and cleaned his hands with fresh juice of a lemon from another pocket.

I greeted them with cheek kisses as Mina said, "You slept in, *ma chérie*. Raphaël already finished breakfast."

"I was up late," I said, pouring myself coffee and settling into a chair.

Mina clucked and took a bite of *pain au chocolat*. "Why?"

"I couldn't stop thinking about the previous gardener." I steadied my voice. "Amber."

Mina blinked, looking confused. "How do you know about her?"

Zut. I searched for a logical and ethical response, but my groggy mind just offered a big blank. "I found her letters."

"Letters?" Mina echoed.

"She wrote about breaking the rules, confronting the ghosts."

"That silly child." Mina shook her head. "Going on about suing the ghosts. Remember that, Bao?"

"Of course." He selected his words with care. "Amber was . . . well, we never warmed up to each other."

"She seemed afraid." As much as I tried to keep my cool, fear crept over me. "Of punishment. What happened?"

Bao wiped croissant crumbs from his chin. "One morning she was simply gone," he said slowly. "We assume she left of her own volition."

"So she just *vanished* after breaking the rules?" I asked, flustered. "How do you know there wasn't foul play?" Unsure how to say "foul play" in French, I translated it as "bad things."

"The girl got in a huff and left." Mina scoffed. "End of story."

"Why would she leave her letters behind?"

In an even tone, Bao said, "She wasn't the most responsible person."

"Ha!" said Mina. "She did a terrible job. She was used to getting what she wanted, being served. Oh, and she was a stingy cook. No oil, no butter, no sugar."

"Well," said Bao. "She had issues around food."

Mina raised her pinky. "The girl was tiny. *Toute petite.*" She paused, then added, "But yes, she was in her own pain."

Sympathy rushed through me. In my old life, I'd had conflicts with my body. Not perfectionist urges, more of a frustration turned betrayal turned *hatred.* I'd resented my breasts—useless, milkless pounds of flesh. I'd despised my uterus for harboring pain and false hope, my endocrine system for triggering ache with no greater good, my pointlessly ample hips.

And worst of all, I'd resented other people—*well-meaning* people— simply for being whole, for having functioning bodies, for failing to understand how broken mine was. Bitterness and shame and heartbreak had drowned out my friendships.

Recalling all that hate now filled me with regret, made me wish I hadn't been so hard on people, so hard on myself. It made me understand how far I'd come—in just weeks. These gardens held healing magic. The *bizarre* parts wouldn't scare me away, damn it.

Mina sighed. "We've all been through our own hells. Some of our own making. Some not so much. What matters is how we get ourselves out."

I appreciated her warmth and wisdom, but I couldn't shake the feeling that she and Bao weren't giving me the whole story.

"Don't worry about it, Eloise," said Bao, his voice gentle. "Just ignore the letters."

Whatever he and Mina might be hiding, the intentions behind their words were clear and kind: They wanted me to stay. They cared about me. We were friends—family, even—and we were all in this together.

Market day was every Wednesday. We always used my atelier as the staging grounds for preparations. The night before, we'd gather jars and bottles, jams and honeys, infusions and balms. The morning of, we'd rise before dawn to cut flowers, make bouquets, snip herbs, and package it all into crates.

The first few weeks, I'd stayed in my atelier to clean up the chaos of stems and leaves and paper and twine while my companions carted goods to the gates and loaded up Antoinette's trailer. By eight a.m. they'd return to my atelier, help me with any remaining cleanup, and then we'd have a leisurely breakfast.

But this market day, I told my friends I wanted to load the trailer too. My plan was to ply information from Antoinette about the *bizarreries* of the garden—Amber's departure, *Les Dames Blanches*, the poison garden, the creepy statues, and maybe even the woodsprite. I'd convince her to let me ride with her to the market, chatting along the way. Maybe I'd even wander the market, gathering intel about the gardens . . . without overt gossiping.

The sun shone as Raphaël and I wheeled our flower wares up the path to the main gate. Meanwhile, Mina and Bao carted bottles of mead and honey and *confiture*. Morning light shone through the jars—golden and ruby and sapphire, liquid jewels.

At eight o'clock Antoinette breezed out of the castle and through the inner gate, dressed in creamy silk, with sunglasses covering much of her face.

"Bonjour," she said with an aloof nod, joining us by the outer gate, which she proceeded to unlock. No chance for awkward cheek kissing with this lady.

Instead of casual conversation, I was swept into a flurry of activity. We loaded the merchandise into a trailer attached to the Peugeot as Antoinette supervised, instructing us to move a box here, a bouquet there. Once everything was loaded, I was sweating and catching my breath when Antoinette said, *"Au revoir,"* and locked the spiked gate—with us on the inside.

"Wait!" I said as she was opening her car door.

She glanced at me, clearly irritated.

"Can I come?" My voice squeaked out like a child's.

"Non," she said simply, then slipped into the car and sped away.

Shell-shocked, I pressed my forehead to the iron bars. "That's it?"

Raphaël answered with sympathy, "A man at the market sells our wares. It's a lot of work, long lines, nonstop customers. This way we can enjoy a nice breakfast."

"But don't you ever want to go?"

The others traded shrugs. "Antoinette prefers that we stay here," said Bao.

"Duly noted," I said, feeling my shoulders tense.

"In the future, just make a list of things you need and give it to me," Mina added. "I'll pass it to Antoinette."

"Is she afraid we'll break the no-gossip rule?" I asked, still clutching the bars.

"Perhaps," said Raphaël conspiratorially. "Who knows—we might plant the seeds of a mess."

I gave a reluctant grin, assuming *semer la pagaille* meant something along the lines of *stir up trouble*.

Mina added in hushed tones, "And who knows what my little finger might tell me."

Right. In English, that would be *a little bird*. I released my grip on the bars.

"*Oh, la vache!*" I said, blowing air from my cheeks in defeat. "Let's have breakfast." I took one last look at the outside world, then followed my friends into the depths of the gardens. My new friendships—human and floral—were what mattered most.

Over the next few days I went about life in Paradise, coexisting uneasily with the *bizarreries*.

Every morning I worked with the compost, then moved through the garden rooms, snipping old blooms, saving seeds, adding fertilizer, watering, weeding, trimming, harvesting—always staying clear of the poison room. I worked and whispered and sang, chatting with my flower friends, ignoring distant under-currents of warnings from the devil's and angel's trumpet, the henbane and hemlock.

In the heat of the afternoons, I retreated to my atelier, referring to Iva's notebooks, poring over her spidery handwriting, soaking in her wisdom, learning her flower lotions and potions. She listed

ingredients for tisanes that could address any issue, whether stem-
ming from the mind, body, heart, or spirit. The tisanes went far
beyond *calme*—promising *courage, amour, beauté* . . . and then there
were the more intriguing ones, like *érotique* and *poussière d'étoiles*—
stardust.

I kept my eyes open for anything about *Les Dames Blanches*, any
hints the trio might be real. But no, in her notebook, the flower
witch stuck to her flowers.

I could almost hear her whispering in my ear as I infused
dried rose and calendula and chamomile in olive and almond oil
for luscious skin and smooth hair. I blended batches of infused
oil with beet powder over low flames, then strained them, added
hot beeswax, and let them cool into shiny lip and cheek balms. I
replenished jars of tisanes from fragrant stashes in cabinets and
blended new batches. Here and there, with a frisson of exhilaration, I experimented with my own concoctions.

In my downtime, I relaxed in my library, flipping through
vintage books, gravitating toward the ornate ones on the ancient
history of the Celtic and Ligurian tribes of southern France. I
searched the texts for some explanation of my goddess sighting,
or why the blue hour was forbidden. Nothing.

Once in a while, I picked up a darker title like *Les Fleurs
Vénéneuses*, with its curious plants ranging from mildly psycho-
active to downright deadly, and their uses in medieval times
when women poisoned abusers and witches entered altered
states. I thought of the poison garden, its exquisite blooms hissing threats.

For comfort, I went to the three beloved picture books from
my childhood that stood face-out on the bottom shelf: *Goodnight
Moon, Home for a Bunny,* and *Where the Wild Things Are.* They'd barely
survived the fire in Denver, and on a sentimental impulse, I'd
tucked them into my duffel bag. Whenever I glimpsed them, I

thanked the distraught Eloise of the past for saving them. These books were part of me even if they'd never be in the pudgy little hands of my own child.

One night after dinner, I came into the library, made myself a cup of *calme* tea, and noticed a gaping void where the children's books had been.

When was the last time I'd seen them? A day or two ago?

It was late and I was tired, so I sipped my flower tea and meandered through a book about Celtic spirituality, then went to bed. Another bizarre thing to ignore.

Two days later, I was searching for a manual on flower distillation when I saw my children's books back in place. I picked up *Where the Wild Things Are*, fingered the worn dust jacket, and noticed brown smudges. Fingerprints. I took a tentative sniff. Chocolate?

I glanced at the large mason jar, half filled with chocolate chip cookies I'd baked. Had the jar been fuller a few days earlier? Had someone been helping herself to cookies and books?

Mystified, I dropped onto the fainting couch and stared at an old, gilded mirror that reflected the windows behind me. And in the reflection, I caught a glimpse of something—a face, obscured by the leaves, half hidden by a waterfall of dark hair.

I spun around, searching the treetops.

A blur of purple fabric and wild hair, bronzed hands and bare feet, scrambling down an oak.

I ran outside, leaned over the railing. Oak leaves hid tiny birds and russet squirrels, but nothing human.

I pressed my fingertips to my temple. Either I was experiencing vivid—and *worsening*—delusions, or a woodsprite was stalking me, or a ghost child was haunting me. And she'd been inside my house, eaten my cookies, taken my books. She'd moved from a corner-of-the-eye glimpse and an echo of laughter to something disturbingly real.

An ache clutched my chest. Arms folded across my center, I doubled over with the familiar beginnings of panic.

Breathe, Eloise. Breathe.

Whoever this girl was—human, imaginary, or fantastical—she was a taunting reminder that I loved children more than anything.

Yet I couldn't bear to be near them.

The next morning, Mina was munching on an apricot jam tartine while Raphaël was helping himself to more granola and Bao was looking at sparrows through his binoculars. I hadn't felt confident enough to ask about the mystery girl last night, and now, in the morning light, it didn't seem as alarming. I sipped my café au lait and sank into the normalcy of breakfast time.

"Look," Bao said, handing me his binoculars. "A nest!"

I wiped buttery croissant crumbs from my hands, then pressed the binoculars to my face, trying to home in on the nest in the branches.

Instead, I caught flashes of color, blue and purple. Leaves hid her face, revealing tanned skin, dark hair. I dropped the binoculars and squinted into the trees, attempting to locate her. "Someone's out there," I whispered.

Ignoring my friends' looks of confusion, I stood up, scanning the foliage, then pushed back my chair and ran into the grove. I paused behind the cypress where I'd last seen the blur of color. Bewildered, I glanced around, turning in a slow circle. Nothing. She'd vanished into thin air. No noise but my breath and the breeze and birds and insects.

My head slumped into my hands. No matter how hard I tried, I couldn't escape children. I doubled over, sinking to the ground, forehead to knees, waiting for the panic to dissipate.

Breathe, Eloise.

A few months earlier, I'd quit my job in Denver over a girl on my caseload. A pale, moon-faced girl with ginger curls and pink eczema on her cheeks and a spark of silver in her eyes—until the spark had been stamped out and her eyes turned a flat, empty gray. It had come down to this: Since I was just her play specialist, not her mother, there was nothing, absolutely *nothing*, I could do to save her. After the other lost children, I'd reached my breaking point. This girl had shattered me.

And now I felt haunted.

It's not her.

This girl in the gardens had dark hair, tangled and wild, in long, loose waves. Figment of my mind or not, she clearly had a spark. A big one.

I stood and straightened up, trying to collect myself, then returned to the others.

Raphaël met me at the edge of the grove, his face worried, then put his arm around me and pulled me in. He walked me to the table, gently sat me down, and rested his hand on my shoulder. "What happened, Ellie?"

His nickname for me usually made me melt, but now I only rubbed my temple.

"What was it, Eloise?" Bao asked.

I let out a long breath and wondered how much to reveal.

"Are you all right?" asked Mina, patting my hand.

I shook my head, stuck my trembling hands in my pockets.

My pulse sped as I thought of the child. The child who *wasn't supposed to be here, damn it.* The child who was, in all probability, a fabrication of my exhausted heart.

Finally, I composed myself enough to glance at my friends' faces, kind and open. "I keep thinking I'm seeing a girl. Or a ghost. Or a . . ." I paused. How to say *woodsprite* in French? I settled on *"un esprit des bois."*

Their expressions held empathy—and deep concern.

"You think I'm crazy, don't you?" My voice hitched.

Mina kept patting my hand. "Of course not, *ma chérie*."

My words came out, halting and slow. "I—I keep catching glimpses of her clothes, her hair. I hear her laughing. And—and she took my cookies and borrowed my books and left prints by the pond. She must be real." I swallowed hard. "Right?"

My friends exchanged glances until finally, Mina spoke. "Listen, *ma chérie*. You've been drinking all that *calme* tea. Perhaps the dreams are slipping into real life."

Bao nodded. "You might consider consuming less of it."

I looked around at their sympathetic faces. "You really think that's it? The blue lotus?"

"Mixed with the mugwort and other herbs, perhaps," said Mina. "Considering their talents. And your sensitivity to them."

Raphaël locked eyes with me, his expression earnest. "Please, Ellie, remember, when in doubt, ignore *les bizarreries*." He paused, and then, looking torn, added softly, "We care about you, *mon amie*. More than anything, we want you to stay."

And he leaned in, planting kisses on my cheeks.

The Poison Bouquet

All week I tried my best to ignore *les bizarreries*.

And during the sunny, blue-skied days, working and eating and chatting with my friends and the flowers, all was well. Paradise lived up to its name.

Nights were when I felt unsettled, when the underbelly of Paradise revealed itself.

When I glimpsed the towers and gargoyles of the château, instead of fairy-tale magic, I thought of Alexandre Dumas's novels involving medieval castles and skeleton keys and island prisons and secret passages and poisons and murder and deception and prisoners tossed into oubliettes—dungeons where they were left to rot.

The girl no longer felt like a whimsical oddity, but a reminder of all I'd lost. And the ghost trio, a reminder of possible supernatural punishment to come.

I stopped drinking *calme* tea but kept catching glimpses of the woodsprite. Which meant she wasn't just a hallucination. And now, without the tea to relax me, I slept in fits and starts, my dreams foggy and elusive.

Was I losing my mind? Every glimpse of her haunted me more and more, pushed me further and further down a dark spiral. I had to take action, understand what was happening. I'd get nowhere with my friends—they clearly cared about me but downplayed the bizarre things in hopes that I'd keep our odd little family intact.

So I formed a secret plan to speak with Antoinette. This time I'd be ready.

On Wednesday morning, mist shrouded the sun as it rose across the valley. Overcast weather was unusual, but in a place that insisted on being sunny most of the time, a little gloom was welcome.

At the front gate, my companions were arranging bottles and blooms in the trailer when I turned to Antoinette. She was supervising in her belted trench coat, holding a black umbrella, and for once, not wearing sunglasses.

"*Bon matin, Antoinette.*" My brain felt sleep-deprived and chaotic, but I had to be strategic. *Casual.*

"*Bon matin,*" she said tersely.

"I just want to say how beautiful it is here." I pasted on a smile. "I love the flowers."

"Evidently, they love you back." Her tone softened the tiniest bit.

I blinked. A compliment was the last thing I'd expected. "*Merci,* Antoinette." Her kindness emboldened me. "There's so much magic here," I added. "Not just the flowers."

Play it cool, Eloise. No direct questions.

She nodded and turned, opening her mouth to bark more orders. Apparently, bonding time was over.

"Also, other things." I lowered my voice in hopes that my friends wouldn't hear. "Like *Les Dames Blanches* and the woodsprite."

"The woodsprite?" Her words shot out, cold and loud, slicing the air like icicles. "What do you mean?"

"Oh," I sputtered. "Just a magical girl, probably my imagination."

"A child?" She spat the word.

In my peripheral vision, my friends had stopped packing and

were watching us. With *alarm*. And I understood, with a sense of crashing and smashing, that I had crossed a line. Maybe even destroyed something.

"Um, you know," I said, walking it back. "The effects of those teas . . ."

Antoinette's rain-gray eyes bored into me. "La Patronne forbids children here."

"Right." *Mon Dieu*, if only I could snatch back my words. "Never mind. Forget I said anything."

Antoinette's gaze rested on each of us. "If you see any children, human or *imaginary*"—and here she glared at me—"report it at once."

"*Bien sûr, Madame.*"

"It would not end well for you or the child."

Her words were a punch in the gut, and judging by the looks on my friends' faces, they felt the same. Without another word, she zipped away in Epona the Peugeot, trailing the scent of flowers and potions, leaving us locked behind spiked bars, goose-bumped in the drizzle.

❀

For days my friends kept me at arm's length. I alternated between feeling hurt and guilty . . . but I was unclear on what to apologize for. Failure to ignore bizarre things? Simple curiosity?

Raphaël no longer showed up for our daily *apéro* or afternoon swim. Bao refrained from offering me nature gifts. Mina withheld laughter and hugs. Meals felt formal, with stilted conversation, limited wine, no eye contact. Their rejection unearthed my insecurities of the past decade—lost friendships, lack of connection, and an aching loneliness—everything I thought I'd left behind.

I kept up with my after-work swims, glancing at the path, hoping Raphaël would appear, ready to *faire la bise*. Alone again, I sank back into the lows of my old life.

The void left by Gaby after she'd given birth five years ago. My closest friend—the one who understood the inner workings of my soul—had crossed to the fertile side of the river. Lush fields, fruitful orchards, bountiful baskets, flowing milk. I'd stayed on my own barren rock.

On the third day of silent treatment, I sat in a pool of river water, leaning my face to the sun.

Relax, Eloise. Relax, damn it.

But without Raphaël at my side, this felt like a bath. And I *hated* baths.

My baths of the past decade had been in the throes of uterine cramping. With blood leaking out of me, I'd beg the hot water to unwinch the torture device in my belly. Part of me wished I'd just pass out and drown in diluted blood. Death by a literal bloodbath.

I stood up, dried off the river water, and started walking—but not toward my lonely treehouse. Instead, I found myself following the voices of flowers, heading toward their château in the beating heart of Paradise.

In the medicinal flower room, my whole body sighed, soaking up the healing energy. Once I asked permission, the chamomile and lavender fairly leapt into my hands, and I plucked a whimsical bouquet.

I tilted my head, listening. Whispers were drifting from the nearby poison garden, dark shadows of voices. Now, instead of feeling scared away by their hissing, I felt an almost hypnotic pull, a deep curiosity.

I followed their voices, feeling the chill as I entered. Walking past the angel's and devil's trumpets, I resisted my reflex to brush the petals, and instead I kept both hands clutched around my bouquet like a talisman. I edged around the statue, feeling her sinister gaze, toward a corner of the garden I hadn't explored on the tour.

I froze. A wilted bouquet lay on the ground. A deadly cluster of angel's and devil's trumpet. Without gardening gloves, I didn't risk touching them, but bent down for a closer look. The edges of the pale petals had yellowed and browned. Someone had picked them a few days ago.

Beneath the bouquet, a bronze plaque peeked through. I pushed aside the blooms with my toe and read the inscription.

> ### HERE LIES A LITTLE ONE WHO
> ### NEVER DREW A BREATH.

Tears clouded my eyes as I read it again and again. Tears for the mother.

My mind drifted back to Iris, when she was alive and growing inside me last year, when I'd dared to be hopeful as the first trimester ended. I'd gone in for the ultrasound alone—Josh had a work meeting. In the dark exam room, the doctor searched and searched with his wand, until finally he said, "I'm so sorry, Eloise. There's no heartbeat."

Staring at the headstone for someone else's child, I let out a quivery sigh, wiped my cheeks, and wondered who had made this. La Patronne? The plaque looked decades old, tarnished green—yet the bouquet was recent. Someone was still mourning.

Which I understood. I, too, was still mourning.

Against the doctor's recommendations, I'd refused a D&C procedure to "remove the dead tissue." Three times was enough. Iris would not be tossed into a medical waste bin. My baby would be buried.

Now, tears streamed down my cheeks as I laid my bundle of chamomile and lavender on the grave of this unknown child. I rocked back on my heels, wrapped my arms around myself. Angel's and devil's trumpet crooned in a dissonant chant that somehow captured the darkness I'd felt back then.

I remembered sobbing alone and obliterating dishes on the patio as I waited for contractions to start. Days later, when they did, I'd drawn a hot bath, and as I was about to step in, Iris slid from me. I could still feel the raw sensation of cradling her in my palms. Most of what I'd held was probably the placenta—Iris herself would have been only a few inches long.

I breathed in the scents of the poison garden, feeling for the mother, trying to imagine how she'd felt holding her own lifeless child. What trimester had she been in? Had it been a stillbirth? Did she have other children? Or had this been her deepest, final hope, like mine? Had the father cried with her? Or had she been like me, cradling her child alone?

My quiet tears were turning into full-blown crying for this mother, drowning out the chorus of poison flowers. I wanted to rewind the years and hold this woman. And maybe hold her now, whoever she was.

I could never forget how it felt to hold Iris that day. I remembered searching the mass in my palms for a head or hands or even a toe. Nothing. Yet in my heart, she was a beautiful child, gazing at me with a universe of love.

Even now, a year later, I felt her turning from warm to cool in my hands. The blood dripping from me as I buried her beneath the lilacs. The emptiness when Josh came home and I told him nothing. The rage of shattering dishes, the sorrow of weeping alone. The pain an uncrossable river.

⚜

During twilight I lay in bed, listening to frogs and crickets, wondering how to ford the river. Until now, things had mostly been going well in the gardens—the healing, the flowers, the food, the friends. I couldn't burn it all down. Somehow, I needed to change my patterns, fly up and out of my old way of being.

Once dusk turned to night, I headed to the fairy-lit dining grove, unsure what might unfold. There were no cheek kisses, only polite *bonsoirs*. Over steaming plates of ratatouille and hon-eyed lamb confit and the heady scent of *herbes de Provence*, Mina asked Raphaël to pass the salt.

I had easier access to the salt. *Much* easier access. Why hadn't she asked *me*? Before he could reach it, I grabbed the salt shaker and gripped it, knuckles white. Was I going to *throw* it?

My companions watched, looking wary.

After a stretched-out moment, I lowered the shaker, released my grip.

Something had to change. I would leave my old self in my old life and see what my new self did.

My new self *sobbed*.

For a long time. In undignified, unfiltered misery. In front of the people I cared about most. I was vulnerability personified.

When I caught my breath, I sputtered, "You want me to leave?"

Through the candlelight, Mina put her hand to her mouth. She hurried over to me, pressing my head against her shoulder.

"I thought we were friends." I sniffled and released a shud-dery sigh. *Mon Dieu*, I sounded like a rejected middle schooler. Still, I kept going. "I like you. And I thought you liked me. You *hurt* me."

She faced the others. "This isn't right, the way we've been acting."

Rubbing his jaw, Raphaël whispered, "Sorry, Eloise. We panicked."

Bao hung his head, then raised his eyes to meet mine. "We didn't know what to do."

At least they were all making eye contact with me now, their faces showing real shame.

I pulled away from Mina, noticing a damp spot on her pink cotton—my snot or tears, who knew. I wiped my face with a napkin, not caring how pathetic I looked. My words came out in a rasp. "I don't understand."

"Eloise," said Mina, "we've been on guard with you. After what happened with Amber." She wrapped me in a hug and I let myself sink into her. "Of course we want you to stay. You've been a breath of fresh air."

"We care about you," Bao added.

"We all like you, Ellie," said Raphaël, his voice raw. "Very much."

"What am I supposed to do?"

Mina sighed. "Just trust us, Eloise. Ignore what doesn't concern you. Follow the rules. Do not go to Antoinette about *anything*."

"Stay on our side," said Raphaël with a pained look. *"Please."*

I pressed my palm to my damp cheek, wanting to drill them with more questions, but questions had gotten me into this mess. I filled my cheeks with air, puffed it out in a slow stream—a French mannerism I'd picked up.

"You belong here," said Bao, as if this were my ecosystem.

My path was clear: I had to prove my allegiance, ignore the bizarre things. Which meant I couldn't ask them about the grave either. If this was the price for living with friends in Paradise, I'd accept.

I gave a weak nod. *"D'accord."* I scooped up the mélange of aubergine and courgette and tomato, dripping with garlicky olive oil.

Raphaël opened a bottle of Rhône red and poured me a glass,

and we resumed our sweet life in Paradise. But I wasn't the same person—something inside me had changed. For once, I'd let my sorrow and anger bond me with people. I'd shown my friends a part of me that even Josh hadn't known.

I'd become a new self in my new life.

Now if I could just obey the damn rules.

13

The Mysterious

The next day, Raphaël and I stood side by side in the atelier, surveying copper vats and tubes. I'd invited him to help me make floral water and essential oil, hoping that with Iva's instructions, we could figure it out.

Her notebooks brimmed with wisdom and advice—she saw flowers as colleagues, best friends, and spirit guides. Little by little, I was learning more nuances of their language, deeper than ever.

Raphaël's head was almost touching mine as we read Iva's delicate writing. A basket of red rose petals sat by my elbow, singing softly in a fragrant cloud. It wasn't the cloying smell of synthetic rose. No, this was an ancient, spicy, mysterious scent, something layered and intricate, like the most expensive wine or chocolate.

Raphaël breathed it all in. "Ellie, I hope you know how bad I feel about our behavior. You didn't deserve that."

He looked pallid and tired, as if he'd lost sleep.

Well, good. I almost felt sorry for him.

"Forgiven." Glancing at the rose petals, I said, "Ready?"

"Ready."

Inhaling the sweet musk, I began to distill the essential oil, listening to the roses' guidance. First, we dropped handfuls of petals into spring water in the two vats. Then I lit the burners with matches—after just three tries—and we waited for the rose-petaled water to boil. We'd already poured cool water into the smaller tubs, which contained the copper coils, and arranged them on iron stands attached to glass beakers and funnels and jugs.

I studied the crescents beneath his eyes. "You okay?"

"Sometimes I don't sleep well."

On impulse, I took a jar of *calme* tea from the cabinet. "Here, have a cup of this before bed." I set the jar on the table. "I made it for you myself. I call it Getting Over Silent Treatment Guilt."

His face fell into his hands. "Oh, Eloise."

"Kidding! It's just *calme* tea."

He quirked a smile, revealing a dimple. *"Merci, ma sorcière."*

My witch. I met his eyes and saw something more than fatigue in his face: pain. "My witchy powers are telling me something else is wrong."

He hesitated. "I'm leaving the gardens soon."

My head spun in confusion. "How will you get out?"

"I'll tell Antoinette." He paused. "I won't be coming back."

My throat constricted. "Because of what I did?"

He shook his head quickly.

Amber's letter came to mind—leaving heaven and entering hell. "Then why?"

"Responsibilities."

"What do you mean?"

"For years I lived in the present here in Paradise. Past and future didn't matter. Only the pleasures of the moment."

"That's the selling point, right?"

"Things change," he said. "Eventually, one needs to think about other people."

"Your parents? Your family?"

His gaze dropped. "Something like that."

An urge to sink down to the floor came . . . and went. In this atelier, I felt strong, as if Iva's spirit were here bolstering me. What Raphaël needed was strength too.

I pulled a jar of tea from the apothecary cabinet. COURAGE. "Try this."

His hands wrapped around mine as he took the jar. For a moment, we held still, our faces close, every cell of my body alive and thrumming.

"The water is boiling," he whispered, removing his hands and backing away.

I shook myself, refocused on the equipment.

The rose essential oil was evaporating up the narrow copper neck and into the pipe. Near the ceiling, the pipe angled downward, directing the essence through the coils, where it was cooled in the water. Finally, the oil dripped through the funnel and into the large glass jars on the floor.

Alchemy. What a strange mix of science and magic.

Raphaël murmured, "Iva said rose makes us brave in life and love."

I inhaled more deeply.

He's leaving. Let him go.

Once the jars of essential oil and floral water were filled, Raphaël left to take a nap in his caravan. I walked along the swinging bridge to my library and brewed up my own cup of courage tea. I noticed the rose petals in the mix, pink and red and burgundy and white. Their scents surrounded me from the tea and the essence that had seeped into me all afternoon.

What was my essence?

It was easier to imagine Raphaël's: kindness. And the layers: joy in fixing what was broken, helping people, making things, being close to the earth, embracing pleasure . . . and a touch of obliviousness at how much he could hurt me.

And the undercurrent? *Le mystère.*

"The most beautiful thing we can experience is the mysterious."

I reclined on my fainting couch and breathed in the mint and lemon peel and rosemary that blended with the roses. *Brave in life and love.* Sometimes I felt that the good witch was whispering in my ear. *Be brave.*

I shook myself back to reality and scanned my bookshelves for something to read, some distraction. A folded paper poked out of *Where the Wild Things Are.*

Strange. I set the book on my lap and pulled out a typewritten letter on creamy stationery.

Dear Eloise,

    May I remind you of the rules. There shall be no roaming during twilight, no gossiping, and no children. Consequences may ensue.

I took a sip of courage tea. Had Antoinette told La Patronne about our conversation? *La Patronne.* It dawned on me that this term for owner or boss could also refer to a patron saintess or patron goddess. I read onward.

    To be clear: The Goddess is not always life-giver.

    In My Hera form, I've prolonged a woman's labor, forced her to wander the earth alone and in pain, then sent a dragon in relentless pursuit of her children.

One may argue that the Goddess is, in Her most powerful form, death-bringer.

Remember this.

Respectfully,

The Goddess of the Gardens

Without the courage tea, I might have packed my bags and gotten the hell out. Instead, I was intrigued. The grave marker in the poison garden flashed through my mind. I could relate to this aspect of the Goddess, the rage I'd felt during my infertility. After each loss, I'd transformed into my own wrathful goddess, cursing fertile women.

Yet there was a point where this goddess and I diverged: I'd never wished harm upon any child. I *loved* kids. Always. All of them. Even if they weren't mine. Even when it killed me to be near them. Was that my essence—what I had to somehow distill?

I wondered if I was moving past the pain, approaching the other side, starting to accept my fate. Maybe one day I could even be near children again.

I'm moving on.

I tried out this idea. It felt liberating, the way a bud might feel as it's gingerly opening its petals, welcoming honeybees and butterflies and sunshine. I felt almost grateful to this furious goddess, this shadow self, this nudge toward the light. *Almost* grateful. Because I also felt an icy, prickling fear.

Were my friends and I in danger? And worse, what if there *was* a child in the gardens? Was *she* in danger?

Thunderheads filled the evening sky. It was only five or six o'clock but as dark as twilight. Still, Raphaël and I went for our ritual swim. We had such a short time left together, why let an impending storm stop us?

We'd just dunked ourselves underwater when a bolt of lightning illuminated the sky, followed by a roar. My body jolted to a new level of aliveness.

"*Zut!*" we said at the same time as the first fat drops fell.

Laughing, we scrambled to gather our clothes. "Want to come over for tea instead, *mon ami?*" I tacked on the "my friend" to clarify there would be no awkward near-kisses.

"*Oui.*" Shivering and dripping, he met my gaze, still grinning, then rasped, "*Mon amie.*"

We jogged to my treehouse, jumping and yelping at each boom of thunder. The entire gardens shook with the force. The air smelled of damp earth and electricity.

Inside my library, I offered Raphaël a crocheted blanket and wrapped another around my shoulders. I wanted to sit with him on the fainting sofa, warming each other beneath blankets. Instead, I kept a safe distance as I boiled the water and lit candle lanterns.

He walked to the bookcase, running his hands along the cloth-bound volumes. In typical *bricoleur* style, he pulled out a pocket-knife and tightened a few screws on the shelves. "Iva and I would sip tea here and read together," he said, wistful.

"I can be her less-wise substitute." I gave him a sidelong glance. "If you'll have me."

"Without a doubt." His eyes met mine. "She was way too wise for me anyway."

When the kettle whistled, he said, "Why don't you change into dry clothes? I'll make the tea."

This man was *considerate*—a fact that sparked another pang over his impending departure.

As I ran up to my dressing room, I noted that most of my

clothes were outside on the line, soaking in the downpour. I grabbed the only thing left in my wardrobe—my little black dress. I rubbed beet balm on my cheeks and lips, then ran a brush and almond oil through my hair.

On impulse, I dabbed rose eau de toilette on my neck. *Brave in love.* Despite myself, my heart flew in anticipation of the coziness that awaited: blankets and tea and candlelight. Just the *bricoleur* and me taking a refuge in the storm. I stared at my reflection in the mirror.

You're friends, Eloise. That's all.

But maybe—

Nope. Just friends. Do not set yourself up for pain.

Back in the warm glow of the library, Raphaël was sipping tea on the sofa. When he saw me, his gaze lingered. *"Très jolie,"* he said softly, then motioned to the pot and second cup on the tray. *"Calme tea."*

"Merci." I gave him an appreciative smile, shaking droplets from my hair.

Through the window, gusts whipped through branches and rain pelted the glass. I counted just one second between lightning and thunder blasts. A deep sense of unease rolled over me. "Is this treehouse safe?"

"I installed lightning rods," he assured me, and explained all the structural engineering principles that made my home secure.

From my spot by the window, I only half listened. It wasn't just the storm distracting me. Flowers were whispering, but I couldn't grasp their meaning. Their tone was *frantic.* Maybe they felt distressed out there in the elements, being flattened and smashed and drowned, poor things. Or were they warning me of something? Their voices reminded me of their warnings in the shower at twilight. But I was inside now, breaking no rules.

I glanced at Raphaël, who had grown quiet, watching me as if

I were a frightened child. "Sit down and have some tea, Ellie," he said gently, filling my cup and refilling his own. "Add extra honey. This batch tastes bitter."

I drew in a quivery breath and sat beside him.

"This treehouse has weathered worse storms, *mon amie*." He held out my cup of tea.

Trying to shake off my dread, I reached for the cup.

And missed.

It smashed onto the hardwood floor, sending shards of ceramic sailing.

Strange. How had I missed the cup? A force, or instinct, or *something* had made me miss. An uneasy feeling grew in my stomach as I gathered the pieces.

"Let me help you." He grabbed a broom and swept up the rest.

Thunder cracked, the sky lit up, and the flowers' voices escalated to a feverish pitch. I held still and listened. And sniffed the air.

The tea puddled before me was not *calme*.

I dumped the shards in the trash and examined the contents of the open jar on the counter. I couldn't detect any of the usual sweet, sunny, appley scents of chamomile or rose or lavender. No, this blend smelled rotten, almost fishy. Had the batch gone bad?

I sniffed again. The foul smell could mean that something in here was bat-pollinated. And I perceived another layer: a honeysuckle-like fragrance with an eerie edge.

I peered closer at the dried flowers—white and lavender and yellow—unfamiliar. I stuck my fingers into the jar to scoop some up.

A force snatched my hand back, as if an invisible *someone* had yanked my arm.

My chest thudded as realization dawned. These blossoms were poison: henbane, devil's trumpet, angel's trumpet, belladonna.

In a panic, I turned to Raphaël, who was just finishing his second cupful.

"Stop!" I shouted in English.

Alarmed, he lowered the cup.

Heat swept over me, as if my head had caught fire. I sputtered the word, the same in French. *"Poison."*

Raphaël's forehead creased. "The label said *calme*."

Dropping onto the sofa, I ran a hand through my damp hair, more frantic by the second. "This makes no sense."

He paled as the gravity of the situation sank in. "Did you drink any, Ellie?"

I shook my head. Had some protective power kept me from drinking it? Still, a sick feeling spread over me as I wondered what might lie ahead for Raphaël.

After a moment's relief, he rasped, "What's going to happen to me?"

I recalled bits of the *Fleurs Vénéneuses* book and tried to stay calm, gently pulling him up. "Let's get you to a hospital. How do you feel?"

"I don't think it's kicked in yet." Still, his words sounded dry and he looked off-balance.

Think, Eloise. Think, think, think. "Can you make yourself throw up?"

With a quick nod, he ran into the storm and leaned over the railing. I averted my eyes and rushed to my atelier to search for an emetic but found no safe option.

Minutes later, I ran back into the library, where Raphaël was gulping water.

"Any luck?" I asked.

"More or less. But I had two cups of tea. Some of it probably made it past my stomach. I'm trying to dilute any poison that's still in there."

I hugged my arms to steady myself. Soon the effects would kick in and everything would be up to me. "You started drinking the tea about a half hour ago, right?"

He nodded, his face naked with fear.

"You might feel symptoms soon. Come on."

We stumbled down the slippery bridges, beneath falling branches and leaves, through pelting rain and shrieking wind, toward the gate.

I prayed that Antoinette would hear the bell ring over the storm. And that she'd let us out.

14

The Dark Château

 ainwater spilled from the mouths of gargoyles perched atop the castle. The château loomed and the Fates watched as I rang the bell, more frantic by the second. Raphaël tried rattling and kicking the gates, to no avail.

Mon Dieu, what if we were trapped in here? And I had to watch Raphaël die? I had no idea how much poison he'd ingested. I struggled to remember the side effects I'd read about. Dilated pupils. Hot, dry skin and mouth. Elevated heart rate. Blurred vision.

When he took over clanging the bell, I stayed close, arm around him, studying his face through the torrent. His pupils were dilated . . . but it was so dark that mine could be too. He was blinking, but so was I, vision blurred from sheets of water. I pressed my hand to his forehead—damp and warm, but so was mine. I grabbed his wrist, felt his pulse—racing, but then again, we'd run here in a storm and he was facing death.

Soaked and trembling, we took turns ringing and shouting alternate plans over the cacophony. The most feasible idea to me was alerting Mina and Bao for help.

"They might hear the bell," I said, looking hopefully toward the path.

"Not from the other side of the gardens during a storm." He

added, "And the hole in the wall is on the far side of the gardens too."

"There's a *hole* in the wall?"

He nodded, as if he'd just forgotten to tell me. "Near the southeast corner."

I tucked this knowledge away and focused on the task at hand. It came down to this: What was the best use of time, before he became incapacitated?

The entire sky lit up at the same time as a deafening roar of thunder.

And a figure appeared at the inner gate, fists on her hips, silhouetted against the lightning. Antoinette. There she stood like a furious apparition born of the storm. She wore a long, black raincoat and a look of disapproval.

"What is it?" she yelled over the wind.

Gripping Raphaël's waist, I stumbled with him toward the inner gate. "He was poisoned! Datura, henbane, brugmansia. He needs a hospital."

With a deep frown, she unlocked the inner gate and ushered us toward the main entrance of the castle—an imposing pair of arched, carved wooden doors at the top of a dozen stone steps.

This was my first unobstructed view of the castle—and it wasn't very clear in the dark storm. But for once, I was inside the inner walls. Tilting my head back, I estimated the château to be three stories tall, not counting the much-higher turrets. Its walls were a patchwork of stucco and stone, crawling with trumpet vines.

Shivering, I paused beside Raphaël at the base of the stairs, assuming Antoinette would rush inside for her car keys.

Yet she stayed at the top, squinting at us through the rain. "Come inside. I will attend to him."

"Drive us to the hospital!" I shrieked, clutching Raphaël.

"Non." Her expression wavered, revealing fear. "There's an antidote inside. It will be faster."

I looked at Raphaël, who was staring into the torrent and muttering.

The hallucinations were kicking in.

Antoinette tore down the stairs, grabbed his arm. I kept mine wrapped around his waist and reluctantly helped heave him up the steps. He needed the damn antidote. Now.

Disoriented, he stumbled, sluggish, speaking to invisible people . . . or *beings* of some kind. Monsters? Ghosts? Spirits of the Otherworld? Goddesses? *Mon Dieu,* who knew what hellish creatures he was encountering in his mind. I couldn't decipher his words through the storm—but one thing was clear: *terror.*

We staggered into a long, wide hallway with high ceilings, our clothes dripping rainwater. This place felt cavernous and dark, lit only by the glow of candelabras in alcoves. The smell of beeswax and candle smoke and musty stone wrapped around us. Music floated from somewhere in the castle's depths—mid-century French music—Serge Gainsbourg singing a melody so lighthearted that it felt ominous.

In the faint light, I could barely distinguish what at first I'd assumed was a narrow carpet, but then realized was an impossibly long knit blanket that ran down the center of the hallway. It emerged from beneath a door on the right and snaked out into the hall, stretching to the far end of the castle, where it vanished around a corner. *Bizarre.*

Lining the walls were paintings reminiscent of the statues throughout the gardens—goddesses enacting vengeance—shadowy scenes of battlefields, fireballs, corpses, blood, whips. I blinked, as if I were hallucinating too, though I hadn't had a drop of tea or even touched the dried flowers. I doubted that smelling it would have affected me, but who knew.

Antoinette ushered us through a door halfway down the hall, into an ornate drawing room featuring a massive stone fireplace surrounded by antique furniture and weaponry. In the near corner sat an easel with a half-done canvas of a furious Aphrodite emerging from a conch shell. The smell of fresh oil paint drifted from a palette on a metal stool.

Antoinette sat Raphaël onto the couch. "Keep him calm. I'll get the antidote from La Patronne."

She breezed out of the room as I tried processing the situation. Was the antidote something La Patronne kept on hand, like an EpiPen? Was she the one behind the blanket? The one painting macabre goddess pictures? I had the urge to run after Antoinette and confront La Patronne, ask her what the hell was going on in Paradise.

"No!" cried Raphaël, cowering, hands over his head. "Please, no, enough death!"

I focused back onto him, tucking a crocheted blanket around his shoulders. His eyes looked both terrifying and terrified, the pupils gaping black holes that overtook his irises. His conversations with invisible beings had escalated to shouting, begging, crying.

"No, I won't let her die. Don't kill me. Is she in danger? Please, no, it's not fair." He lashed out, punching the air. "Why? Death, why have you come for me? For her? Why? Oh, she's so young."

"Shh, it's okay," I said in a soothing voice.

He sank into the sofa, sobbing, defeated.

Goose bumps prickled my skin. I could almost believe there were unseen creatures here, intimidating him, laying bare his worst nightmares.

Antoinette swept into the room with a vintage black leather bag, as if she were a 1950s doctor making a house call.

Upon seeing her, Raphaël shrieked and shrunk away.

Undeterred, she sat beside him. "That's enough," she said, silencing him.

He rubbed his eyes and grabbed my hand.

From the bag, Antoinette removed a syringe and a vial of liquid.

Panic rushed through me. I couldn't let this woman—this personal assistant to an eccentric recluse—inject him. "No, wait." I grabbed her wrist. "Give me your keys. I'll take him to the hospital."

She shook her head, lips tight. "The clinic in town has no antidote. It would take forty-five minutes to get to the nearest hospital. By then he could be in heart failure." Her eyes narrowed. "Does one want this on one's conscience, Mademoiselle?"

I eyed the vial. "What is it?"

Antoinette gave a frustrated sigh. "Physostigmine. An antidote to plants that contain tropane alkaloids. It's found in Calabar bean and manchineel trees."

It felt both reassuring and unsettling to hear this technical language, as if she were a biochemist in disguise. I pressed my hands to the *bricoleur's* feverish face. "Raphaël, do you want Antoinette to give you the antidote?"

He was oblivious to my words, arguing and pleading with a ghost.

I closed my eyes, listened to the hum beneath the wind and rain and music. The flowers' voices were calling out, ever so faintly, *Yes, yes, yes.*

"Do it." I pulled the blanket from his shoulders and offered her his arm. His bicep was muscled and tan, so healthy and strong—a stark contrast to his vulnerability.

I winced as Antoinette pierced his flesh and pressed the plunger.

He met her eyes and screamed.

❧

I couldn't tell whether Raphaël's cries came from physical or emotional—or spiritual—pain, but after a torturous wait, they subsided. His pupils shrank and his fever abated and his pulse rate returned to normal.

Thank you, thank you, thank you, I whispered to the universe and the flowers and any other helpful forces out there.

Antoinette brought out a tray of tea. *"Calme,"* she said.

"Are you sure?" I asked, sniffing the pot and inspecting the damp blossoms with my fingertip. Yes, it was the familiar chamomile and rose and lavender with touches of skullcap, passionflower, valerian, and blue lotus—and yes, it might bring him down from the panic-inducing hallucinations.

Still holding him, I moved the cup to his lips and soothed him as if he were a child recovering from a nightmare.

Antoinette sat across from us in an antique tufted chair. "La Patronne is disappointed in you."

"What?" I sputtered.

"She asks how one could let this happen."

"She thinks *I* did this? Let me talk to her."

"Non. She is resting."

I let my head fall backward, staring at the ceiling. Had I slipped through a rabbit hole? "The tea was labeled *calme.* I've been using it since I came." I struggled not to sound defensive. "But tonight, the tea changed. Or someone changed it."

Antoinette clucked. "You must have refilled the jar with the wrong blend from the atelier."

I scanned my memory. True, I had topped off near-empty jars, using Iva's larger containers. But I couldn't have done *this.* And why would there even be a poison blend in my atelier? Or anywhere in the gardens? Iva never would have made a tea like this. I shook my head. "That's impossible."

"Apparently not." Antoinette frowned. "La Patronne will forgive your trespasses and allow you to stay. *If* you abide by her rules. For now, this has been punishment enough."

Punishment? I sank back into the sofa, exhausted now that my adrenaline rush had faded.

In silence, we sipped the tea, which calmed me and made Raphaël doze. I kept a close eye on him, checking his vitals.

In the silence, I heard a noise down the hallway. A door closing? Footsteps? I eyed the doorway.

Antoinette stiffened.

I leveled my gaze at her. "Tell me about La Patronne."

Antoinette's lips remained sealed, and her grip around the cup tightened.

Lowering my voice, I asked, "So it's just you two in this giant castle?"

She set her cup of tea in the saucer. "Only the more re-cent sections are inhabited. The oldest medieval parts are left alone."

I glanced around the room, taking in the flails and swords and brass-studded whips on the walls, and trying to glimpse more of the Aphrodite painting in progress. "Who painted that? And who knit that long blanket?"

Antoinette flicked her eyes around. "La Patronne made an exception letting you in her château. Do not disrespect it with questions. And needless to say, one will not gossip about what has occurred here tonight."

I rubbed the tension from my neck, wondering how the hell she thought I'd keep living here after this. Part of my mind was already planning to pack up and find a hotel in town.

Antoinette sipped her last drop of tea. "Look. He is fine. And twilight has ended. The storm has passed. You may leave now." She nudged him.

His eyes opened and locked onto mine. They were confused

and full of questions . . . but he was back. "What happened?" he rasped.

"Let's get you home," I said. "I'll explain on the way."

And we trudged out of the château, clinging to each other.

Alive.

15

To Stay or Not to Stay

t breakfast, the sun was shining over the gardens which were strewn with fallen branches and debris. I was ravenous after skipping dinner the night before. As we devoured croissants and honeyed yogurt and stone fruit, Raphaël and I recapped the events of the previous evening with Mina and Bao, who listened with wide-eyed horror.

Raphaël had made a complete recovery, his body and mind once again intact as he sipped his coffee. I'd tried to convince him to stay at my place last night, but he insisted he was fine to sleep alone in his caravan. It was hard not to be offended at his adamance.

But now, as he munched on his *pain au chocolat*, he gushed gratitude. "Eloise saved me."

"Well," I said, "Antoinette would claim that I poisoned you. And that she saved you."

"Either way," he said lightly, "I survived."

"Do you remember your hallucinations?"

He hesitated, then forced a laugh. "The usual nightmares from hell."

I sensed he was holding back. His conversations with the ghosts had centered around themes—not just death, but fear of death coming for himself . . . and for *her*. Whoever she was.

His ex-girlfriend? That might explain why he didn't want to talk about it.

Mina gave Raphaël another hug—the fiftieth so far this morning—and kissed his head. "Bao and I will wash dishes. You two relax."

I gave a grateful smile, too tired to protest.

Raphaël leaned toward me, took my hands. "*Merci, ma sorcière.* You must have been so scared. But you stuck with me. You rose to the occasion."

"Of course. What else would I do?"

He paused, his eyes glassy. "Not everyone can face pain and death with a clear head."

Our hands stayed interlocked. We looked at each other with this new bond, something so much bigger and deeper than that kiss we'd been avoiding.

"Should I leave the gardens too?" Quickly, I added, "Not with you. I'd just find a hotel and go from there."

His brow wrinkled. "Why would you leave, Ellie?"

"We're trapped in a locked garden with poisons and punishments. Why *wouldn't* I leave?"

"We're not trapped. I'll show you the hole in the wall."

"How reassuring." I breathed in. "But what if that poison was meant for me?"

Raphaël said gently, "Maybe you just made a gaffe, like Antoinette said."

"A gaffe?" I echoed in disbelief. "Of the murderous variety?" I knew in my bones that I hadn't made a gaffe. I knew my flower teas inside and out. Someone else had switched them. "I am *not* the one who poisoned you."

"*D'accord,*" he said, holding my gaze. "I believe you. You're my flower whisperer, after all. And in the end, you *saved* me."

I crossed my arms. "Well, I'm talking to Antoinette today. Giving her my notice."

Looking torn, he opened his mouth to say something, then closed it again. Finally, he said, "Mina and Bao will be sad to see you go. You're like an arthritis-free, American version of Iva, you know."

His words warmed me, but not enough to cancel out the chill of last night.

I spent the morning working near the entrance so that I could intercept Antoinette. The jar of poison tea sat beside me as I tended to pink and red oleander bushes. When she appeared, I stood up with the jar. "Antoinette!"

She walked through the inner gate, locked it, then paused beside me. She was perfumed and lipsticked, and her hair was swept in an elegant braided bun—as if everything were normal. "How is Raphaël?"

"Shockingly, he's okay." I paused. "Considering his near-death experience."

She waved away my words. "Oh, he's faced death before. And poisoning."

"What?"

"Outside the gardens, before he came. Periwinkle. Yew. This was cake in comparison."

I furrowed my brows. "What are you talking about?"

"Never mind."

I'd get nowhere with her, so I simply handed her the jar. "I'm giving you my notice."

She regarded the poison flower blend. There was an uncomfortably long silence.

"He could have *died*, Antoinette."

She opened the jar, sifted through the dried petals and leaves. "Oh, this isn't enough to kill anyone. And look, there are harmless flowers mixed in. Black lilies and pansies. No one's life was in danger."

Dizzy, I pressed my fingers to my temple. So was this some kind of warning? Meant for *me*?

"La Patronne would like you to stay." Another beat. "Mademoiselle, have you felt the healing effects of the gardens?"

"Well, yes, but—"

She held up a finger. "If you leave, all of this healing will unravel. You will go back to being a broken, lonely, sad, angry woman. You will leave heaven and go to hell."

Her words felt like a curse.

I studied her face, even though sustained eye contact with her scared me. "What happened to the previous gardener? Did she get poisoned too? Is that what you meant by *'She is no longer here'*?"

Antoinette barked a cold laugh. "Of course not. She left. I don't know how. I didn't let her out of the gates. As far as I know, she is alive and miserable in Iowa. She wasted her chance in Paradise. And now it is gone forever." She gave me a measured look. "Is that the fate you want?"

My mouth had gone dry. "I'll think about it."

"I'll assume you're staying unless I hear otherwise. Is there anything else?" she asked, tucking the jar under her arm and unlocking the main gate. "Anything you need from town?"

What a mundane question after our bizarre conversation. But come to think of it, there were things I needed—and part of me welcomed the return to normalcy. "It's my turn to cook soon. I'll need some ingredients."

"Now, you know that normally one gives requests to Mina and she passes them to me. That is how one does it. However, I will make an exception today." She pulled a tiny notebook from her handbag. "Go ahead."

As she jotted down my ingredients, I looked at her timeless

pencil skirt and silk blouse and scarf and wondered about her. Had she come here to heal too? And *mon Dieu*, if this was her healed version, what had her broken version been like?

After the final ingredient, I asked, "Why does La Patronne want me to stay?"

Antoinette sighed. "It's difficult to find new workers. And it's a risk. The previous gardener was a mistake. But you—despite your flaws, you have something special with the flowers. Something that Iva had too. You have much to offer the gardens. If only you stop challenging the rules and asking questions."

What a roundabout compliment. I'd barely said *merci* when she slammed the gate shut between us, locked it, and slipped into Epona the Peugeot. Moments later, the engine roared to life and the mysterious personal assistant vanished down the road.

Later that morning, kneeling in the edible flower garden with Mina, gathering sticky calendula blooms, I told her I was thinking about leaving.

Her eyes filled. "Because of last night?"

"Of course."

A pause. "Please stay."

My throat ached. This was my friend, the closest one I'd had in years. "I can't. It felt like *punishment*. Intended for me."

She said nothing, only bit her lip.

"Listen, Mina." I blew air from my cheeks. "Before the poisoning, I found a disturbing note in my library."

"Oh, Eloise." She gave me a pleading look. "Ignore it."

I pulled the folded-up letter from my shirt pocket. "Read it."

Mina adjusted her head wrap, a sunburst print of gold and orange. "I'm sorry, but no."

My stomach sank. Her way of dealing with fears was to ignore them. She wasn't gaslighting me, but trying to protect me the best way she knew how. Trying to make me feel safe enough to stay.

She plucked more calendula, then looked at me with shiny eyes, her expression vulnerable. "Life is better with you here. I've never had a friend like you." Her chin quivered, a little earthquake spreading out until her entire body trembled. "I understand you're worried, *mon amie*." She pressed the heels of her palms to her eyes. "But please don't be scared away. Please."

I couldn't help it, I reached for her and wrapped her in a long hug.

"Eloise," she said into my shoulder. "You have the power to transform darkness to light. Hurt to healing."

"Don't forget *merde* to *fleurs*," I added with a wry smile.

She gave a sob that morphed into deep belly laughs. "You're a woman wise in flowers. You belong here."

I thought of what Antoinette said about my healing unraveling if I left. About the hell of my old life that would await. About my potential here in the gardens. I thought of the warmth of Mina's embrace, my friendship with her and Bao and Raphaël. The stark contrast with the loneliness of my life before.

The flowers were murmuring: *Stay, stay, stay.*

"Okay," I said. "I'll stay. For now."

Once our baskets were brimming with calendula and our tears had dried, Mina and I rested on a stone garden bench, where she morphed back to her usual exuberant self. "*Alors*, Eloise, you're cooking tomorrow night! Are you ready?"

"All set." I leaned against her. "I've taken care of the ingredients and everything."

She raised her brow. "Really?"

My companions had given me time off cooking duty to get settled—or more likely, grasp their high French cooking standards. Amber's bare steamed vegetables and mushy quinoa had traumatized them.

"I've been studying cookbooks," I assured her. "It'll be a surprise."

"Oh, no it won't, *ma chérie*, not for me. You need help on your first try."

Feeling nervous, I recited the menu as if I were back in my waitressing days. "For an appetizer, cremini tartes with Gruyère and rosemary. Cream of asparagus soup with fresh lemon and garlic. Sautéed chicken stuffed with basil and goat cheese and toasted almonds in a citrus wine sauce on a bed of herbed orzo. Arugula with fresh lemon–olive oil dressing and shaved Asiago. A variety of cheeses and warm baguettes. For dessert, a cinnamon-almond-peach crumble with whipped Chantilly cream."

The crumble was my American touch. I didn't want to tackle apple pie, but peach crumble was an old farmers market favorite.

She nodded at each item, although she looked confused over my generic-sounding "peach dessert"—I had no idea how to say crumble.

"Sounds good," she conceded.

I felt myself glow . . . now if I could just pull off *making* it.

"And for the special touch?" she asked.

I blinked. "Isn't this *whole meal* a special touch?"

"I know you want to impress Raphaël."

"Pardonne-moi?"

"You think Bao and I don't notice?"

"Notice what?"

"You two. The way you act around each other. Those little swims you take?" Her eyes crinkled.

"He's leaving soon. It doesn't matter."

She waved away my words. "Well, he's here now, my dear."

I scrambled for another excuse. "He just feels obligated to hang out with me since you and Bao are a couple."

"Wait." She studied my face. "You think Bao is my boyfriend?"

I nodded.

She laughed. "Bao is attracted to men. Only men."

"Oh." So much for my naive assumptions.

"We're best friends, like family. Humans need touch, you know. We need to feel loved. Even if it's not by a lover." In French the word *lover* seemed far less cringy: *amant*.

She slung her arm over my shoulders. "Now you and Raphaël, you're friends, and you're on the road to being *amants*."

I flushed. "I'm too old for him."

"Ha! How old are you?"

"Thirty-seven."

"And he's thirty-three."

"Right, but he's a *young* thirty-three and I'm an *old* thirty-seven."

"*Ma chèrie* Eloise, I was twelve and my husband was fifty when we got married. Now *that's* too old."

It surprised me when she laughed and then I laughed, and then we leaned against each other, and soon we were all-out crying.

Before I could follow up, she slapped my knee and asked, "What's the real reason you're not with him?"

I paused. "My body and I—we've been through a lot of pain. I don't know if we're ready for pleasure yet, at least not with someone else."

She nodded, as if it made sense to refer to me and my body as "we."

"Anyway," I continued, "he'll be gone soon."

"Life is complicated sometimes."

I studied the half-moons of dirt beneath my fingernails. "Why do you think he's leaving?"

She pressed her hand over her mouth. "It's not my place to say."

"The no-gossip rule?"

She took my hand and stood up. "Perhaps if you open up with us, then we will do the same."

Opening up. My gaze rested on a pink rosebud, just beginning to spread its petals. I let my fingers brush over it as Mina led me toward the chive blossoms.

"Sprinkle those over the chicken," she instructed. We moved on to the orange nasturtiums. "Serve these with the salad, along with calendula petals. Thyme and savory flowers on the *champignon* tarte. Sugared rose and violet petals on your peach dessert."

She held my hand the entire time. After just a few weeks, I was well accustomed to her touch. Sometimes I even found myself reaching out to pat her shoulder or nudge her with my elbow or slip my hand into hers.

"Oh, I'm so happy you're staying, *ma chérie*." She squeezed my hand. "Now, can you remember all this, or should I write it down?"

"I'll remember."

Leaping over Fire

The next day, from afternoon through twilight, I cooked and sweated in the kitchen, keeping the door propped open. I downed three glasses of sauvignon blanc to calm my nerves, extra-jangled because, as Bao had informed me, this was the feast for the summer solstice. Apparently, Iva used to build a bonfire and oversee festivities. Somehow, my friends had faith I could fill her shoes.

I wondered if I *was* trying to impress my *bricoleur*. I thought about him as I tossed petals onto the food like confetti. Could I dare to grow closer to him? His departure would hurt more, but it would be an easy way out.

For the centerpiece, I chose roses for courage in life and love. I lit beeswax pillars that filled the grove with a warm, honeyed scent. I'd stuck a small white peony behind my ear, its perfume mixing with candle smoke. Above, the Milky Way leapt out, a ribbon dense with stars.

Once we were seated around the table, I poured an *apéro* of champagne, then Mina raised her glass to the night sky and said, "'The cosmos is within us. We are made of star stuff.'"

"Carl Sagan?" said Bao.

"Bien sûr."

When our champagne flutes were empty, I brought out a bottle of Beaujolais with the first course—cremini tarte—and with bated breath, I waited for my friends' reactions.

Raphaël closed his eyes for his first bites.

Mina winked at me. "Listen to him, Eloise."

At that he moaned. Orgasmically.

I broke into helpless laughter and dug in, feeling a rush of thanks for my friends, and for the tarte, buttery and flaky and baked to perfection.

By midnight, I was a flushed and happy hostess, having witnessed many moans over my food—and having drunk much more wine than usual.

Carrying lanterns, glasses of brandy, and the guitar, we all walked uphill toward the terraced meadows to make a bonfire. The castle stood dark against the starry haze, as if watching us live out our lives. Whether it was a benevolent or malevolent watcher depended on which part of the Otherworld I focused on. At the moment, I saw only beauty.

Still, part of me felt nervous. In the aftermath of my last fire, I'd been alone and half crazed in smoke from my burned-up life. And that had ended with sirens.

My *bricoleur*, it turned out, had lugged firewood up here earlier today. He'd set up a teepee of wood and kindling, encircled by stones and ready to be lit. Farther out were four inviting oak stumps to sit on.

When I set down my lantern, he said, "Light the bonfire, Ellie."

It touched me that he thought I was capable of initiating the ritual.

Still, a tremor ran through me as my mind returned to the fire in Denver. The night after I'd run into the pregnant girlfriend, I'd awoken at three a.m. from dreams of *merde* and *fleurs*, and on the spot, I scribbled out a CV. The résumé of ashes had felt like a riddle, so I'd taken a gamble, grabbed matches and fuel, then headed into my backyard.

I met Raphaël's encouraging gaze. "I'm not great with fire."

He pulled a piece of kindling from the pit. *"Bois de cœur. So rich in sap, a spark will light it."*

I took the heartwood, breathed in the mysterious scent of pine resin, then moved its tip over the lantern candle. When I laid it on the other kindling, flames spread, and soon the bonfire was blazing.

What a contrast to my last fire. That night I'd clutched the CV containing my melodramatic qualification: *I feel closer to flowers than to any living human.* No actual job experience or references. Not even my neighbor, a hermit retiree, would vouch for my green thumb, even after my gifts of bulbs and cuttings. I'd crumpled the paper, tossed it into a pasta pot, and after four tries, lit a match. My résumé had soon become ashes.

Mina handed us yellow-blossomed sprigs of Saint-John's-wort. "Iva had us throw this into the flames to let go of bad energy. To welcome new beginnings."

We tossed in the plants, watching sweet, piney smoke rise into the night sky.

Back in Denver, I hadn't stopped at the résumé of ashes. I'd thrown in my childhood artwork that I'd intended to frame for nursery décor. Onesies naively bought during my first pregnancy. The baby blanket I'd quilted for the second pregnancy for good luck. Sexy lingerie from my bridal shower. Files labeled Fertility Supps, Endo Diet, Energy Work, Acupuncture, Misc Alt Med, IUI, IVF, Scans & Tests, Laparoscopy, Therapy, Adoption. Lovers, children, family . . . *be gone, all of it!*

I leaned my head back to the summer solstice moon, imagining what this same moon had seen that night across the sea: a crazy lady—red eyes, tangled hair, spark-burned pajamas. But inside, I'd teetered on the edge, as if this job in France would be my last-ditch effort to preserve my sanity, avoid becoming a friendless, bitter old lady, a crone without love or wisdom.

Flames danced into the Provençal sky, orange against black. I could feel Raphaël's gaze on me, and my face grew even warmer.

Mina's voice broke the mesmerizing quiet. "Listen, you two." She gave us pointed looks. "Iva told us that *les amants* must leap over the bonfire."

In my peripheral vision, I caught Raphaël staring—a bit mortified—at the fire.

Mina let out a whoop of laughter. "Of course we wouldn't let you two catch yourselves on fire, would we? Look at that!"

True, the flames were leaping high, bright and hot, not welcoming to any *amants.*

"I'd wait until the fire has calmed a bit," Bao recommended.

Raphaël and I traded amused, somewhat awkward, glances.

I let myself take one last look back at the desperate woman I'd been in Denver, holding my picture books over the fire in the pasta pot. I'd been just about to toss in *Goodnight Moon* when sirens wailed and lights flashed. Behind my neighbor's window: her scrunched-up frown, her finger wagging in disapproval. Holding on to my single thread of hope—Les Jardins du Paradis—I'd made my way toward the firefighters as my old life smoldered.

Now, jasmine blooms whispered, *Let it go.*

The ashes of my old life drifted away. Here I was now, a flower whisperer in Paradise, surrounded by friends and a potential *amant.* I imagined the moon looking down, nodding in approval.

With some drama, Mina stretched, yawned, and walked over to kiss my cheek. "*Merci,* my dear. Everything was *magnifique.* Iva would be proud."

She pulled up Bao and interlocked arms with him. "We'll clean up the kitchen. You two relax."

Raphaël stood to protest, but she pushed him down.

As Mina and Bao walked downhill, my *bricoleur* and I lingered, heads craned back to the sky. Cradling his guitar, Raphaël finger-picked some playful jazz melodies, and when I asked about them, he answered with pride—songs of the beloved Romani-French musician Django Reinhardt.

Our conversation drifted from music to stars to firelight, souls to flowers to trees, animals to stream to stone. The elements of our days, our lives. What had I talked to people about in Denver? Politics? News? TV shows?

I didn't ask him about his upcoming departure, just immersed myself in the present. If one cannot fix something, one must find joy in the moment, right?

Raphaël and I sipped brandy and moonlight into the depths of night. I fed more wood into the fire, and he plucked guitar notes like stars. When dawn was brightening the east and the fire had calmed to coals, we stumbled to our feet.

I took his hand. "Want to take the leap?"

His eyes locked onto mine. *"Oui."*

Holding hands, we backed up, then ran and jumped over the coals, landing with laughter on the other side.

We walked downhill, skirting the flower château, past the compost area, into cedar groves. Passing the harpist, I clutched his hand tighter.

"Everything okay, Ellie?"

"The statues freak me out," I said, using the slang term *flipper*—less dramatic than admitting they *terrified* me, especially after my rule-breaking and *Les Dames Blanches* sighting and the poisoning. *"Vachement,"* I added with a wry grin, trying to lighten things up.

"Oh, you'll habituate to them." He leaned into me.

"Oui, bien sûr." I tried to keep sarcasm out of my tone—he seemed so sincere. Above the treetops, the turrets of the castle now evoked

secrets, nightmares, poisonings, prisons, disappearances, death, and dark fairy tales like Bluebeard's wife.

Would I really habituate? *A place of power. Power to heal or to harm.* How unnerving that this sense of wonder and danger could co-exist. Two sides of the same *médaille,* in Antoinette's words.

I said nothing more about my fears, focusing instead on the magic of this summer solstice, the beautiful *bricoleur* at my side.

When we reached the turnoff for my place, I whispered, *"Bonne nuit, mon chéri."* My tone was playful, but I'd wanted to call a man *mon chéri* ever since high school French class.

He kissed my cheeks, made firm lip-to-skin contact, longer than ever before. He fingered the peony petals in my hair, kissed them, then moved his lips to my earlobe—giving me delicious shivers. "Eloise, you have seduced me with flowers."

Laughter burbled up inside me—this was ridiculously romantic. I refrained from jokes about poison flowers and moved my own lips to his stubbled cheek.

I considered letting my lips drift to his—but no, this night had been too exquisite. Even though, in the eyes of ancient nature spirits, we were lovers, I couldn't risk pain and heartbreak.

So I pulled away and bid him *bonne nuit* and floated back to my treehouse.

"You have seduced me with flowers."

I slipped out of my clothes and crawled into bed. I crossed my arms, one palm on each breast. Peonies infused the air. I melted into the most decadent sleep.

Greeting each other at breakfast, Raphaël and I stretched out the cheek kisses. And when he served granola sprinkled with pink rose petals, I read it as a sign. We exchanged goofy grins through coffee steam while Mina scribbled memoir notes and Bao pored over a pocket guide to mushrooms.

After shit-shoveling duties, I headed for the medicinal garden, imagining my swim with Raphaël after work. It was a dizzy, tingly feeling—something I hadn't felt since, maybe, a middle school slow dance.

Were my soul-case and I ready for an actual kiss?

In my peripheral vision, I registered something in the mud of the riverbank—footprints. Small human prints.

Curiosity took hold and I veered off the path to investigate, stepping on stones to avoid scuffing the tracks. They were formed by bare feet. Unlike the smudged prints by the pond, these toe prints were distinct, the curve of the arch and the heel well defined. Not from an animal. And far too small for an adult.

The woodsprite. I imagined the sound of the mud squishing between tiny toes. It made my chest ache.

At the same time, my mind cleared. This was solid evidence that the girl was real.

I sat down on a rock, motionless, as if waiting for rare wildlife to appear. Nearby stood the mermaid statue that I'd thought had moved on my first day—but maybe it had been the girl.

Who are you? Why are you here?

I pulled the goddess booklet from my pocket and found the mermaid drawing while keeping an eye out for the girl.

```
Melusine, Goddess of the Springs. My father
was forbidden from entering the room where My
sisters and I bathed. He did . . . and I took
    revenge by trapping him inside a mountain.
   When our mother found out, she turned Me
   into a mermaid. I now protect the rivers.
   I do not regret leaving that man to die.
```

A common thread ran through these goddess descriptions—noble rage from a damaged psyche. I scanned the area again for the girl, resting my gaze on the INTERDIT sign atop the cliffs across the river. *Forbidden.* A threat? Or a warning? What if she'd gone there? She could be in danger.

I hopped stones to the opposite bank, then scrambled up ten feet to the ledge, noting a lack of footprints, although the gravel here might not show them. Up close, the sign looked old, with worn, weathered edges. Overgrown rosemary shrubs flanked a cave entrance, and as I brushed by, they released pungent scents.

Catching my breath, I peered into the darkness. As my eyes adjusted, I realized that although the entrance was small, just four feet high, it led to a taller, wider tunnel, going deep into shadows.

I stepped back, mystified, and glanced at my surroundings, wondering if there might be a more detailed sign in the foliage. A few feet to my right, I glimpsed something hidden in the shrubs. I pushed aside the rosemary and saw a bronze plaque.

HERE LIE THE BONES
OF THOSE WHO BROKE THE RULES.

My heart froze. I fingered the rosemary blossoms, breathed in their clarity. But their whispers were clear too: warnings. Something dangerous lurked ahead.

What if the girl had ventured inside?

"Bonjour?" I called into the darkness. A ghostly chill drifted out. "Is someone in there?"

No answer. But of course, she wouldn't answer. She was well practiced at hiding.

Her prints were real. She was real. And the powers in this garden were adamant: Children were forbidden. Breaking the rule would not end well for the child.

I had to make sure she wasn't in there. Realizing I'd need a light source, I clambered down the steep rocks, hopped from stone to stone across the river, and grabbed a solar lamp from the path. Then, panting, I crossed back over the water and scrambled up to the cave.

I glanced over my shoulder at the sun-sparkled stream, and beyond, over the tree canopy, at the château guarding its secrets. I thought of Eve in paradise, unwilling to follow the rules, and Pandora, unable to keep the box shut.

I stepped around the FORBIDDEN sign and ducked into the void.

My solar light flicked on. The lamp emitted a tiny glow, weaker than a flashlight, but my eyes soon adjusted. I followed the tunnel, walking more upright as the ceiling height increased to a comfortable six feet.

I ran my hand over the cold stone walls, noticing the air growing cooler and damper, and the tunnel angling downward. I felt uneven stone beneath my feet. In places, I ducked where the ceiling lowered. From time to time, I glanced back, but there was no one, nothing, just me and my breath and pulse.

Where was this tunnel headed? How far did it go? How long would this light last? It had only had a couple of hours of morning sunlight to recharge. Why was I risking this job? And my friendships?

I stopped in my tracks. Flouting the rules was a betrayal to my friends.

But a child could be in danger.

Standing there, deep in the earth, I wondered: Who did this child belong to? What would I do if I found her?

By now, the rosemary's warnings had faded. There was a distinct absence of flower whispers. I shivered in the cold silence. I forged ahead, curving this way and that, deeper and deeper. I was just about to give up and turn around when I took a step . . .

. . . into nothing.

I fell.

17

The Oubliette

It was a long fall, long enough that I understood I could die at the bottom.

At times in the past, I'd been scared of death, knowing my genes wouldn't live on. I'd failed at a key definition of life: the capacity to reproduce. I used to fear being forgotten, not even living on in the heart of an adopted child. After years of failures, I'd shifted to almost welcoming death. At the lowest points, I'd wished for it.

Now, all I could think was: *I want to live.*

With shocking impact, I landed on my feet. My legs bent at the knees, but my whole body felt the smack, from my soles to my crown. I dropped onto my side, cradled my head in a fetal position.

I tasted dirt, grit. I lay there, breathing, aware of my heartbeat. Were my bones shattered? Was I paralyzed? What to do next? Weren't you supposed to wait for help if a spinal injury was possible? But who would come? At least my brain was working well enough to worry about this stuff.

I opened my eyes. Complete darkness. The solar lamp must not have survived the fall. Or else a concussion had blinded me.

I tried moving. First my fingers. They worked. Then my toes. All good.

Pushing myself to sitting, I felt sore throughout my entire body, but only a three or four on the pain scale. I pressed my abdomen to check my internal organs. Just the achy aftermath of a fall.

I brushed my hands over the ground, located the lamp, fumbled with the switch. No luck. I shook it. Nothing. I took out the batteries and stuck them back in. Still, darkness.

Dropping the lamp, I stood up, reached out a shaky arm, and felt the stone wall. I stretched my fingertips upward along the wall but only touched stone. I moved my hands over the surface, which formed a circle around me, maybe five feet in diameter.

A hole.

Raising my arms along the wall, I forced myself to jump. My legs protested and buckled. Again, I jumped and my hands still touched only stone. I tried again and again, cursing with each landing.

So I was in a deep hole, at least eight feet deep, probably more, but no more than fifteen because wouldn't that have resulted in at least a broken bone?

Trapped in the dark in a hole in a tunnel.

No one knew where I was.

No water, no food.

I was dressed for a summer's day, in shorts and a T-shirt. It had to be in the fifties in this underground cave. But it wasn't an ordinary chill. There was something phantasmic about it, as if ghosts were drifting by, as if this were a tomb.

HERE LIE THE BONES
OF THOSE WHO BROKE THE RULES.

I hugged myself, rubbed my goose-bumped arms, wishing for flower whispers. Maybe their voices couldn't carry all the way down here, deep underground. Silence pressed in on me.

I could almost hear, beneath my breath and heartbeat, the hiss and hum of bones, voices from the dead, ghosts from beyond, trapped with me.

Biting back tears, I tried to stay rational. When would my friends start searching? They'd notice I wouldn't be at lunch— but sometimes I ate lunch at home. It wouldn't be until Raphaël came to our after-work swim that alarms would be raised. They'd spend the early evening looking for me. Had I left footprints leading to the cave entrance? Probably not. I'd been walking on rocks, preserving the child's footprints as evidence. And once I'd climbed the cliff, the gravel might not hold prints.

At what point would they think of the tunnel? Would that even occur to them? Or would they assume I'd just left . . . like Amber did? Had she been trapped in this hole too? When the next gardener came, would Antoinette say that I was simply no longer here? How long would it take to die of thirst? What would it feel like?

Panic crashed over me.

I clawed at the smooth stone, desperate for a handhold.

Mon Dieu. An oubliette.

The French origin was *oublier—to forget.* I had fallen into a medieval dungeon, where prisoners were left to die.

Supernatural punishment? The consequence of defying the FORBIDDEN sign? Words from the Goddess of the Gardens surrounded me like cold mist, eerie whispers from beyond.

```
One may argue that the Goddess is, in Her most
  powerful form, death-bringer. Remember this.
```

I yelled for help. *"Au secours!"*

My voice echoed back.

For a long time I yelled, until I was hoarse.

I wanted to live. I wanted to live in moments of dappled light and babbling streams and herbal teas and crème brûlée. I wanted the comfort of Mina's arm around me, the odd nature gifts from Bao, the quiver in my core from Raphaël's eyes. And so many flowers!

Eventually, I paused, my throat raw. I wished for just a sip of water. Would my shouts even travel outside? Tears and snot streamed down my face, and soon I was gasping in guttural sobs.

My last moments on earth couldn't be alone in the darkness of a tomb.

Time passed.

Memories drifted in and out.

Scenes from my old life floated to the surface.

Back in Denver, I'd fallen into a kind of oubliette.

My mom had raised me to identify problems and find solutions. But despite extreme efforts, there had been no solution for me . . . and there was no solution to being stuck in this oubliette.

Still, I wanted my mom here. I drew my knees up and buried my head in my arms like a child trapped in a nightmare.

I want my mom. I want my mom. I want my mom.

I conjured her up—sensible, short gray hair and sympathy wrinkles. Until this winter, our phone conversations had followed the same pattern, circling through the labyrinth haunted by my own Minotaur: infertility.

She'd suggest IVF or surrogacy, and I'd remind her of the astronomical costs; then she'd suggest gluten-free or paleo or keto diets, and I'd remind her I'd tried all that; then she'd suggest another go at adoption, and I'd remind her of the heartbreak of a failure—on par with miscarriage. *Antidepressants?* she'd suggest. No, I'd respond, they could hurt a fetus. A therapist? The good ones weren't accepting new clients or didn't take my insurance. Focus on the kids on my caseload? But they weren't *mine*!

The conversation would end with me telling her I felt trapped in a dark place with no way out. And she'd whisper in the tenderest of tones, *"There's always a way out, honey. Always."* My poor mother. Fixing her child's pain was an impossible task. Still, when we're trapped in a dark place, we just want our moms, don't we?

And here in the oubliette, I realized what I wanted: my mom to sing me lullabies . . . not to solve anything, but to comfort me, to bring me back to that intimacy of mother and child. I wanted a mother's love, distilled to its essence: *I am here and I love you.*

I was supposed to be loving my own child, singing and comforting her. But since there was no child, I closed my eyes and sang to myself.

> *How can there be a cherry that has no stone?*
> *How can there be a chicken that has no bone?*
> *How can there be a story that has no end?*
> *How can there be a baby with no cryin'?*

For a long time, I sang, tears streaming down my face. There was something pure about this sorrow, no resentment or blame or rage. Just compassion and a simple acceptance: Life had not gone according to plan, and that was okay.

Now, if I could just get out of this oubliette so that I could live it.

I sang and sang. Every so often I wondered how much time had passed. Minutes? Hours? I finished the last verse of "Scarborough Fair."

> *Remember me to one who lives there*
> *She once was a true love of mine.*

I stopped singing, licked the tears.

A voice broke through the darkness, a voice from above, a small, thin voice: *"Encore!"*

❧

I opened my eyes. The darkness was no longer complete. A faint light shone from above. I looked up, searching for a face to go with the voice. Nothing. Just the weak light—maybe from a solar lamp?

Gathering my wits, I shouted for help. *"Au secours!"*

"Chante!" The voice commanded me to sing.

A little girl. The woodsprite?

"Who are you?" I called.

No answer. "Are you still there?"

"Oui."

"Can you get your parents?"

No answer.

"Your uncles or aunts?"

No answer.

"Are you still there?"

"Oui."

"Can you get someone to help?"

No answer.

"Please?"

No answer.

"Are you still there?"

"Oui."

I was about to ask her to move closer, show her face . . . which made me realize this little girl was already too close to the precipice. "Stand back. Don't fall in. Are you being careful?"

"Oui."

How could I convince her to get help? "Still there?"

"Oui." And then, "Sing!" And then, "Please!"

I weighed my options. She was a stubborn child who wanted a song. She had all the power in the situation. I had one bargaining chip.

"If I sing, will you get help?"

"*Oui.*"

I sang "Scarborough Fair" again. At first my voice shook, weak and tired. What was I doing, trapped here and forced to sing to a child? At the mercy of a child *who wasn't supposed to be here.*

Little by little, my tone changed into something tender. A child was listening—a child who wanted to hear me, a child who held my fate in her hands.

I found myself singing *as if.*

As if she were my own little girl.

As if I were telling her: *I'm here and I love you.*

When I finished, after a beat of silence, she said, *"Merci."*

"You're welcome. Will you get help now?"

"*Oui.*"

Silence. "Are you there?"

No answer.

"Be careful!"

No answer.

Once again, the darkness was complete.

I waited. And I waited.

And I sang.

18

The Woodsprite

he minutes ticked by, slow and excruciating.

Would the girl get help? From whom? What if La Patronne or Antoinette discovered her?

And then there was light.

And footsteps.

And a man's voice calling out, "Eloise?"

"Bao?" I yelled. "Is that you?"

"Eloise! *Oui!* I'm coming!"

Moments later, a bright beam shone on me. I squinted, blinked. He pointed the flashlight onto his face, and there was Bao, kneeling at the edge, twelve feet above.

"Bao! Thank God!"

He lowered a rope and harness—tree trimming equipment. "Are you hurt?"

"I'm okay."

"Good. Put on the harness while I brace the rope."

Trembling with gratitude, I buckled the harness.

"Okay, now I'm lifting you up, Eloise."

In fits and starts, I rose, circling and swinging and trying to control my ascent, reaching for the wall with one hand, and with the other, gripping the rope. Shaking with relief, I reached the top, grateful for Bao's strong arms pulling me onto solid ground.

I hugged him, smelled his sunshine and sweat and citrus soap.

Catching his breath, he patted my shoulder. "It's okay. You're okay." He offered me a water bottle.

"*Merci.*" I chugged it, wiped the water and tears from my chin. Disoriented, I looked around for the girl.

"*Alors*, let's go." He stuffed the equipment into a rucksack. "Okay to walk back?"

"I'm fine."

"Want me to get the others?"

"Really, I'm fine. I just need to rest."

He kept an arm around me as we walked up the dark passageway. I felt stiff and sore, and my legs dragged. Bao's flashlight shone on the walls. Who had made this tunnel . . . and why? Who else had gotten trapped in the oubliette?

I kept my questions to myself, overwhelmed with gratitude for Bao and the sunlight ahead and the warm, fresh air wafting inside. I kept saying, "*Merci, merci, merci.*"

This kind, reserved scientist had become my hero. And the mystery girl *who wasn't supposed to be here* had become a heroine of sorts.

It wasn't until we walked past the INTERDIT sign, into the blazing sunshine and rosemary-scented air, that I asked, "The little girl—is she yours?"

Bao's forehead wrinkled. "What girl?"

"The girl who came to get you. Don't worry. I won't tell Antoinette."

He tilted his head. "I'm not sure who you're talking about, Eloise."

"I'm worried about her."

Shaking his head, he said, "I don't understand."

I rubbed my face. "How did you know I was down there?"

"I heard singing. In English. I deduced what had happened. I got rescue equipment."

"But there was a girl."

"I'm sorry, Eloise." A pause. Looking pained, he pressed his lips together. Eventually, he said, "Maybe it was a hallucination?"

I sighed, then let him lead me across the stream by the elbow. I was ready to show him the girl's footprints, but they were gone, scuffed by his larger ones.

As we walked to my treehouse, flower voices welcomed me back to the sunlit world. I took in every petal, every leaf, every butterfly and birdsong, so much light and color and pattern. I'd been in the oubliette for eight hours, and my brain felt overloaded now with so much intricacy.

"Can I bring you food?" he asked in his soft voice.

"*Non, merci,* Bao. I'll have cookies and tea." I gave a weak smile. "There has to be some labeled 'Recovering After Nearly Dying in an Oubliette.'"

"Good idea."

I hugged him goodbye, swung by the *toilettes*, splashed water on my face, then walked up the swinging rope bridges. I headed straight to the library and found a jar of *calme*. It was between *érotique* and *poussière d'étoiles*—stardust—both of which piqued my curiosity. I hadn't dared try either yet. What if *érotique* made me spend *all day* with that shower nozzle? What if stardust sent me on the wildest of mushroom trips?

I made myself a small cup of *calme*, checking that it smelled like the familiar rose, chamomile, and lavender blend.

I grabbed a handful of sugar cookies topped with rose petals— which I'd made yesterday, a lifetime ago. I sat on the balcony eating cookies, sipping tea, and processing. What flowers might come from the *merde* of being trapped in an oubliette?

And it hit me: Pain of all sorts had separated me from my parents, my ex, my old friends. I would *not* let that happen with my new ones. I'd let pain bring us closer. I'd open up. I'd reach for Mina's hand. I'd offer Bao gifts in return for his nature treasures. And with Raphaël, I'd move from cheeks to lips. Why would they trust me with their secrets if I wouldn't trust them with mine?

Peace swept over me as the *calme* took effect. Yes, from here on out, I'd let my pain be a force of bonding, not isolating.

I took another sip and saw a face in the trees, just twenty feet away at eye level.

The girl.

First came the impulse to thank her.

Next, the impulse to question her.

Next, the urge to protect her.

Throat still raw, I sang "You Are My Sunshine," "Here Comes the Sun," "Keep on the Sunny Side." I noticed the sun theme and realized how mind-shattering it had been to be stuck in darkness.

The girl settled in the crook of three branches like a squirrel, listening.

I was an average singer. I could carry a tune and had a decent range but mixed up words and hummed lines I'd forgotten. She seemed content with my mediocrity.

I tried not to stare at her dark curtain of hair, her golden face, her crown of asters. She was too far away for me to see if there was scarring around her eyes or if one of them was glass.

She raised a pair of binoculars, aimed them at me.

Still singing, I looked away as if cloud gazing and moved on to "Octopus's Garden," aware of her examining my face close up.

The binoculars, I realized, most likely were Bao's. Had she taken them in secret, as she'd done with my books? Or had he loaned them to her? If so, why would he lie? Well, if she belonged to him, it made sense he'd hide her.

Were Raphaël and Mina covering for him?

After "Morning Has Broken," I stopped singing—my voice was exhausted and I worried she'd get bored.

As if in the presence of a wild animal, I stood up with caution, then went inside for my children's books. Back outside, I propped them beside the cookies.

What are you doing, Eloise?

I caught a glimpse of her watching me. I went back inside, leaving the door ajar, and lay down on the fainting sofa, just five feet from the open window.

I closed my eyes and waited.

Soon footsteps came up the bridges. I opened my eyes a crack, and through the window I saw her, a girl of about five or six, creeping toward the table. She grabbed some cookies and the books, then sat down. After a moment, I stood up and watched her flip through pages and munch cookies as she sat cross-legged on the balcony floor. Mahogany hair fell over her face.

She turned the pages of *Where the Wild Things Are* in order, talking to herself in dramatic French about *les monstres*. There was something indescribably moving about this child pretending to read—something about the way she widened her eyes and said her throaty r's and pursed her lips to say her *eu*'s and imitated an adult's voice with her tender one.

This was not a feral child. This was a child who had been read to with care. I imagined Bao would make a good father figure, teaching her about wildlife.

I dared to walk to the window for a closer look.

Just a few feet away now, she pushed her hair from her face.

I stared, transfixed. There was no scarring. Only smooth, fawn-soft skin and brown eyes and rosy cheeks. This was not the girl from the photo.

Yet the binoculars were Bao's, I was sure of it. They hung at her neck, and every so often, when a bird rustled in the trees, she raised them to her face.

When she'd gone through all three books and finished the cookies, she stood up.

I had to do something. I rushed from the window to the open doorway, and at the movement, she jumped.

Our eyes met. Hers widened in alarm.

"Wait!" I said, running outside . . . but she was sprinting down the bridges.

"Merci!" I called after her. "For saving me!"

She kept running, quite fast, considering the swinging surface beneath her.

"Be careful!" I called.

She kept running.

Let the child go, Eloise!

"Come back!" I had to find out more about her. Even as my words tumbled out, I balked at my desperation. "I'll read to you! I'll sing!"

She turned to look back. She'd reached the ground now, wavering by the base of the tree. "Promise?"

She doesn't belong here.

I heard myself call out, *"Oui!"*

She might be in danger here.

"Where do you live?" I asked.

"On a farm. Outside the wall."

"How did you get in?"

"A hole."

"Do your parents know you're here?"

Panic gripped her face. "Don't tell anyone! Don't tell La Patronne! Promise?"

Do not promise this child anything, Eloise!

Mouth dry, I swallowed. "Promise."

And at that, she ran into the woods.

I absorbed the idea that she came from outside the gardens. She knew about La Patronne, who clearly had a reputation in town for prohibiting children. And maybe locals heard rumors about the child-hating goddess? I had no idea.

First step, make sure the girl is safe.

Second step, make a boundary: maternal feelings forbidden.

19

Shaken Up

After the blue hour, I headed toward the dining grove, my body less sore thanks to a warm, honeysuckle-scented shower. The sliver of moon was setting and the sky was rich indigo, its first stars materializing. As I glimpsed the cave entrance across the river, I felt a tingle of fear, a memory of the oubliette. Farther on, the stone goddess with her harp and ghoulish smile only magnified it.

It was a relief to enter the candlelit clearing where Raphaël and Mina sat at the table adorned with late-blooming poppies, and Bao was setting down a steaming pot. I let it soak in: the yellow and purple print of Mina's dress, the scents of nutty soup and pines, Raphaël's smile.

When Mina saw me, she leapt to her feet, wrapping me in a hug that smelled of hibiscus and mint, her favorite iced tea blend. She planted kisses on each cheek. "Eloise! Thank goodness you survived! Are you hurt?"

"Just a little sore."

Raphaël rushed over and took my hands. "Bao told us what happened. You must have been terrified."

Before I could answer, Mina embraced me again. "Oh, *ma chérie!* We wanted to see you, but Bao said you needed rest." She kept a firm arm around my shoulder.

Raphaël asked, "How are you feeling?"

"Better, now that I'm out. Thanks to Bao."

"That's my job," Bao said with a modest grin. "Taking care of wildlife."

"We wildlife do tend to disregard signs."

I considered mentioning the girl—Bao must have already mentioned her—but no one brought her up. Apparently, this fell into the category of *things to ignore.*

Well, I'd promised her I'd keep quiet. And I kept my promises to children. If Bao claimed she was a hallucination, so be it.

He humbly pointed out the dishes, made from ingredients he'd foraged himself. Fresh watercress sprinkled with toasted nuts and deep red berries. Roasted chanterelles topped with herbed cheese. Spiced acorn-porcini stew with chives and crème fraîche. Sautéed dandelion greens. A duck egg omelet sprinkled with wild onion blossoms. A whimsical forest feast, smelling earthy and ancient, of trees and rivers.

I was moaning over the chanterelles when I remembered my epiphany. *Open up.* I downed my glass of mead, then opened my mouth to see what would come out. "So, I applied for this job after I ran into my ex-husband and his pregnant girlfriend."

The others perked up, curious, as I rambled on. I attempted to make it a funny story, exaggerating my bloody foot and the girlfriend's perfection, but it came out disjointed since I avoided my defective uterus. There wasn't context.

No matter. They appreciated my efforts. Mina clucked. *"Alors,* now you're available for a better man!" She eyed Raphaël, not so subtly.

I plowed onward through my past, offering a lighter, cleaned-up version of reality, skirting around my reproductive woes. I was heading down the tunnel, only willing to go so deep. But even with my sputtering descent, our conversation turned more intimate.

Out of the blue, Raphaël said, "Lucie was a dancer."

"Lucie?"

"My ex-girlfriend."

Ah, the one he'd made the vardo for.

He continued. "She danced through life. She only wanted happiness."

"So sad, what happened." Mina shook her head. "Poor thing."

Raphaël lifted a shoulder. "And the ones she left behind . . . it wasn't easy for us."

I offered a look of sympathy and chose words without ambiguity. "Is she deceased?"

The trio nodded, faces solemn.

So the vardo wasn't a result of pining over a breakup, but honoring a death. I wanted more details, but then Mina brought up her family in rural Senegal—she'd left sorrow in her wake too. She talked about sisters and brothers she'd lost contact with. They were still children to her—she had no concept of them as adults. Her voice held a mix of sadness and nostalgia over their shenanigans.

"Did you put all this in your memoir?" I asked.

"*Oui!* And it's almost done."

I tried to remember how to say, *I can't wait,* and settled on, "I expect it with impatience," to which Mina beamed.

When we were on the dessert course—wild strawberries drizzled with honey from this very garden—I turned to Bao, basking in that buzzy, lovey feeling after so much mead. "I noticed the photo of a girl on your shelf."

He glanced at Mina and Raphaël, whose faces softened.

"Her name is Vivienne," Bao said. "She turned twenty-six last month."

Cricket songs rose and fell as I absorbed this. "A family member?"

"Someone forever linked to me."

Again, silence.

"A friend?" I ventured.

He shook his head. "But I think of her daily."

I wanted to ask about her scars, who she was to him. But he hadn't pushed me to explain why Josh and I had divorced. And no one had pushed Mina to detail why she'd fled Senegal.

The back and forth of friendship was returning after all these years. It felt good to fall into this rhythm, this intuitive drumbeat of human connection.

Years earlier, it had been like this with Gaby, something like falling in love, but with a friend. What we'd had together felt somehow more real and deeper than even my marriage with Josh. Our friendship had begun in a waiting room as our husbands jerked off to online porn, our bond born of laughter and tears. A pang hit me, this ache of missing her, this fierce regret.

I ate my last strawberry and let go of my questions, trusting that at some point my friends would enlighten me.

After dessert and brandy, Bao and Mina left for their snug homes, but Raphaël lingered. "Can I walk you home?" he asked, like a teenager. He was gazing at me—really *gazing*—as if my face were a full moon or a crystal ball. "I mean, you might still be shaken up from all that darkness."

"*Oui, merci.* I am very shaken up."

And I did feel shaken up . . . in a glittery way, like a snow globe.

He offered his hand and I took it. His hand was soft and rough at once, calloused and tender. He held my hand with the perfect grip—not tight or sweaty—just cupping it.

Electricity zinged between our skin.

As we walked, we drifted closer, until the sides of our bodies were touching. I slowed the pace, savoring the magic. My whole self, every nerve ending, was coming to life. *I expect this with impatience!*

When I laughed, he asked, "What's so funny?"

"I haven't felt this way in a long time."

"Me neither."

I'm ready. For a kiss, at least. I'd seduced myself with showers and flowers. My brush with death had increased my sense of urgency.

Raphaël and I reached the path that led to my treehouse, then faced each other. I soaked up the scene: the Milky Way, the night breeze, the scent of rose, the river music.

I stepped closer, until we were just inches apart. He reached his hand behind my neck, and his fingertips sent glorious shivers down my spine. I moved my head toward his . . . and we were kissing.

Raphaël kissed me as if we were a miracle.

Our lips touched, softly at first, his lower lip grazing mine, petal against petal. Then, like a tendril of vine, my tongue explored his, and his, mine.

We closed the space between us, formed a little cave of warmth and breath and skin. He tasted ambrosial, all nectar and honey, and my lips grew plump against his, as ripe as the cherries in our orchard. We kissed and kissed and crested waves from whimsical to wondrous, passionate to playful, starry to silky.

His hands cradled my face, brushed along my neck, down my shoulders, over my hips. Everywhere he touched lit up. My body became flowers, a garden in bloom after a harsh winter.

I wrapped my arms around his waist, pulling him closer, moving my mouth over his jaw, his neck, his earlobe. I wanted to continue our kissing on my sofa, draw it out and sink into it. I wanted his bare skin against mine, on velvet, in candlelight.

I asked myself, *Are you willing to risk this?*

Oui!

"Want to come up?" I murmured.

"Oh, Eloise." He trailed his fingertips down my arms and squeezed my hands. Then, as though it were a struggle, he let go and stepped away. "I can't."

I bit my lip. "You can't?"

"I'm sorry."

"Oh." I waited for an explanation.

None came. My chin quivered, my hands shook. I had the urge to smash something. I'd finally felt ready for kissing, and now . . . rejection.

"I'm so sorry, Eloise. I have to go."

In a trembling voice, I whispered, *"Bonne nuit."*

"Bonne nuit, Eloise." Shoulders slumped, he turned and walked away, disappearing into the shadows.

Once I was alone, the tears came.

That kiss had meant everything to me.

Apparently, not to him.

❦

I dropped to the earth, leaned against a pine trunk at the edge of the path, and touched a finger to my lips, still sensitive, still craving his. Jasmine whispered comfort, and river sounds lulled me. I hugged my knees to my chest and took a quivery breath, gathering strength for the walk home.

And then my eye caught something gleam in the underbrush, by the light of solar lamps.

Crawling closer, I saw it more clearly: a bronze dagger.

I picked it up, ran my fingers over its cold, ornate surface, thinking it could date back to the nineteenth century, based on the patina. The hilt was shaped like a goddess, robed from the waist down, a belly pooch hanging out, breasts visible, one hand holding a dagger, the other at her chin, as if she were thinking, *Hmm, whom shall I kill next?*

My pulse quickened as I pressed my fingertip to the dull point. Had *Les Dames Blanches* dropped this on their twilit walks? Had it been an accident . . . or a warning?

The dagger fairly vibrated with a dark energy. My inclination was to drop it, but what if the woodsprite came across it? I couldn't leave a weapon lying around. I shook myself, then brought it home, where I set it on a high shelf in the library, out of a child's reach.

I boiled water for a tisane, shaken. My hand hovered between COURAGE—in light of the eerie dagger—and SWEETENING SORROW—in the aftermath of the failed kiss. The silent message behind the dagger terrified me, but Raphaël's rejection felt worse, threatening to plunge me back into a lonely, sad, bitter crone state.

I drizzled honey into my tea, felt the plants melt into me—holy basil, Saint-John's-wort, passionflower, rose, cacao. Little by little, it sweetened my sorrow over the kiss that had felt so luscious, so breath-taking, so *right*. Our first and last kiss. A bittersweet thought.

Later, I lay in bed, wondering how the hell I'd face the *brico-leur*. I stayed awake into the depths of night, torturing myself by reliving the kiss.

And all the while, part of me tensed from the chill emanating from the dagger. It was potent, like black smoke, or the musky scent of deadly angel's trumpet, a dark force wafting up from the library, through the branches and into my open window.

With the bedspread pulled up to my chin, I waited for morning to come.

❋

At breakfast sunlight shone through pine needles and coffee steam. I struggled to let go of my unease, breathing in the comforting scents of toasted baguettes and almond croissants and apricot confiture. I'd avoided the dagger entirely this morning, not even entering my library. And I'd avoided the memory of the kiss, at least until now, confronted with Raphaël's empty chair.

The longer it stayed empty, the more my anxiety grew. By my second café au lait, I was nearing panic. Was he too scared to face me after the awkwardness? Had he just left the gardens without a goodbye? After all, he'd warned me he was leaving sometime soon.

Bao was puttering in the kitchen and Mina reading at the table, as if this were a normal morning. She flipped through a book about trees, jotting notes in her spiral notebook.

"So, what are you doing, *mon amie?*" I tried sounding casual, but my voice came out hoarse.

"More revision notes." She smiled, marked her page with a sprig of lavender, then tucked the notebook into her pocket and the pen into her headscarf. "Fact-checking baobabs."

"Oh," I said. "Interesting." *Act normal, Eloise.*

Chest tight, I kept glancing at the path, willing the *bricoleur* to appear. "So, where's Raphaël?"

"It's the weekend." She dipped her tartine into her café au lait. "Free time."

I clutched my cup. "Where did he go?"

"Sometimes he sneaks out for the weekend."

It was hard not to take this personally. "Why?"

She shrugged and munched her tartine.

I could understand her lack of response. When you're in a four-person family in a locked garden, privacy matters. Talking behind each other's back could destroy everything. Still, I cursed the no-gossip rule. "Maybe he's left for good." My voice broke.

"Oh, Eloise," she said softly, "I'm sure he'd say goodbye first."

Bao emerged from the kitchen with his mushroom tea. "Why don't you ask him about it when he gets back?"

I forced a nod. I'd become used to spending free time with Raphaël, distilling flowers, having picnics, soaking in the river. This weekend stretched ahead, lonely and barren.

And then it occurred to me: What if Raphaël had disappeared like Amber? What if he was in a danger that Bao and Mina couldn't see? Made some transgression we didn't know about? Worse, what if he was paying the price for me taking the dagger? After all, he'd been nearly killed before by poison, probably meant for me.

If the Goddess of the Gardens, in some form, was spying on us, she'd know about Raphaël and me—our *apéros*, our swims, our kissing. She'd know that hurting him would hurt me. Her note warned of dire consequences. Raphaël's disappearance could be a consequence.

A sick feeling settled in the pit of my stomach. Yet Mina and Bao just calmly ate. They were kind and well-intentioned but stuck in their habit of turning a blind eye to the disturbing parts of the gardens. I wondered about previous employees here—maybe Amber's disappearance wasn't an anomaly.

I couldn't interrogate my companions—they'd only clam up—so I conjured up a nonchalant voice. "So, no *bricoleur* this weekend. Hopefully, nothing breaks." As if it just occurred to me, I said, "Was the previous *bricoleur* as talented as Raphaël?"

"Bricol*euse*." Mina corrected me with a look of pride. "Handy-*woman*."

"And yes," said Bao, "she was quite competent, although not as creative as Raphaël."

"French?" I ventured casually.

"Canadian," said Bao. "Mary Martin. A bit older, in her sixties."

I nodded. *Keep it casual, Eloise.* "Guess she's enjoying retirement in Canada."

"Who knows," said Mina with a light shrug.

I made a sympathetic sound. "Too bad you don't keep in touch."

After a beat, Bao said, "She left abruptly. No time to leave us her address."

"Oh," I said, keeping a tone of mild interest.

Mina sighed. "Unfortunately, she had a disagreement with La Patronne."

"The details were vague." Bao sipped his tea. "Something about Mary being disloyal."

I said nothing. So Mary Martin had left the gardens without a goodbye, just like Amber. And no one had heard from her since, just like Amber.

Mina puffed air from her cheeks. "We liked Mary, but she could be hardheaded, right, Bao? It was probably for the best. And Raphaël has been an incredible replacement."

Sometimes I felt so close to my friends—my new *family*—but at the moment, I couldn't relate to them in the slightest. It appeared that foul play hadn't occurred to them. Beyond all reason, they chose to see only the happy, healing parts of these gardens and ignore the dark underbelly.

Later, washing dishes, I asked, "You really think Raphaël just took a weekend getaway?"

My vulnerability must have come through, because Mina pulled me in for a hug. "Oh, *ma chérie*, you care deeply about him, don't you?"

I said nothing, afraid I'd start crying.

"I'll take you bird-watching this afternoon, Eloise," Bao said, patting my shoulder.

Mina gave me a tender look. "And you can make flower art with me."

I breathed out. *"Merci, mes amis."*

Maybe distracting myself was the best course of action for now. Still, I couldn't help imagining the medieval punishments my *bricoleur* might be facing—poisonings, oubliettes, daggers, or worse.

And I couldn't help reliving that exquisite kiss. The devastating aftermath.

My questions and fears swirled together, cold and dark and hidden.

20

Lavender Tears

Instead of working in the gardens, I baked brownies in an attempt to let go of worries I could do nothing about. A mental health day of sorts. I craved chocolate, warmth, and comfort food.

I brought the steaming pan from the stone kitchen to my treehouse, and on the deck table, I arranged twelve chocolate-cinnamon brownies on a cake stand and covered it with a bell jar. On impulse, I set up the picture books beside it, with a pot of cooled tisane for *l'amitié*—friendship.

The flowers offered me encouragement, the chamomile surprisingly loud for such tiny blooms. Their wishes echoed through the garden. *Find the girl, talk to the girl, be with the girl.* I was vague on their motives, which made me worry they knew something I didn't—that the girl was in danger.

I thought of the dagger, a warning message, still sitting high on the bookshelf, exuding creepy energy. The threatening note left by the Goddess. The icy reaction of Antoinette when I'd mentioned the woodsprite.

My eternal weak point: helping a child in need, no matter how hopeless the situation, no matter how much it drained me. Hurt me. There were children I'd tried so hard to save through my job, only to be met with frustration, even devastation.

But what if this girl truly needed saving? I had to meet her, understand what she was doing here, who she belonged to, assess the risks.

I sat on a deck chair, peering into the forest, sipping tea and letting chocolate melt on my tongue. Through leaves, I glimpsed the crumbling castle turret, distant and dark against the bright morning sun. After an hour, I considered bringing everything back inside, but despite myself, I stayed.

The taste of cinnamon and chocolate made me think of another dark-haired girl, Emilia, who was the same age as the woodsprite. In my old life, I'd watched her grow on social media, from big-cheeked baby to bright-eyed toddler to curious preschooler. I'd "love" each post and then I'd cry. Sweet little Emilia had ended my most important friendship and caused me so much pain.

Children caused me pain.

Parts of me fought inside my chest. The part that wanted nothing to do with the girl in the gardens. And the part that needed to protect her. And another, elusive part that just wanted to follow the flowers' advice and be with her.

Risk the pain, whispered the violets.

I took another bite of brownie. Six years earlier, Emilia's mother was the one who'd taught me the magic of cinnamon with chocolate. After crossing paths at the infertility clinic, Gaby and I had quickly become best friends . . . and then she got pregnant. IUI had been her only hope, and it had worked, and I was happy for her. She and her husband had immigrated from Oaxaca, and spent most of their meager income on infertility treatments. Without documentation, they hadn't qualified for adoption or even fostering. That was why I could spend time with Gaby as her belly swelled, why I threw her a baby shower with pink balloons and cinnamon hot chocolate.

Tasting the zing of cinnamon, I remembered the mix of anticipation and dread I'd felt in those weeks before Gaby's delivery, knowing that her child would change everything. Oddly, the feeling was similar to how I felt now, waiting for the woodsprite on my treehouse deck.

It was all for naught. I waited the entire morning, but she never appeared. At noon I ate a third brownie and headed down the bridges to meet Mina for the mysterious flower art.

Maybe I'd scared off the girl. Maybe her parents weren't letting her come anymore. Maybe she'd never return. Maybe that would be for the best.

But maybe she'd fallen into the hands of the Goddess of the Gardens.

Find her, the flowers whispered. *Find her.*

Mina and I sat at the sun-warmed stone table in the yellow garden. The day had melted into one of those Provençal afternoons of soft blue skies and honeyed light captured in a Cézanne painting.

"Feeling better about Raphaël?" she asked gingerly.

I didn't want to go down that road again, so I just nodded. I'd have answers in a couple days. *Patience, Eloise.*

I ran my hand through the rainbow array of blooms in our basket. We'd chatted with the flowers as we gathered them—they seemed eager to play their part.

My eyes rested on Mina in her tangerine headscarf and brass earrings. She looked so concerned, I gave her a grateful smile. "So, how do we do flower art, *mon amie?*"

"However you want. I like to make mandalas." With deft movements, she arranged white peony blooms in a circle on the table, filling in the top half with asters and harebells and flax in all shades of indigo. In the bottom half, she added dried grasses to form a cone-shaped house. "*Et voilà.* My childhood home." Playfully, she added twig stick figures. "Me and my brothers and sisters."

A wistful look swept over her face. This was her before, I realized. Before she married the old man. "*Magnifique, mon amie,*" I said.

This flower mosaic reminded me of art therapy I'd witnessed before leaving my play specialist job. I'd been working with nine-year-old MacKenzie and her support team of therapists. She'd been traumatized after witnessing her bio mom's boyfriend commit horrible acts of domestic violence. The mother refused to press charges, and despite court orders, she stayed with her abuser, exposing MacKenzie to daily terror. So the court placed the girl with a loving foster family.

I remembered holding back tears as she'd drawn the phases of her traumatized young life with crayons, then narrated them, then had the therapist narrate them back. Those intent gray eyes, those eczema-pink cheeks, those ginger curls. I'd wanted to fold her into myself, hold her and hold her. The therapy had worked wonders. I'd never forget how she'd floated outside, light as a butterfly, eyes sparkling silver.

"Your turn, *ma chérie,*" said Mina.

I tried to recall details of the therapy, realizing I'd need to improvise. "This will be a story."

"Good, I love stories!"

Taking a long breath, I arranged honeysuckle blossoms into the shape of a bridal veil inside a ring of cheery marigolds. And I began: "Eloise grew up an only child and wished she had sisters and brothers to play with. When she got married, she was so excited to be a mother. She imagined a house full of kids."

I scooted clockwise, giving Mina a playful hip bump.

And then I clammed up. Why would anyone want to know my life story? There was nothing brave or noble about it—just an amicable divorce, no deaths of any legally defined humans. But a voice rose inside me: *When you want a baby more than anything, even though she dies when she's just three inches long, you* need *to mourn her, damn it. You need to mourn them all.*

I wondered about Mina's life story, her memoir. Hers would be one that I'd want to read. That the world would want to read. But mine? Rage would infuse it. The reviews would be two-star, about how whiny and privileged and angry I was. More than concerns of boring or offending people, I feared I'd reveal an ugly, unfixable part of myself. The secret part that cursed pregnant women.

A shameful example: Back home, when I'd seen a news story involving an impoverished, desperate woman in a war-torn country clutching her baby—when a decent human would feel moved to donate or help—I'd felt only fury. Why did *she* deserve all the sympathy? At least she had a baby. At least she had someone to love so deeply and unconditionally . . . and someone to love her back in equal measure. At least she had the chance to fulfill her biological purpose of life on earth. At least she wasn't an evolutionary dead end. Where were sympathetic news articles about what *I* was going through?

Of course my rage was always tempered with shame. I couldn't spew my toxic energy all over my nice, normal, fertile, socially conscious Denver friends. After things had ended with Gaby, I'd hidden the growing darkness inside me, and instead I skimmed the sunny surface and, little by little, bowed out of more and more parties and showers and potlucks and coffee dates. Until one day I had no friends. And not long after that, no husband.

I glanced at Mina beside me, waiting with patience and openness. The flowers, too, urged me onward. With a sigh, I made a new circle with the deepest purple peonies and poppies. Inside, I arranged four reclined stick figures on a bed of black flowers.

"It was very hard for Eloise to get pregnant. And every time she did, her babies died inside her. She kept their names secret. Iris, Violet, Sage, and Zinnia."

With a deep sigh, Mina pulled me close.

It felt strange to speak my children's names aloud, to another human. Since the world considered my babies medical waste—and would have claimed it too early to determine their sex—I'd kept them hidden. Only I knew that Violet and Zinnia were the first two girls, then came Sage, the boy. Then Iris, who had come on the heels of the failed adoption of Melvin from Honduras.

I added one more stick figure, standing up. "And there was Melvin, who she tried to adopt, but then he was gone too."

I paused, blinking back tears. The red tape had unraveled on his end after I'd fallen in love with his shock of black hair in the photo and decorated his room with a quetzal bird theme and bought our plane tickets. The aftermath felt like holding a lifeless baby in my arms.

We scooched to the left and I made a circle of pine needles and bloodred geraniums. Inside were tears of lavender blossoms.

"Eloise was sad and angry." I forced myself to go on. "She wanted her babies so badly and she lost them all and it hurt so much." A long breath. In. Out. "So she smashed her dishes. She smashed her marriage. She smashed her friendships. She smashed her life."

Mina kept her arm around me.

Next, I made an airplane of sage leaves flying over an ocean of asters. "And then she flew to the gardens. Here she felt free and full of hope. Here she can heal."

I turned to my friend and leaned my head against hers, letting our temples rest together. "*Alors*, now you can narrate this back, *mon amie*."

As she did, a strange sensation came over me, hearing her tell my story. I felt Mina's tenderness for Eloise, who had tried so very hard to make a family, put her whole heart and soul into this endeavor.

Mina even remembered each of my children. Hearing her say their names lifted the floodgates. For a while, we hugged, and then I sniffled and wiped my nose. "Want to try?"

And she told me the flowered story of her life.

"Once there was a girl named Mina. She liked to read books and write stories and play with her cousins and brothers and sisters. Then her mother died and she felt sad. When she was twelve, her father arranged for her marriage to an old man. Nine months later, she was in labor. But her hips were too small and her body didn't know what to do, and after days of pain and blood, she gave birth to a dead baby. Little Mina almost died too. She knew that if she didn't leave, this would happen again. She ran far away. It took her years, but she made it to the Gardens of Paradise."

She echoed my words. "And here she can heal."

A new round of tears stained my face. *Mon Dieu*, how I loved this brave girl named Mina. As I narrated her story back, my voice shook with emotion.

At the end, we surveyed our stories, hers taking up half the table's circumference, and mine the other half. The heartbreak of our lives, joined together and transformed into flowers.

We held each other until she broke the silence. "We are sisters."

"Sisters?"

"We understand each other."

It felt as if she'd given me a giant present wrapped in a shiny bow. As I wondered how I could possibly reciprocate, I found myself asking, "When can I read your whole story?"

"Soon."

"How long have you been writing it?"

"Oh, twenty years."

"Wow. And it's nearly ready?"

"The truth? It's been nearly ready for a decade. I can't stop fixing a word here, a comma there. Writing it has lifted a weight off me. But there is still some left."

"What would help lift the rest?"

She watched a lizard dart through our flowers. "Sharing it. I've read it to the plants, of course. They give it five out of five stars." She tossed her head back in laughter. "Now the question is, what will humans think?"

"Have Bao and Raphaël read it?"

She glanced in the direction of their homes. "No."

"Are you scared?"

"Terrified."

"Maybe you could share it with me first. And if that feels right, you can share it with Bao and Raphaël, and if that feels right, then with more people."

She made a face. "You really want to read it?"

"More than any other book in the world." I was not exaggerating. "I expect it with impatience, *mon amie*."

The brownies were all intact when I returned to the treehouse. I ate one, watching the foliage, trying to accept that the *esprit des bois* might never return . . . but that felt utterly *wrong*.

Find her, whispered the flowers, a chorus of chamomiles rising.

I dug deep into my battling emotions. I wanted the girl gone. I'd come here to escape children. I couldn't bear failing to save another child. So why didn't I give up? What *was* it about this girl?

I sang "Parsley, sage, rosemary, and thyme," imagining blossoms carrying my song over the wall to her.

As the sun set, I sipped friendship tea and my mind went back to art therapy with MacKenzie. Her therapist had said the next steps would be helping her integrate who she was now, after witnessing the abuse, with who she was before.

Tears stung my eyes. Even recalling what had happened next probed a tender wound.

MacKenzie had been on a healing path when, three months later, the court returned her to her bio mom, who had met court requirements for her own therapy. Yet for weeks after that, the woman had missed her appointments, and when she finally brought MacKenzie in, the girl was visibly retraumatized, dark circles beneath downcast gray eyes, bleeding eczema. In a weak voice, she whispered, "He's back."

I'd quit my job that day.

When my mom had asked why, I told her I couldn't work with children while I was dealing with infertility. But it was so much bigger and deeper. It was knowing I'd give my right arm for a child—I truly would. It was knowing I was *this* close to scooping up MacKenzie and riding into the sunset. It was knowing I'd go to jail if I did, while her bio mom could damage her, over and over, and *still* have her returned.

It was enough to transform a person into a wrathful goddess.

I wiped my tears and breathed in the scent of lavender. Channeling a woman wise in flowers, I held MacKenzie's silver eyes in my mind and sent her strength to reclaim her spark.

Reintegration.

How could I integrate my own before and after selves?

Before the infertility and pain and loss.

After the infertility and pain and loss.

I thought about little girl storyteller Mina and grown-up writer Mina, how they were reconnecting, here and now, in the gardens.

I thought about little girl Eloise wishing for a family full of children and adult Eloise understanding she could accept what the universe offered and find another way. Beyond all reason, my mind landed on the brown eyes of a certain woodsprite.

Of course the girl might not come back. And there was the question of whether I could protect her—but deeper still: If she did return, could I handle it, knowing that at any time she could leave? Could I trust that my heart would survive?

I headed to the kitchen to make a chocolate-themed dinner for Mina and Bao. We could all use some theobromine—food of the gods—to release happy neurotransmitters. The star of the feast would be chocolate-chili *mole* that I'd learned by heart from Gaby. The cinnamon and cloves and raisins and toasted almonds and twenty other ingredients made her feel close.

Later, when Bao and Mina moaned over my dinner, I wished Gaby were here. Maybe even her daughter too.

And, of course, Raphaël. Fear for him skirted the edges of my consciousness. Our predecessors had both disappeared under questionable circumstances. He could be next.

There was nothing I could do but wait until Monday to see if he returned. And if he didn't, what would I do? Ring the bell and hope Antoinette would let me out? Find the hole in the wall and run the hell away?

Dread fell over me at the thought of what awaited.

Past midnight, I grabbed the jar of tisane labeled COURAGE. As it brewed, I paced around my library with pent-up energy. My gaze landed on the maintenance Raphaël had done—making the windows open more smoothly, oiling the door hinges, tightening loose screws. He loved puttering around under the guise of fix-it tasks that morphed into his personal *bricoleur* duties to me.

Mon Dieu, I missed him.

I missed the feel of his lips on my cheeks, lingering. The way his hands grazed my arms, my back, my shoulders. And even though we'd only kissed on the lips once, I missed it. I wanted to do it again and again, for longer and longer. I wanted his lips, soft against mine, exploring my neck and collarbones. I wanted him folding his body into mine, his hands cupping my face, his fingertips trailing my skin, leaving shivers in their wake.

The more I relived the kiss, the more certain I was that he'd felt it too. But something had stopped him. Maybe something that had nothing to do with me.

I ran my fingers over his handiwork on the bookshelf and noticed, with a start, that the dagger was gone. My stomach torqued. Had the woodsprite taken it? But I'd put it on a high shelf. She would have had to drag a chair over to reach it.

I racked my brain for when I'd seen it last—earlier this afternoon, so it must have gone missing during twilight or later. Had I somehow misplaced it? Or had someone come to reclaim what was hers?

A tremor ripped through me. It felt violating, the idea that the Goddess of the Gardens had invaded my home, walked across this very spot. I imagined the figures in white spying on me, watching my comings and goings, peering at me as I slept.

Frantic now, I took a candle lantern and ran from room to room, searching. Jasmine blooms whispered: *Go to bed. Leave it.*

But I couldn't. The courage was already flowing through my veins. I kept searching, the lantern casting huge, strange shadows. Anyone could be hiding there. Or lurking in the woods, lying in wait.

No sign of the dagger in my atelier or bedroom. Heart pounding, I climbed to the topmost structure, the dressing room with the mirrored vanity.

In the flickering candlelight, a thick piece of paper rested beside the mirror.

I stepped closer and gasped. The note had been *stabbed* with the dagger. The tip of the blade was lodged a half inch into the oak surface, piercing the paper. I pressed my palm against my chest.

Leave it, whispered the jasmine. *Leave it.*

The lantern trembled in my hand, making shadows quiver, huge and gaping. How could I not read the note? How could I leave this grisly still life untouched, in my own home?

Scars

I pulled the dagger from the wood, which took effort. Someone had put extreme force behind it. With a shudder, I set it down beside the lantern, imagining the rage fueling this strange act of violence.

When I unfolded the impaled paper, out fell a blossom. Milky yellow, veined in red-purple. Poisonous henbane. My throat constricted as I read the typewritten words.

Dear Eloise,

One must remain loyal to the Goddess at all costs.

Remember that healing may turn to harming whenever I wish.

Perhaps the time has come to tell you about the Furies.

We are the Goddess of Vengeance and Justice.

In this manifestation, We wear long black robes. We weave venomous snakes into Our hair. We carry brass-studded whips. We cheerily oversee punishments in the Underworld.

"For what crimes?" you might ask.

Breaking Our simple rules.

Respectfully,

The Goddess of the Gardens

Fear prickled my neck, and I looked out the open window, as if murderous Furies could fly right inside. Whoever was behind the typewritten letters and booklet had plucked goddess attributes from across cultures, combining them into her own bizarre, dark version.

Trembling, I picked up the dagger, studied the goddess on the hilt, her spine-chilling smile that said, *Whom shall I kill next?* I re-read the letter, wondering what twisted mind had written it.

Without warning, blood dripped onto the paper, red and blossoming like a rose. I sucked in a breath and looked for the source.

But wait.

The blood was dripping from my own hand. I must have nicked it with the dagger blade. I ran my finger lightly over the tip and the edge. Whereas before, the blade had been dull, it was now as sharp as a scalpel. The edge had sliced my palm, diagonal along the lifeline.

I pieced together the events. Someone had found the dagger on the shelf, sharpened it, then moved it here as a warning. She might have even used the knife sharpener in my atelier. Anger tore through me at the thought of someone invading my sacred space for such a brutal task.

I let the dagger fall with a clang and then stumbled to the armoire. I grabbed a white washcloth and wrapped it around my hand, applying pressure, feeling the sting, watching the crimson stain grow. My heartbeat quickened as I noticed my trail of blood across the room, glistening now in the candlelight.

Once the bleeding had slowed, I examined the wound—not deep enough for stitches. I tossed the henbane into the trash can, then picked up the dagger, unsure what to do with it.

My fear for Raphaël grew. What if he'd been . . . *disappeared*? What if he'd gotten warnings that he hadn't heeded? What if he'd broken a rule? Or what if he was paying for my sins?

And what about the woodsprite? She embodied a broken rule. I hadn't seen a glimpse of her for days now.

I stuck the dagger and bloody note into the drawer, then walked back to the library, carrying the lantern, trying not to shiver. Thankfully, I had no symptoms of poisoning—the dagger must not have been dipped in anything, and any henbane residue on the blade must not have been significant. I cleaned the wound and wrapped my hand with a cloth napkin. Tomorrow I'd find some actual bandages and Iva's herbal antibiotic.

For now, on the fainting couch, I sipped one cup of courage tea after another, willing its powers to flow through me.

On Sunday a layer of pearly clouds hung over the gardens, a relief from near-constant blue skies, a gloom that matched my mood. I spent the morning in my atelier, in the flow of my creations. Little by little, the flowers pulled me out of my dark place.

Following their guidance, I blended a new tisane with violets, poppy, skullcap, linden blossoms, yarrow, hawthorn berry, and rose. I channeled compassion as I thought of the mother laying flowers over her baby's grave, of La Patronne's nightmares, even of the angry goddess with her threats.

I labeled the jar HEART-MENDING. Something light inspired by the darkness of the note and dagger. After all, my job was turning *merde* to *fleurs*, blood to beauty, harming to healing.

That afternoon I showed the jar to Mina and explained that La Patronne could take it to prevent nightmares.

"You're wearing Iva's shoes," said Mina with a wink. "They look good on you."

I'd explained the filling-one's-shoes idiom, but she only sort-of got it. *"Merci."*

On the verge of handing her the jar, I realized a conversation with Antoinette could be a way to get information.

Ghosts didn't leave footprints and daggers and notes. Humans did. There had to be real people behind these *bizarreries*. And the personal assistant had to know about it. If Raphaël had been *disappeared*, she'd know about that too. I'd have to be subtle, catch her off guard, tap into her humanity.

Hugging the jar, I said, "I'm giving it to Antoinette myself. And she can pass it to La Patronne."

Mina raised an eyebrow. "Well, Antoinette would prefer it if I—"

"Listen." I raised my chin and channeled my best Antoinette impression. "Of course, normally, one must follow the chain of command. However, one must make an exception for the good of La Patronne."

Mina laughed, linked her arm in mine. "Well, she might be annoyed, but what can she do?"

I grinned, thankful my friend wasn't protesting. Maybe I evoked sympathy, with my heartsickness and bandaged hand, which I'd told her was a simple accident. "Let's go, *mon amie.*"

At the front gate, she rang the bell, and after a short time, Antoinette emerged from the castle, dressed in a linen pantsuit the color of crème caramel. She unlocked the inner gate, breezed through, and locked it behind her—as if we might dart through and invade the castle.

She wasn't wearing sunglasses today. Her eyes were naked, her look of disapproval crystal clear. "One is supposed to come alone."

"*Desolée,*" said Mina, not looking very apologetic. She pulled a folded-up paper from her skirt pocket. "Here's our grocery list, Madame."

I studied Antoinette's bare face as they talked about restocking jam and honey, lotions and potions, and Mina jotted down notes.

When they finished, I handed Antoinette the jar labeled HEART-MENDING. "La Patronne should take this before bed to prevent nightmares."

She gave a clipped *merci* as she took it. Her steely eyes were as guarded as ever, and the grooves between her brows ran deep from pain or fear or anger—it was hard to know, since she offered so little of herself.

Letting vulnerability into my voice, I said, "Please tell La Patronne I understand how it feels to have a broken heart. For years on end."

A curt nod.

It struck me how much Antoinette knew about my own heartbreaks. "You and La Patronne listened to my cover letter, right?"

She nodded again, her expression softer.

I'd poured out my guts in that letter. Since I'd burned the résumé to ashes, I'd tape-recorded the cover letter, thinking it might give me an edge over the competition. Assuming these people in Paradise were old-school, I'd dug out my ancient tape player and only cassette, which contained my mom's lullabies. With a sentimental pang, I'd recorded over them—I had no child to hear them anyway.

Mina gave me a confused look and broke the silence. "What cover letter?"

"I can recite it for you." Even many weeks later, I still remembered it by heart, in all its melodrama. Before they could decline, I launched into the letter, hoping it would tap into Antoinette's fragile thread of empathy.

"Your job ad intrigued me," I began, staring at her, "especially the part about absolutely no children. Flowers are my children, the only ones I will ever have." I steadied my voice. "I've grown them from dead flesh and blood. If you provide me with a composting bucket, sawdust, and seeds, I will make flowers, per your job description." I paused to calm the quiver in my chin. "I will put my entire heart and soul into this task."

In my peripheral vision, Mina put her hand to her mouth in some mix of astonishment and sympathy. But I kept my focus on Antoinette. Her rainy eyes shone, and her expression cracked a bit.

I wanted information, but now, more than that, I wanted to let our pain connect us. I recognized something in her, something I could relate to, something beyond sorrow—an echo of resentment. This life she'd been given was not what she'd wanted. Had she ever had children? Had she longed for them? Had she ever been married? Did she long to be? Did she have family? Friends? Was she close to La Patronne? Was she lonely?

If I hadn't come here, I might have still been stewing in bitterness. I'd even felt a lonely resentment during my marriage. Oddly, the closest I'd been to Josh was the night we'd decided to separate, the night of the failed enema, when we'd realized we were buried in a pile of crap. Infertility, and all the shit that came with it, had pushed us apart rather than bringing us together.

Which made me think about Raphaël and me. The kissing. The rejection. His leaving. If he did return safely, then did we have to push each other apart?

I studied Antoinette. Clearly, she was well practiced at keeping everyone at arm's length. Beneath the veneer of cool elegance was a heap of *merde* that she hadn't transformed. Maybe I could help her. After all, this was my impossible marvel.

Gently, I said, "Antoinette, maybe you could also use some heart-mending tea."

Emotion flashed in her eyes. Then she composed herself. "The state of my heart does not concern you."

"But you know I can relate, right?"

Her lips pressed together.

I thought of the vehemence in her warning about the consequences of a child in the gardens. She must have had some trauma around children too. Taking a tentative step toward her, I said, "If you ever want to talk, I'm here for you."

A heaviness undercut the buzz of insects.

Beside me, Mina shifted her feet and cleared her throat, obviously uncomfortable with the direction this was going.

Antoinette looked away, face flushing. "Occupy yourself with your own onions," she snapped.

My onions? I could only assume she meant something along the lines of *mind your own beeswax.*

Breathing out, I pressed my hand to my face, then noticed her staring at my bandage. "I got cut. With a dagger."

I sensed Mina's shock but kept my eyes trained on Antoinette. Her cold gray eyes gave nothing away. She said only, *"Tant pis."* Too bad.

"I found it on the path near my treehouse," I said slowly. "I'm not sure what to do with it."

"Put it back where you found it," she said with an icy glare. "These things do not concern you."

She turned to leave, but I caught her arm with my bandaged hand. "You know that Raphaël is planning to leave," I said.

She wrenched her arm away. "Of course." She paused. "He is making a mistake, but he is free to go."

If he'd been disappeared, nothing in her expression betrayed it. "Have you been looking for a replacement?" I asked.

"Not yet," she said in a wary voice.

I tilted my head. "Maybe you could invite Mary Martin back to fill in. I'm sure she misses it here."

Mina drew in a breath beside me.

Antoinette raised her chin. "Mary Martin was disloyal. La Patronne will not invite her back."

"Oh, too bad." I kept my tone light. "She might be bored in retirement, back in Canada—"

"Enough!" Antoinette's facade shattered. "The woman is never coming back. She is gone. In a dark place. Just like the previous gardener. Now, *ça suffit.*" *That's enough.* Her words sliced like blades.

She turned on her heel, the jar of tea under her arm as she unlocked the interior gate and stormed up the stairs, vanishing into the château.

I hugged myself, hearing the echo of her words. *A dark place.*

Metaphorical . . . or literal?

Once the door slammed shut, Mina widened her eyes. "Oh, *mon amie*, what's gotten into you?"

I leaned my head back at the castle turrets, releasing a long sigh. "I just want to understand what's going on."

Mina took my hand. "I'll tell you. Antoinette is the shadow to your light. The darkness has hardened inside her for decades."

She spread her other arm wide toward the jasmine and honeysuckle. "You've tapped into the gardens' power to heal. Just like Iva." She paused. "Iva said that Antoinette can only access their power to harm. The most you can do is ease her pain with teas."

"I wish there were more."

After a beat, Mina slung her arm around me, lightened her expression. "Ready for bird-watching with Bao, *mon amie?*" she asked, ushering me along the path. "It will be wild," she added with a wink. "Prepare yourself."

Bird-watching with Bao not only distracted me from the enigma of Antoinette and the absence of Raphaël, but was, indeed, *wild*—or at least a surprisingly captivating activity.

I'd always associated bird-watching with earnest retirees, but now I got a glimpse of its allure. It gave you a stealth mission. In addition to birds, I watched for the woodsprite.

Bao and I did spot all other manner of forest creatures—snakes, frogs, rabbits. Every so often he'd find a pretty pebble or snail shell, which he'd gift me and I'd admire, then stick in one of my khaki pockets.

From his own vest pockets, he pulled out two small sketch pads and an array of colored pencils, and together we drew birds. He was the gentlest of teachers.

We rested by an oak, sipping bottles of homemade hibiscus-mint tea. He offered me a spring roll, translucent and filled with rice noodles, pork, cucumber, cilantro, and mint. Then he held out a tiny jar of peanut dipping sauce. Of course I moaned as I bit in, and he laughed.

"This is incredible," I said. "Seriously, Bao, why did you leave your family's café?"

He stared at the treetops. "I wanted to be in nature. With animals and plants and fungi, rivers and rocks and soil. Away from children."

"What?" I froze, mid-bite. "Why?"

"One day at the café, a little girl was dancing around. She seemed so happy, I didn't say anything, even though the place was busy and she was in the way. I was carrying a tray filled with bowls of pho."

I listened with my entire body, holding still. Bao rarely spoke so much at once and, even more rarely, revealed anything about his past.

"Normally," he continued, "we would have served them at just the right temperature. But the restaurant was busy and backed up. In the kitchen, the bowls of pho had cooled before I could deliver them. So I'd microwaved them. But for too long."

He stopped speaking and collected himself. His entire body shook with emotion.

My own muscles tensed. I could guess where this was headed and wanted to hug him, tell him he didn't have to continue.

He kept going. "I was hurrying as I brought out the tray. I didn't see her twirl in front of me." His voice faltered. "I ran right into her. Tripped. Soup spilled all over her face, into her eyes." He sniffled, tears welling. "She was in the hospital for a long time. One of her eyes got infected. She—she lost it."

I reached out, put my arm around his shoulders.

"I destroyed her perfect face." His voice broke. "I destroyed her life."

I thought of the girl in the photo, the scar tissue, the glass eye. *Vivienne.*

He pulled a tissue from his pocket, wiped his face, blew his nose. "And that's why I came here."

I patted his back and thought of things to say: *It wasn't your fault; her parents should have been watching; shit happens.*

He released a long sigh. "I could no longer look at children's innocent faces. I felt an unbearable guilt." He wiped more tears. "I gave my savings to her family for reconstructive surgeries. I couldn't live with myself. It was a nightmare. I hoped I could forget everything here in Paradise."

I took his hand, searched his face. "Can you?"

"No." He rubbed his eyes with the heel of his other hand. "Vivienne's family forgave me. Vivienne forgave me. That's why I have her picture. They give me updates."

"And how's she doing now?"

"They say she's fine. But I can't believe it. They're trying to make me feel better."

I looked at him. I thought he'd just been a quiet naturalist, but his whole life had been built around this single tragedy.

The hand the universe had dealt him. "That picture—when was it taken?"

"A year after the accident."

"She looks happy."

"I've looked at that picture thousands of times, and each time she looks more beautiful to me. I feel like . . . in an odd way . . . she's my daughter. Even though I've only seen her in person once. The day it happened."

"Maybe she really is fine, Bao."

I thought of the stories we tell ourselves—the stories we build our lives around.

The story I'd told myself that my friends in Denver had abandoned me, when in fact I'd abandoned them. My sex toy friend? She'd texted me afterward, but I'd been too embarrassed to reply. The story that I was a sexless old crone. The shower spray alone could attest to its falsehood. The story that I could only be happy in life by being a mother. I'd had plenty of moments of soul-lifting joy these past weeks.

And the story of Gaby—*oh, Gaby.*

I released a breath. "I came here because of the no-children rule too. I've tried everything but can't have my own. I used to think my entire life was pointless."

I met Bao's eyes, full of empathy. He pulled something from his pocket and handed it to me—a white feather, pure and hopeful.

Running my fingertips along it, I felt invisible wings spread. I rose above the old stories, seeing rivers of possibility flowing before me.

I spoke in a voice that didn't sound like mine. Lower and firmer. "We need to let our stories go."

A bird fluttered past—black plumage with iridescent purple and green, and a bright yellow beak.

"Look, a starling!" he said.

I raised my binoculars to watch it land inside a tree hollow. "Is that yarrow in its beak?"

"Starling males adorn nests with fragrant plants to attract mates," said Bao in his naturalist voice.

"Seduced by flowers."

He went on to elucidate the many talents of starlings.

And just like that, our heart-to-heart was over.

Back at the treehouse at sunset, the three-day-old brownies remained untouched under the bell jar, beside the books. A sad still life.

I thought of my mom saying, *"There's always a way."* And my advice to Bao about letting our stories go. Words sprouting shoots. I made some *esprit clair* tisane. *Clear mind.* Or *light spirit.* Or maybe a mix of both. I breathed in the steam of rosemary, holy basil, and spearmint.

I munched on a brownie, sipped tea, and let it lighten and clear my mind—which drifted back to the moment I'd held Gaby's newborn as she whispered, "Oh, my Eloise. One day you will be *una mamá chingona.*" One bad-ass mom.

But I couldn't handle watching her breastfeed—the way Emilia locked eyes with her mother as if she were everything. The way Gaby's dark, shiny veil of hair fell over the baby, just the two of them creating their own world.

I'd told myself I was romanticizing it—some women hated breastfeeding, some didn't have enough milk, some got horrible infections. Still, watching Emilia grow up would only hurt more every year. So I'd made excuses and canceled plans. Regret consumed me, but I'd told myself our friendship was an impossible task.

Now, sipping *esprit clair*, my shame dissipated, leaving only clear-eyed love. I calculated that Emilia would be starting kindergarten in the fall. On an impulse, I ran to my library, opened the stationery drawer, and pulled out some old, yellowed postcards with photos of flora and fauna. I wrote the first one to Gaby, in our signature mix of Spanish and English, asking to be her daughter's eccentric, Francophile *tía*. The next one, to my mom and dad, thanking them for their nurturing. And next, to Josh, non-snarkily wishing him well—after all, he'd been through hell too.

I realized I knew my grumpy neighbor's address in Denver, just next door. I wrote her a postcard telling her it was never too late to plant flowers. I signed that one with affectionate *gros bisous*—big kisses. Then I tucked aside a bluebird card for Bao.

Tomorrow I'd give the mail to Mina to give to Antoinette to stamp and send off. Thinking about the postcards flying across the ocean gave me a sense of freedom.

At the blue hour, I stationed myself in the dressing room atop my treehouse and peered out the window, watching the river path where *Les Dames Blanches* had appeared before. Where I'd found the dagger, now inside the drawer with the blood-stained note.

Soon I registered movement far below on the riverbank— glowing white figures, three of them, drifting along like ghosts. *Les Dames Blanches.*

I craned my head out the window, wishing for binoculars. Once again the figures were cloaked and hooded, faces hidden.

They paused at the turnoff to my treehouse grove, heads bent, as if searching the ground for something . . . the dagger? I bit my lip. Antoinette had told me to put it back where I'd found it. *Merde.*

When the white glow vanished around the bend, I flipped through the goddess booklet, looking for clues to understand what the hell was going on. The macabre illustrations brought out the dark facets of these goddesses but led me nowhere.

I closed the booklet, shook myself. *Ignore the* bizarreries, *Eloise.* Still, I couldn't help watching for more glimpses of the trio through the indigo light. I whispered to the jasmine blooms, asking them to protect Raphaël, wherever he was. And the woodsprite, whoever she was.

Behind the Waterfall

aphaël wasn't at breakfast on Monday morning.

My heart sank and fear loomed. The sky weighed gray and heavy, drizzling a steady rhythm. Someone—Bao or Mina—had strung a canvas tarp to the trees. Rain tapped overhead as I sipped Vietnamese coffee, creamy and sweet with condensed milk.

Despite the gloom, I tried to stay light. I pulled the postcard from my pocket and handed it to Bao. "For Vivienne."

His surprise softened into a pensive expression. "*Merci*, Eloise. I just might write her."

We drank coffee in quiet camaraderie, but whenever I glanced at Raphaël's empty seat, unease swept through me.

I regarded my friends' faces over croissants and bowls of plump apricots and granola. They showed no sign of worry. Bao was telling Mina how lichen was a symbiotic combination of algae and fungi, and she was musing over how to use it as a metaphor in her memoir.

Remembering the gifts stashed in my other pockets, I pulled out muslin bags of *amitié* tisane. Friendship. I'd made it Sunday morning, using Iva's recipe as a base but tweaking it to fit with my friends. I also had one for Raphaël as a peace offering, but it stayed in my pocket.

"*Merci,*" I told Mina and Bao, handing them the bags. "You've made me feel like part of a family."

"Of course, sister." She wrapped me in a giant hug.

Bao breathed in the scent of the tea, looking moved. "We're glad you're here."

"Me too." I refrained from asking about Raphaël, even though he was front and center in my mind. Instead, I said, "It's mostly Iva's recipe, but I've been experimenting more with my own."

"What kind?" asked Mina.

My gaze landed on my *bricoleur's* empty chair. "The latest is called: Reducing Angst About Your Missing Former Potential *Amant.*" I used the word *angoisse* for angst, which felt extra melodramatic in French.

She and Bao glanced at each other, passing invisible messages. She turned to me. "Raphaël returned late last night. He's sleeping in now."

Relief swept over me. He was safe. Then anger swelled—I'd worried for *nothing.*

As if seeing inside me, Mina said, "It's okay, sister. When he wakes up, talk to him."

After breakfast I moseyed over to Raphaël's caravan. The drizzle had turned to cool mist. I whistled under my breath, telling myself I'd do my composting duties, then get on with my day. If he came out, I'd talk to him, although I cringed at the awkwardness that would ensue.

Of course his *toilettes* structure was gorgeous—carved wood painted in swirls of gold and burgundy and forest green. I opened the polished wood throne, took out the waste bucket. I couldn't quite grasp my feelings toward Raphaël at the moment—a mix of relief, sadness, and anger. I wanted to cry and scream and fall into his arms all at once. Just when I thought I was moving on, letting go . . . I found myself overwhelmed before a pile of *merde*.

I had a bad track record for dealing with shit. After the last miscarriage, my doctor had suggested another procedure to get rid of my endometrial lesions and cysts. The night before the surgery, I was supposed to do an enema to clear out my guts, but I couldn't get the damn thing in. Josh had been playing *The Legend of Zelda*, riding his horse, Epona, through the countryside. He'd been no help. He finally paused the game and said, "I think it's time to give up."

He'd meant not only our baby quest but our marriage.

I left Raphaël's *toilettes*, scrunching my nose and carrying the bucket of sawdust and *merde*. I slowed as I passed the caravan, wishing I could just knock on his door and throw my arms around him. But he'd rejected me. He'd left without a word. His message was loud and clear.

Knock, knock, knock, whispered the flowers.

But no. There was another voice inside me, an echo of Josh's words that night.

"I think it's time to give up."

Words I could never forget. Words that had ended my marriage. Words that had brought out the monster in me—after years of loss and loneliness that was what I'd become. A monster. I cringed, remembering how I'd thrown the enema at Josh in response. Then he'd cried and I'd apologized and sat stiffly beside him. With an odd detachment, I'd watched him weep, wondering what was wrong with me. I couldn't make a baby. I couldn't bond with my husband. I couldn't even use an enema. I was, in all ways, full of crap.

The vardo door creaked open. Raphaël appeared in his boxers, rubbing his eyes, half awake. I took in his bare chest, broad shoulders, biceps. All that muscle and warm skin, sunlight reflecting off soft hairs. Again, I had the urge to run into his arms, breathe in his smell, kiss his lips, pick up where we'd left off.

He smiled and said, *"Bonjour,"* in a groggy voice.

"Bonjour." I stopped there, not trusting the chaos inside me. Anything could spew out—tears, shouts, or kisses.

Throat aching, I jogged away, the bucket banging against my leg.

Back at the compost heap, panting and sweating, I poured out the bucket's contents, jabbing at them with a pitchfork, trying to imagine how the hell flowers might grow out of this mess.

By midday I still didn't feel ready to face Raphaël, so I made myself a Nutella-baguette sandwich and hibiscus tea at my tree-house. The mist had drifted away, replaced by gossamer light through leaves. Bad weather in Paradise was as fleeting as my moods.

In the afternoon, I cleared out scum from the ponds, with frogs and fish for company. After work I was heading home when I spotted my *bricoleur* sitting on a rock by the river.

"Eloise!" he called, motioning me over.

I hesitated. Part of me wanted to run home. Part of me wanted to yell at him. Part of me wanted to hurl myself into an embrace. I forced my legs to walk toward him, slowly. He moved in to *faire la bise,* and I offered only air kisses.

"Ça va?" he asked gingerly. *How* am *I? Really?*

I fought the urge to walk away and hole up in my treehouse.

Be honest, Eloise. Be vulnerable. Be real.

Don't be a monster. Don't throw the enema.

"Hurt," I said. "Hurt that you left so suddenly." I stared at a pair of mallards shaking their tail feathers. "And I was worried something happened."

"Oh, Eloise." He blew air from his cheeks. "I'm so sorry. I never meant—" He ran a hand through his hair, then rubbed it over his face. "My situation is complicated."

I waited, feeling off-balance.

"It was a last-minute decision to go. Unexpected. Nothing to do with you, I promise. I was in Lyon. I have commitments there. I should have explained." His words sputtered out, all stops and starts. "It wasn't fair to you, Ellie."

"*Merci.*" I waited for more details.

None came. "I really missed you," he said, looking full of regret. "*Vachement.*"

I couldn't bring myself to banter. Or admit that I'd missed him too.

"After we kissed—" he began.

"Forget about it," I interrupted, feeling my cheeks heat up. I couldn't handle reliving the humiliation. He was still keeping secrets from me. There was no point in rehashing the kiss. He didn't feel close enough to be honest and open. "It's water under the bridge."

He tilted his head. "What bridge?"

Clearly, the idiom didn't translate. "*Please.* Just forget about it."

After a long moment, he said, "Want to swim?"

I took a deep breath. I could either accept our casual friendship— or run home.

I pulled off my shirt. He glanced away, as he always did. I stripped down to my sports bra and underwear and entered the cool water.

We floated in sunshine, keeping conversation on the surface. I gave a shallow recap of the flower art and bird-watching, and he mentioned the rainy weather and bad traffic around Lyon. When he asked about my bandaged hand, I just said I'd cut myself.

He drifted beneath the waterfall, and after a beat I followed, holding my breath as I ducked under. Inside, it felt like a little cave, the close space forcing us together.

He studied me with his golden-forest eyes. "Why did you really come here, Ellie?"

I'd told Mina and Bao, and it had brought us closer. It could take my friendship with Raphaël to a deeper level too. And what a relief it would be. Maybe if I opened up to him, he'd reciprocate. Maybe there could be more kissing.

But it had felt so natural to tell Mina and Bao, flowers and birds leading the way. Now, I was floundering.

Cross the damn river, Eloise.

I closed my eyes and began. "I came because of the no-children rule."

A pause. The waterfall pounded around us. "Really?"

"I didn't want to be near kids. Not even passing them on the street."

Another pause. "So—you don't like children at all, even nice ones?"

I measured my words. "I didn't like how I *felt* around children."

Tentatively, Raphaël asked, "Why?"

Where to go next? Should I just lay my defective womb on the table? I hated explaining my losses in the language of biology and medicine, when it should be done in flowers, the language of the heart. I wanted to bring him to the mandalas, lead him through step-by-step.

I was about to plunge in when he said, his words barely audible, "So you don't see yourself as a mother . . . ever?"

"I don't." To my surprise, I was able to state this fact without a quaver in my voice.

"Oh." After a long moment, he said, "I need children in my life."

His words felt like a kick to the gut. I hugged myself tightly, recovering my breath. Emotions flashed through me—rage, then sorrow, then acceptance. There would be no kissing. There would be . . . *nothing.* "So why are you here, Raphaël?"

"My life was different when I came." He paused. "Yesterday I was making arrangements for a new home."

"Okay," I said, trying to process. My insides felt empty. Even a casual friendship would be pointless. "When are you leaving?"

"In a week."

The rush of water felt too loud and close. I ducked out of the cascade and stumbled to the shore. I put my clothes on over my still-damp skin, avoiding the *bricoleur's* eyes.

As I was walking away, he called out, "Eloise, wait!"

Slowly, I spun to face him.

"I wish," he said.

"What?"

"I just—*wish.*"

"Wishing doesn't get you much in life, Raphaël."

I walked away.

From my treehouse perch, I gazed through branches, toward the river path, waiting for Raphaël to leave—I didn't want to run into him on the strange errand I'd planned. Once he headed home, I took the dagger from the drawer. The women in white had clearly been searching for it, and there was no point being on their bad side.

By the path, I dropped to my knees in the spot where I'd found the dagger. I was slightly worried the woodsprite might come across the weapon, but hopefully the ghost ladies would retrieve it at twilight in a couple of hours. On impulse, rather than passively leave it there, I raised it over my head, and with a grunt, plunged it into the dirt.

I was careful not to injure any plants. Still, the flowers murmured their surprise around me—this wasn't characteristic Eloise behavior. But it felt cathartic, expressing my frustration, and not just over Raphaël's deal-breaker about children. I was also sending the Goddess my own message: I would not meekly accept her threats.

Not to mention, if the woodsprite was in danger, I'd do everything in my power to protect her. Every bloom in this garden, except the poisonous ones, was cheering me on.

Find your girl.

During sunset I sat alone in the dappled pink light of my porch, scanning the trees, drinking courage tea, and eating stale brownies. Maybe the woodsprite wasn't a fan of brownies. French kids probably had more refined palates.

I glanced at the castle turrets through a gap in the trees, felt a shiver. I took another swig of courage and resolved to make double chocolate chip cookies next.

Twilight came, but the woodsprite didn't.

Don't give up, whispered the flowers. The chamomiles, with their cheerful innocence, were especially vocal. *Find her.*

I stationed myself at my uppermost window, keeping an eye out for *Les Dames Blanches*. Maybe they were the Triple Goddess of the Gardens. Maybe they'd left the notes. Maybe they'd plunged the dagger.

When they appeared, I shivered and watched them with binoculars borrowed from Bao. Still, their faces were shrouded. They moved in and out of shadows, sometimes obscured by bushes and branches. One of the figures leaned over and picked something up, then kept drifting along.

As I walked to dinner an hour later, the dagger was gone. I

wrapped my arms around myself as I passed the eerie harpist. *Les Dames Blanches* weren't statues or ghosts—they were real enough to make footprints, throw stones at Amber, stab a dagger, leave poisonous flowers, and write threatening notes.

What else were they real enough to do?

Wild Thing

The next afternoon, I set out fresh-baked cookies and milk beside the children's books on my balcony table.

I pushed away thoughts of Raphaël as I waited. Dinner the night before had been awkward enough—anyway, he'd be gone soon. Then it would be the comfortable friendship of me, Mina, Bao . . . and Raphaël's replacement. And maybe the woodsprite?

I ate a warm cookie, then belted out "Yellow Submarine."

What the hell are you doing, Eloise?

One last try. Please.

Soon, to my astonishment, leaves rustled. My heart fluttered, as if I were about to view a rare bird. And there she was, watching me from a nearby branch.

"Milk and cookies?" I offered.

She descended the oak and ran up the rope bridges. I couldn't help smiling. I appreciated the kind of kid who *ran* everywhere, as if walking was just too boring. Why not run?

Once she reached the balcony, breathing hard, she plucked a cookie with filthy hands. She wore a too-big Jimi Hendrix T-shirt and frayed orange shorts. *"Merci."*

"You can have more."

She took another. *"Merci."* She took a big bite and grinned. She took another.

A neon sign flashed in my head: *Danger.*

My intention might be to keep her safe, but this was not my child. This child might be here without her parents' knowing, eating sweets without their permission. I was complicit . . . in *something.*

This wasn't just a quick chat with a lost toddler. This was the beginning of *something* with a needy child. It terrified me.

"I want to be sure you're safe," I said as she took a swig of milk, leaving a charming mustache. "Do your parents know you're in the gardens?"

"My papa knows," she said, spewing crumbs. "He says to make sure La Patronne doesn't catch me."

What a bizarre situation. But the locals probably understood the risks better than I did. This man wouldn't let his daughter come here if she'd be in danger. And if she was going to be here, she'd be safer with me.

"You're sure?" In Denver my friends wouldn't let their five-year-olds walk down the block alone. And this girl must be at least a half mile from home. "Really?"

She nodded, shrugging a shoulder.

Maybe it was a cultural difference. After all, we were in a farming region in rural southern France. She didn't seem neglected—sure, her hair was a mess and her clothes were disheveled, but so were mine.

As she munched on a cookie, she did a little pirouette.

"Hey," I said, "were you watching me by the mermaid on my first day?"

She gave a guilty grin.

I wanted to interrogate her, piece together the puzzle . . . but now she was flipping through *Where the Wild Things Are*, pointing with her chocolatey hand. "What's his name? Does that boy really have a tail? What kind of trees are these? Is that opera cake? Does this forest have moths? Are these monsters nice or mean?"

I let myself fall into banter. Five-year-olds are *all questions*. All curiosity. Taking in the strangeness of this blue-green planet and making sense of it.

"*Alors,*" I said, "this is Max. He's wearing a wolf suit, so it's just a pretend tail."

I studied the foliage, wondering if the woodsprite wanted the genus and species. "I think they're imaginary trees."

She nodded, accepting the answer.

I tried to remember what opera cake was . . . a fancier, French version of tiramisu? "*Oui,*" I said. "That could be opera cake."

"*Délicieux!*"

"*Oui.*" I hoped she didn't expect opera cake next. I'd been thinking of Rice Krispies treats. Not that Rice Krispies even existed in small-town France.

I continued. "Probably the forest has moths, but they're hiding in the leaves."

She searched for moths in the forest illustration. "*Oui.* The moths are hiding." Looking concerned, she asked again about the monsters. "Are they like La Patronne?"

"I don't know."

"But will they hurt the boy?"

"At first the boy thinks the monsters are scary. Then he tames them. So in the end, they're nice, I guess."

She considered this. "I'm not scared of these monsters. I could tame them too. And I'd like to climb those trees, even though they're imaginary."

She looked at me with eyes wide, making it clear she wanted me to read the book. I took a deep breath. Reading the book would be a contract. This wouldn't be a friendship I could abandon. "Want me to read it?"

"*Oui, s'il vous plaît.*" The way she used the formal "please" so delicately and earnestly—it made my chest somehow expand and contract at once. I took a deep breath and let my heart grow until it felt outside of our bodies, holding us and the treehouse and forests and gardens.

In my most theatrical voice, I translated the story into French, relishing the drama and rhythm of Maurice Sendak's words. Part of me was evaluating the woodsprite, as I did with kids on my caseload.

This close, I could tell she was well cared for—a mouth full of brushed baby teeth, white and polished. She smelled like lavender soap and orange blossom shampoo.

Her social-emotional skills were on-target, or even advanced, for a five-year-old—she was chatty, with normal eye contact. She had excellent fine motor skills, deftly turning pages and pointing. And of course, her large motor skills were impressive, evidenced by her finesse climbing trees and running up the rope bridge. Her cognitive skills were advanced—her questions demonstrated critical thinking, creativity, connection to the story, curiosity. She listened with clear comprehension, absorbed in Max's adventures, her facial expressions reflecting his emotions.

When I finished, the woodsprite declared, *"Encore!"*

I flipped back to the beginning, appreciating that the book was now smudged with layers of chocolate fingerprints. I hoped her father wouldn't mind her lack of appetite for dinner. I hoped he wouldn't be upset when she told him about the American woman feeding her sweets and monster stories. She'd only mentioned her father, no mother.

"Make sure to check with your papa that it's okay for you to be here."

Mouth full, she nodded.

I read the first line: *"The night Max wore his wolf suit and created mischief of one kind . . . and another . . ."*

My woodsprite tilted her head and glanced into the trees, eyes widening.

I noticed nothing but an owl's hooting.

"I have to go," she said.

"My name is Eloise," I called after her.

"My name is Sabine." She swiped the air with an imagined monster paw. "But you can call me *La Chose Sauvage*."

Wild Thing.

"*Enchantée, ma chose sauvage.*"

As she vanished into the trees, I shouted, "Be careful!"

It always annoyed me when mothers said this at playgrounds, but Sabine's situation was different. This child could be in real danger.

The next morning, the mistral was blowing, cool and dry, from the north. These winds created the honeyed light of Provence.

Inside I held the secret seed of my encounter with Sabine. *Sabine.* The girl had a name. She was human. I kept this knowledge between me and the flowers, whispering about her cleverness and charm.

Over granola and yogurt and cherries, Mina frowned at the tension between Raphaël and me. After breakfast, with Baudelaire's poetry beneath her arm and the wind whipping her headscarf, she approached me as I carried buckets of composted soil to the indigo garden.

"What's going on with you and Raphaël?"

"We kissed. Then he ran off. Then we talked. We need different things in life."

She scoffed. "Like what?"

"He wants kids. I can't give him kids. It's impossible." I squinted as the wind blew grit into my eyes. "I'm not signing up for a broken heart."

She tilted her head. "Talk to him, sister. Tell him how you really feel."

"There's no point. He's leaving."

"Maybe you have more in common than you think."

The mistral breeze whipped through leaves despite the walls around Paradise. Iva had said that these winds swept away bad energy. Maybe they could clear the awkwardness with Raphaël and give me peace when he left.

Together Mina and I spread rich, new soil where I planned to bury iris bulbs in the fall. Next spring, when they'd emerge, Raphaël would be a distant memory, but I'd still have Mina, Bao, and maybe the woodsprite.

First, I needed to make this place safer for her. I had the urge to dig up the poison garden and plant sunflowers over it. Of course La Patronne wouldn't be on board—after all, the grave was still tended to . . . perhaps by her? I'd just make Sabine promise not to touch the poison flowers.

The tunnel was another matter—I had to block the entrance, which meant I'd need the *bricoleur's* help.

Before lunch, I caught Raphaël on the path by his workshop. Seeing me, his face softened, as if we could just have a heart-to-heart, make up, be friends again. As if his words hadn't touched my deepest, rawest nerve.

All business, I said, "Will you help me board up the entrance to the tunnel?"

His brow creased. "I would, Eloise, but La Patronne won't allow it."

"Why?"

"Who knows. I suggested it already. She believes the *Forbidden* sign is sufficient warning."

"*Alors*, let's put a barrier around the oubliette."

"I don't know if she'd accept that either."

"Does she have to know?"

He blew a puff of air. "I suppose not." His gaze rested on my face, as if searching for the intimacy we'd had just days earlier.

I averted my eyes. "Why don't you get the equipment? Meet me at the tunnel. *Merci."* I attached no *"mon ami."* We were not friends. He was just a *bricoleur* whose services I needed.

❀

Fifteen minutes later, Raphaël was walking across the stones toward me, cedar boards and rope over his shoulder and the tool belt around his waist. The mistral winds toyed with locks of his hair, rippled his shirt. Despite myself, I felt a pang watching him, so earnest and helpful, so muscled and skilled. So oblivious to how he'd hurt me.

As he climbed up the rock outcropping, I had an impulse to hug him. Instead, I said, "Let me take some of those boards."

Breathing hard, he shook his head. "It's okay."

When we'd first met, he'd avoided my eyes. Now it felt as if he could *only* look at me. His expression was an open doorway, an invitation: *Come back in. Let me back in.*

"Allons-y," I said, turning away. "Let's do this."

I brushed a hand over the rosemary, breathed in its clear scent, and glimpsed the plaque.

HERE LIE THE BONES
OF THOSE WHO BROKE THE RULES.

Raphaël noticed me eyeing it. "You've read the inscription?"

"Oui." My gaze swept over the castle turrets in the distance, feeling their darkness.

"Greeting card material, huh?"

I refused to engage in playful banter. "My bones could be lying there now."

As we entered the tunnel, Raphaël flicked on a flashlight, letting his other hand hang by his side, available for me.

I hugged my bare arms. The dank, musty air brought back memories of being trapped.

He gave me a sidelong glance. "You okay, Eloise?"

"Let's just get this done."

Soon I spotted the shadow of a hole ahead. We approached, side by side, my pulse racing as he shone his flashlight beam to the bottom. "I can't believe you didn't get hurt."

"Got lucky."

"Who knows where this tunnel leads." Kneeling, he pulled out a hammer, a saw, and a box of nails. "Outside the walls?" he mused. "Medieval castles often had secret escape passages. Maybe this hole trapped enemies in pursuit."

I shivered. "Or held prisoners."

He took off his long-sleeve shirt, handed it to me. "Here."

"Merci." I wrapped myself in its scent of lavender soap and sunshine and sweat. The shirt sparked a chain of reactions in my body that brought me to a whole new level of heat.

He's an impossibility, Eloise. Let him go, damn it.

I helped rig up a barrier of rope and wood. He insisted I wear his work gloves, claiming that his own fingers were so calloused, no splinters could get through. Once we finished, I gave a nod of approval.

"We have materials left over," said Raphaël. "If there are more holes, we can block them too." He offered a sideways glance. "I'm your personal *bricoleur*—your wish is my command."

I averted my eyes, feeling the ghostly chill drifting through the tunnel. This place felt like a tomb. I fought the urge to run back outside—I had to be thorough, for Sabine's sake. "Okay. Let's keep going."

Onward we walked, deeper and farther, as the tunnel curved here and there. He attempted more banter but petered out when I didn't reciprocate.

"Look," I said when another shadow materialized.

Raphaël strode ahead and shone his flashlight beam into the hole. With a sudden cry, he stumbled backward, the wood clattering to the ground, the flashlight rolling to a stop at the edge. His face held the same terror as his night of hellish hallucinations. *"Mon Dieu."*

I grabbed the flashlight.

"Non." He scrambled to block me. "Eloise, don't look inside."

I looked inside.

24

The Bones

At the bottom of the oubliette, a human skeleton was curled in a fetal position, as if sleeping.

The eye sockets were black holes that sucked my breath away.

The skeleton looked adult-sized, half covered with scraps of clothing and clumps of dark hair and glints of metal. Patches of mummified flesh and tendons clung to the bones.

I pressed my hand to my forehead, fighting the nausea. "Amber?"

Beside me, Raphaël shook his head. "She wouldn't have decomposed this fast."

"The handywoman?"

"Looks older than five years." He raised his fist to his mouth. "A medieval prisoner?"

I shuddered. "I doubt any clothes and hair would be intact." Then I whispered, "Here lie the bones of those who broke the rules."

"But who?" said Raphaël.

"That's a men's belt buckle. The hat looks like a man's, old-fashioned. And the boots are big."

"Maybe mid-1900s?"

"Sixties or seventies," I guessed. "Look at the avocado polyester, the wide collar."

I'd never seen a dead body before—my grandparents had been cremated. I tried wrapping my head around it: *This was once a man.* A man who had suffered a terrible death. A death I'd barely escaped.

Tears burned my eyes. I reached for Raphaël.

He pulled me close, wrapped his arms around me.

We were in the Underworld, land of death and darkness, encountering its horrors. The *harming* that was the flip side of *healing.* The shadow face of this place of power.

I let his warmth soak into me, his smell of pine and sap and comfort. "What now?"

He let out a long breath. "We make a barrier."

"Would that incriminate us?" I knew nothing of small-town French police proceedings. "Should we report it first?"

"Probably doesn't matter." He rubbed his face. "It happened so long ago."

My impulse was to go straight to the cops. "Think it was an accident? Or murder?"

"*Alors,* someone knew about it. Someone who made that plaque." He ran a hand through his hair. "Someone's been keeping secrets for decades. And I doubt that someone would be happy to have them exposed."

"Let's get this covered and leave. Then we'll figure out the next step."

Within ten minutes, we'd set up the barrier. I quickly whispered, "Rest in peace," then added, "Let's go."

"What if there are more holes? Or skeletons?" Raphaël squinted deeper into the tunnel. "The plaque implied there could be more. *Those* who broke the rules."

I bit my lip. "But we're out of wood."

"We could check, then come back if we need to."

I thought of Sabine. Now the danger was not just an oubliette, but the trauma of finding skeletons. "Okay, let's take a look."

Our hands stayed interlocked—this felt necessary, even though it further entangled us. I couldn't shake the feeling we were walking through a *crypt*. On instinct, I listened for guidance from the flowers. Nothing. I was beyond their reach.

I was about to suggest turning around when the flashlight beam landed on something ahead: an ornate door made of ancient wood. A carving of a plump toddler with wings filled the door—cherub or gargoyle, I couldn't tell, but its devilish smile made my skin crawl. I ran my hand over the wood, splintering and rotting. I tried turning the green brass knob. Locked.

"Where does this lead?" I whispered. "A tomb?"

"No idea."

Did Antoinette know about all of this? Did La Patronne?

I felt desperate to return to the surface. "Let's go."

I loosened my grip on Raphaël's hand, but he kept his firmly around mine. By the time we reached the surface, we clung to each other with equal force, tethers to the sunlit world.

Outside, I blinked and breathed in the humming, buzzing gardens. Raphaël's hand stayed interlaced with mine as we scrambled down the cliff and across the stream.

We sat side by side on a warm boulder. I was still shaking from the cold, the dark, the death. I didn't resist when he wrapped an arm around my shoulder and rubbed my back.

I leaned into him, craving comfort and warmth. I could almost hear phantom whispers floating from the tunnel, like echoes of the ghosts Raphaël had spoken with when he was poisoned.

"Hey," I said hoarsely. "During your hallucinations, you kept saying, 'She's so young,' and pleading to someone not to kill her. Or you." I turned to him. "Remember?"

He breathed out. "I think I was talking to . . . Death."

A chill crept over my neck. "Who was the *she*?"

He opened his mouth to say something, then closed it.

I didn't push him. I could only assume it was his ex-girlfriend.

"I just remember feeling terrified," he said finally. "There were dark forces. Even Antoinette transformed into a monster."

I recalled how he'd shrunk away from her.

His voice softened. "But one thing stands out from that night. You were made of flowers. Rose, lavender, chamomile . . . you even smelled like them. And you were lit up, like flowers in sunshine. Glowing." He paused. "You still are."

Warmth spread through my body. Did he really see me this way?

He turned to me, our faces close. "Will you stay in my life, Ellie? After I leave?"

The flowers whispered, *Yes, yes, yes.*

I wanted to lean in just a few inches, touch my lips to his, but part of me held back. *He needs children.*

Still, I wanted to kiss him. It had felt so good. More than good. Otherworldly. "Listen," I said, gathering the courage to be vulnerable. "I need to know. Was—was there a problem with our kiss?"

His face fell. "Oh, Ellie. It was the best kiss of my life. And that scared me."

My heart skipped a beat. "Why?"

His expression was raw and earnest. "Because I—I've never felt this way about anyone. This closeness. This passion. But I knew I had to leave." He brushed his hand against my cheek. "It seemed too painful to get more involved."

I noticed he said nothing about children. Maybe he'd decided he was getting ahead of himself. Maybe I was getting ahead of myself too. Maybe that was something we didn't need to worry about now.

He stroked my hair, rested a hand on my shoulder. "This isn't fair to you. I know that. I'm sorry. I just—I just want to be near you. All the time."

His anguish seemed genuine. We both had our secrets, but our chemistry was undeniable—like flowers in a tisane bringing out the other's magic. Maybe we could just take what each other had to offer.

"Let's try being friends," I said.

"Okay," he murmured.

I stared at his lips, so full and tender. When they'd met mine that night, it had been pure stardust. I pressed against him and whispered, "Maybe with some kissing."

Smiling, he tucked a strand of hair behind my ear, kissed my cheek for a long moment. *"Merci."* His breath was warm at my ear.

I melted into his touch but forced myself to say, "On one condition."

He kissed my other cheek. "Anything, *ma sorcière.*"

"One must not mention children." *Mon Dieu,* my rule-making made me sound like Antoinette or La Patronne. But it was the only way this friendship had a chance. The only way I could let our lips touch with abandon. Flushing, I added, "And one may not ask why."

He cupped my face and said under his breath, "One is in agreement."

I wrapped my hands around his waist and pulled him close, feeling our chests warm against each other, his back muscles rippling against my palms. I brought my lips to meet his, fully and completely.

And we were kissing. A kiss unlike any other I'd had before—at once softer and deeper and *more real.* A kiss that tasted of darkness and light. A kiss of two people who had been to the Underworld. And survived.

🏵

Eventually, with reluctance, I pulled away from our kiss. I couldn't ignore the stark reality. "Raphaël. We have to do something about the skeleton."

He stroked my arm. "Like what?"

"Tell the police. Right now."

"Okay." He hesitated. "But it's been there for half a century."

"This isn't ancient archaeology." I stood up and straightened my clothes. "It could have been murder."

"Ellie, if we go the police, our life in the gardens might end. Mina's and Bao's too." He stood up beside me. "The repercussions could be huge."

I squeezed his hand. "Let's talk with the others first."

"At dinner tonight," he said, and after a lingering kiss, headed to his workshop where broken irrigation pipes awaited.

But I couldn't return to my own work. How could I weed or dig, knowing what was underground?

I found Mina and Bao in the grove having lunch: an elegant *salade Niçoise* of hard-boiled eggs, tuna, and black olives atop lacy lettuce, alongside a crusty baguette.

"Join us," said Mina with a warm smile.

As I sat down, Bao poured me a glass of chilled lemon water. "Help yourself."

I sipped, then set down my glass. "Raphaël and I found a dead body in the tunnel."

They glanced at each other, raising their brows.

"A dead body?" Bao echoed, then sipped his water.

"A man's skeleton," I said. "Probably there for fifty years. At the bottom of an oubliette."

Mina clucked. "How terrible." She lifted an olive to her mouth.

My stomach tightened. There was something *off* about their

reactions. A lack of shock. A lack of questions. It was as if they already knew.

"Here," said Mina, "have some salad."

"Salad, *really?*"

She sighed. "Just ignore—"

"I can't ignore this." I stared in disbelief. "I was stuck in that oubliette for hours. I could have ended up like this skeleton. I deserve the truth."

Mina rubbed her forehead, glanced at Bao. "Of course you do, sister. It's just that we adore you. We want you to stay."

I clutched my glass. "I'll only consider staying if you're honest with me."

Bao answered in an even voice. "Mary Martin found the body five years ago."

"The handywoman?" I asked.

Bao nodded. "Antoinette assured her it was a proper burial, registered with the authorities—a traditional grave for an old relative."

"Seriously?" I raised a doubtful eyebrow.

Mina shrugged. "Some kind of Celtic cave burial."

"Apparently," Bao continued, "Mary kept pushing, demanding to talk with La Patronne, threatening to involve the police." He sighed. "And then, just as we told you, one day she was gone."

"Disappeared?"

"She never said goodbye," Mina admitted. "But Antoinette said she just quit."

"What if it was murder?" I pushed. "And what if the same thing happened to Amber?"

"This is why we didn't tell you the details." Mina's face grew heavy. "We knew it would upset you."

I took another sip. "I'm getting answers."

"Listen, Eloise—" Bao began.

"I'll be careful," I said. "I won't jeopardize our lives here. But I have to find the truth."

❁

Late in the afternoon, I sat alone on the treehouse porch, thinking about the skeleton. At the bottom of it, I had to know whether the gardens were safe. But I had to be subtle. La Patronne and Antoinette couldn't know.

My heart leapt when the woodsprite materialized among the trees, swung for a minute on the swing Raphaël had made, then ran up to join me. As we munched on caramel swirl brownies, I made her promise not to go into the tunnel again.

"*D'accord,*" she agreed with a shrug.

"Or the poison garden."

"I'm not allowed in there anyway." She gave a dramatic shudder. "Even passing by it gives me goose bumps." Or, literally, *chicken flesh.*

"Agreed." I breathed out. "Hey, did you check with your papa about coming here?"

"It's fine."

I would have felt better meeting him, but this would do for now.

After stuffing the last bit of brownie into her mouth, she announced, "Time to play!"

Magic words. An excuse to forget the disturbing discovery—for a little while, at least.

We descended the swinging bridges. The first peach light of sunset filtered through leaves, casting an ethereal glow.

This was my element, letting children lead me into their imaginary worlds. Now I was just another kid, or at most an eccentric aunt . . . *not* a wannabe mom with an urge to wipe chocolate from her daughter's chin.

"You, too, are a *chose sauvage*," declared Sabine, raising a stick like a monster's staff. "We are a family of wild things!"

"*Oui.*" I lifted my paws with a gentle roar.

Sabine echoed my roar with her throaty French *r*'s.

Conversations with five-year-olds felt almost sacred to me. Over the years, I'd noticed that if I truly listened and engaged, they seemed like weird little Buddhas. There was layer after layer to their endless chatter—bizarre symbolism and imagery galore. Their questions were a starry sky of koans, spiritual riddles that turned logic on its head and brought enlightenment. It was as if every five-year-old was on an illuminating mushroom trip and—if I was game—would bring me along for the ride.

With ceremonial flair, Sabine handed me a stick.

I held it up. "Let the wild rumpus start!"

I said *rrroompoos* in English with a French accent—the Frenglish word I'd invented. Sabine hadn't questioned it, simply incorporated it into her own vocabulary.

We jumped and paraded and swung from trees and howled to the sky—not too loudly because of La Patronne. The woodsprite heeded her papa's warnings.

I almost wished Bao and Mina and Raphaël would hear our wild *rrroompoos*. I didn't like keeping the woodsprite secret, but I'd promised her.

"Now, stop!" Sabine commanded, echoing Max's words.

I stopped dancing mid-twirl. I'd forgotten how bossy five-year-olds were.

Instead of going to sleep as the monsters did, we leaned against a chestnut tree and she wove me a wildflower crown. I wondered who had taught her this skill.

"For you." She placed the crown on my head.

"*Merci*, Wild Thing." I'd also forgotten how generous five-year-olds could be.

"You can be king of the wild things with me, Eloise."

"*Merci*, King."

"Now, sing!"

And I sang . . . softly, as she commanded, so that La Patronne wouldn't hear.

La Patronne. Would she—or whatever dark forces existed here—hurt a child? As much as I tried to keep it whimsical, I had the duty to keep the girl safe. *Not* a maternal feeling, just a responsible adult feeling.

After my song, I said, "Tell your papa I'd like to talk with him, okay?"

She nodded and continued weaving her own flower crown.

Still, I had to do *something* to understand if she was in danger. My thoughts came together in a rough plan. The market would be tomorrow. I'd sneak out and walk to town. My objective was simple—to research and gossip the hell out of the situation.

25

Gossip

The hole in the wall was barely big enough for my hips to fit through—an awkward maneuver in my little black dress. I'd need to blend in with French women at the market, so my usual khaki attire wouldn't work. On the other side, I brushed stone dust from my dress and breathed in the predawn scent of freedom, cool and dewy.

"Ready to do some espionage?" Raphaël asked. Last night, after I'd recapped my talk with Mina and Bao and explained my plan, he'd insisted on coming.

We hurried around the outside of the wall, glancing over our shoulders, then walked toward town, ducking behind trees when we heard the occasional car. The sun rose over the hills, spilling light over meadows, and my nerves settled as we put more kilometers between us and the castle.

When Epona the Peugeot appeared in the distance, we hid behind a blue tractor at the edge of a massive field of lavender.

I noted the key in the ignition. "The locals are trusting."

He laughed. "No one's about to steal a lavender harvester. And no one locks anything around here. Antoinette being the exception."

I lifted a playful eyebrow. "Let's drive the rest of the way in the lavender-flower-mobile."

"We wouldn't attract any attention that way," he said with a wry grin.

We watched Epona speed by, pulling the trailer, and once it vanished around a curve, I started walking. He grabbed my hand and drew me close, the scent of lavender surrounding us. "Hey, remember what you said about the kissing benefits?"

A smile spread over my face. "Remind me."

He wrapped his arms around my waist, pulled me closer. I kissed each cheek, then his closed eyelids, the pulse points on his neck, his ear lobes. As if he could stand it no more, he pressed his lips to mine. We kissed for a stretched-out moment, hands skimming each other's contours, lavender murmuring around us.

Finally, I paused to catch my breath, feeling my heart race and heat flood my body. As much as I wanted to lie down with him in a row of lavender blooms, we had a mission. I leaned against the sun-warmed metal of the tractor, palm on his chest. "We've got some gossiping to do."

He trailed his fingertips along my sweaty clavicle. "But you smell so good," he whispered. "Like a love apple."

I laughed and tugged at his arm. *"Allons-y, mon chéri!"*

We walked down the road, hand in hand, the scent of lavender cradling us. An hour later, we rounded the final bend.

Perched atop a hill, the town of Sainte-Marie-des-Fleurs shone in the early morning hours, ancient buildings illuminated as if in a spotlight. Climbing up the steep paths and steps, we passed creamy limestone houses with periwinkle-blue shutters and wrought iron balconies and pots of scarlet geraniums.

Once we reached the main square, I turned in a slow, dazzled circle. Striped awnings covered outdoor cafés, where servers arranged chairs and tiny tables toward the plaza like a theater-in-the-round.

Around the central fountain, vendors set up tablecloths and umbrellas, foods and wares: olive wood bowls, pottery, baskets, soap from Marseille, dried lavender sachets, olive oil, dried herbs, truffles, cheeses, sausages, olives. Fruits and vegetables glistened, artfully arranged as if for a still life: cherries, straw-berries, apricots, melons, lettuce, bell peppers, aubergines, cour-gettes, artichokes, tomatoes, basil, onions, garlic.

What a strange feeling to be outside the gates of Paradise, dropped into the hustle and bustle of other people's lives.

Beside me, Raphaël had been the excited tour guide on the way through town, but now he turned serious, motioning to the far end of the square. "The *Paradis* booth is over there. We can't let Antoinette see us."

"Got it." I spotted the booth, where she was arranging bouquets into baskets. An unexpected wave of pride rushed through me at our flower wares shining their magic for all to see.

I gave my *bricoleur* a sidelong glance. "First stop, the internet."

Slinging his arm around my waist, he led me to a tiny café that rented computers by the half hour. We ordered espressos and leaned together, sharing an old monitor and worn keyboard. His proximity gave me flutters—despite our morbid investigation, my body wanted more kissing.

First, I checked my bank account and bills, as Raphaël politely looked away. I nearly gasped at how fast my debts were decreasing. I'd be back above water within a year.

Next step, Amber. Nervous sweat dripped down my sides as I pulled up the most *à la mode* social media site for twenty-somethings and entered her full name. Instantly, her profile popped up. Twenty-three years old. Iowan native. The latest entry was dated yesterday.

My body melted with relief. "She's alive."

Shoulder-length, pink-streaked hair framed a narrow chin, pert nose, and lips in a strained pout. Pretty, except for the hollowness—sunken cheekbones, empty gaze, ribs curved beneath a cropped tank, skeletal clavicles. A strand of pearls hung around the tendons of her neck. There was something haunting about her, corpse-like.

As I scrolled through her updates, my insides clenched. Every photo had been taken in a bedroom with the curtains drawn, her cropped shirts different, but her zombie expression unchanged.

Raphaël shook his head, visibly upset. "She's gone downhill."

I translated the captions aloud to French.

U don't understand the miracle til its literally slipped thru ur fingers

When u leave the garden's, ur literally the walking dead

After u taste paradise everything else taste's like literal crap

I sucked in a breath, recalling Antoinette's warnings. *If one leaves heaven, one enters hell.* Here was living proof. Or, more like half-dead proof. Something heavy settled in my stomach—a mix of sorrow and dread.

"Poor girl," said Raphaël.

Did he worry his own healing would be undone when he left—whatever it had entailed?

I closed the tab, desperate to erase Amber's images. Would that be me if I left?

He sighed. "Mary Martin next?"

"It's a pretty common name," I said, doubtful we'd find much. We'd pried more details about her from Mina and Bao, but nothing substantial. Sure enough, the number of Mary Martins online was overwhelming, even when narrowed to Canadians.

"I have an idea." I brought up my email account. "My ex's best friend is a PI. Maybe he can help."

"*Vachement cool.*" Raphaël looked impressed.

"Indeed." I typed a quick email to Josh, first wishing his new family well. Then I copied my scant details about Mary Martin and asked him to snail-mail me any information his buddy came up with. I finished the email: I'm happy here. I'm healing.

It felt good to press Send. A peaceful closure. "Now, on to the deaths and disappearances."

Raphaël leaned forward, typing keywords in French.

But we found no records of sales of the estate or previous owners' names or deaths or disappearances. Not even a Celtic burial.

"Most of this stuff happened pre-internet," Raphaël said, deflated.

"*Pas de problème, mon ami.*" I slung my arm around his shoulder. "Next step, gossip."

We emerged into the sunshine, finding the market more crowded now. Throngs of people had come from surrounding villages— and the biggest draw was Les Jardins du Paradis. A crowd had gathered around the booth, the young vendor efficiently tending to eager customers. Antoinette was nowhere to be seen.

Raphaël and I moved from booth to booth, tasting samples of lavender honey, currant jam, spiced olives, truffle-infused oil. I introduced myself to each vendor, engaged in friendly chatter for a bit, then mentioned I worked at Les Jardins du Paradis. At that, the vendors clammed up.

Raphaël hung back—still not 100 percent on board with breaking the gossip rule—as I tried more subtle approaches. Channeling a simple tourist, I asked vendors about the crowd by the Paradise booth. No one offered new information, only affirmation that the gardens produced special plants.

Just past the woven hats, stood the *saucissons* vendor, a grand-fatherly octogenarian with a warm yet no-bullshit smile.

"Have some." He sliced a dried sausage. "*Allez-y.*"

As Raphaël and I sampled a mind-boggling variety—herb-encrusted, pepper-coated, hazelnut—the old man chatted. He looked quintessentially Provençal with his gray beret, worn cardigan, and large, pink-tipped nose, as if he'd just played a game of pétanque.

When he asked if I was enjoying my vacation, I admitted I worked at the gardens.

"Eh bien, dis donc!" he said. *Well, ya don't say!* "The mysterious gardens. How are they treating you, Madame?"

"Actually, I have some questions, Monsieur."

The man raised his bushy white brows. "Perhaps I can help."

No convincing needed. "I heard there were a series of disappearances and deaths there."

He nodded, a spark in his eyes. "The estate was in the same family for generations. People envied them because of the special plants." He spoke as if he had all the time in the world.

I flicked my eyes toward the Paradise booth. Still no sign of Antoinette.

The old man stroked his chin. "And then, back in, oh, the 1960s, I'd say, the owner died in a car crash. I knew the man. Faithful customer. His death was suspicious—failed brakes, even though he'd just tuned up the car."

I lowered my voice. "Murder?"

"Who knows?" He smoothed his mustache. *"Eh bien,* not long after his death, one of his business associates started courting his widow. A greedy man. Lawyer. Never liked him."

The vendor clucked, fed me more *saucisson.* "Of course he just wanted that estate. And its powers. His new wife died soon after they married. Fell down the cellar stairs."

"Murder?"

"Bah, neither of the accidents made sense. And wouldn't you know it, her new will gave the lawyer the estate. He stayed on with the three girls, poor things."

Handing me more *saucisson*, he leaned in. "And then, what do you know, a year later, the man disappears."

My heart pounded as Raphaël asked, "No body found?"

He shook his head. *"Rien."*

Raphaël and I traded meaningful looks.

The man placed another sliver of *saucisson* in my hand. I was eating way too much of it, but this stuff was in its own exquisite, artisanal realm.

The vendor continued. "No one looked very hard. The lawyer was an outsider. Not friendly. No one liked him much. He was even estranged from his own family in Paris."

"And the girls?" I asked.

"Went to live in Paris with an elderly aunt. Only relative. Never heard from them again. The estate remained abandoned for, oh, about five years. Then they must have sold it."

"To La Patronne?" I calculated this would be the early 1970s.

He nodded. "A secretive lady. No one knows her name. She never shows her face in town. Sends her assistant to do everything."

"Antoinette Beaulieu," I said with a sigh.

He laughed. "Oh, I've tried to gossip with her. But she's as cold as ice."

"What do you know about the Goddess of the Gardens?" I asked.

"*Pff*, so many rumors have floated around." He leaned in, tapping a finger to his lips. "If you ask me, someone's playing games over there, pretending to be a goddess. And using those plants to play with one's mind, if you know what I mean."

He raised a bushy brow. "Of course some people believe it's really magic."

I dove to the heart of things. "*Alors*, Monsieur, do you think there's anything truly dangerous there?"

He waved away my question. "*Bof*, it's all in people's minds. The deaths and disappearances happened decades ago. Ancient history. Someone over there just wants to keep up the *illusion* of danger. It gives them power."

I breathed out with relief, then glanced around, worried we were monopolizing him. "Monsieur, why are you the only one willing to talk about this?"

"*Bah*, people fear vengeance. From La Patronne or the Goddess or *Les Dames Blanches* or whoever." He gave an exaggerated shrug. "But I'm an old man. Not scared of much. Already outlived my time." He thumped his chest. "The *saucissons* keep my heart healthy."

I leaned in. "Monsieur, tell me more about—"

He widened his eyes, gesturing behind me.

A hand gripped my shoulder. I spun around.

It was Antoinette, pink-faced and furious.

Merde. Adrenaline shot through me.

Raphaël looked like he might be sick.

"Enjoying the market?" Antoinette's words were daggers.

I forced a nod.

She glared at the market vendor, then back at me. "Gossiping?"

"No, not at all. He was just talking about the good old days."

The old man nodded along. My hands shook as I guilt-bought a ridiculous number of *saucissons*.

"Here," I said, sweat trickling down my torso, "have a *saucisson*, Antoinette."

She shook her head. "Go on, walk back to the château now."

I glanced at Raphaël, who shrugged an uncertain shoulder.

We headed out of the market as the *saucissons* vendor called after us, "*Bon courage!*"

26

Stardust

Think the scary Goddess stuff is just an act?" Raphaël asked as we walked back to the château.

"Possibly," I said, swinging my hand in his. The sausage vendor had pulled back the curtain and lightened my fears. Maybe someone in the gardens—a *broken* someone—was just playing games. "That would be a relief."

"Agreed."

We were heading down the driveway, beneath the arch of plane trees, when Antoinette sped by with Epona pulling the trailer. As we helped her unload the empty crates, she said in a cool voice, "You may stay in Paradise. If you remain loyal."

It appeared we were forgiven. After all, there were no actual rules about leaving the garden. Maybe she believed my lie about the vendor sharing old-timey stories. Maybe she hadn't heard any gossip. Maybe she thought Raphaël and I were just on a romantic outing.

And maybe she recognized her strange bond with me. Maybe she believed that I was the light to her shadows, that she needed a flower whisperer to make healing teas. Maybe La Patronne did too. My talents were valued here, a kind of leverage.

Later, in the dining grove, we sat with Mina and Bao, who'd made a lunch of cured ham and brie on baguettes with sliced tomatoes drizzled with olive oil.

"For future lunches, let's have *saucissons*," I joked, laying my stash on the table.

Raphaël and I shared our intel, and by the end of lunch, we'd all reached a tentative consensus: The deaths had been unsettling, but if they'd been committed by the stepfather—well, he'd disappeared. And if he was the guy in the oubliette—a *murderer*—then maybe he'd gotten what was coming.

As far as Amber, at least she wasn't dead. Although we felt disconcerted by her downfall, it didn't change Raphaël's mind about leaving. But her hollowness made me reluctant to leave. *Heaven to hell.*

Anyway, I had nowhere to go, no life to return to, no other way to reduce debt. My French work visa was contingent on this job. My life in Denver was ashes. Here, I was healing myself, discovering pleasure, exploring the language of flowers, and making friends, including—beyond all belief—a *child* friend.

I'd be sad to see Raphaël go, but we could meet for espressos and kisses in town. And if he entered hell upon leaving heaven, I'd heal him with bespoke flower teas.

The *saucissons* vendor's belief made sense—someone with a big ego was playing power games. I didn't have to engage. I could ignore *les bizarreries*, which was what my friends had encouraged me to do all along. And I could sneak out whenever I wanted. I had the power here. Except for the poisonous ones, the flowers were on my side.

The only real risk was getting too close to the woodsprite. And that was a matter of maintaining boundaries. We could just have fun together, especially now that I knew we were safe.

As we washed dishes, I turned to my friends, wanting to hug them. They were family, and this was our flowered nest, and we were in it together. Drying the last plate, I said, "From here on out, let's just enjoy Paradise."

❀

Over the next few afternoons, before my swim and *apéro*, I waited on my porch, and every day the woodsprite came for a magical *rrroompoos*.

She'd appear among the trees, scoping out my home, making sure I had no visitors. She was stealthy, blending into shadows, tiptoeing through underbrush. And then she'd run up the bridges like a puppy. I had the feeling if I'd opened up my arms, she'd run straight into them and I'd pick her up and swing her around.

Instead, I kept my arms crossed against my chest.

Boundaries.

She'd skid to a stop, stuff chocolate into her mouth, and then, sparked by theobromine, our wild *rrroompoos* would begin. Sometimes she charmingly referred to herself in third person as Wild Thing. I loved these things five-year-olds did, which, if done by an adult, might be a sign of narcissism or drug use.

She complimented me often: *"Your cookies smell marvelous, King Eloise."* Or, *"You look like a beautiful butterfly!"* Or just, *"Good job, Eloise!"* Or, the one that really got me: *"Wild Thing feels joy in her heart when she's with you."*

I'd sent a note home with her, introducing myself and asking permission for her to spend time with me. Sabine just reported back that her papa said it was fine. I chose to believe her, to simply be her friend, not her babysitter or play specialist or social worker—and definitely not her mother.

She chattered and sang as we swung and played, composing rambling songs inspired by melodies she'd learned from me. Sometimes she'd sing them under her breath and other times belt them out, increasing in volume until she remembered La Patronne and dropped her voice to a whisper.

She chatter-sang about her friends: *My friends bring me special stones / my friends spin me around / my friends paint with me / I love my friends / and my friends love me.*

She chatter-sang about her relatives: *My cousins throw me the ball / my aunts dance with me / my uncles do silly tricks / my cousins play cards with me / my grandma makes yummy food / my grandpa gives me too much candy / I love them / and they love me.*

She chatter-sang about her papa: *My papa tells funny jokes / my papa lets me dance on his feet / my papa plays a pretty guitar / I love my papa / and my papa loves me.*

She never chatter-sang about her *maman.*

Sometimes I watched her and thought: *"And Max, the king of all wild things, was lonely and wanted to be where someone loved him best of all."*

Sabine wasn't lonely. She had her friends and relatives and father, whom I thought were all real but wasn't quite sure.

Loneliness wasn't a part of her . . . but *longing* was.

I recognized it as though she were holding up a mirror.

I could see longing in her face when we said goodbye every day.

"Until tomorrow, my wild thing."

"Until tomorrow, my wild thing."

Later that Saturday, at the cusp of twilight, I stationed myself in the library. If I was going to stay in the gardens, research was in order. It might help me find some kind of truce in this game I'd gotten into with the Goddess. I picked up a cloth-bound, century-old book with the gilded title of *The Triple Goddess* and flipped through it by lantern light.

It described versions of the ancient Triple Goddess, her common threads across cultures—destiny, weaving, fertility, fruits, flowers, serpents, maidenhood, motherhood, cronehood, the capacity for both wrath and kindness. The Norn in Norse cultures; Parcae among the Romans; Morrigan among Irish Celts; *Les Dames Blanches* in France; Matronae all over ancient Gaul, Italy, Spain, Britain, and Rhineland; Slavic versions with different local names; and the southern French Three Maries. Greek culture alone had multiple versions, including the Fates and the Furies.

I looked up from the book at Iva's tea jars. POUSSIÈRE D'ÈTOILES. *Stardust.* It exuded an aura of magic—just what I needed now, since logical research was getting me nowhere.

I thought of the Carl Sagan lines Mina liked quoting: *"The cosmos is within us. We are made of star stuff."*

I scooped out a generous spoonful, noting the beige powder—possibly ground mushrooms—along with blue and orange petals, dried ginger and lemon peel, and unknown grassy herbs.

After it steeped, I ventured a taste. A zing, a sweet depth, and a *soul-expanding* feeling.

As I sipped, I imagined the faces of the Triple Goddess throughout my life, homing in on the mother facet. Since I was unable to have the children I craved, maybe she'd twisted herself to fit the situation. During the worst of it, maybe *I'd* become the child to protect—and she had, in fact, managed to keep me alive. Her rage had prevented me from drowning in an opioid stupor. In an odd way, maybe she'd saved me by keeping me furious—she'd driven me to smash things.

I found myself whispering to this face of the Goddess: "Thank you for your help in the past. But now I'm asking you to step down from your angry role. I need the kind protector to take the lead."

To my surprise, she said, *I thought you'd never ask!*

To the other faces of the trio, I said, "Thank you, crone, for showing me how to heal. And thank you, maiden, for giving me hope."

I glanced out the window into the night sky. What a strange—

yet natural—feeling, to be talking to facets of myself and facets of the stars all at once. I focused on the loving parts. *Protector of mothers and children. The benevolent face. The compassionate hand . . .*

A bud was loosening, opening, petal by petal, welcoming honey-bees, releasing its essence, facing the light. We would find a way to live in harmony in these gardens. *We*, of course, meaning the Triple Goddess inside and outside of myself, in all her forms.

The mistral winds vanished the next day, leaving behind the bluest of skies and the most lemony of light. In the late afternoon, Sabine showed up at my treehouse with a third of her hair in a multitude of braids. Bright orange fabric was wrapped in a big bow around her head, someone's effort to make the abandoned hairstyle presentable.

Understanding dawned.

I could imagine what had happened like a film clip. *Someone* had been styling her hair. The woodsprite had lost interest, then *someone* had decided to finish braiding after a break. Then my wild thing had refused round two.

Around her neck were Bao's binoculars, which, I realized, had not been swiped but loaned.

She carried a small house, the size of an orange, made of twig and twine. *Brindille et ficelle.* A château fit for a royal fairy family—a smaller version of the one in Raphaël's shed.

Setting the tiny house on the table, she helped herself to a chocolate cupcake.

I ran my fingers over the fairy palace, emotions battling inside my chest. "Who made this?"

"My papa." She gave a proud smile. "He made it from *brindille et ficelle.*"

Mon Dieu.

I half listened as she chatter-sang. *"My papa made a fairy palace / and this is a dollhouse for the palace / and the fairy children play with it all day long . . ."*

Sabine wasn't the daughter of local farmers. And she wasn't a wild thing. She was *ours*, here in the gardens.

And Raphaël . . . was her *father*.

Amour

As Sabine spewed cupcake crumbs, I replayed conversations with Bao and Raphaël and Mina. Of course they'd lied. I'd made it clear from day one that I didn't want to be around kids. Raphaël had tested the waters to see if I might change my mind. And Mina had urged me to talk with him. I should have known Bao was in on it, between the binoculars and the oubliette rescue.

Raphaël was a *father*.

I stared at his daughter, singing to herself with her chocolate-smeared mouth and orange bow and braids poking out.

The stakes were high for my *bricoleur*. Why *wouldn't* he keep her secret until he was certain he could trust me? And I had a bad track record—I'd divulged my child sighting to Antoinette. No wonder my friends had freaked out. *Mon Dieu*, I'd even told Raphaël that mentioning children was forbidden.

Sabine made a theatrical frown. "My papa says we're moving soon. But I'll make him change his mind. I'm tricky that way. We can't leave without the fairy palaces, so I'll hide them. The big one too. This is the little one. The bigger one is harder to carry, but I'll do it."

I recalled the fairy palace in Raphaël's woodshop—at least two feet tall.

"I'll hide it here tomorrow," she said. "And when my papa tries to leave, I'll say not until we find my fairy palaces."

I had an urge to scoop her up, twirl her around. Instead, I

folded my hands in my lap. "*Ma chose sauvage*, we need to tell your papa that we're friends."

"*Mais non*, Eloise!"

This poor child, living here *in hiding*. How had Raphaël let this happen?

But I couldn't judge. I'd been deceiving him all this time, allowing his daughter to deceive him.

"Sabine, listen. Tomorrow, I'll explain to your papa that we're friends. Everything will be okay. *Ça va?*"

She stroked her chin. "I want to be there when you tell him."

I nodded, not quite thinking it through.

An astute negotiator, she added, "And I want us to eat chocolate chip brownies. The three of us. *S'il te plaît.*"

I looked at Sabine with a new tenderness. What a relief it wasn't my sole responsibility to keep her safe. The others understood the situation far better than I did.

How long had she been hidden here? And why? Raphaël had come about five years ago—had he brought her with him? Had Iva and Amber known about her? Who was Sabine's mother?

I considered the paths ahead. If Raphaël left, he'd take Sabine, with or without the fairy palaces. Which would, despite the boundaries I'd set, break my heart.

❀

Alone during dusk, I sat by my dressing room window. For the first time in ages, I let my mind return to the ritual that Gaby's aunt had led, to cleanse our spirits and divine our futures. At the end, she'd offered me a riddle of sorts, something hope-inducing and heartbreaking at once.

I shivered in the breeze through the open window. Stars and planets had materialized. Was my fate somehow written in the cosmos, a puzzle waiting to be solved?

Heading to dinner, I couldn't help seeing everything in a starry new light. As I passed the harpist statue, she smiled darkly. And I smiled back lightly.

Entering the grove, I studied my companions around the candlelit table. What a secret burden they'd been carrying. I felt like hugging them all.

I assumed Sabine was in bed. Other than dinner times, I rarely saw all three of my friends gathered together. Someone must have been in charge of her at any given time during her waking hours. But of course, she was mischievous enough to slip away to see me.

I wanted to shout the truth from the treetops. Still, I had to proceed with caution rather than charging through the china shop.

During dinner I said nothing about our woodsprite. I sipped my rosé and complimented Raphaël on his ratatouille, made with aubergines and courgettes and tomatoes and *herbes de Provence* from this garden—savory, thyme, basil, fennel, lavender, marjoram, parsley, oregano. And I almost cried over his baked rosemary-lemon fish, wrapped in little parchment packages and tied with string like farewell gifts.

I asked Mina how her memoir was progressing, and she said in a giddy voice that she'd almost completed the final touches. "It will be ready for you to read soon, sister."

Bao patted her shoulder with pride.

For the cheese course, Raphaël had pressed violets and nasturtiums and chive flowers into the *chèvre*. A message to me? Seduction by flowers? For dessert, he served a rose crème brûlée topped with sugared petals—courage in life and love. Definitely a message.

As we were kissing goodnight, I whispered to the *bricoleur*, "Come to my porch tomorrow after work. I have something to tell you."

His face lit up. "I'll come by after I finish packing."

I'd thought he'd wanted me to give him a child one day . . . but he already *had* the child. He only wanted to know if I could love her.

On the way home, I paused by the river. The moon had set and the Milky Way stretched across the sky.

I'd finally, *finally* learned to be happy without a child . . . and then the universe had dropped one into my treehouse. This child was no longer in the world of fairy tales or nameless local farmers. Sabine had entered the realm of real life and the pain that could come with it. And yes, I could embrace being the zany aunt . . . but I'd *miss* her.

I'd miss her father.

Could I convince them to stay?

Should I?

Back at the treehouse, I stood in candlelight before Iva's jars of tea. My eyes swept over the labels, past SWEETENING SORROW and HEART-MENDING, and landed on AMOUR.

I brewed an entire pot.

That night in my sleep, the *amour* tea brought me fully back to the divination. The dream was vivid, as if I'd traveled back in time to relive it.

Gaby's aunt—a *curandera* from Oaxaca—had ushered us into the tiny bathroom of her mobile home in Colorado and, with reverence, lit candles and copal incense around a greenery-filled vase. Gaby went first, clad only in her underwear, stepping barefoot into the beige plastic shower. Her *tía* chanted prayers in Mixteco, whacked Gaby with fresh, pungent rue, then spit mezcal over her in great gusts. At the end, she announced that she saw a vision of Gaby with a baby at her breast.

My turn next. As the *tía* chanted, each blow of the plant bundle resonated in my core. My body was soaked and goose-bumped, my spirit scrubbed clean. Afterward, I waited to hear what the *tía* would say about my own destiny—whether there would be a child in my future too.

❋

Sparrow songs tugged me from my dream.

It felt like swimming up from ocean depths. Part of me resisted, trying to sink back down.

My unconscious self had clearly held on to that ritual in the trailer, every word, every detail. Still, I wasn't ready to relive it in its entirety. Part of me couldn't bear to hear the *tía* pronounce my destiny again.

As I walked to breakfast, my mind drifted to Sabine's wood-sprite eyes, bright brown and ever curious. I couldn't shake the regret—she wasn't joining us for meals . . . because of *me*. Sabine was why Raphaël often grabbed a second bowl of granola and dashed back to his vardo. She must have felt so left out.

Sitting at the table with my café au lait and almond croissant, I wanted to hear her cheery chatter-songs over meals, see her *chocolat chaud* mustache.

Later in the morning, as I mixed the compost, I thought of the journeys of our *merde*—microorganisms breaking it down with pine dust, generating nutrients, creating humus, allowing new soil to cradle seeds and feed tender shoots and let flowers bloom.

Maybe it was last night's tea, but I saw *amour* everywhere—not just the flowers' love for the shit, but love among birds and seeds and trees and mushrooms and humans and squirrels and moss and stones and river and light . . . so many intricate pathways flowing throughout the gardens.

When the sun was low and glinting pink, the woodsprite ran up the rope bridges. Mina must have undone the braids. Sabine's hair was back to its endearingly messy state. I folded my arms and smiled and gestured to the chocolate chip brownies with my chin.

"*Bonsoir, ma chose sauvage,*" I said.

"*Bonsoir, ma chose sauvage,*" she said.

"Is your papa coming?"

"*Oui.*" She bounced, giddy. "He doesn't know I'm here. He thinks it's just you. But I ran ahead in secret."

My heart pounded in nervous anticipation. I shouldn't have agreed to Sabine's plan. I should have talked to Raphaël, just the two of us.

"There he is!" She pointed through the trees, then put a chocolatey finger to her mouth. "Shhhh." She moved around the corner to hide, her brown eyes wide, as if this were a surprise *rrroompoos.*

I ran a hand through my hair. *Mon Dieu,* how would Raphaël take this? It would be understandable if he felt upset. Furious, even.

He walked up the swinging bridges, waving.

I drew in a breath and waved back.

Sabine crouched around the corner, suppressing a laugh. She had let go of any fears her papa would be angry, while mine had grown.

I watched the *bricoleur* ascend, recalling the first time I'd seen him. Those sexy, calloused hands.

He moved closer. His hair was damp—I could see the comb lines. He'd taken a shower, changed into clean clothes, scrubbed his stubbled face. When he leaned in for cheek kisses, I smelled cedar soap and let my lips linger.

Faces close, I saw Sabine's eyes in his. His had only hints of brown, forming a woodsy hazel, but something about the spacing and shape and *spirit* of their eyes was the same.

With a monstrous roar, Sabine leapt out.

Raphaël jumped.

So did I, even though I'd been expecting it.

Sabine broke into giggles.

Biting my lip, I watched Raphaël.

He stood before us, blinking.

In a flash, Sabine took advantage of my arms not being crossed—she plowed into me like a tiny football player and threw her arms around my waist and smiled sweetly at her father.

Raphaël's knees buckled. He stumbled backward into a chair, staring at us.

Say something, Eloise!

Sabine clung to me like a baby animal. Around us, the leaves fluttered and the river flowed and the sun shone, as if our human worlds hadn't been turned upside down.

I sat down beside the *bricoleur* and Sabine hopped into my lap, arranging my arms around her. Her message was clear: *We are besties.*

Raphaël's face contorted.

"Are you okay, Papa?" Sabine asked.

He sniffled, rubbed his damp face.

She moved into his lap, wiping the tears. "Are you sad, Papa?"

"Just a little, my bunny." He kissed her head, then looked up at me. "Mostly happy."

"Me too," said Sabine.

I let the *amour* and fear rush through me. "Me too."

Next step: *explaining.*

I braced for it while Sabine rearranged herself onto my lap and grabbed a book, flipping through it with gusto.

"I suspected she might be spending time *near* you," Raphaël began, "but more like *spying* on you. It didn't occur to me you'd become friends."

"It happened so fast. In less than a week. I thought she lived on a farm. I didn't know you were her father until yesterday."

He regarded his daughter, a creature of mystery. "The other night, she was singing about her wild thing friend on the Yellow Submarine. A mix of French and English. I asked where she'd learned it."

He paused, as if weighing whether to say more.

"And?"

"She said her *maman* sang it to her."

"Oh." I breathed in the orange blossom scent of her hair.

She tilted her head up, as if on cue. "I'm a baby robin and you're my nest."

Mon Dieu.

My chin quivered. I wanted to call her my little bird, kiss her feather-soft head. At the same time, I felt a panicked urge to cross my arms, fold my hands, put distance between us.

Which at this point was impossible.

If I Die

t dinnertime, when Sabine and Raphaël and I walked together into the grove, Mina hooted with delight. Even Bao let out a whoop.

As we filled them in over summer squash soup, they beamed.

Once Sabine fell asleep in her chair after the soup, Mina eyed Raphaël. "*Alors*, are you still leaving tomorrow?"

I held my breath.

He looked at me, his expression soft. "We can wait a couple months."

My whole body gave a satisfied sigh.

At breakfast the next day, our woodsprite was giddy, chatting up a storm, circling the table as Raphaël told her to sit down and finish her *pain au chocolat*. So endearingly *paternal*.

Late that afternoon, while Sabine was helping Mina crush basil and garlic with a mortar and pestle for *pistou*, my *bricoleur* and I brought our *apéro* to the indigo garden—his favorite, tucked between the white garden and the poison garden. All morning I'd been feeling fluttery about this impending tête-à-tête.

Raphaël and I settled side by side on a bench as a blue butterfly meandered over flax blossoms. I sipped my rosé, holding my glass up to let light shine through. A toast to the universe.

"So, Raphaël, how did Sabine come to be here?"

He watched a bee move from one harebell to another. "I didn't know of her existence until last year."

I blinked. "Really?"

"Remember Lucie, my ex-girlfriend?"

"The one who danced through life."

"She was Sabine's mother." He took a breath. "Six years ago, I was diagnosed with stage four colon cancer."

I stared at his profile, his jaw set like stone. "What—" I started, then stopped. "How—?" There were no words. He would have been twenty-seven and facing death.

"I had severe pain in my abdomen. They did scans and found tumors on my colon, liver, lungs, and lymph nodes. The survival rate was dismal. Since the cancer had already spread quite a bit, my oncologist said that statistically I had less than one year left. That I should enjoy the remaining time I had on earth. Not quite in those words," he added with a half smile.

"Mon Dieu." Antoinette's words came back to me: *"He's faced death before."*

"The chemo was hell. Pure poison."

Poison. She'd mentioned yew and periwinkle, the plant origins of chemo drugs. So, she'd known about his personal hell, just as she'd known about mine.

"It crushed me," he said in a raw voice. "Lucie couldn't handle it. She was five years younger than me, scared of sickness and pain and death. One night I mentioned that if I somehow survived, I might need a colostomy bag for the rest of my life. The next morning she was gone."

"She couldn't handle the *merde.*"

He gave a resigned nod. "She was a good person but so young— it was too much for her. I never heard from her again. I'd never felt so much despair. Then, after a few months, scans showed the tumors shrinking. My doctor recommended surgery to remove the remaining ones. But the next scans showed no tumors. My blood tests were clean. I've been in remission ever since."

I pressed my hand to my cheek. "What a miracle."

"It felt that way. But on the other hand, when there's a 5 percent survival rate, *someone* gets to be in that 5 percent. Why not me?"

An impossible marvel. I tried making sense of the timeline. "So, Lucie was pregnant with Sabine when she left?"

He stroked his chin stubble. "She must have been early on. I didn't know. She assumed I'd be dead soon, so she never told me. That's what her relatives say, at least."

"Sabine sings about them."

"*Oui.* They thought I was dead, didn't even know my last name. Lucie hadn't put my name on the birth certificate. Maybe she felt ashamed she'd left me. Anyway, she died on impact, so they couldn't ask my name."

He rubbed his face, steadied his voice. "She skidded into a tree on a stormy night. Sabine was still a baby—thankfully, she wasn't in the car. Her grandparents are her legal guardians. They live in a Romani encampment outside Lyon."

"That's where you went that weekend."

He nodded. "Sabine woke up missing them and asked to visit."

"They've raised her with love."

"They have. But their lives aren't easy. When the government breaks up one camp, they have to move to another. There's poverty, discrimination. Earlier this year, her uncles lost their construction jobs. The family was barely scraping by, performing music in plazas. They tracked down Lucie's friends and found out my last name. They hoped my parents might offer financial support for Sabine. But surprise . . . I was alive and well."

I watched an orange-tipped butterfly as I did the math. He'd come here about five years ago, no guarantees for the future. "So, you'd been in the gardens for years already."

"*Oui*. After my brush with death, I didn't want to spend life in a desk job. I worked for an environmental organization but wanted to work outside with my hands. Make things. When I came here, it felt perfect. I loved Bao and Mina and Iva. They helped me through the uncertainty, celebrated every time scans came back clear. Iva's concoctions helped too. And the garden itself healed me."

"So you just met Sabine this year?"

He nodded. "I visited her on weekends in the winter, and then she started coming here for weekends in the spring. She loved it, became quick friends with Mina and Bao. We grew so close so fast. She became everything to me."

My eyes filled—I understood on a heart level how this could happen.

He gave me a warm, knowing look. "So I asked her family if I could bring her here for the summer. It was against the rules, but I figured if we got caught, I'd just lose my job and leave the gardens with Sabine. A reasonable risk. And honestly?"

He dropped his voice. "I felt scared to leave the gardens for good. I didn't know what might happen. I still don't. I might be back in the *merde*." He paused. "Like Amber."

"I get it." I swirled my rosé. "Did Iva know Sabine?"

"I wish. Iva had already left and we were waiting for her replacement. Mina and Bao were on board with hiding Sabine for a few months. And to Sabine it felt like a game. Unfortunately, we had to keep her hidden when Amber came."

"You didn't trust her?"

"With good reason." He pressed his fingers to his temple. "When she discovered Sabine, she blackmailed us."

My jaw dropped.

"Bao gave her a pearl necklace—an heirloom from his grandmother. In exchange, Amber said she wouldn't tell La Patronne."

No wonder Raphaël had been skittish about me. Any sympathy I'd had for Amber dissolved. "What a jerk."

"She felt upset when I rejected her advances. But she wasn't someone I connected with." He ran his thumb along the stem of his glass. "I needed to be with someone who could relate, in some way, to what I'd been through. Anyway, she took it personally. I think her pain drove her to blackmail us."

"Very understanding of you." A part of me couldn't help thinking, *Oh, Amber, maybe you* did *deserve a curse.*

"Otherwise," he continued, "hiding Sabine here has worked out fine. We slip through the hole in the wall to visit her relatives. Antoinette and La Patronne have no idea. But this can't go on forever. Sabine starts school in September, less than two months away—and she should be with other kids." He paused. "I have to take the risk and leave."

"Will she live with you outside the gardens?"

He nodded. "She'll visit her relatives often. It's important they stay close." He paused. "If I die, my daughter needs to be loved."

If I die . . . what a terrifying *if* at age thirty-three.

Overwhelmed, I sipped my rosé. His situation scared me but made me see him in a new light. He knew how it felt to have your body betray you. To be dealt an unfair hand. To be in pain, naked beneath a hospital gown, stripped of dignity. To look death in the face. To feel alone despite a partner. To have your partner leave you. To know your child could be torn away.

He knew the risks of loving.

"I'm sorry I didn't tell you. I didn't want the cancer to affect how you treated me. It makes me feel so . . . exposed. I wanted to put it behind me. It's hard for me to talk about."

His hand was resting between us on the stone bench. I put mine over his. "I'm sorry you went through that." I struggled for words. The woodsprite's face came to mind, her exuberant life force, her affection for her papa. "I'm glad you and Sabine have each other."

He squeezed my hand, looked at me with no hesitation, no half-truths, no holding back. "You mean a lot to her, Ellie."

I forced myself to keep hold of his gaze.

He tilted his head. "You mean a lot to me."

Now would have been a good time to lean in for a kiss. But I had to get the *merde* out of the way.

"I adore Sabine," I began. "The reason I felt terrible around children—it's because I can't get pregnant and stay pregnant."

Understanding filled his face.

"I lost my babies when they were still inside me. Zinnia, Violet, Sage, and Iris. And in a different way, I lost Melvin, the boy I tried to adopt."

He set down his rosé and put his other hand on top of mine.

"Here's the thing," I continued. "I *love* children. My job was even playing with kids. And it almost killed me that I couldn't have my own."

I paused and sipped my wine. "Then, my first weeks here . . . I was *happy*, without my own child. I realized it was possible. I felt free. But then I met Sabine. And it scared me to get close to her, but I mostly felt amazed. For the first time in ten years, I could just enjoy being with a child." I gave a half smile. "It helped that I thought she was a magical woodsprite at first."

"Sorry we didn't help you out there."

I moved closer, touching my lips to his. Now our kissing felt even deeper and more real. No more secrets. No need to hold back. I kissed him harder, pulled him toward me.

He drew back. "Listen, Ellie, can we take things slow?" He

cleared his throat. "I really like you." Another throat clear. "I'm just a bit nervous, out of practice."

"So am I." I gave him another long kiss, then forced myself to withdraw. "*Oui*, slow is good."

Part of me was screaming, *Really, Eloise? Slow is good? He's leaving in two months! How can you take it slow?*

He put his finger to my lips. "Shh, hear that?"

Sounds came from the poison garden. Footsteps, leaves rustling. I squinted through the morning glory trellis. Someone was in there.

I tiptoed to the plant wall, peering over hydrangeas. Antoinette was snipping devil's trumpet with bare hands.

Raphaël rested his palm on the small of my back.

I pushed aside leaves to get a better look.

At my movement, Antoinette whirled around and locked her gaze onto mine.

I offered an awkward wave. "*Bonsoir, Madame.*"

Raphaël's hand tensed on my back.

Antoinette narrowed her eyes and straightened up, one hand holding the datura blooms, the other raising the scissors in an almost threatening gesture. "La Patronne is quite put out." Her voice quavered. "One has entered the tunnel and gossiped in town. And now one is spying."

With a rush of indignance, I said, "Then why hasn't she asked one to leave?"

A long pause. "For better or worse, Mademoiselle, you have talents with the flowers." Her voice softened a notch. "Your heart-mending tea has helped La Patronne."

Part of me felt a strange compassion for the mysterious boss, yet part of me wanted to send her my own rule: *One must not enter my home and leave creepy notes and poisonous flowers.*

"Still," Antoinette added, "La Patronne's patience has limits."

Her face shone pink, damp with sweat, twisting with emotion, her cold mask falling away. Something guttural, almost bestial, crept into her voice. "She could snap. She has done so before."

Goose bumps sprung up on my arms. La Patronne wasn't the one who would snap. *Antoinette would.* They were one and the same.

I felt sure of it. Antoinette was the one mourning a baby, cutting a fresh bouquet for the grave.

After a stretch of silence, Raphaël told her, "Please tell La Patronne not to worry. We'll stick to the rules."

"She's keeping a close eye on you." With a curt nod, Antoinette turned away.

Now it was crystal clear what she meant: *I'll* be keeping a close eye on you.

Tugging my hand, Raphaël led me back to the bench.

I whispered, "You think Antoinette might actually be La Patronne?"

"Why would she pretend?"

"A power trip? Playing games?" I sucked in a breath. "But think about it—no one has ever seen La Patronne. And the way Antoinette talks about her—it's bizarre."

He wrinkled his brow. "Then who else is living in the château?"

True, someone else was there. Or at least *had been* there. That night in the castle, I'd heard footsteps in the corridor, a door closing. *"Les Dames Blanches?"*

He gave a short, uncertain laugh. "Seriously, Ellie?"

Whatever the explanation, Antoinette seemed more and more like someone to pity. We'd pulled back the curtain, revealed the scary Goddess to be a flawed, perhaps traumatized, human. I shook myself. "Listen, what matters is Sabine. Whether she's safe."

"Agreed. I think she's fine."

"You think Antoinette heard us mention her?"

He squeezed my hand. "We were being quiet."

"You're right." Still, a power coiled inside me, a snake ready to pounce at any threat to my woodsprite. "I just care about her. So much it scares me."

"I know, Ellie. I know."

Wee Cabbage

While Sabine was bird-watching with Bao the next morning, Raphaël invited me to his vardo. At the threshold, he took a deep breath and opened the door—Dutch style, carved and painted with gilded swirls, something from a fairy tale. "I've been wanting to invite you in, but Sabine's stuff is everywhere."

And it was. Pink hair bands and stuffed animals and picture books were strewn around, as if mistral winds had whipped through the six-by-twelve-foot space.

"It's like a big fairy palace," I said, and he laughed.

Straight ahead stood an elevated bed with fringed burgundy velvet curtains and luxurious bedding in deep reds and forest greens. My imagination ran wild. This was the perfect bed for a night of unbridled passion followed by extreme coziness.

Take it slow, Eloise.

But it would be magical to wake up here with my leg tossed over my *bricoleur's* hip.

SLOW, Eloise!

To the right was a wide bench covered in padded velvet and piled with pillows—where Sabine slept, I assumed. To the far left was a chest of drawers, the woodwork and artistry exquisite. And to the near left, an elegant cast-iron woodstove holding a copper teapot.

My *bricoleur* had created *wonderment*. "So this is what's inside your soul-case, Raphaël."

He grinned enough to show a dimple. "It was my way of grieving," he said, tidying up toys and books. "After I moved here, I ran into a friend of a friend at the hospital where I get my scans. He told me about Lucie's death, but for whatever reason, he didn't mention her baby. The world outside felt cruel, so I retreated even further."

A refuge for the broken.

He ran his hand over the carved arch above the bed. "I researched Romani vardos, tried to make every detail authentic."

He rearranged cushions, folded a blanket. "When Sabine appeared, I realized the vardo would be perfect for her. A way to stay connected to her roots. It was like a part of me knew all along that I was building it for her . . . even though I didn't know she existed."

That made a strange kind of sense. "Well, it's magnificent, beyond anything I'd imagined."

I moved farther inside. Just a few steps brought me to the other end, at the edge of the bed. The chest to the left held a woman saint—dark-skinned, with flowing black hair, a white flower tucked behind her ear, a gold crown, and turquoise and white flowered robes. A gold chain with a star charm was draped around her hands, which were held in prayer. Two feet tall, she stood on a pedestal of pink and red roses.

"Sainte Sara," said Raphaël, following my gaze. "Patron saint of the Romani people. Lucie made pilgrimages with her family to honor her every May. The town isn't far from here. They say that in the time of Christ, when the Three Maries were coming ashore as refugees, they were caught in stormy waters."

"I read about them. A version of the Triple Goddess."

He nodded. "Sainte Sara brought her little boat out to help, but the sea was so rough, she couldn't reach them. In desperation, she threw her cloak to the waters. It transformed into a raft to bring them ashore. A miracle."

I moved closer to the saint, noticed pebbles and seedpods and dried blooms around her pedestal. Offerings from the woodsprite, no doubt.

"Sabine talks to her sometimes," Raphaël said, arranging the stuffed animals.

My heart melted at the thought of Sabine chatting in earnest with Sainte Sara. "Exactly how much longer do I have with you two?"

"She starts school in two months, second week of September. That's when we'll move into the cottage. We were planning to stay in their encampment till then." He took my hand. "But things have changed."

Two full moons from now, they would be gone.

"She'll be safe here?" I tightened my grip on his hand.

His brows knitted. "I think it's reasonable to keep her here now that we're all looking out for her. She adores you—I can't just tear her away."

I breathed out in relief. If he'd assessed the risks and deemed his daughter safe, that would suffice. Earlier, when I'd told Mina and Bao my theory that Antoinette was La Patronne, they'd taken it as more evidence that she was just playing games, no real threat.

Still, that power stayed coiled inside me, ready to protect my woodsprite.

Raphaël stroked my palm with his thumb. "I wish we could stay longer, but I have to put her first."

"Of course." A lump formed in my throat. *Two more months.*

He wrapped his arms around me. "Before Sabine I thought, *If I die, I die.* But now things are different. Whatever happens, she needs a family."

I drew him closer, until his wet cheeks were against mine. "So many people love her."

"I know. But I want to see her grow up. I want to make stuff with her. One day I want to make stuff with her children. I want to make stuff with *their* children."

Our foreheads fell against each other and his voice dropped. "I have nightmares. I die and Sabine's wandering alone, calling out for me."

My stomach knotted. I couldn't help going down the dark road of what-ifs. I pulled him in, until the lengths of our bodies were touching. "Maybe it's about trusting in the universe . . . but having a backup plan."

"*Oui*," he murmured, lips grazing my hair. His trembling calmed, leaving a stillness between us.

I tucked my chin into the crook of his neck, breathed in his scent of heartwood. At the core, this wasn't about us. It was about our woodsprite. "You're a good father."

At summer's end, Sabine and Raphaël would walk out of the gardens. And cancer might be a constant threat for him. Could I let myself grow closer, knowing it might end in more loss? Could I invite uncertainty back into my life—hope and fear?

My mind circled around the divination from Gaby's aunt. A marvel that no longer seemed impossible. A seed of hope that had been growing in darkness. And now it was poking a tender shoot into the sunlight, asking the sky, *What if, what if, what if?*

Over Raphaël's shoulder, I took another look at Sainte Sara. She was also called Sara-la-Kali, possibly influenced by the goddess Kali, in India—the origin place of the Roma. Although nuanced, Kali was most famous for death and destruction. Sara, on the other hand, was known for brave compassion.

That's what I would choose, heading into future storms.

❀

I'd never imagined how *fun* it could be to shower a child with French terms of affection. Mina and Bao offered a buffet to choose from: my little cabbage, my little shrimp, my little chick, my little she-wolf, my little flea, my bunny.

Now that Sabine's existence was out in the open, she ate breakfast, lunch, and her pre-twilight dinner with us in the grove. My wild thing was a natural performer, turning every meal into a dinner theater event. She embodied a scrappy young Édith Piaf in her busking days, belting out "La Vie en Rose," accompanied by Raphaël on guitar.

When she'd catch sight of the moon, she'd declare, "Ah! *La lune! La lune!*" and sing her own meandering version of "Au Claire de la Lune," which morphed into a wild *rrroompoos*.

Before bed, she'd yawn and swipe the air with her wild thing paw and give a sleepy, throaty *"roar!"*

Sometimes, out of the blue, she'd say, "Speaking of . . ." when no one had been speaking of it. "Speaking of cake, Eloise, we should make an opera cake today!"

She rotated among a smattering of books—*African Folktales* with Mina, *Flora and Fauna of Provence* with Bao, mid-century American picture books with me, and the Madeleine series with Raphaël. She had a penchant for acting out the scenes, even livening up Bao's nonfiction selections with her wild boar imitation.

We'd take turns watching her throughout the day. Every morning when Raphaël would ask, "What chores do you want to do first?" she'd respond, "Saving the day!" After flying around like a superhero, she'd choose compost duty so that she could be near me, *merde* and all.

She took me on mystery flower treasure hunts to discover the hidden ones "invisible to human eyes," she said with wide-eyed drama. "But we're wild things, so we can see them!" We followed gossamer voices to flowers I'd never seen or even heard of, petals the elusive color of dawn, nectar scented with the Otherworld, voices like echoes of harps, urging us to pluck them and dry them in the sunshine of my atelier.

One afternoon Sabine and I munched on fresh-picked cherries between stanzas of "I Gave My Love a Cherry." My voice cracked with emotion as we sang the last verse—she belted it out in English with her French accent and five-year-old earnestness.

A cherry when it's blooming, it has no stone
A chicken in the egg, it has no bone
A baby when it's sleeping, does no crying
The story of my love, it has no end

When she asked what it meant, I explained, "They're riddles, things that seem impossible. But they're not. How can there be a cherry without a stone? When it's in flower form. Remember back when the cherry trees bloomed?"

She nodded and cuddled deeper into my lap.

"Well, each of those blooms turned into a cherry. In the spring, each flower was still getting ready. If you're patient, you'll notice things can grow and change into something delicious."

By the time twilight turned to night, Sabine would be asleep in the caravan—she slept like a rock—and the rest of us would gather in the dining grove, chatting about our wee cabbage. She'd sparked transformation in the others too.

Mina tossed an arm around Bao. "Oh, remember how you treated her like she was made of glass at first?"

He recounted how much Sabine had reminded him of Vivienne, so innocently brave—and he'd steeled himself for the moment she'd get hurt. Little by little, he'd grown closer to her, realizing that when she scraped a knee or stubbed a toe, he was more than capable of making her feel better. And pho turned out to be her most beloved food, their favorite dish to make together.

"Children are resilient creatures," he concluded.

Raphaël gave him an appreciative grin. "Sabine and Bao have

a sweet relationship founded on scientific identification of flora and fauna."

With a wink, Mina said, "We need to get her some khaki outfits with lots of pockets."

Bao sipped his Beaujolais, his expression pensive. "Bad things happen, people get hurt. We take refuge. Then we forgive ourselves and others and the world. We focus on the good things. And make them even better. Sabine taught me that."

Mina patted his knee. "I was nervous around her at first too. You all know I had painful memories. But it's so easy to laugh with children, and I love to laugh."

I smiled. "I thought I couldn't be around kids anymore until Sabine."

"Our little bird," said Bao.

"Our little shrimp," said Raphaël.

"Our little flea," said Mina.

"Our little wild thing," I finished.

If only this could last forever, I thought, sinking into this fragile moment in Paradise.

The Divination

he moon waxed and then waned—the Holly moon of July, named for the tree that offered protection, according to the ancient Celts.

Here and there, I caught eerie glimpses of *Les Dames Blanches* from my treehouse window. They dropped no more weapons, showed no signs of interest in me. I assumed that beneath their white cloaks were humans, playing their bizarre games. Still, I was careful to break no rules other than the inevitable no-child one.

The comforts of Paradise wrapped around my little family, and we relaxed into our flowered nest. Despite Herculean efforts to stay inside the eccentric-aunt box, I was feeling more and more like Sabine's *maman* every day.

Antoinette made Raphaël repair the hole in the wall, watching him like a bird of prey to make sure he was thorough. She'd deduced the hole's existence after our market outing and admonished us for keeping it a secret, claiming that Paradise could be overrun if outsiders discovered it. After it had been sealed, Bao assured us we could use ropes and harnesses to climb over the wall if needed.

Otherwise, our interactions with Antoinette were just as business-like as ever. At times moments of warmth even slipped into our conversations. She'd thank me for my healing teas . . . on behalf of La Patronne, of course. Or she'd admire how the flowers were thriving under my care. And sometimes, when she let vulnerability leak out, I'd feel for her. Maybe her game playing gave her a sense of control. Maybe, in a twisted way, it had saved her from her own oubliette.

Early one morning, a banging noise broke through my dream. Someone was rapping on my bedroom door. I pushed up the eye mask and squinted at the windows. Sunrise reflections bounced off glass, making it impossible to see the person. The Goddess?

The knob turned back and forth and the door rattled in its frame. After the dagger incident, I'd been locking up every night. I rubbed my eyes, cleared my head. Grabbing a silver candelabra as a weapon, I called out, "Who is it?"

"Sister! It's me! Open up!" Mina's voice was urgent.

I opened the door and pulled her inside, locking it again behind her. Not that it would do any good. If anyone wanted to get inside, all it would take was a rock through the antique glass. Maybe just a pebble with some force.

I turned to Mina, who was holding a massive pile of paper. Carefully, she placed it onto my bedside table, eyeing the foot-tall stack with pride and exhaustion.

My mouth dropped open. "Your memoir?"

"I stayed up all night revising." Her tired face beamed. "It's finished."

I threw my arms around her. "Can I read it?"

"*Mais, bien sûr!* That's why it's here. You'll be the first person to read my life story."

I ran my fingers up and down the edges, absorbing the immense work it represented. A memoir twenty years in the making. I flipped through with reverence, observing the neat cursive, the page numbers carefully handwritten in the upper right corners. *In Search of Paradise*, she'd titled it.

"I'm honored, *mon amie*." I placed my hand over the manuscript, almost feeling its breath and pulse. "Can you tell the others I won't be working today?"

She wrinkled her brow. "Why?"

"I'll be reading your book."

Suppressing a smile, she nodded. "Enjoy."

Once she left, I cozied up in my library with cup after cup of tisane. As the sun rose higher outside the windows, I read and read. The others brought me breakfast and lunch and an *apéro*. Briefly, I stretched my legs with Sabine in a mini dance session in the woods.

But most of the day I was with young Mina in rural Senegal, and then heading north with her, through the dry dunes of the Sahara, past the goat-covered argan trees of Morocco, and then on a stomach-turning boat ride to Spain. And along the way, I shook with fear as she faced the cruelty of humanity—witnessing her companions beaten and shot dead, evading sex traffickers, making daring escapes. And my chest warmed at the compassion of strangers who risked their lives to help her reach safety. At the end, I breathed the deepest sigh of gratitude when she arrived in the soft sunlight of southern France. Here her memoir concluded, at the gates of Paradise.

I reclined in the chaise longue and let her story settle into my bones as I watched *l'heure bleue* descend. I thought of this extraordinary woman who called me sister, now awaiting my response in her little hobbit hole. My heart felt tender and full—shattered and put together again, chapter by chapter, over the course of a day. The course of a life.

I had to restrain myself from running out into the twilight to Mina. Once the last indigo bits of daylight had turned to darkness streaked with moonlight, I walked outside and down the path, past the kitchen where Raphaël was making dinner, all the way to Mina's house.

I knocked on her round, wooden door.

When she answered, I threw my arms around her. "The world needs your story, sister. How can I help?"

My lantern lit up her delighted face. She ushered me inside her candle-filled home. Illuminated inside and out, she settled onto her sofa and patted the cushion beside her, and together, notebooks and pens in hand, we mapped out a plan.

All week, Mina and I spent every spare minute together, editing her memoir. We decided that once Sabine and Raphaël left in a month, she would buy a laptop in town and dictate her manuscript while I typed. We'd research agents and editors at the local library, then send off query emails. The thought of our next steps made Mina giddy and nervous, and I kept assuring her how much her story would mean to the world.

Mina and I hoped this project would soften the blow of Sabine and Raphaël leaving in September. Bao, of course, insisted he'd pitch in with publishing research—we'd need to keep ourselves occupied when our nest was empty. And in the meantime, for the next month, Mina would do the final polish.

Even with the plan, we knew this autumn would hurt.

On the first of August, Mina made a cheery announcement at breakfast. "Time for the harvest feast!"

I cupped my warm café au lait, still groggy. *"Pardon?"*

"Halfway between the summer solstice and fall equinox," she said, stirring sugar into her espresso.

Bao sipped his condensed-milk coffee. "Iva celebrated all the seasonal festivals."

I thought of our summer solstice ritual, how my life had changed since then. The odd thought struck me: *Iva would be proud.*

This woman wise in flowers might even welcome me into her flower witch club.

I licked foam from my lip. "How do we celebrate?"

"We feast tonight, *bien sûr*," said Mina.

"A feast!" cried Sabine, leaping from her chair and doing a comical disco dance. "With chocolate?"

"Double chocolate brownies," I assured her.

Mina offered me a mischievous smile—she had something up her sleeve. "And I'm preparing you a flower bath."

My mind went to her clawfoot tub nestled in jasmine blooms.

"*Merci*," I said, feeling undeserving. Why did a vague guilt, even shame, come over me when people did kind things for me?

"Can I have a bath too?" said Sabine.

"But you always run away and hide at bath time." Raphaël ruffled her hair.

"Well, maybe I like *flower* baths!"

Bao leaned in toward our little shrimp. "How about you and your papa and I go to the orchards to pick fruit instead?"

Sabine made a face.

I tugged her ponytail. "We'll give you a flower bath another time, *d'accord?*"

She did three pirouettes and collapsed, dizzy on the ground. "Soon, *s'il te plaît!*"

"Soon, my bunny," her papa assured her. "Now sit down and drink your *chocolat*."

Mina turned to me. "*Alors*, after breakfast, get your towel and robe and meet me at my place."

She and Bao and Raphaël exchanged secret smiles that left me wondering what they were up to.

It wasn't till I was on the way to the hobbit hole, wearing my robe and carrying my towel, that I remembered I hated baths. I paused by the river, fighting the urge to run back to my treehouse.

But thinking of Mina, I took deep breaths and forced myself to keep going as sunflowers urged me onward. *Tournesols* in French, meaning *turn toward the light*.

Outside her home, she greeted me with a hug and led me around back toward the tub, chatting about how Iva had made her a flower bath once and now she wanted to do the same for me.

Then she stopped in her tracks and clutched my arm. "Sister, why do you look like someone just died?"

I exhaled. "Baths remind me of pain and blood and loss. I'm sorry. I don't know if I can do this."

She took my hand and clucked with sympathy. "We'll see."

I rambled on. "If you're trying to thank me for helping with your memoir, you don't have to. I love your book. It's not work—"

She shushed me, pulling me along.

We reached the bathtub, tucked into jasmine trellises. The water was deep and steaming and scented with chamomile and rose and lavender. Fresh pink and red petals had been arranged into a heart, floating on the surface. The olive wood slab was set across the lip of the tub, holding a clay teapot and cup and vase of chamomile blossoms.

"I don't deserve this," I said.

"Why on earth not?"

"I failed, over and over." I heard the words come out of my mouth, without entirely understanding them. Just when I thought I was whole, another broken part of myself emerged. "I couldn't do what's supposed to come naturally. I just . . . *failed* at the most basic thing in life."

And as the words came out of my mouth, I realized who I was talking to—someone whose body hadn't delivered a live baby either, through no fault of her own, of course. For my friend, I had nothing but compassion. Why not for myself?

Mina pressed her palms to my cheeks. "You are perfect, sister."

I hugged her, my face damp. "You're better than perfect."

I turned to the steaming tub, taking in the heart made of petals my friend had so carefully arranged . . . for *me*. Of course I wouldn't reject this gift. "*Merci*, sister. Now, if you'll excuse me, I'm going to take a bath."

With a smile, she turned away and vanished into her hobbit hole.

I untied my robe, draped it on the nearby stump, and tested the water with my toe. Hot but not too hot. I stepped into the tub and slid my body underwater as steam moistened my face and heat softened my muscles. I poured a cup of tea—lavender, rose, and chamomile—which Mina must have steeped ahead of time and added to the bathwater too. Submersed to my neck, I sipped the tea, feeling the flowers enter me inside and out, working their magic.

Bravery in life and love.

This bath felt different from those of the past decade—this one immersed me in love. I dipped my head, then rose back to the surface. Ages ago, I used to love baths. In my teens, I'd pour salts into the hot water and luxuriate, eating chocolates and reading books, not even caring if the edges got wet.

How to integrate my before self and after self? I recalled the art therapy with MacKenzie. Her therapist had told me the next step, which had never come to pass as far as I knew, once she was returned to her bio mom. MacKenzie would have drawn a picture of her before self, before the trauma, then torn it into tiny pieces, mixed it into a wet glue solution, and brought up a thin layer of goo with a screen. After the brand-new paper dried, she would have drawn a picture of her integrated self over it.

With a pang, I sent her a flower message of hope. Then I picked up a chamomile blossom, symbol of innocence and purity. I tore the tiny white petals from the sunshiny center and let them fall into the bath. One by one, I tore apart the rest of the blooms, dozens of them.

Their essence melted into the water and absorbed into my pores. The tea slid down my throat, warming my center. The torn-up petals were creating something new.

I saw my before self—young Eloise with her hopes for a family full of children—then I saw myself now. My two selves merged into something whole, something that understood that life might not fulfill expectations, yet was still a miracle.

I fell into a trance, slipping back into the ceremony with Gaby's aunt, deeper and closer to her divination. As in my dream, the details were vivid, from the yellow towel she wrapped around me after the *limpia*, to the gap between her teeth as she'd pronounced my fate. With a huge smile, Gaby had translated: "My *tía* sees beautiful brown eyes on the face of a beautiful girl."

For a moment, I'd seen those brown eyes too. Melted into them. Then rational thought had broken through. Here was the impossibility: Josh and I both had blue eyes, so there were only recessive genes in the mix. Barring any rare mutations, a brown-eyed girl made of egg and sperm from a blue-eyed couple was impossible. There would be no brown-eyed daughter in my future.

Breathing in scents of chamomile and rose and lavender, I drifted out of my trance, back into my body soaking among flowers. Now I felt only peace as I remembered how, a couple of months later, Gaby had called to say her *tía's* prediction had come true—she was pregnant—on the same day I got a negative result.

Over the years, I'd tried to forget my own divination. It wasn't until much later, filling out adoption papers, that I'd wondered if a brown-eyed girl would come our way. I was thrilled when we were assigned Melvin from Honduras, but after four months of hoping and dreaming, the adoption fell through. I'd never even gotten to meet him, but the loss wrecked me.

My heart couldn't withstand any more attempts. The brown-eyed girl faded away.

Now, behind my closed lids, amid sweet flower whispers, I saw those beautiful brown eyes.

Sabine's eyes.

After the bath, I worked in the color-themed gardens in a blissful daze, a profusion of sunflowers chattering with me.

But as I walked by the entrance to the poison room, a chill shook me.

Out walked Antoinette.

We nearly crashed into each other. My heart raced as I sputtered an apology. *"Oh, pardon. Desolée,* Antoinette.*"*

She blinked, looking disoriented and shaken, a crack splitting through her icy facade. Of course she still exuded impeccable mid-century style in her signature silk skirt and low heels and matching handbag. Yet grass stains marred the knees of her stockings, and strands fell from the twist of her white-blonde hair. Makeup was smeared over puffy, red eyes.

She straightened her shoulders. "What are you doing here, Mademoiselle?"

"Tending to the flower rooms." I hoped she wouldn't accuse me of spying.

Her voice emerged, fragile. "There is no need to go into this particular garden."

"Bien sûr."

I peered behind her shoulder, spotted a fresh bouquet of

datura on the grave marker. "The baby buried here—was it yours, Antoinette?"

She staggered backward, as if she'd been hit.

I reached out to steady her, felt her arms shaking. Compassion swept over me, a bond forged by secret grief.

"I'm so sorry," I whispered. "I can only imagine how sad you feel, even all these years later."

"No, Mademoiselle. You cannot."

"My own babies—they never drew a breath either," I said, thinking of the epitaph on the grave.

She rubbed her eyes. "Your babies were conceived in love, were they not?"

I paused. The centrifuged sperm injected into me wasn't exactly an act of love, but yes, Josh and I had loved each other, had wanted a baby to love too. Finally, I nodded.

"The baby in that grave was not," she said. "Quite the opposite."

Understanding sank in. I wanted to hug her, but of course, she'd never let me. Instead, I hugged myself. "I'm so sorry, Antoinette. Can I help you in some way? Maybe make you a tisane for . . ." I faltered.

For what? Dealing with the aftermath of a rape, decades later? I could only guess at some kind of violence. And in response, another kind of violence came through in the angry Goddess notes, the enraged statues. "For whatever you survived, Antoinette," I finished.

She looked back at the grave. Then she teetered away, as if she could fall at any time, then vanished through the wall of cypresses.

Seeing her so broken made me understand: *I am whole.*

Handfasting

ina intercepted me on the way back from the gardens, but I said nothing about Antoinette, feeling the need to honor her secret, our twisted bond.

I simply gushed about the bath as my friend glowed. And then, in stops and starts, I told her about the brown-eyed girl.

She made the connection at once. "Sabine!"

I gave a cautious nod. "I'll be her eccentric American aunt and she'll be my woodsprite niece."

"Oh, you'll be more than that."

"The *curandera* might have just felt she'd be an important child to me." My body tensed with the familiar fear of hope. "That's all."

Mina made a doubtful face. "We'll see."

Later that afternoon, Sabine was jumping up and down, begging to help Bao and Mina prepare the harvest feast. The *plat principal* would be a Provençal daube, flanked by roasted carrots and *pommes de terre*, the beef soaked in Syrah and crushed garlic and garden-picked herbs, then roasted for hours. Mina agreed to let Sabine help but claimed that three cooks in the kitchen were enough, shooing Raphaël and me away.

No shooing needed.

We headed to the river. For weeks we'd snuck in kisses but stopped there.

Now, at the water's edge, every cell in my body—and every bit of ether in my spirit—felt ready to move to . . . *something more.*

Once we'd stripped to our underwear and waded in, I looked at his damp chest and could stand it no longer. I pulled him beneath the waterfall. Inside this little heart cave, I kissed him, longer and deeper than ever before.

He met me with equal desire, clutching my waist and pressing my body against the length of his.

After a moment, I forced myself to pull away and fixed my gaze onto his. "Raphaël, I want you."

He looked shocked, in a good way, a dazed smile spreading.

I'd never expressed such urgency to an *amant*. And why hadn't I? It lit a bonfire inside me, as if my entire core were heartwood.

His voice emerged, low and gravelly. "I want you too, Ellie."

Resisting the overwhelming urge to touch him, everywhere, *immediately,* I hugged myself over the thin, damp fabric of my sports bra. "But first, you need to understand what you're getting into."

He gave a nod, endearingly earnest.

"I think I'm better now." I hesitated, searching for words. "But in the past, sex hurt."

His expression softened and he drew me close. "I'm so sorry."

"Merci," I said, hot tears in my eyes. "I just want you to know, in case, well . . ." My voice tapered off.

He pressed his hand to my cheek. "There's something I should tell you too." After a beat, he said, "Before the cancer treatments, the doctors warned me that afterward, I might not—" He stumbled over his words. "I might not regain normal sexual function."

I put my hand over his. "And?"

"Well, I have no idea about my sperm count or fertility. And I haven't been with a woman since the diagnosis. But as far as I can tell, it's all working. Still, you should know, I might feel nervous if . . ." He cleared his throat. "Not to be presumptuous."

"It's not presumptuous." I leaned in, letting my lips graze his. "And you're not alone. I'm kind of terrified too."

Now would be the time a normal couple would chat about condoms. I dredged up the awkward words. "Obviously, pregnancy isn't something we need to worry about."

He gave a wry smile. "And we've both been celibate or monogamous for years."

I anticipated the feel of him inside me, touching me and filling me. A thrill shot through me—my shower escapades times a hundred. And when his lips met mine, times a thousand.

I sank into the warmth of his kisses, so safe and comfortable, but with an edge of exhilaration. As he pressed his body to mine, our sighs turned into something almost incandescent. Our kisses grew deeper, more urgent than any kisses of the past.

We pulled our bodies closer as the waterfall rushed beside us, cool river flowing over hot skin. Desire swept through me and the last of my fears dissolved. Judging by the blissed-out look on his face, so did his.

I paused to catch my breath, noting that so far everything was indeed in working order on his end. Mine too.

"It works," I said, pressing my forehead to his, feeling a laugh burble up.

"It does," he said, laughing along with me.

I'd never felt closer to him, and part of me wanted to try more, *right now* . . . How good would actual *sex* feel with him? I glanced at the sky, now a ripe shade of peach, the sunlight angled and golden. Dusk would come soon, but I didn't want this to end. I grazed my lips over his neck. "Want to go to my place for an *apéro, mon chéri?*"

Tilting my chin, he found my lips again. *"Oui, ma chérie."*

I remembered the first time I'd seen him, carrying the tray to my treehouse, how I'd thought he was young and carefree, while I was an old, dried-up crone. And now, I could only imagine what had been going through his mind.

As we walked along the path to my place, hand in hand, I whispered thanks to the flowers and spirits of the gardens. Despite the shadows here, there were forces of *amour* rooting for us.

❧

Our *apéro* involved a great deal of Kir-flavored kissing on my treehouse porch until the sun dropped behind the castle turrets. *L'heure bleue* was descending. Inside the library, I lit candles while Raphaël walked to the bookshelves and brushed his fingers over the bindings.

His hand rested on my old copy of *Home for a Bunny* and he picked it up, skimming the pages by candlelight. His face softened. "Sabine tells me this story sometimes, but she changes it. When the bunny finds his home, you're always there."

Part of me wanted to spill out the *curandera's* divination, but part of me held back, thinking it might pressure him. I filled a pot with water and lit the antique stove. *"Amour* tea?" I tapped the jar of petals, feeling playful.

"Perfect." Raphaël walked over, kissing my neck near my earlobe.

His touch sparked a cascade of thrills in my center. Lightheaded, I grabbed the jar, savoring his hands grazing my hip, my shoulder, my waist. I relished this casual way *amants* touch each other.

Mon Dieu, why weren't we naked yet?

Take it slow, Eloise.

When the tea had brewed, I poured it into porcelain cups and drizzled in lavender honey. The taste was exquisite but different from what I remembered. I could distinguish the expected rose and jasmine . . . but earthier undercurrents added mystery to the mix. It brought heat to my chest, opened my heart, but more than that—somehow, it elevated my senses. I savored the steam against my lips, the taste of flowers on all parts of my tongue, the warmth of the cup between my palms, the evening breeze through the window, the buzz of the gardens.

Vaguely, I considered checking for poison, but a chorus of flower voices encouraged me to drink it. Not to mention, neither of us would have forgotten the foul odor of the poison blend. Raphaël, especially, would have spit it right out. No, this tisane was something else entirely.

After our first cups, I poured us seconds, adding plenty of honey.

We sat side by side on the velvet sofa and sipped and stared at each other. It was titillating, letting this desire build. In blue light through the windows, in the candle glow, my *bricoleur* looked sexier than ever. I could smell his scent of sunshine and river water, with the slightest trace of salt and mineral.

In this state—both ethereal and visceral—it appeared his skin was *shining* from within, golden and rippled. I reached out to touch his forearm, and my fingertips moved over his skin ever so lightly. What a miracle that his flesh existed so close to mine. I closed my eyes and sank into the deliciousness.

When I opened them again and registered his face, his expression was clear . . . *desire*, pure and simple.

Mon Dieu, I wanted my skin against his, all of it.

Take it slow.

With reluctance, I pulled my hand away and finished the second cup of tea.

"This tea . . ." He set down his cup and gave me a sumptuous kiss, his hand cupping my chin, my cheek, running down my neck, along my collarbone. "You blended it?"

"Iva did." Quivering at his touch, I glanced at the jar. And that was when I saw that it was not, after all, *amour* tea. It was labeled ÉROTIQUE.

"Ohhhh." I buried my face in my hand. "Wrong tea."

He glanced at the jar and laughed. *"Eh bien, dis donc!"*

Well, ya don't say, indeed.

"Sometimes I feel like Iva's spirit is here, doing things," I said with a tickle of amusement. "Like moving my hand to the tea of her choice."

"Sounds like Iva."

Our mouths found each other again, lips and tongues tasting, exploring, sending electricity through my body. His calloused hand moved from my neck down to the top buttons of my shirt.

His voice was a raw whisper. "Are you okay with this?"

"Oui." The word came out raspy. "Are you?"

"Oui." He explored me with his fingers in long, luxurious touches—the brush of a petal, the graze of a feather. In the dim lighting of the treehouse, everything felt like a dream. Breathy sighs, hot skin, soft lips. Our bodies holding each other, moving together, becoming waves.

"Feel okay?" he whispered.

"Mmmm." There was no pain—*no pain!*—only this . . . *succulence* spreading through the very core of me. I pulled him closer, feeling something in my center gather force. My eyes closed and my entire being focused on this power inside. The sensations grew more intense, hotter and deeper, building to a crescendo.

And now, I felt it with every molecule of my body: *We are whole.*

Afterward, we lay in the twilight, intertwined on velvet, currents moving through us.

My eyes flickered open and landed on the *érotique* tea.

Merci, Iva. Merci beaucoup.

❁

Later, I walked with Raphaël to the harvest feast, our hands inter-laced, feeling playful and light. As our arms swung together, he asked, "You know what this day is about in Celtic traditions, be-sides feasting?"

"Tell me."

"Matchmaking."

"Ha!" So that was why Mina had given secret looks to Bao and insisted Raphaël and I go off on our own. "That explains a lot."

"And it's a time for handfasting, when couples decide to try out being together for a year. To see if it works." He slowed down and looked at me.

Was he proposing a *handfasting*?

"You're leaving with Sabine in five weeks," I reminded him. Yes, I was counting.

"I could visit you when she's with her grandparents. And you could visit us on weekends." He paused. "If you'd want that."

My chest expanded. *"De tout mon cœur."* With all my heart.

He stopped in his tracks and pulled me in for a kiss, full and sensuous—our own secret handfasting contract. And for the rest of the way, we sealed our contract again and again, every few paces.

Everything felt so safe and warm and right that I didn't even feel the usual chill passing the harpist statue. Pleasure eclipsed fear. Yes, I was getting very good at ignoring *les bizarreries*.

When we entered the grove, a sleepy-yet-giddy Sabine ran into our arms and made us swing her around.

"What took you so long, Papa?"

Raphaël ruffled her hair and gave me a meaningful look.

Smiling to himself, Bao poured some Côtes de Provence red, while Mina watched us over the platter of *la daube* with a satisfied, almost smug expression. Our matchmakers.

I looked around at my friends, wanting to press pause and bask in the beauty. This all felt precious and precarious, as if we were just peaking at the top of a Ferris wheel and a tiny part of me was bracing for the descent.

The Face in the Window

ime moves differently when you're forging relationships in a nook of the Otherworld. Time is at once sped up and slowed down. Time stretches to accommodate tête-à-têtes by candlelight and flower crown parties and soaks in the stream and dances in moonlight and wild *rrroompooses* beneath trees.

And time shrinks: Just a season in the gardens is enough time to fall in all kinds of love.

Sometimes I looked around the table at my friends with awe. Mina had grown brave enough to share her manuscript with Bao and Raphaël, who loved it as much as I did.

Bao had received a warm letter back from Vivienne, saying she would be backpacking around Europe this fall and hoped to visit him. He was already gathering nature treasures for her.

"Remember, the woman has to fit all this stuff in her backpack!" Mina said, laughing.

In one summer, she and I were sisters. Bao and I were besties. Raphaël and I were *amants*. And Sabine was my woodsprite.

No more poison blooms showed up. No more menacing notes. No more daggers . . . which made it easy to ignore the bizarre things and rules—they couldn't darken our joy. We saw the garden through rose-colored glasses. *La vie en rose.*

I experimented with petal blends for Antoinette, to help heal her trauma. We didn't speak of it again, our encounter outside the poison garden, the devastating truth she'd shared, but she thanked me for my efforts and said the tisanes had been helpful. I wished I could sit down with her to do flower art, but we were still far from that kind of relationship. Tisanes were the best I could offer now.

For the entire first weekend of September, I holed up in my atelier, making lotions and potions with copper vats and glass tubes and baskets of blooms. The mystery flowers from treasure hunts with Sabine had dried, and I spread them out on the worn oak table. They were clearly of distinct varieties, but I'd found nothing about them in Iva's notebooks or flower guides, and without internet, I couldn't even determine their genus or family. Orchids? Asters? Salvia? There was something unearthly about their colors, as celestial and iridescent as butterfly wings.

So I closed my eyes, breathed in deeply, and asked the flowers for guidance.

La vie, la vie, la vie.

Listening to their whispers, I infused them in honey that Bao had collected. Their ethereal voices made me smile, their intricate scents of sky and sea, forest and meadow, earth and star, mushroom and moon, spider silk and galaxy. From a deep soul-place, I thanked them for bringing their full talents into this elixir. *The Mysterious.*

Afterward, my pen hovered over the label, then my hand wrote of its own accord: La Vie. The script was confident, though I wasn't sure of the purpose of this potion. I set the flowered honey on the windowsill in the sunshine. It would need time to infuse, and maybe once it was ready, I'd understand its powers.

Then I moved on to floral waters and essential oils of the familiar lavender, chamomile, and jasmine. I blended them together with the rose concoctions that Raphaël and I had made, then poured the liquid through funnels into tiny antique atomizer bottles. I channeled love from the flowers the whole time, through my heart, into my alchemist potion.

I brought the atomizers to the dining grove on Monday morning and in the dappled light, presented them to my friends. "I call this potion *L'Amour Fort*." Strong love.

They sniffed their bottles in delight.

"Lavender for love and devotion," I said. "Rose for love and courage. Chamomile for love and renewal. Jasmine for love and luck."

Sabine squealed and leapt up, spraying the flower concoction until we were immersed in a love mist.

Once her papa made her sit down and drink her *chocolat*, she looked at me solemnly. "I will carry *L'Amour Fort* with me everywhere I go, Eloise." She kissed the bottle. "Forever."

The others laughed, charmed, but she continued to look at me with her brown eyes brimming with the gravity of *l'amour*.

When I had one week left with Raphaël and Sabine—just a quarter of a moon cycle—a letter came from Josh. Mina passed it to me at breakfast, and I stared for a long moment at his familiar scrawl. I'd forgotten about the email I'd sent him weeks earlier. I took a long sip of café au lait, braced myself, then tore open the envelope.

> *Hey El,*
>
> *Glad Paradise is treating you well. Thanks for the cool postcard, that meant a lot to me. Things are good here. It's a relief that you're okay with my situation. I swear it was an accident and I'm really sorry it hurt you. Damn it, El, I wish you could be a mom. You'd be a really good one. You deserve all the good things. I mean that.*

So, I just heard back from Alex about the Mary Martin thing. It's weird. Eight years ago, she left Canada to work at the same place where you work. She sent Christmas cards to a few family members every year. But then she stopped sending them about five years ago. No one knows why—seems like no one was really close to her.

Anyway, hope that helps. Alex says no worries about paying him. Honestly, we're a little freaked out, though. Any idea what happened to this lady? Stay safe, El.

Josh

Merde.

While Sabine was playing with her stuffed animals in the pines, I translated the letter for the others, trying to keep my voice from shaking.

Afterward, the silence stretched out, only cicadas and bird songs filling it.

Finally, Raphaël said, "You think something happened to her?"

Pressing a hand to my mouth, I nodded. "I think I'll leave the gardens next week too."

"What?" Mina looked devastated. "Are you sure?"

I nodded, heartbroken at the idea of leaving, but grateful Sabine and Raphaël were already planning to move out. "These gardens helped me heal. You all helped me heal. I believe that will last."

"You could stay with us in our cottage," my *bricoleur* said, his face all tenderness.

"*Merci.*" My chest clenched. "At least until I figure out next steps." I didn't want to be presumptuous—not to mention that my time in France would be limited without a work visa.

Wrinkling his forehead, Bao turned to Mina. "Maybe we should talk about leaving too."

She rubbed her face. "I don't know."

The gardens had been her refuge for decades. Of course it would be emotional to consider leaving them.

Bao said, "We're healed too, Mina. Sending that postcard to Vivienne made me realize it. And cooking with Sabine. And reading your memoir."

Mina nodded slowly. "And I'm ready to share my book with the world."

"We can tell Antoinette tomorrow," I said, feeling almost sorry for the personal assistant.

A gloom hung over us all day, the knowledge that we'd leave the gardens soon, probably never to return.

At twilight we all squeezed into the kitchen, wanting to spend as much time together as possible this week. Our woodsprite was helping Mina and Bao make her favorite dinner, pho. Bao's childhood comfort food *was* comforting—rich, steaming beef broth with ample noodles, topped with basil, lime wedges, sliced chilis, and heaps of bean sprouts.

A breeze swept through the window, and with it came the voices of lilies and lotus, orchids and jasmine—expressing a chaotic cacophony of emotions from scared to sorrowful. I assumed it was in response to my plans to leave. I'd spent the day whispering my goodbyes to them, telling them how it would break my heart.

Now, I ignored their voices, focusing instead on making things feel safe and normal for Sabine, chatting about school supplies and first-day outfits as she tore basil into a clay bowl. Mina was offering to braid her hair for the first day of school when out of nowhere, something crashed.

I jumped. So did the others, faces alarmed.

It took a moment to process what had happened. Sabine's bowl of basil had fallen to the tile floor, shattered in a violent blast against the clay tiles.

"You okay, my bunny?" Raphaël wrapped an arm around her.

Sabine's expression was strange, a mix of fear and curiosity. Eyes wide, she pointed at the open kitchen window.

"What is it?" Still holding her, he looked outside.

I followed his gaze, squinting into the dusky forest, seeing only shifting blue shadows of leaves and trunks and branches.

"A face," said Sabine. "I saw a lady's face."

My hand flew to my mouth.

Bao pulled a flashlight from his pocket and shone it into the grove. "Nothing out there."

"What did she look like?" Raphaël struggled to keep his voice calm.

"Like a grandmother. With a white hood."

Raphaël and I exchanged glances. It could be her imagination— we'd read plenty of fairy tales together. Then again, it could be one of *Les Dames Blanches*.

Mina grabbed a cleaver and barreled outside as Bao followed. "You two stay with Sabine," he said over his shoulder.

"Don't go out!" cried Sabine. "The twilight rule!"

"It's okay," Raphaël said in a soothing tone.

I wasn't so sure. This was new territory. We held our wood-sprite, glancing out the windows. Of course she was a fountain of questions, which we answered with "I don't know."

When the others returned, I asked, "Anything?"

They shook their heads. "We checked the dining grove," Bao said, panting. "And the hobbit hole and yurt and caravan. All clear."

My treehouse was the farthest. The women couldn't have reached there so fast, right?

Raphaël must have sensed my thoughts. "Ellie, stay with us tonight?"

Sabine hopped on one foot and then the other, hands in delighted fists beneath her chin. *"Ouiiiii!"*

"Merci." I met Raphaël's gaze and pulled our wild thing close, letting her nestle into me.

When dusk turned to night, we ventured into the fairy-lit grove with bowls of pho. We ate quickly, looking over our shoulders, trying not to let our woodsprite see how shaken we were. It seemed that *Les Dames Blanches* had broken an unspoken rule of sorts. They were supposed to stay by the river, away from the safe little nest we'd created.

Tears filled my eyes. "I think we should leave in the morning."

"Me too," said Raphaël, kissing his daughter's hair.

Mina's and Bao's eyes shone as they held hands and nodded in solidarity. "We'll all leave," she said, voice breaking.

"We'll use the ropes and harnesses," Bao said gently.

After dinner Raphaël and I walked beneath a smattering of stars toward the caravan. He carried a sleeping Sabine, and I leaned into him, my arm around his waist.

Jasmine blooms murmured goodbyes, their voices sweet and sad—and fearful.

Vanished

I'd envisioned my first full night with Raphaël a bit differently, all heat and passion, without a little woodsprite present. But here she was, snuggled between us, piled in with a dozen stuffed animals.

Her eyelids drifted closed over a satisfied smile. "We're a wild thing family."

Raphaël and I kissed her hair and exchanged tentative looks over her head.

And you're her eccentric aunt, Eloise. Nothing more. Don't get any ideas.

Part of me asked: *But why couldn't we be a wild thing family?*

The answer came with a shot of fear: *What if things didn't work out? What if I lost another child?*

It could wreck me forever.

When I awoke, little hands were clutching my cheeks. My lids fluttered open, and there were Sabine's brown eyes, inches from my own. "She's awake!" she declared to her papa, then turned back to me. "Ready to play?"

Raphaël was making tea at the cast-iron stove, scents of rose and cacao and jasmine filling the vardo. He gave me an apologetic smile. "I tried to let you sleep in."

I pulled Sabine in for a hug, then propped myself up on the feather pillows. It was half-light outside, the trees bathed in pinkish dawn, the sun on the brink of rising, early birds singing.

Raphaël put a clay cup of tea in my hands. *Amour.*

"*Merci,*" I said, my voice hoarse. I'd slept well last night, considering the circumstances. A light rain had tapped on the vardo, lulling me back into sleep whenever I'd awoken. "We have a big morning."

My woodsprite misted us with the *Amour Fort* spray, which she had indeed been carrying everywhere. While I had tea in bed, she flipped through illustrated fairy tales. The warted witches made me recall a chapter from the Triple Goddess book. Centuries ago, with the decline of nature spirituality, the nuanced Goddess had morphed into an evil witch, representing only the darkest aspects of the crone part of the triad—death and danger and destruction.

Sabine asked me to read "Hansel and Gretel," pointing to the witch and commenting that she didn't actually deserve to be pushed into the oven. "She's like the monsters in *Where the Wild Things Are.* Just scary at first, but inside she's nice and lonely."

"Very reassuring." I sipped my *amour* tea. "*Alors,* let's change the ending."

We decided that Hansel, Gretel, and the witch baked an opera cake together instead, which reminded Sabine that I was supposed to make an opera cake with her. "Today!"

"How about next week?" We'd have to wait till I had access to video tutorials on making it—basically, tiramisu on steroids.

After the fairy tale, we headed to the dining grove. The sun was grazing the treetops now, shining comfort into the gardens. Moisture from last night's drizzle was evaporating in a silvery mist. Pure magic. Did I really have to leave?

Mina and Bao were already in the dining nook with a steaming pitcher of coffee and an array of stone fruit, baguettes, croissants, confitures, yogurt, granola, almonds, and vases of sunflowers. A gorgeous last meal, but my stomach filled with nerves.

After cheek kisses, I said, "I'll pack my bag first. Then I'll be able to relax and enjoy breakfast with you."

Mina stood up and adjusted her layers of lemon-yellow cotton. "Oh, I'm coming too, sister."

"My bodyguard?"

She grabbed a bread knife. *"Oui, c'est ça."*

Raphaël looked at us with concern. "Want me to come?"

"Stay with Sabine," I said. "We've got this."

In the morning light, everything felt so idyllic. I wondered whether Mary Martin might have just gotten tired of polite Christmas cards. And Sabine might have imagined a face in the shadows. Maybe everything was fine in Paradise after all.

When we reached my treehouse, Mina plopped into a chair on the porch. "Shout if you need me."

"Merci, sister."

I headed to the bedroom first, pausing to take a birth control pill, which I'd skipped last night. In a whirlwind, I stuffed my belongings into my duffel, then headed to the library, where I retrieved my books for Sabine. On impulse, I deposited my favorite jars of tea into the bag too.

In my dressing room, I added containers of beauty balms along with my little black dress. I left my grubby underwear and khaki drab in the closet—an excuse to swing by some local boutiques.

Last stop: the atelier. I breathed in the mystical smell of years of flower concoctions. I wanted to take it all: the copper vats, the tubes, the beakers. Instead, I tucked handfuls of lotions and potions into my duffel, followed by Iva's notebooks—she'd want me to have them.

I surveyed the loot. Too greedy? No, just careful. Despite my confidence that we were healed, I wasn't taking any chances. If needed, we'd ration out these elixirs for years to come.

Mina chuckled when she saw me lugging my bulging bag down the swinging bridge. "You're leaving with a lot more than you came with, sister."

"I know." I gave a sheepish grin. "It's severance pay. We deserve it after dealing with the Goddess of the Gardens, right?"

Mina laughed and tilted her head to the sky. "'The wide world is all about you: You can fence yourselves in, but you cannot forever fence it out.'"

"Tolkien?"

She nodded.

I leaned in for a hug. "*Alors*, let's eat breakfast and get you packed too."

I took one last look over my shoulder at the treehouse, the spiral shower, the heavenly *toilettes*. Teary-eyed, I walked with my sister to the grove where our little family was waiting.

The morning grew breezy, foliage shifting around us during breakfast. On high alert, I jumped at every branch creaking, every lizard skittering. We were so, so close to escape, I dreaded something going awry.

I took a long breath and focused on my companions around the table, trying to enjoy our last meal. We opened almonds with a vintage nutcracker and mused over life in the outside world.

"We could all live together in a giant treehouse," suggested Sabine. She'd already eaten and was hulling more almonds. The hard shell was intact, while the silver-green hulls were falling through her tiny fingers. "My papa could build it."

As we laughed, Raphaël said, "We could consider living near each other."

"Without a doubt." Mina's eyes watered.

I felt raw, at the brink of an uncertain future. My friends, too, seemed tentative, fearful, hopeful, wistful, and excited, all at once.

After Sabine grew bored of hulling almonds, she shoved them into her pockets and fussed over her stuffed animals, arranging them in a bag with noses poking out. "So they can breathe," she said, businesslike.

"*Bien sûr,*" said Bao.

Our woodsprite slapped her forehead and let out a dramatic, "Oh *no!*"

My heart raced as I scanned the foliage for a hooded face.

"What's wrong, little bird?" asked Bao.

"My big fairy palace," she cried. "We have to bring it!"

Raphaël raised his brows. "Too hard to get it over the wall, my bunny. Maybe we'll come back for it. If not, I'll make you another one. Anyway, we brought the tiny one."

She shook her head emphatically. "The big one's special. Magical."

I hugged her. "I know it feels like we're leaving magic behind. But the magic's inside us."

She allowed me to comfort her, which comforted me as well. Then she went back to her stuffed animals and chatter-singing. Crisis averted.

I returned to my granola just as Mina and Bao were finishing theirs. They stood up with empty bowls. "We're going to pack now," said Bao, stretching.

Mina deposited their dishes at the washstand. "Leave the dirty dishes for *Les Dames Blanches* to clean up," she said over her shoulder.

Joking about the Goddess doing menial labor, she and Bao set off.

Just as they were rounding the bend, Sabine leapt up, spilling animals from the bag. "Can I help them pack, Papa?"

He did the French air poof. "Just don't get in their way, *d'accord?*"

She bounded after them, their laughter still drifting behind.

Raphaël stuffed the animals back into the bag.

"Make sure they can breathe," I said with a grin.

Showing a dimple, he settled back into his chair and sipped his coffee.

"What about the vardo?" I asked. "It's yours, right?"

He rubbed his face. "We'll come back for it."

"Maybe with the police?" I suggested.

"*Bonne idée.*" He let out a soft laugh, then met my eyes through coffee steam. "Maybe we could set up the vardo by the cottage I've rented. It could be your own little atelier. If you'd like."

"I would like that. *De tout mon cœur.*" With all my heart.

He beamed. "You'll need a job to keep your work visa. How about a bilingual preschool teacher? That was more or less your job before, wasn't it?"

In the same ballpark. "More or less."

"You already have experience and education in the field." He paused, gauging my expression as I tried to process.

He ran a hand through his hair. "Sorry, *ma chérie.* Maybe you don't want to be around children. Sabine could just be an exception?"

"Maybe." I considered telling him about the *tía's* divination. No, too presumptuous. "She's like the niece I never had. Or the goddaughter. Or *something.*" Flustered, I forced myself to wrap it up. "We have a bond."

He raised his brows. "That is evident."

I envisioned Sabine inviting friends over, a bunch of little ones playing in the yard. "You know, maybe I *could* handle being around kids. Maybe it would be fun. *Vachement* fun."

Excitement built in his eyes. "I could build a playground."

"We'll have an *apéro* every sunset."

"And when Sabine is with her grandparents," he said with a gleam in his eye, "you and I can get naked and drink *érotique* tea."

His words lit a fire in my core. "Speaking of which, I brought the tisanes and elixirs." I gestured to my duffel, nearly bursting at the seams. "Right there."

"It would take a lifetime for us to use all that."

"Well, I was worried. Heaven to hell and all that."

He leaned in close. "We've healed ourselves. That will last, I can feel it."

I pressed a hand to his stubbled cheek and kissed him on the lips. Warmth spread through me as we settled back into our chairs and sipped coffee, dreaming of possibilities.

Out of nowhere, as Raphaël was talking about his cottage rental, my stomach clenched. I straightened up, looked around, interrupted him. "What's that?"

He tilted his head. "What?"

I closed my eyes, heard the flowers murmur with urgency. No doubt about it—these were warnings, echoing through the garden like alarm bells.

My stomach tightened further—something was very wrong. In the velvety darkness behind my lids, I saw two brown eyes. "*Sabine.*" I opened my eyes. "You're sure she's with Bao and Mina?"

Confusion clouded his face. "She was going after them."

"But did they acknowledge her?"

He frowned. "They were seconds away."

I leapt to my feet, nearly knocking over my chair. "I'm going to check."

"I'll come too." He put a hand on my shoulder. "I'm sure everything's okay."

But I was already running out of the dining grove. As I skidded around the bend to the main path, I almost crashed into Mina, loaded with bags and a suitcase. Bao was beside her, carrying two small duffels, with coiled rope over his shoulder. I peered behind them.

Nothing.

Raphaël's eyes darted around. "Where's Sabine?"

Alarm flashed over Mina's face. "With you, right?"

Raphaël and I exchanged panicked glances.

Sabine is gone.

34

Into the Underworld

Sabine!" My companions cupped hands around their mouths. "Sabine!"

As if from a distance, I heard Raphaël's frantic voice. "Maybe she's at the caravan."

"I'll go with you," said Bao. "Mina and Eloise, stay here. In case Sabine comes back."

I said nothing. My own mouth had frozen, my body solidified. The world around me muffled. *Another loss. Another loss. Another loss.*

A violent stab in my belly made me double over. *What if I lose her?* My knees gave out. I sank down, forehead pressed to the mud.

Mina crouched beside me and rested her palm on my back. "Get it together, sister." Her voice sounded faraway. "Your girl needs you."

I tasted earth and grit. "I can't—"

"Listen." Her hands gripped me. "I needed a mother when I was a girl. And Sabine has you. Protect her." She yanked me to standing. "Now find your girl."

All around, flowers echoed her. *Find your girl.*

My feelings crystallized: *I love this child like my own. And I will fight for her like my own.*

I took a long breath. *"Merci,* sister."

Moments later, Raphaël jogged around the bend. "Footprints.

Sabine's and a woman's. Heading from the shed. We followed them back here."

Muddy from last night's rain, the path held a woman's prints. "Low heels," I noted. "Just one pair."

Bao wrinkled his forehead. "But look, the prints end here."

Pressing a hand to her mouth, Mina said, "It's as if they just flew away."

My stomach torqued as I thought of the hooded face at the kitchen window. Threats ran through my head in a jumble. *The Goddess of Vengeance . . . oversee punishments in the Underworld . . . breaking Our simple rules.*

"The fairy palace was gone," said Bao. "They must have taken it."

"What now?" Raphaël looked as if he might collapse.

I straightened, drew in a shaky breath. "We look for more clues."

As I scanned the ground where the dining grove met the river path, I imagined the sequence of events: Sabine must have pretended to follow Mina and Bao but secretly gone to retrieve her fairy palace. The woman had intercepted her at the shed and led her back along the path. Then, when they were nearing the grove, the woman had led her off the path, into the foliage, so that Raphaël and I wouldn't spot them.

Beside me, just off the path, grasses and wildflowers were flattened, and something tiny and light-colored stood out from the underbrush. "An almond!" I said.

"Sabine had a pocket full of them," Raphaël said under his breath. "Look! Another . . . and another."

A trail of almonds. Judging by the plants that had been tamped down by feet, it looked like it led upstream toward the waterfall. We bolted through the damp foliage, following the trail that ran parallel between the stream and path.

"'Hansel and Gretel' was fresh in her mind," I said, tears brimming.

We ran along the river and reached the waterfall. It stopped here. I looked across the water, my gaze landing on the cave entrance.

Mon Dieu, had the woman taken Sabine into the tunnel?

Raphaël hopped across the stones to the other side of the stream while I grabbed a couple of solar lights from the path's edge. Then I ran after him. The almond trail picked back up on this opposite bank. Footprints marred the damp sand and gravel, heading up the cliff toward the tunnel entrance.

"They went inside," said Raphaël, his voice heavy with fear.

I handed him a solar light.

"You two follow the trail," said Mina as she stepped ashore with Bao. "We'll get help."

"We'll go over the wall with ropes." Bao's face steeled in determination. "Then we'll run to town."

Raphaël nodded, already ducking into the tunnel.

Mina gave me a quick, frantic hug. "Find our girl, sister."

Flowers urging me onward, I stepped into the darkness after him. I prayed our solar lamps would stay lit—they'd had only a few hours to recharge.

We fell into a swift pace as Raphaël called, "Sabine!"

His voice echoed off the low ceiling and rounded walls. The tunnel smelled musty, of stone and secrets, bone and darkness. Soon the trail petered off—an ominous sign, but maybe our woodsprite had run out of almonds. As we jogged around the first oubliette barrier, I remembered my mother's words: *There's always a way out.*

There had been. *Sabine.*

Beside the hole, Raphaël stopped in his tracks. "What if she was pushed in there?" Trembling, he looked inside. "Empty." His voice shook with relief.

I exhaled, and we clutched hands again, forging onward. I

heard Sabine's voice in my head and stifled a sob. *"Wild Thing feels joy in her heart when she's with you."*

Moments later, Raphaël's lamp flickered out.

Merde. This left only mine.

At the second oubliette, he peered inside. "The skeleton's still there. Sabine isn't."

A moment of relief, then panic returned. As we forged ahead, I talked to Sabine in my mind. *We're on our way, we'll find you, we love you.*

Soon the tunnel ended at the ornate, rotting wooden door. The carving of the sinister gargoyle-cherub grinned at us. I rattled the knob, pushing the door with my weight, then hurling my body against it in desperation. After Raphaël couldn't budge the door either, he reached into his jeans pocket and pulled out a pocket-knife. I clutched my solar lamp as he unfolded the screwdriver.

"The hinges are on the other side." Hands quaking, he gestured to the antique keyhole. "I'll take off the knob, tinker with the locking mechanism. Then maybe—"

My solar lamp flickered off, leaving us in complete darkness. *"Merde."* I shook the lamp, trying to eke out more charge. Nothing.

"I can still do this," he rasped. "It will just take longer."

Energy coursed through my body. "Back up and let me try something first."

I felt for the rotten spot below the knob, memorized the location, and stepped backward, stabilizing my back left foot. Then, with eyes closed, I kicked with my right. The sole of my foot connected with the wood, making a splintering crack. Ignoring the pain, I bent down to explore the damage with my fingers. "It made a hole."

I stuck my hand through and reached up toward the knob on the other side. My fingers rested on the metal handle of a skeleton key. I gripped it and turned, hearing the lock slide away. Whispering thanks to whatever power was watching over me, I extricated my hand and turned the knob.

The door creaked forward.

With a sharp intake of breath, Raphaël took my hand. Bracing myself, I stepped through the doorway.

A faint light shone from overhead. It took a moment to make sense of things. "We're in a cellar," I whispered.

"There must be a staircase," said Raphaël.

Which meant there was a house above. But there were no houses within a mile of the tunnel entrance. Unless . . . "The château?" I ventured.

"Must be."

We stumbled toward the hint of light.

"Sabine?" Raphaël called.

I cried out as I tripped over something—metal, from the clank of it.

"You okay?" Raphaël asked, steadying me.

"*Oui.*" I reached down, felt the contours of the object. "A lantern."

And where there was a lantern, there might be a match. I ran my fingertips over the packed dirt floor and breathed out in relief when they landed on a matchbox.

"And matches." I lit one on the first try, then scrambled to open the lantern and light the candle. I held up the lantern, illuminating the cellar—an eerie space, about twenty square feet. The walls were stone, and old junk was piled all around, with a cleared pathway leading to a spiral staircase ahead.

The market vendor had said that years ago a mother of three girls had fallen—or been pushed—down the cellar stairs. I shivered at the chill of her ghost.

"Maybe there's a weapon here," I said, glancing at wooden chests and broken chairs. Nothing looked promising.

Meanwhile, Raphaël was rushing around, checking behind crates and falling-apart bookshelves. "No sign of her. Let's go up-stairs."

"Wait." My gaze landed on a smooth, glossy square marker, flush with the ground in the corner. I moved the lantern closer, shining light onto a stone grave.

HERE LIE THE BONES OF A DISLOYAL ONE.

A shudder passed through me. The marker looked modern, no signs of age or wear. It could have been made within the past five years. I recalled Antoinette's words: *"Mary Martin was not loyal."*

Mon Dieu. The handywoman.

A wave of nausea.

Raphaël, now at my side, wrapped an arm around me. *"La bricoleuse."*

Trembling, I clutched his arm. "Let's go."

We ran to the staircase, narrow and medieval—a cylindrical space with small steps spiraling around a stone hub. Trailing bees-wax smoke, we climbed by twos up the worn stone. This staircase must have been used every twilight—the route of *Les Dames Blanches.* And maybe Antoinette was among them, dressed in a hooded cloak.

When we reached the door at the top, I gripped the lantern like a weapon, turned the knob, and pushed it open.

35

The Crumbling Turret

Before us stretched a long hallway, about ten feet wide and a hundred feet long—its floor, walls, and ceiling made entirely of raw stone. This didn't feel like the same château we'd visited on the night of the poisoning—none of the elegant tiles or high ceilings or tall windows. Narrow slits showed the thickness of the bare stone walls. The atmosphere pressed on me, cold and suffocating, like a prison.

Yet this had to be the same castle. Morbid paintings lined these walls too, and the same narrow blanket ran down the hallway. Antoinette had said the château was a patchwork built over the past millennium. Only the Renaissance parts of the castle were inhabited, but the medieval parts were abandoned. That was where we must be.

I tilted my head, noticing sounds floating from somewhere down the hallway . . . faint music. The surreal sensation from the night of the poisoning rushed through me, and I recalled the scratchy old melodies. I homed in on the song playing now—Édith Piaf belting out *Rien de rien. Non, je ne regrette rien.* No, I regret nothing.

"Sabine?" called Raphaël. The word echoed off the walls.

Our surroundings seemed even stranger by weak daylight, without shadows from candlelight obscuring them. I bent down to touch the blanket, soft between my fingers, an arm's length wide but longer than this hallway. It was knit in pastel blocks with irregular edges. A *baby* blanket grown out of control. Antoinette's handiwork? I felt goose bumps spread. Was this another twisted form of mourning her own lost baby?

Raphaël jogged down the hallway, alongside the blanket, calling out, "Sabine!"

I followed, heart thudding. The flowers urged me onward, their voices floating through slit windows.

As we ran, I glimpsed paintings of death, violence, and enraged goddesses—each one pale and blond. A crow-woman flying over a battlefield, dropping firebombs. A woman smiling, blood dripping from her teeth, standing over a king, his crown askew, his ear torn off. A woman in a black cloak, silver snakes woven into her hair, circling a brass-studded whip above her head.

The outfits and scenarios differed, but every single goddess was a younger version of Antoinette.

In horror, I clutched Raphaël's hand. "Look."

"It's all Antoinette." He drew in a breath. "So violent . . . If she has Sabine—" His voice broke.

"Let's check these rooms." The search felt overwhelming, but we had to start somewhere.

I darted into a doorway, a gallery dimly lit by narrow medieval windows and filled with statues—an array of goddesses, all strikingly similar to Antoinette. She must have modeled for the statues in the gardens too—I hadn't realized the resemblance until now.

As we frantically checked behind pedestals, calling for Sabine, I recognized goddesses from my leather book. The deer-woman was the Goddess of Woodlands, who had caught the eye of an evil magician. When she rejected him, he turned her into a deer, protector of the forests.

Beside her, a statue with empty eye sockets, holding her eyeballs in her palm—the Goddess of Vision. After a king had repeatedly tried to rape her, she finally tore out her eyes and gave them to him. He didn't bother her again. After that, blind people came to her to get their sight back. The pattern was clear—each goddess had her own story of how she found power from her violation.

We were about to head back into the hallway when I glimpsed a giant statue of Antoinette perched on a pedestal, holding a bouquet of trumpet blossoms with a victorious expression. Something about it made me pause. This statue was not in my book—I would have remembered it. Breathless, I skimmed the placard, as Raphaël looked over my shoulder.

THE GODDESS OF THE GARDENS OF PARADISE.
AS A GIRL, SHE CAUGHT THE EYE OF HER
STEPFATHER. HER MOTHER WAS DEAD AND
COULD NOT PROTECT HER. SHE TOOK HERBS
TO END HER PREGNANCY. AFTERWARD,
STILL BLEEDING, SHE LURED THE MAN INTO
A TUNNEL AND FED HIM POISON CAKE. TO
KEEP HER SISTERS SAFE, SHE PUSHED HIM
INTO AN OUBLIETTE, WHERE HE SPENT HIS
LAST DAYS IN A NIGHTMARISH STUPOR.

"Antoinette killed her stepfather," he rasped.

A chill gripped me. Here was proof. The man in the tunnel had broken the rules—*the rules of being a father*. Antoinette had committed murder. Premeditated. Twice. Maybe more. "We have to find Sabine," I said. "Now."

Back in the corridor, we started down the hallway toward the music, but just steps away was another doorway. Inside, a spiral stone staircase rose into shadows. I locked eyes with Raphaël. "The music or the turret?"

"The turret," he said, already climbing. "It feels like—a prison."

The voices of flowers rose, almost shrill in their insistence: *No, follow the music.*

But he was nearly at the top, taking two steps at a time. We could just do a quick check, then continue down the hallway toward the music. I stumbled up after him, certain that this was the turret that had conjured gargoyles-come-to-life in my imagination.

My sense of dread grew as we approached the top. Flower whispers morphed into warnings, rising to a feverish pitch. *Go back down!* It felt as though a tourniquet was tightening around my chest. "Let's turn around, Raphaël."

"We're almost there."

"But—"

"You can go back, meet me down there."

No, I couldn't leave him alone. I kept going, despite the warnings. We reached the top stair, which opened into a room of about twenty by fifteen feet. Slits of daylight shone through thick walls, slicing through smoke from candles and burning plants—some kind of incense?

Shelves lined the stone walls, overflowing with flasks and beakers and jars of powders and leaves and petals. Bottles of hand-blown glass—green and blue and amber—held murky liquids. On a wooden table, antique gas burners simmered with copper pots of oils. Dried plants hung from the ceiling.

An apothecary. The shadow version of my atelier. The flip side of the coin, the hidden underbelly, the dark reflection. While my workshop was all healing plants and sunshine . . . this place held potions sparked by shadows. A place of harm.

I hovered by the doorway, feeling the draft. Now the voices

of my healing flowers were drowned out by the ominous hisses of belladonna, datura, brugmansia, henbane, hemlock. The hisses of the poison garden. *Leave. You are not welcome here.* This apothecary clearly belonged to whoever had made the poison tea. Antoinette?

"Wait." I reached for Raphaël's arm, but he was already barreling deeper into the room, calling for Sabine, checking behind tables and cabinets.

In a corner sat a tin bucket of water, positioned beneath a hole in the ceiling. Yes, this had to be the crumbling turret, the one that exuded darkness.

He headed toward an ancient iron door at the far end of the room. Since the turret was self-contained, this had to lead to a small room or closet. *Mon Dieu*, what if Sabine was in there?

I held my breath as he opened the door and looked into the darkness. From across the room, I could barely make out the shadowy forms of brooms, vats, shelves of jars. A storage closet. My heart thudded as he moved deeper into the shadows.

Someone rushed out from the darkness and hit him over the head. He fell limp to the stone floor, just inside the closet doorway.

With a cry, I ran toward him.

And out stepped Antoinette. She was barefoot, cloaked in black, one of the Furies come to life. Her hair stuck out like a grisly crown. She wielded a studded whip in one hand and a war club in another. A club slick with Raphaël's blood.

Before I could reach him, she slammed the iron door and locked him inside with a skeleton key from a ring looped around her forearm.

"Raphaël!" I shouted, keeping a distance from her weapons.

No answer.

As she blocked my path to the closet, I recognized the hilt of the dagger sheathed on her belt. She was no longer the coiffed, silk-clad personal assistant. No, she was the enraged goddess, the maleficent crone, no trace of human connection in her eyes.

"Where's Sabine?" I yelled.

"The question is, what are you doing in my château?"

"Let Raphaël out." I struggled to steady my voice. "Tell us where the girl is. Then we'll leave."

"I am the Goddess of the Gardens." Her expression was feral, as if she were possessed. "And children are forbidden in my realm."

"Raphaël!"

No answer.

Antoinette's eyes seemed unfocused, as if in another world. Darkness had overtaken the irises—the pupils dilated into gaping black holes. Was she hallucinating? And it hit me. The blooms she collected from the poison garden weren't just to adorn her baby's grave. They were for *herself*.

She looked like she'd stepped out of the *Fleurs Vénéneuses* book, a frenzied medieval witch reveling in her altered state. Beside her, small pots on the burners contained beeswax and olive oil, infused with an array of poisonous blooms. She must have been making balms for skin absorption that offered psychedelic effects without the risk of death.

But why so much? I recalled that one could build up a tolerance to the active alkaloids, requiring bigger doses. But if she made plant potions, why would she need me to make her tea? Maybe she only worked with plants with powers to *harm*. I was the one who brought out talents of the healing flowers.

"You have broken my rules." Her skin shone with oil in the dim, smoky light. "There are consequences."

Stalling, I racked my mind for a way out. "So you really think you're a goddess?"

"I *am* the Goddess of the Gardens. My flowers strengthen me. For decades, they've increased my powers."

She was so far gone, completely deluded, impossible to reach with rationality. "Let him out, Antoinette!"

"You have defied me. Your precious one will suffer."

"Is the girl in there too?"

"A child in the gardens breaks the rules. One must face the consequences."

"Where the hell is she?" I yelled.

"Why do you care?" Antoinette said. "She's not your daughter. From what I remember, you're sterile."

I flinched, tears burning my eyes.

Yet beneath Antoinette's cruelty, traces of pain showed on her face. She was still furious over her own lost child, still brimming with darkness. The harmful side of the coin.

She'd barricaded herself in a castle in response to her trauma, created a bizarre and frightening world. I'd come so, so close to taking that route, fencing myself in my own lonely little place in Denver, alienating myself, drowning in my suffering.

"She can't be yours," Antoinette hissed. "Why pretend?"

I saw my woodsprite's brown eyes, woven into my fate from the beginning. "Sabine has always been mine."

And then I lunged.

In one swift motion, Antoinette cracked the whip. It sliced through my shirt and seared my bicep. I stumbled, clutched my arm, blood seeping through cotton. I backed away to the opposite corner, beside floor-to-ceiling shelves of glass jars and bottles—filled, no doubt, with poisons. This woman might have been a quarter century my senior, but she knew how to use this weapon. And it was deadly. Just six inches higher and it could have opened my jugular.

She grabbed a dried bundle of datura, lit it with a candle

flame, and shoved it beneath the iron door where my *bricoleur* was trapped. Then she filled the gap with rags.

Horror filled me. The smoke would quickly fill the closet—poisoning or suffocating Raphaël, or both. And what if something caught fire? If he was unconscious, he could burn to death.

Think, think, think. What was her vulnerability? I took in her bare feet, the long toes, high arches, network of veins. The Achilles tendons, rising from soft heels into lean calves. I recalled the pain of the shard in my own bare foot from the stoneware I'd shattered in Colorado.

I glanced at the shelves beside me, holding hundreds of bottles and jars.

Enough to destroy a person's soles.

The energy of a goddess flowed through me—but not the nurturing, compassionate aspect. No, this was the violent, furious part that had smashed dishes after the deaths of my babies and friendships and marriage.

But the energy felt different now. In the past, without a child to protect, the anger had twisted and turned in on itself, making me the victim, multiplying my own suffering. Now I had a reason for the rage. Someone to keep safe.

Keeping my eyes on Antoinette, I grabbed a bottle of amber liquid and threw it at her.

She ducked, covering her head.

It shattered on the stone wall, exploding in countless splinters. Alarmed, she glanced at the floor, glittering with broken glass. Her bare feet stayed glued to their spot.

I tossed another bottle. And a jar. Liquids pooled and powders coated the stone floor.

She sheltered her face as glass exploded, shards sticking to her hair, her skin, her cloak.

From the behind the door, Raphaël coughed and said in a muffled voice, "You okay, Eloise?"

He's alive. This knowledge fueled me. *"MAGNIFIQUE!"* I sang back and hurled a pottery jar. "Is Sabine in there?"

"No," he shouted, coughing.

"Hang on!" I yelled, and I hurled a couple glass vials at Antoinette's feet.

"Stop!" she shrieked.

I hurled three flasks.

"They're centuries old! And years of work!"

"Toss me the weapons and the keys. And tell me where Sabine is."

Her black-hole eyes flared and her mouth narrowed into an iron line. Still, her anger was no match for mine. Mine was the anger of a mother protecting her child, and it had no walls, no floor, no ceiling.

I fired off ten jars with the staccato of a machine gun.

As she ducked and dodged, her dark eyes filled with terror. Now she was scared . . . of *me.*

"I can do this all day long, Antoinette."

Tears flowed down her cheeks. She was losing control of the situation, and possibly of the entirety of Les Jardins du Paradis.

"The weapons and the keys," I yelled. "And Sabine's location."

I threw two ceramic bowls and a pitcher.

With a cry of surrender, she tossed me the weapons and key ring, which clanked on the stone floor. I picked them up and crunched over to the iron door in my thick-soled boots, watching her the whole time.

"Which key?" I demanded, flipping through dozens.

She narrowed her black eyes at me. "The small brass one."

The moment I unlocked it, Raphaël stumbled out, coughing in a cloud of noxious smoke. Blood trickled from his head. With a hazy expression, he surveyed the destruction. Then he noticed my arm, coated in blood. "What happened?"

"The whip." I handed the weapons to him, my eyes on Antoinette. "Now where's Sabine?"

"I have no idea what you're talking about."

"We know you took her!"

"I did no such thing."

"Get inside," I commanded, lifting a stone mortar over my head as a weapon.

With a scowl, she obeyed. "The wrath of the Furies will fall upon you and those you love."

I slammed the door behind her and locked it, then took Raphaël's hand—it was too hot, too dry. I registered his dazed look, large pupils, flushed face, the blood matting his hair, the lump already growing at his temple. "You okay?"

"That smoke." His words slurred. "Poisonous?"

"*Oui.*" I rubbed my forehead, trying to quell my panic.

"I can feel it already, Ellie." He sank to the stone floor, letting his head fall forward.

I crouched beside him, stroked his cheek. "You inhaled it—the effects are having a faster onset." Tugging his hand gently, I said, "Come on. Let's get our girl."

His eyes welled. "You have to leave me."

"I can't." My voice broke, my own tears spilling over. "I can't, Raphaël."

But he was right—he was in no shape to run through a castle. If our woodsprite had a chance, I'd have to find her myself.

He gave my hand a weak squeeze. "Find Sabine."

I clutched his face, kissed him, then arranged the weapons in his lap and put the key ring in his hands.

His words creaked out. "If I die—"

"You won't." A sob escaped me.

"Be her mother." His head flopped back against the wall and he lost consciousness.

"I'll find her," I said between gasps. "And I'll come back for you." Another desperate kiss, then I descended the staircase.

Back in the hallway, I took a long breath and homed in on the flower voices, drifting from open windows. *Follow the music.*

Through a blur of tears, I did.

The Other Sisters

I left behind the dankness of the Middle Ages, running into the Renaissance part of the château. The stone floor transitioned into russet tile and stucco walls, with huge windows ushering in daylight as the music grew louder, closer.

Did parts two and three of the Goddess trio await? If Antoinette was the hurt-maiden-turned-angry-mother-turned-cruel-crone, then how would these other two women manifest? And did one of them have Sabine?

Fear winched my chest.

I passed macabre paintings of Antoinette-as-goddess, slowing down only to scan the rooms. There was a giant dining hall with a massive table and formal chairs, wavy glass windows revealing a neglected courtyard. Next, a mildewed library of leather-bound books, dust motes illuminated. Musty bedrooms with canopied beds and mirrored dressing tables. An old-fashioned kitchen with scarred butcher blocks and blackened stone ovens. Smelling ash, I shoved fairy-tale images of witches and fiery ovens from my mind.

No sign of Sabine anywhere.

Desperation growing, I followed the music, the flowers' guidance. A melancholy piano melody rang out and Edith belted out "Mon Dieu."

Time to start or to finish
Time to illuminate or to suffer.

I ran past more rooms, becoming more frantic as I called for Sabine. I skidded around the corner, noting that the blanket disappeared beneath a door halfway down the hall. Was that where the music was coming from? Beyond, at the far end, stood a massive arched door—the main entrance.

Chest pounding, I paused at the doorway to the parlor where Antoinette had taken us the night of the poisoning. Nightmare memories flooded back. The room looked different with sunlight streaming over tufted chairs, inlaid chests, jacquard curtains, medieval weapons, taxidermied peacocks, animal figurines, bronze busts.

Again, there was the smell of fresh paint. Venturing farther inside, I saw, in the near-left corner, a woman painting at the easel. My heart stopped.

She wore an artist's smock, flecked with vibrant paint, and her gray-streaked hair was wrapped into a high, messy bun. Her back was to me, but I had a full view of the painting: Aphrodite emerging from a shell, with garish reds and greens replacing the classic peachy pastels. And she didn't look like a goddess of love and sex . . . no, she looked mad as hell.

"Hey!" I yelled.

The artist turned to face me. Her mouth dropped open. There was something profoundly eerie about her, as if she were a dollhouse figurine come to life, as if she weren't quite part of this world. She might have spent her life here, painting creepy goddess portraits.

I planted myself in front of her. "Where's Sabine?"

She gripped her paintbrush and palette with white knuckles. "So sorry, Mademoiselle." Her voice emerged timid. "I don't know who you mean." Her brow creased. "Do not hurt my sisters." She spoke in delicate, formal French, barely loud enough to be heard. "Please."

"Where the hell is the girl?" I shouted.

She startled. Her ghostly face turned pink as tears filled her eyes. Something about her chin and cheekbones looked familiar—a softer version of Antoinette's face. I recalled the sisters mentioned in the gallery, the ones who needed protecting. According to the market vendor, three orphaned sisters had gone to live with their aunt. Had they come back? Did they live here in secret?

"Perhaps my elder sister, Antoinette, knows."

I grabbed her shoulders and shook her. "Where's the girl?"

The woman let out a bewildered yelp, the whimper of a caged animal. "Perhaps she is with my younger sister." Her voice trembled. There was something disturbingly innocent, even naive about her. "Jacqueline has been acting strange all morning. We didn't see her at breakfast. We just left her alone while she played the phonograph. Which is curious, because she rarely listens to Édith Piaf—"

I released my grip and raced out the door. Farther down the hallway, "La Vie en Rose" rang out from behind a closed door. The blanket vanished underneath it. I turned the knob and braced myself, then opened the door.

Inside, Sabine was mid-twirl.

My woodsprite was . . . *dancing?*

Édith Piaf's voice blared from a phonograph while Sabine sang along, spinning.

Once she slowed down, she regarded me, dizzy and sweaty. Then she hurled herself at me. "Maman!"

Maman?

Overwhelmed, I melted into her, holding her close, pressing her face into my torso. After a moment, I drew back, taking in her lit-up eyes, beautiful and brown. I held her little hand firmly in mine. I had to get her to safety, then go back for her father.

"Where's Papa?"

"Nearby. I'll get him soon." I studied her face. "Are you okay, my wild thing?"

She nodded and smiled at a middle-aged woman in a crocheted cardigan, sitting on a tufted sofa. Again, I had the ghoulish sense this was an old-fashioned doll come to life. She held knitting needles in her hands, and the working end of the impossibly long blanket in her lap.

Something cold crept up my spine as I realized she evoked the Fates weaving destiny.

She set down the needles and clasped her hands in delight. Thick, dark hair shot through with silver cascaded over her shoulders, almost reaching the sofa cushions. Her face was pale, her expression preternatural, as if she were half phantom. "Welcome!"

"This is my new friend, Jacqueline," said Sabine with pride. "We're having a wild *rrroompoos*."

There was something deeply unsettling about both the knitter and the artist. I didn't trust either of them. Staying on guard, I turned off the phonograph music to clear my thoughts. Maybe Mina and Bao had returned by now, hopefully with backup. I could leave Sabine with them and come back for Raphaël.

Meanwhile, Sabine had pulled the atomizer from her pocket: *Amour Fort.* Strong Love. "I sprayed Jacqueline, and it made her extra nice."

The knitter gave a smile that reminded me of the cherub's on the tunnel door. Her eyes shone, the same periwinkle shade of her sweater.

"What happened?" I asked Sabine, keeping a grip on her hand and glancing at the doorway.

Her gaze lowered. "I'm sorry." She gave a dramatic sigh. "I went to get my fairy palace, and that's when I met Jacqueline. And she surprised me, so I sprayed her with the love potion. And I told her I was sad we couldn't take the palace. And she said she knew another way out and we could bring out my palace and come back to you."

"Why didn't you tell us?" My voice shook with emotion.

"I knew you wouldn't let me."

I filled in the blanks. She'd gotten distracted in the castle and lost track of time. Of course it wasn't the five-year-old kid's fault.

"Sabine *wanted* to come with me." Jacqueline spoke in a child-like way, almost singsong, her voice high and wispy. Spectral. "I've always wanted a little girl friend. A baby niece. I've been waiting so, so, so long."

I shivered as the meaning behind her words sank in. This woman was operating with the mind of a little girl herself. A girl who might have spent a bizarre life locked in castle grounds.

"What are you doing with her?" I asked Jacqueline, not sure what kind of answer I expected.

"Hiding. My eldest sister would be angry. She can't know about Sabine."

I had to get my woodsprite out of here. I gave her a quick hug. "I'm so glad you're okay."

"I heard your voice in my head," she whispered in my ear. "You were singing to me."

My throat ached with love. I wondered if she would call me *Maman* again, or if it had been a slip. The word felt right.

Then she cried, "Your arm!"

"I'm okay. Now let's go, my bunny."

"I need my palace!" She tried wriggling away, but my hand clamped around hers.

"We'll come back for it."

"Don't go," Jacqueline pleaded in a haunting voice.

I looked back and saw her lower lip quivering, a child on the verge of a tantrum. These younger sisters were prisoners of sorts, or at least in emotional shackles. "Is Antoinette keeping you here? She's La Patronne, isn't she?"

"That is what she calls herself." Her eyes shone and her hair spread like gossamer silk of spiders. "Don't go," she begged, evoking the monsters at the end of *Where the Wild Things Are*. She was lonely and trapped on a château island, her own kind of oubliette.

"I'm sorry," I said, pulling my woodsprite into the hallway.

"But this is for you, Sabine!" Jacqueline followed us out, dragging the blanket. "I've been knitting it for a long, long time. I thought you'd be a baby, but you're perfect now. A girl who can talk and dance and sing."

Mon Dieu. This blanket might have been started for Antoinette's baby, decades ago. "We'll come back for it," I said, leading Sabine toward the front entrance.

"Mais non!" shrieked the knitter. "You cannot leave!"

I considered taking her on alone, but I wanted to protect my woodsprite from violence. Ignoring the woman, I bolted toward the front doors, pulling Sabine along.

We were nearly there when another voice called out. *"Excusez-moi!"*

I looked back and saw the artist, her hair mussed, smock disheveled, face blotched. An uncanny apparition. Were these sisters the three-headed hound of Hades? Hell-bent on preventing us from leaving the Underworld?

"I'm afraid you must depart," she said in her oddly quaint voice.

"That's our plan," I said, wary.

"Oh, good. Because my sister is quite angry."

Alarm shot through me. "She's not locked in the turret?"

"Goodness, no. She's looking for you. And she's a bit put out."

Fury

In desperation, I tried the handles of the massive front doors. Locked.

Merde. I'd left Antoinette's key ring with Raphaël. Sweating, I glanced over my shoulder. No sign of Antoinette yet. How the hell had she escaped? And had she hurt my *bricoleur*?

I turned to the artist and knitter, standing behind us. "Give me a key!"

No response, just wide-eyed stares.

"Antoinette has the only key," said the artist.

Jacqueline nodded. "Camille and I never leave Paradise."

"Not since we were girls," added the artist.

I shuddered. These were willing prisoners. For life. Had Antoinette brainwashed them?

But there was no time for questions. I ran a hand through my hair and looked at Sabine. She'd quieted down, finally grasping my urgency. "We have to climb out a window, my bunny."

I pushed back the heavy curtains of the nearest window. With a grunt, I tried to open it, but it was painted shut. I blew out in exasperation and turned to the sisters. "Which window opens?"

Blank, doe-eyed stares. Had they really been locked in Paradise for *decades*?

"Which window?" I yelled.

"Perhaps you could try the one in the study." Camille gestured with her chin.

"But I don't want them to leave!" cried Jacqueline, blocking the doorway, raising her knitting needles like weapons.

I shoved her aside. Her needles clanked to the tile as I pulled Sabine into the room. I pushed open the window, then picked her up and set her onto the ledge. I kept my hands on her waist, assessing the six-foot fall to weedy earth below. I leaned out the window, lowering her, and letting her drop the last meter. She landed on her feet, then looked up at me, full of trust.

I was about to jump out when Jacqueline's hand clamped onto my arm. "Please don't go."

I wrenched my arm from hers. "We'll send someone back for you." Then I dropped from the windowsill.

Heart pounding in my ears, I stared at the two locked gates ahead of us. I considered leaving Sabine in this side yard, hidden behind a cypress, as I headed back for her father. But no, what if the knitter absconded with her again? The woman was now looking out the window, crying, "Don't leave me, Sabine."

I studied the interior gate, not as intimidating as the exterior one. One step at a time. I scanned the side yard and spotted a pile of gardening equipment—spades, shovels, watering cans, all rusted and abandoned.

"Stand by that cypress," I told Sabine, then picked up the biggest shovel and started smashing the lock.

Glancing over my shoulder, I saw that Jacqueline was standing beside my woodsprite. She must have climbed out too, but at least her knitting needles were in her hair now, holding up a heavy bun. She ignored her artist sister calling out from the window: "Jacqueline, come back!"

"Do not move from that spot, Sabine!" I called out.

Jacqueline held her hand and rambled about Antoinette,

which I half listened to as I battered the lock. At least if she was talking, I'd know she wasn't running off with Sabine.

"We need to watch out for my eldest sister," said Jacqueline in that eerie voice. "Her flower potions give her the powers of a goddess."

Clang. With all my strength, I smashed the shovel against the lock. No luck.

"That's how she rules over us in the gardens," continued Jacqueline.

Whack.

"We go out every twilight to the river. An in-between place at an in-between time."

Crack.

"The door to the Otherworld is open, so Antoinette absorbs more power."

Bang.

Finally, the lock gave out. I kicked the gate open, then wiped sweat from my eyes and pulled Sabine through. Jacqueline followed, and behind her, Camille, who had also come through the window. Our weird entourage.

I ran with Sabine to the exterior gate. "Stand back again." I pointed to the Fates fountain. "Go behind there."

She obeyed, and the sisters went to either side, like creepy bodyguards. I held the shovel over my head and bashed it against the lock, over and over.

Again, Jacqueline thought this would be a good time to chit-chat. "I'm sorry I scared Sabine at the kitchen window. I was curious. I wanted to play. So I snuck back this morning. And we became friends. But I didn't mean to scare anyone."

Muscles screaming, I pounded the lock as my mind took in the knitter's words. Everything she said had a bizarre logic.

She kept talking as I beat the lock until the wooden handle of my shovel cracked. *Merde.*

I ran back through the interior gate to grab another, and was just paces away from the garden tools when the front doors creaked open. Out stepped Antoinette, looking ten times angrier than Aphrodite emerging from a shell. She towered at the top of the stone staircase. A Fury, embodied.

Her face shone red and sweaty, her black cloak rippled in the breeze, her silk blouse clung damp, her hair fanned out, clumped and wild. Her feet were bare and bloodied, swollen and pink. The key ring was now looped around her belt, and she held the studded whip at her side, its tip stained with my blood.

Terrified, I glanced at Sabine, who'd stayed by the exterior gate, at least a dozen yards away. On either side, the sisters held their hands in protective gestures. Still, when it came down to it, their loyalty might lie with their lifelong jailer.

I looked back at Antoinette and tried to inch toward the shovels for a weapon.

She struck her whip, and even though it fell ten feet short, I jumped away.

"Do not move," she commanded. She was channeling the most enraged aspects of the goddesses—the ones who rained firebombs and tore off ears and murdered enemies. I could almost believe she'd used supernatural powers to escape the turret.

Maybe I could bring her back to a rational, human plane of existence, tap into the personal assistant role, find our tentative bond. At some point, the hallucinogens had to wear off. I steadied my voice. "Is Raphaël okay?"

A sinister smile, straight from a goddess statue. She slid her dagger from its hilt, held it up to show its blade glistening with fresh blood.

Nausea filled me. Raphaël's blood. Whose else could it be?

No, no, no. I let out a sob. "What the hell did you do to him?"

She raised her chin. "He is in a dark place, just as others who have been disloyal."

I wanted to storm her, push her down the steps—who cared if she killed me. But there was Sabine. And my *bricoleur* had told me to be her mother. *"If I die . . ."*

"Let Sabine and me go. We'll never come back."

She tilted her head. "I think not."

Red-hot rage filled me, but I held back. Stalling could be my best option. I'd lost any sense of how much time had passed since Mina and Bao had left. An hour? Two? I just needed to keep Sabine and myself safe until they arrived with the police.

"I can help you," I said. "You and your sisters."

She barked out a laugh and descended the steps, dagger raised.

I braced myself, stepping backward toward the shovels, and stole a quick glance at Sabine. If I died, what would happen to her? The sisters might keep her here, another prisoner in the château.

Something rumbled down the driveway. Something big and loud.

Antoinette looked over my shoulder. I followed her gaze. Through the rows of plane trees lining the driveway, a huge machine rolled toward us. Red and bright and enormous. Some kind of tractor, ten feet tall. Like a lavender harvester on steroids. But the lavender harvest was done. Maybe a grape harvester?

As it barreled down the driveway, Mina's and Bao's heads poked out the vehicle's windows. My heart leapt. They must have found it on the roadside, key in the ignition, thanks to trusting local farmers.

My friends were saying something, but the engine noise drowned it out. They waved us away as they built speed toward the main gate.

Alarmed, I looked at Sabine by the Fates fountain, but the artist was pulling her to safety.

Meanwhile, Antoinette stood frozen halfway down the staircase, dagger raised. Her eyes looked wild, savage, bestial.

The harvester crashed through the gate with a crunch and clang of iron.

Mina climbed down and immediately ran to the woodsprite, who fell into her arms. I called to her, "Get Sabine out of here!"

She hesitated, casting a fearful glance at Antoinette, then swiftly led our girl to the harvester. As Antoinette shrieked about her destroyed gate, Mina helped Sabine climb into the harvester, then sat beside her, prepared for escape, waiting on standby.

Meanwhile, the other sisters watched, hovering at the boundary, like dogs with electric collars. I kept an eye trained on Antoinette even as Bao ran toward me, drawing me into a relieved hug.

He glanced at her, looming like a statue above us, halfway up the staircase. "Where's Raphaël?" he whispered, fear in his voice.

"Injured, maybe even—" I couldn't bring myself to finish. "Last I saw, he was in the turret."

Antoinette's voice cut through. "You have destroyed the gates of Paradise. You have broken my rules. There are consequences." In one sudden motion, she descended more steps and cracked the whip, slicing into Bao's calf.

His legs gave way and he dropped to the ground. Blood seeped out, staining his khaki pants.

When I bent over to check his wound—which was dangerously deep—Antoinette climbed back up the steps, as if onto her pedestal. I glared at her, towering above me, larger than life, containing entire storms of rage. But I felt myself growing bigger too, strengthened by love for my wild thing family. I channeled my own Triple Goddess—the wise crone, the bold lover, the protective mother.

Before Antoinette could attack again, I ran up the dozen stairs, barreling straight at her. I tackled her legs, pulling them from under her. She fell on top of me, and together we tumbled down the stone staircase. As we fell, the back of my head cracked against a step, pain surging through my skull. My lower arm snapped as Antoinette's weight fell onto it.

At the bottom, I lay for a moment, dizzy, fighting unconsciousness, pressing my fingers to blood pooling in my hair, feeling my arm throb, pain shooting through my bones.

I blinked, registering Antoinette's movement beside me. As she reached for her whip, I rolled on top of it and clutched the tail end with my good hand. She climbed over me, pinned me to the ground, sitting on my torso, black cape spread over us. With her other hand, she held the bloody dagger over my chest.

38

La Vie

roaning in pain, I held up my other hand to stop Antoinette, but my broken arm wasn't working. I tried clutching her wrist, my grip fragile. Her strength seemed superhuman, as if those plants had given her truly dark powers.

The dagger inched toward my chest. I couldn't hold her off much longer.

Bao staggered into my peripheral vision. He shoved her, but she stayed firmly on top of me. Again and again, he tried pushing her off, attempting to knock away the dagger.

Still, she kept me pinned, dagger raised, determined, invincible. The dark energy of the Furies streamed through her, and she emitted a guttural growl.

"Bao!" From a distance, Mina called out, "My arthritis remedy!"

Really? Now?

Bao pulled it from his pocket—the tiny bottle of chili oil. "Close your eyes, Eloise," he yelled, unscrewing the lid.

I obeyed and a moment later heard Antoinette's piercing scream. "My eyes! My eyes!"

I wriggled out from under her and opened my eyes, panting. She was clutching her face, shrieking from the burn of the chili oil Bao had hurled at her. I scrambled to grab the abandoned dagger with my good arm.

Bao, meanwhile, had tossed aside her weapons. He pulled out a roll of twine from another pocket. "Let's tie her up."

I grabbed the key ring from her belt and stuck it into my pocket, then we tied her wrists behind her back to the cast-iron railing. There she slumped, her eyes red and tearing and swollen, face blotchy.

My dizziness was abating, though my head ached and my lower arm pulsed along with the gash on my upper arm. "I'll get Raphaël."

"You'll need help," said Bao. "Mina can wait in the harvester with Sabine. Then we'll all go to town, get the police."

I nodded, praying my *bricoleur* was alive.

Bao had already cleaned his hands with fresh lemon juice and was now pulling a handkerchief from his pocket. In deft movements, he wrapped my gash and then wrapped his own with his backup handkerchief.

Wiping blood on my pants, I turn to Antoinette. "Where's Raphaël?"

"I cannot be restrained," she cried, tugging at her ropes.

Setting my chin, I turned to Bao. "Give me that chili oil."

As he reached for it, Antoinette squeezed her eyes shut and shrank away. "In the turret."

Bao kept his hand hovering over his pocket as I asked, "Alive?"

"Maybe dead." She gave a vicious grin. "Maybe unconscious and bleeding out."

My insides clenched.

She seemed to relish my anguish. "He's not long for this world. There was a nice little fire when I left him. And those potions you threw on the floor are quite flammable."

As if her words were a curse, an explosion blasted from the turret. The tower crumbled further, flames and smoke rising. The earth beneath me trembled with staccato booms.

With a cry, I raced through the doors into the château, skidding alongside the blanket. Smoke was already filling the hallway. I doubled over, coughing, but kept running toward the turret. I held my broken arm close to my side, flinching at the impact of every step.

"I'm coming!" Bao's voice rang out behind me. His feet pounded the tile in a lopsided rhythm from his injured leg.

When we reached the base of the turret staircase, the smoke hung thick. Eyes burning, I started up the stairs, but the heat pushed me down. I broke into a coughing fit.

"You can't go up," Bao wheezed. "You'll die."

"I have to." I pulled my shirt collar over my mouth and started upward again.

Bao yanked me back by my arm. "Eloise! If he's up there—I'm sorry. He's gone."

With a sob, I wrenched my arm away, headed back up.

I held my *bricoleur's* eyes in my mind, foresty golden-green. His narrow waist with the tool belt slung around it. His tanned, calloused hands, ready to fix anything.

Another explosion. A blast of heat knocked me over. Flames and smoke poured down the staircase.

I forced myself back to standing. Coughing, I folded my arm over my face and kept climbing.

"Eloise! Your girl needs you." After a round of hacking, he shouted over the roar of the fire, "That's what Raphaël would want."

I hesitated. He was right.

My *bricoleur* had told me this himself. His last words to me. *"Be her mother."*

An impossible weight filled me. A soul heaviness. I let myself stumble down the staircase, into Bao's arms. As he held me, I sobbed into his shoulder. "I loved him."

"I know." He drew back, looked into my eyes. "And you still have his daughter to love." Ever so gently, he led me away from the staircase. "Let's go. We'll find a window."

Limp and numb, I let him guide me into the nearest room—the gallery of statues. He pulled me toward the slit windows at the far wall. Daylight streamed inside, illuminating columns of smoke.

Through a blur of tears, I noticed red pools staining the stone floor. A trail of them, leading across the room. I tried to wrap my fuzzy brain around it.

"Blood," said Bao, following my gaze.

A shred of hope cut through my grief. "Raphaël's?"

I followed the blood to a window behind the deer goddess statue, and saw, on the floor behind it, my *bricoleur*.

My heart flew.

"Raphaël!" I dropped to my knees beside him.

He lay motionless on the stone, forehead bleeding and more blood seeping from his abdomen. He must have been too weak to escape out the window.

"Raphaël." I pressed my fingers to the pulse point at his neck, desperate to find some sign of life.

My eyes met Bao's. "I think there's a pulse. Weak but there."

I moved my cheek to my *bricoleur's* mouth, felt the slightest breath. With my good hand, I applied pressure to the belly wound as Bao pressed the head wound. I took in Raphaël's state, his clothes charred and bloody, burns on exposed flesh. Should I do CPR? Give him first aid? Or just get him the hell out?

"Raphaël," I whispered, moving my lips toward his, ready to resuscitate.

His lids fluttered open and his eyes met mine—he was dazed but conscious.

"Ellie," he said under his breath, and launched into a round of coughing.

Bao said, "Let's get him outside."

I gave Raphaël a kiss, then helped lift him up, tucking my good arm under his shoulders. As we wrangled him onto the stone sill, the pain in my broken arm made me gasp. There was no glass in these medieval slits, but their narrowness proved challenging.

I squeezed out beside him, then dropped down six feet, cradling my broken arm as the ground jarred my bones. I reached out my good arm to steady Raphaël as Bao lowered him out. He landed with a thud beside me, half conscious, and I held him as pain shot from my wrist to my shoulder.

Bao dropped beside us, flinching and clutching his bleeding leg. We supported Raphaël with our arms around his waist and half dragged him through the weedy side yard, around the castle.

Another explosion tore through the tower, the boom ringing in my ears. I looked back to see the entire turret ablaze, charred stone and flaming debris tumbling down the hillside, black smoke rising.

When we reached the front of the castle, Mina climbed down from the harvester, ran toward us, and threw her arms around Raphaël.

I caught Sabine's eye as she sat high up in the driver's seat, waving. I hoped she couldn't tell how severely injured her father was. I waved back, singing to her in my head: *You'll be okay. We'll be okay.*

As Bao and Mina tended to our *bricoleur*, I glanced at the staircase, expecting to see Antoinette slumped by the entrance. But she was gone. Her twine restraints were pooled by the iron railing.

My blood froze and I scanned the grounds, bracing for her to appear as a Fury.

Only the artist stood there, pulling the long blanket from the smoking château and piling it beside her. "Oh, good," she said. "The *bricoleur* is alive."

"Where are your sisters?" I called out.

"Well, Antoinette escaped and flew off." She gestured over the plane trees.

I spotted a dark, distant form against the blue sky. A bird of prey? Or . . . Antoinette? I remembered the Furies, bat wings sprouting from their shoulders. I shook myself. "And your other sister?"

"Oh, here she comes." Camille glanced down the garden path. "I worried she might run off with the girl, so I gave her a job. She likes feeling helpful."

Jacqueline approached, carrying the bags we'd left in the grove.

Keeping an eye on her, in case she got any ideas to abscond with Sabine, I turned my attention back to Raphaël. He lay on the ground, still half conscious as Mina pressed her palms to his abdomen and Bao wrapped gauze around his head.

"Think he'll make it?" I asked, hugging myself.

Mina's lip quivered. "It's bad, sister."

Examining his injuries through tears, I realized it wasn't just one stab wound in his gut, but multiple deep punctures. His shirt was soaked with blood that gushed and pooled around him. Overwhelmed, I tried to help stanch the bleeding as his chest rose and fell with ragged breath.

"Let's take him to the hospital," Bao said. "In the Peugeot."

Right. We had Epona the convertible. I flipped through Antoinette's key ring from my pocket. Only ancient skeleton keys.

Sirens sounded in the distance. A sweet sound of hope. Someone must have seen the smoke and called emergency services.

"Stay here," said Bao. "I'll meet the ambulance."

"And I'll go to Sabine," said Mina. "She must be scared."

I observed Raphaël's pulse and breath, applying pressure and ignoring the searing pain in my arm. Judging by the sirens approaching, I figured that within five minutes, we'd have medical help. If he could make it that long.

Beneath the siren's wails, I heard something else: flower whispers. They were rising in a chorus.

La vie. La vie. La vie.

Of course! My gaze landed on the bags Jacqueline had brought, now piled between the Fates fountain and the massive heap of hand-knit blanket. And yes, my duffel full of lotions and potions and tisanes sat there, as if waiting for me.

I ran to the pile and frantically unzipped my duffel, then dumped out dozens of jars and bottles, until I found the golden elixir labeled LA VIE. The potion I'd made from honey infused with mystery flowers.

I grabbed the bottle, knelt beside Raphaël, then unscrewed the lid and breathed in the otherworldly scent—the *life-giving* scent. Whispering a prayer, I parted his lips with my fingertip and drizzled the golden elixir onto his tongue.

Then I cradled him in my arms. The emergency vehicles had arrived, and Mina and Bao were talking to the paramedics, gesturing toward us. In the moments waiting for their approach, I kissed my *bricoleur*, channeling all that was good and loving and healing in these gardens, letting it flow through me into him.

How strange that my journey here had begun with smoke and sirens, and now it was ending with the same. With all my heart—*de tout mon cœur*—I wished for my *bricoleur* to be part of the next journey, *la vie* in the wide world with our wild thing family. Our future flashed before my eyes, a vision vastly different from the desperation of my fantasies in the past. This was a new dream, brimming with the wisdom of stars and choices.

I checked his pulse again. Surprisingly strong. And his breathing now was steady and rhythmic. His bleeding had stopped.

"The most beautiful thing we can experience is the mysterious." This, *this* was The Mysterious. I let out a sob of hope as he squeezed my hand.

"Merci, ma sorcière." His voice sounded powerful, astonishingly so. The voice of someone who would live.

A laugh of joy burbled from my center. "Years ago," I said, "I was given a fortune that a beautiful brown-eyed girl was in my future."

Raphaël opened his eyes, now lucid and sparkling with wonder. "Sabine."

I gave him a smile brimming with *amour fort*, strong love, something you find after venturing through grief and loss and pain . . . and reaching the other side.

"So our destinies are knitted together," he said. "Like a really, really, really long blanket."

"Exactly." I laughed, eyeing the huge knitting project by the Fates. "And now we get to see how it all unfurls."

I leaned closer, and as our lips touched, the garden whispered songs of impossible marvels, of rosemary and thyme, of stones and cherries.

The story of my love, which has no end.

Epilogue

How We Become Flowers

Three years later

In the twilight of our farmhouse gardens, surrounded by loved ones, I let out a happy, drowsy sigh. Lavender bouquets adorned the plank table for our summer solstice celebration. The opera cake was eaten, its chocolatey remnants strewn across the wood, mingling with glasses of champagne, sugared rose petals, half-melted beeswax candles.

Fireflies drifted over the meadow, where a pyramid of logs and heartwood waited beside bundles of Saint-John's-wort, ready to transform into a bonfire later tonight. A waxing gibbous moon rose above Le Château du Paradis in the distance. Flower gardens stretched in every direction—our seeds had come from Paradise and still held magic. In fact, they multiplied magic.

The laughter of flowers and children drifted across a patch of chamomile. Sabine was playing with her cousins and Gaby's daughter on our fairy-themed playground. My parents had been delighted to accompany the girl—Sabine's new *amie américaine*—on the flight over, fully embracing all facets of their grandparent roles.

The evening was warm enough for me to wear a fitted, skin-baring white top that showed some midriff—because why not embrace my firm breasts and smooth belly? There were benefits to being an adoptive mom—body of a maiden, heart of a mother, mind of a wise crone. Three in one.

Raphaël stroked my shoulder with those calloused, *bricoleur* hands—they still had that certain *je ne sais quoi* that quickened my heartbeat. He had healed beautifully from his wounds and burns. And over the past three years, his scans had come back clean—cancer was no longer a lurking shadow. Still, if it returned, we'd face the *merde*, strengthened by flowers.

Across the table sat Mina and her editor, chatting about her book tour. *In Search of Paradise* had been released last year in several languages to high acclaim, and she was now at work on her next book. The book clubs and bookworms of the world now said, "I expect it with impatience!"

Bao and his adorably nerdy paleontologist boyfriend sat beside them, examining seedpods by flashlight with the assistance of Vivienne, a wildlife biologist. Nestled against Bao's pocketed chest was his baby girl—a beagle puppy, snoring softly after a day of playing with the kids. Beside them were three sets of grand-parents, bonded by their adoration of Sabine.

Gaby couldn't come because of lack of documentation, but she'd video-chatted with us during dinner, giving Spanish-accented greetings in French, which she'd been learning in hopes of visiting one day. She was happy my mom and dad could be stand-in grandparents for her daughter, who'd never met her own *abuelos* in Oaxaca.

At the other end of the table were more friends and neighbors, along with Romani aunts and uncles, singing and playing violin.

It was a very, very, *very* long table—essential for our constant stream of guests. Everyone wanted to visit a flower farm called Les Jardins d'Amour when lavender was blooming and rosé was flowing.

Along with the table, we'd built an array of *uniques et rustiques* structures to accommodate visitors. After converting the barn to my bilingual nature preschool, we'd made a hobbit hole, tree-house, and yurt. And of course, there was our beloved vardo.

Now an artist residency, Le Château du Paradis had a different feel. The turret was destroyed, but the rest of the castle had survived the fire. Its furnishings and décor—including the morbid paintings—had been thrown away due to smoke damage. Antoinette had never been found, yet somehow, fresh bouquets of angel's and devil's trumpets showed up every so often on the grave in the cordoned-off poison garden. Always at twilight.

Works by resident artists now filled the gardens and castle. My favorite pieces were done by Vivienne, who was pursuing a hobby of botanical illustrations. Bao declared them brilliant and hung her work around his home. She looked radiant, hardly a trace of childhood scars, wearing the pearl necklace that Amber had once taken as blackmail. I'd messaged my predecessor on social media, suggesting that the return of the necklace could be her first step out of hell. Upon the heirloom's return, Bao had gifted it to Vivienne.

"*Maman! Papa!*" Eight-year-old Sabine ran up and hopped onto Raphaël's lap, leaning her head against mine. Her chestnut hair had grown thick and long, and her limbs had stretched like a sapling's branches. She'd kept her imagination and spirit and penchant for theatrics.

She played with my hair as she chatted and munched on sugared rose petals. "The kids are all ready to start dancing, okay, *Maman*?"

The word still filled me with gratitude. *Every time.*

"Perfect, my wild thing." I brushed my lips over my daughter's forehead. My only child.

Every once in a while, I'd feel a pang that I hadn't held her as a baby, hadn't felt her kick inside me, hadn't fed her milk from my breasts. But in whispered conversations before bed, holding hands in the dark, I would tell her, "You grew in my heart instead of my belly."

And she'd say, "I always wanted a *maman* like you."

"And I always wanted a daughter like you. I saw your brown eyes even before I met you."

"I heard your voice even before I met you. It sounded like flowers."

Now Sabine leapt up and twirled. "Time to dance!"

As she bounded away, my *bricoleur* leaned over and gave me a kiss that tasted of champagne. Then he followed her, guitar in hand, toward her aunts and uncles and cousins. When the music began, grandparents and friends rose from the table in twos and threes to join the dancing.

I lingered at the table, sipping stardust, listening to the music and stream and crickets, and most of all, the whispers of flowers.

Author's Note

Dear Reader,

As you might have guessed, Eloise's struggles were inspired by aspects of my own experiences. If you're dealing with these issues, my heart goes out to you—I hope this story helps you feel less alone as you navigate your own path. We each have our own way of resolving our reproductive challenges. In my family's case, we adopted our now-teen son from Guatemala—he's our happy ending. (He has the most beautiful brown eyes.) May you find meaning in your own journey, and please know that I'm offering my hand to hold in spirit.

With love,

Laura

Acknowledgments

Writing this book meant venturing into new grown-up territory, which made the support I received all the more precious. My longtime writing group guided me with big hearts and brilliant minds: Laura Pritchett, Todd Mitchell, Karye Cattrell, and Claire Boyles.

Endless gratitude for beta readers and consultants who helped me strengthen the story and write aspects outside of my own experience. *Merci beaucoup* to Saikou Jatta, tour guide extraordinaire in Senegal, for fascinating cultural insights; Saly Sane, my *chère amie* from Senegal, for generous laughter and conversation; Phuong Nguyen for sharing her interesting and moving family history; Esther Vincent for highly useful feedback on the French elements of the book and more; Megan Flamant, lifelong friend and go-to *sommelière* for wine pairings in Paradise, who offered valuable advice; Carrie Visintainer, longtime writer friend, herbalist, and forager, for helpful insights; Erin Han, avid reader and writer friend, for sharing experiences with cancer in an honest and beautiful way; poet Lara Payne for weighing in on infertility aspects and more; Gloria García Díaz, *querida amiga*, translator, writer, collaborator, and kindred spirit, for feedback on cultural aspects of fertility challenges; Richele Kuhlmann, creative travel partner, for all things design.

Bisous to my agent, Kim Lionetti, who saw the spark of possibility in my story and expertly guided me, and to Maggie Nambot, her *assistante merveilleuse*, and the entire BookEnds team. Bouquets of gratitude to Lizzie Poteet, my magnificent editor—without her inspiring vision, this book would be a weedy, overgrown mess of a garden! Savannah Breedlove, production editor, and Taylor Ward, senior publicist, have been gems at Harper Muse—and I'm grateful to the whole team for the warm welcome and supportive atmosphere. To my generous launch team, early reviewers, and writing community: You have my eternal thanks!

Secret kisses to the roses and lavender and chamomile in my healing garden—friends who uplift my spirits! Although some flowers in my book, like angel's and devil's trumpets, are aligned with darkness for story-telling purposes, they deserve thanks too—my Indigenous friends in the Amazon value sacred flowers like brugmansia (*floripondio*) in their healing practices.

Big thanks to my "found family": Annie and Alain Thille, my French *maman* and *papa*, and my *frères*, Rodolphe and Damien, for so many warm welcomes; María Virginia Farinango, my Ecuadorian *hermana* and coauthor of *The Queen of Water*, for showing me how to heal through sharing stories, and for shedding light on emotional recovery in survivors of child trafficking; the late María Chiquita López Martinez, Fidelina López López, and the late Epifania García Díaz—Indigenous Mixtec and Mazatec healer friends in Oaxaca who treated me like a granddaughter and had an immeasurable impact on my life; Andrea Mummert Puccini, writer and sister since age twelve, who was diagnosed with metastatic cancer as I was revising. Andrea, I hope my love for you has infused the story—thank you for letting me be part of your journey.

Gratitude to my whole family: my aunt, Liz Neal, and cousins, Kate Myers and Kelly Small, for decades of encouragement; my husband, Ian, for being my *bricoleur* and loving support; my parents, Jim and Chris Resau, and my brother, Mike—adopted from Korea—for showing that family runs far deeper than blood and genes. My wonderful mom empathized with my own infertility and adoption journey and was invaluable in helping me revise this book.

Most of all, I want to thank my son, Bran. You are my treasure at the end of the journey. Thank you for being my child, written in the stars and born in my soul.

Discussion Questions

1. What makes Eloise burn down her old life and start anew? Have you (or someone you know) ever done this or wanted to?

2. This book is full of Goddess mythology. Which manifestations of the Goddess interested you the most? How do these versions relate to Eloise's healing?

3. The job ad requires the "impossible task" of turning *merde* into *fleurs*. How does Eloise ultimately achieve this? Has life ever handed you hard stuff that you've transformed into something beautiful?

4. Les Jardins du Paradis is a "refuge for the broken." How does Eloise form friendships and connections with her "broken" companions? How does she overcome her isolation and cross the metaphorical river with her new friends? How do they help each other heal? What role does Antoinette play in her journey?

5. How does Eloise feel about her body after years of miscarriages and infertility? She compares her relationship to her body as friends who have been in a standoff for years. How does she become friends with her body again? What are the cascading effects of this? Have you ever felt a sense of betrayal from your body? How did you manage that?

6. Describe the ups and downs of Eloise's burgeoning relationship with Raphaël. What vulnerabilities, fears, and assumptions do they each bring? How do they overcome

the challenges and create a true bond? How did you feel about their romantic trajectory?

7. How does Eloise feel about children at the beginning of the book? What caused her to feel this way? How do her feelings change over the course of the book, especially after meeting Sabine? To what extent did the role of the wood-sprite and her backstory surprise you?

8. How did you feel about the role of magical flowers and Eloise's role as flower whisperer? Can you relate to her bond with nature in some way? Have you felt healed by natural teas, herbs, and concoctions? Have you ever participated in mystical healing rituals?

9. How does the dark underbelly of Paradise reveal itself over the course of the story? How did you feel about the Gothic and darker mythological elements? How did you feel about the climax and ending? Which aspects were you expecting and which surprised you?

10. Many aspects of the lush castle garden setting tap into a desire for wish fulfillment. Which elements resonated most with you? (The gourmet meals? The magical flowers? Sunset *apéros*? A charming treehouse? Others?) Describe your dream refuge.

Please visit Laura's website for recipes, a playlist, and other treats: www.LauraResau.com

About the Author

Photo by Tina Wood

Laura Resau is the author of *The Alchemy of Flowers*, her debut novel for adults, and eleven acclaimed books for young people. Her novels won five Colorado Book Awards and appear on best-of booklists from Oprah, the American Library Association, and more. Trilingual and with a cultural anthropology background, she's lived in Provence and Oaxaca, and now teaches creative writing at Western Colorado University. You might find her writing in her cozy vintage trailer in Fort Collins, Colorado, where she lives with her rock-hound husband, musician son, wild husky, a garden of healing flowers, and a hundred houseplants.

Connect with her online at lauraresau.com
Instagram: @lauraresau